Praise for *Chronospace*

"Not only a story about time traveling and multiple worlds, but also a look at how science fiction inspires scientific endeavors . . . *Chronospace* demonstrates Steele's growth as a writer."
—*Steven Silver Reviews*

Praise for *Oceanspace*

"Steele's descriptions of the ocean depths and the unknown possibilities down there are first rate."
—*The Denver Post*

"Steele's account of the undersea research facility that is the real star of this book is so thorough you'd think he had visited the place. The plot is complex and the characters real. There aren't many people writing fiction grounded in realistic scientific explanation. Allen Steele is among the best."
—*St. Louis Post-Dispatch*

"The closest thing in years to [Arthur C.] Clarke's *The Deep Range*. Steele has done his technical homework thoroughly and he writes with an eye to pacing and dry wit. Hard SF adventure doesn't get a whole lot better than this."
—*Booklist*

"Steel's new novel mirrors his award-winning work . . . tightly crafted, highly atmospheric . . . The high-tech detailing of oceanic habitats is first-rate, and Steele efficiently and effectively evokes the cold, dark, and unrelenting alienness of the world deep beneath the sea. This novel is perfect for whiling away a plane trip or a stormy night."
—*Publishers Weekly*

contin

ChronoSpace

ALLEN STEELE

ACE BOOKS, NEW YORK

CHRONOSPACE

An Ace Book / published by arrangement with the author

PRINTING HISTORY
Ace hardcover edition / May 2001
Ace mass-market edition / February 2002

Part two of this novel originally appeared in a slightly different form in the October/November 1997 issue of Asimov's Science Fiction.

Visit our website at
www.penguinputnam.com
Check out the ACE Science Fiction & Fantasy newsletter!

ISBN: 0-441-00906-9

ACE®
Ace Books are published by The Berkley Publishing Group, a division of Penguin Putnam Inc., 375 Hudson Street, New York, New York 10014.
ACE and the "A" design are trademarks belonging to Penguin Putnam Inc.

PRINTED IN THE UNITED STATES OF AMERICA

10 9 8 7 6 5 4 3 2 1

CONTENTS

Fools rush in where angels fear to tread.
—ALEXANDER POPE

The boy began climbing the mesa shortly after sunrise, stealing away from the village while his mother was making breakfast for his sisters. It wasn't long before she noticed his absence; he heard her calling his name, her voice echoing off the sandstone bluffs of the canyon he called home, but by then he was almost a third of the way up the narrow trail leading to the top of the mesa.

Darting behind a pile of talus, he cautiously peered down at the adobe village. Pale brown smoke rose from fire pits within its circular walls, and tiny figures moved along the flat rooftops. There was no sign of pursuit, though, so after a few minutes he emerged from hiding and continued his long ascent.

He had hiked to the top of the mesa several times before, but always in the company of his father or one of his uncles, to set traps for tassel-ear squirrels and desert rabbits. The tribal elders had decreed that children were never to leave Tyuonyi alone, for it was only within the settlement's fortified walls that they were safe from the Enemy. Yet the boy was never very obedient, and he had been plotting this journey for several weeks now. He knew of a stand of juniper trees that grew on top of the mesa. Although the morning was warm, the first frost had come to the canyon a few days ago, and juniper berries would now be sweet enough to eat. He had bided his time until his father and uncles went away on a hunting expedition, then he made his escape from the village.

The boy was little more than five years old, but he was almost as strong as a child twice his age; the soles of his bare feet were tough as leather, his small body accustomed to the rarefied air of the high desert. He scurried up the steep path winding along the mesa's rugged cliffs, barely noticing the escarpments that plunged several hundred feet to the canyon floor. When he became thirsty, he paused to dig a small cactus out of the ground; he pulled its quills, peeled its skin, and chewed on its pulp as he continued his lonely trek.

It was shortly after he passed the landmark his father called Woman Rock—a sheer bluff scarred by an oval-shaped crevasse that bore a faint resemblance to a vagina—that he came to the place where deep blue sky met the ground. Suddenly, there was nowhere left to climb; the terrain lay flat, covered with mesquite and sage, with only blue-tinged mountain peaks in the far distance. He had reached the roof of the world.

The boy grinned broadly. He would find his juniper berries and stuff himself to his heart's content, then he would swagger back down the trail to Tyuonyi, where he would regale his sisters and the other children with his tale of adventure. In his mind's eye, he saw the tribal elders, impressed by his courage and fortitude, inviting him into their kiva, where he would undergo the sacred ceremonies which would affirm his status as a man. His mother and sisters would be proud of him, and when his father returned . . .

His father would probably tear off a willow branch and whip him to within an inch of his life.

Realizing this, the daydream vanished like so much cookfire smoke. Well, for better or worse, he was here. The least he could do was find a juniper tree.

He walked over to a nearby mesquite and lifted the flap of his loincloth. A thin yellow stream of urine irrigated its roots, and he sighed with satisfaction. The sun hadn't yet climbed to its zenith, and he had plenty of time to find the object of his desire. Once he had eaten, perhaps he would locate a shady place to take a nap before . . .

A vague motion caught the corner of his eye.

The boy instinctively froze, not twitching a muscle as his dark eyes sought the source of the movement. For a moment he thought it might be a bird or a lizard, yet as he listened, he couldn't detect any familiar animal sounds. Had it only been . . . ?

There. Just to his left, about twenty paces away. A strange rippling pattern, like the forms hot air makes as it rises from sun-baked ground.

Turning very slowly, the boy studied the apparition. He half expected it to vanish any second, the way mirages always do when the breeze shifts a little, yet the pattern remained constant, spreading out before him like a wavering, transparent wall . . .

No. Not transparent . . . reflective, like the shallows of the creek that wound through the canyon. Indeed, he could see the reversed image of a nearby tree against its surface.

Remaining absolutely still, his heart thudding against his chest, he regarded the manifestation with dread and fascination. Then, ever so carefully, he knelt and, without taking his eyes from the strangeness, picked up a stone. Gathering his courage, he hesitated for another moment, then he leaped up and hurled the rock at the wall-of-air.

The boy had always possessed a keen eye. He had learned how to kill lizards when he was only three, and more recently had refined his talent to the point where he could knock a squirrel off a tree branch from twenty paces. The stone he threw now hurtled on a straight trajectory toward his selected point of reference, the center of the air-wall where the juniper tree was reflected . . .

The rock hit something that wasn't there. It made an odd hollow sound, and in the briefest of instants, the boy glimpsed concentric whorls spreading outward from its point of impact. Then the rock bounced off the invisible surface and fell to the ground.

He was still staring at the place where stone had fallen when a ghostly hand touched his left shoulder.

"Go away, kid," a voice said, in a language he couldn't understand. "You're bothering me."

The boy leaped straight into the air. When his feet touched ground again, he was already running. His terrified scream echoed off the canyon walls as he sprinted back down the trail, the coveted juniper berries utterly forgotten.

A few moments passed, then the air shimmered around the place where the boy had stood. Thousands of tiny mirrors gradually assumed a man-shaped form until it solidified into a figure wearing a loose-fitting environment suit. He raised his gloved hands and pulled off his hood, then grinned at the invisible wall.

"Did you ever see someone run so fast?" he asked. "I bet he's already halfway home."

"That wasn't a very nice thing to do," a woman's voice said within his headset. *"You could have hurt him."*

"Oh, don't worry so much. Just gave him a scare, that's all." Tucking the hood beneath his arm, Donal Bartel wiped sweat off his shaved head as he walked to the edge of the mesa and peered over the side. Although he could see the top of the trail, the boy was nowhere in sight. "All right, he's gone. Let's finish up here."

He turned to watch as the spectral wall began to materialize, taking the form and substance of a saucer-shaped craft. Perched above the rocky ground on five petal-like flanges, its electrochromatic outer skin resumed its natural appearance until the vessel's silver hull dully reflected the hot sun overhead. Hemispherical pods beneath its lower fuselage emitted an amber glow which pulsated within the craft's shadow.

"You've got everything you need?" From within the single porthole on the *Miranda*'s low turret, the timeship's pilot peered out at him. *"We could stay a little longer, if you think we're not going to be bothered anymore."*

Donal pondered Hans's question as he unzipped the stealth suit and shrugged out of it. The suit was useful for hiding from contemporaries, but in the desert heat it threatened to suffocate him. "He's not coming back, but once he tells his folks what he's seen up here, someone might come up to investigate."

"I agree." The woman who had spoken earlier was climbing down a ladder set within one of the landing flanges. "The Anasazi are a very wary people. Someone down there might think the boy saw a scout from an enemy tribe."

Donal nodded. For the last two days, he and Joelle had studied this isolated settlement of pre-Pueblo native Americans. Seven hundred years from now, this place would be identified on maps as Burnt Mesa, overlooking Frijoles Canyon within the Bandelier National Monument, not far from the town of Los Alamos, New Mexico. By then, the village of Tyuonyi would be a collection of ancient ruins carefully preserved by the United States government. The site would have a gift shop and a museum, and thousands of tourists would visit this place every year to saunter among the crumbling remains of what had once been a thriving settlement.

Yet their mission hadn't been merely to record what Tyuonyi had looked like when it was inhabited. Twentieth-century archaeologists had already done that task, three hundred years before the *Miranda* had traveled back through chronospace. There was also the enduring controversy over the forces that had brought an end to the Anasazi civilization. Some CRC researchers, holding to theories first advanced during the late twentieth century, believed that some tribes had begun raiding others, committing atrocities that went beyond rape and slaughter to include ritualistic cannibalism. This was what had eventually forced many tribes to abandon their adobe homes and seek refuge in cliff dwellings; the Tyuonyi villagers had already built their own Long House within the talus walls of Burnt Mesa. Indeed, the very word *Anasazi,* given to the pre-Pueblo tribes by the nearby Navajos, meant "Ancient Enemy."

"We might learn more if we stayed longer, but . . ." Joelle Deotado pushed back her long blond hair as she gazed at the distant village. "I don't want to risk exposing ourselves, and we may have done that already." She glanced over her shoulder at Donal. "You might have done the wrong thing, but it probably doesn't matter. They would have found us sooner or later."

"I'm sorry it worked out that way, but . . ." He shrugged. "You're right. We've been compromised. Better pack up."

"Very well," Hans Brech said from within the timeship. *"I'll begin laying in a return trajectory, if that's what you want."*

"That's what we want." Joelle walked toward the miniature cameras and listening devices they had concealed within foliage upon ledges overlooking the village. As expedition leader, it was her decision whether to call off a survey. "Let's get ready to go."

Donal sighed as he neatly folded the stealth suit. He had donned it when the motion sensors they had placed around the top of the trail detected the approach of the native boy. When Brech put the *Miranda* in chameleon mode, the timeship should have been adequately disguised, the energized fractal coating of its outer hull enabling it to blend in with its environment, yet the boy had the eyes of a cat and the curiosity to go with them. Joelle might not have liked the way he chased him away, but . . .

Something flashed. For an instant, he thought it was sunlight reflecting off the *Miranda,* until he realized that it was coming from the wrong direction, about 30 meters from the timeship. He turned his head, looked that way . . .

"Donal!" Joelle snapped. "Do you see . . . ?"

"I see it," he whispered.

Just above a large boulder near the top of the trail, not far from where the boy had emerged, a bright halo of white-yellow light had flickered into existence. About three meters in diameter, it surrounded an indistinct form lurking within its nucleus: a bisymmetrical figure, vaguely human-formed save for the pair of broad, winglike shapes that expanded outward from behind its body.

"Hans, are you getting this?" Donal spoke quietly, not daring to move a muscle. "Tell me it's not a hallucination."

"I've got it." Brech's voice was subdued. *"Sort of. I mean, it's not registering on . . . no, there it . . ."*

Then, just as suddenly as it appeared, the haloed figure vanished.

Not all at once, though. When it disappeared, Donal noticed that the nimbus seemed to collapse into itself, much as if it had created a miniature wormhole. As it did, sand and gravel were sucked into the vortex, and the surrounding scrub brush was violently yanked toward it. A half second later, there was a loud thunderclap as air rushed in to fill the vacuum. Donal's hands went to his ears as Joelle yelled something unintelligible.

No one said anything for a moment.

"Was that an angel?" Joelle asked softly.

"If it was," Brech said, *"then it's another good reason for us to leave."*

PART 1

MONDAY TIMES THREE

Monday, January 12, 1998: 7:45 A.M.

The train from Virginia was crowded, as it always was during morning rush at the beginning of the week. Murphy could have driven into D.C., and in fact had left his home in Arlington intending to do just that, but when he heard on the radio that an accident on the Roosevelt Bridge had caused traffic to back up on the Beltway, he changed his mind at the last minute and decided instead to catch the inbound Metro from Huntington Station. Under normal circumstances he would have sat out the jam, but his meeting was scheduled for eight o'clock sharp, and this was one appointment for which he dared not be late.

So he sat nervously on the plastic seat, hands folded together on his briefcase, jostled every now and then by the man next to him reading the *Washington Post*. As the train rumbled through the long tunnel beneath the Potomac, he contemplated his reflection in the window. The face which gazed back at him was still young, yet rapidly approaching middle age; he saw creases where he had never noticed any before, a hairline subtly receding from his forehead and temples, dark circles beneath eyes that had once been curious and lively.

Was this just the Monday blahs, or was he was getting old, and more quickly than expected? It had been only seven years since he had left Cornell University, moving his wife and infant child from Ithaca to Washington so he could take a job with NASA. He'd had a beard then, as he recalled, and his eleven-year-old Volvo had still sported a peeling Grateful Dead sticker left over from some grad-student road trip he had taken with Donna. That seemed like a hundred years ago; the beard was long gone, he had traded in the trusty Volvo for a Ford Escort that promptly broke down once every three months, and even the Dead were no longer around. All that remained was another overworked and underpaid government bureaucrat, indistinguishable from the dozens of others riding the train to work.

He only hoped that, when the day was done, he'd still have a job to which he could commute.

Just as Murphy was checking his watch for the tenth time since boarding the Metro, the train began to decelerate. A few moments later, the next station swept into the view. Rushing past businessmen in overcoats, students in parkas, and shabby-looking street people, the train gradually coasted to a stop in front of the platform.

"L'Enfant Plaza. Transfer to all lines. Doors opening on the right." Again, Murphy found himself wondering whether the train's voice was recorded.

He pulled on his gloves, picked up his briefcase, stood up, and joined the line of passengers shuffling out of the car. Once on the platform, he quickened his pace; buttoning up his parka, he marched through the exit turnstiles, then jogged past the ticket machines to the long escalator leading up to E Street. Muted winter sunlight caught random flakes of snow drifting down through the entrance shaft; he pulled up his hood against the harsh wind and ignored the homeless people begging for spare change at the top of the escalator.

He was almost running by the time he covered the two city blocks that separated L'Enfant Plaza from his place of work. A long, eight-story glass box, NASA headquarters was as soulless as any of the other other federal offices surrounding the Mall, but at least it didn't have the paranoid Post-Apocalypse-style of government buildings erected during the late sixties and early seventies, when government architects were obviously planning for civil insurrections by excluding ground-floor windows and limiting the number of entry doors. Digging into his coat pocket, Murphy pulled out his laminated I.D. badge and flashed it at the security guard behind the front desk, then sprinted for the nearest elevator just as its doors were beginning to close. He glanced at his watch; just a minute past eight. No time to visit his office; he reached past the other passengers to stab the button for the eighth floor.

The elevator opened onto a long corridor decorated with paintings of Saturn V rockets and Apollo astronauts being suited up. Murphy tugged off his coat as he strode down the hall, carefully noting the coded signs on each door he passed. In the seven years he had worked at NASA, he had been to this floor only a few times; this was the senior administrative level, and you didn't come up here unless you had a good reason.

The boardroom was located at the end of the corridor, only a few doors down from the Chief Administrator's office. The door was half-open; he could hear voices inside. Murphy hesitated for a moment, then took a deep breath and pushed open the door.

Three men were seated at the far end of the long oak table that took up most of the room; one chair had been left vacant between them. Their conversation came to a stop as Murphy walked in; everyone looked up at him, and for an instant he felt a rush of panic.

"Dr. Murphy, welcome. Please come in." Roger Ordmann, the Associate Administrator of the Office of Space Science, pushed back his chair and stood up. "You're running a little late. I hope you didn't have any trouble getting here today."

"My apologies. There was a . . ." No point in telling them about his decision to take the Metro. "Just a problem with traffic. Sorry if I kept you waiting."

"Not at all." Ordmann gestured to the vacant chair as he sat down again. "The Beltway can be brutal this time of day. At any rate . . . well, I believe you already know everyone here."

Indeed he did. Harry Cummisky, Space Science's Chief of Staff, was the man who had hired Murphy seven years ago. Although only a few years older than Murphy himself, he was the person to whom Murphy directly reported. Harry gave him a nod which was cordial yet nonetheless cool. If it weren't for Murphy, after all, he wouldn't be here today.

Next to him was Kent Morris, the Deputy Associate Administrator of NASA's Public Affairs Office. Murphy knew Morris less well; they had met only three weeks ago, during NASA's annual Christmas party. Morris seemed affable enough then, but there was a certain edge to him that Murphy instinctively disliked. As it turned out, his feelings were correct; Morris had just transferred over to NASA from the Pentagon, where the PAO was more inclined to scrutinize civilian employees for possible security breaches. It had been a little less than a week after the Christmas party when Morris had blown the whistle on Murphy.

As for Roger Ordmann . . . although Murphy had only met him once or twice before, he knew him all too well, if only by reputation. The former vice president of a major NASA contractor, Ordmann had been recruited to the agency by the Chief Administrator after Dan Goldin himself had come aboard during the Bush administration. Ordmann was a company man; he followed Goldin's visionary lead without having much of a vision of his own, beyond making sure that Space Science continued to be sufficiently funded through the next fiscal year. Courtly, urbane, and soft-spoken, he could nonetheless be unmerciful when it came to dismissing any personnel in the Washington office who roused his ire.

"Yes, sir. I know everyone." Murphy draped his coat over the back of his chair; there was a long, expectant silence as he sat down. Now it seemed as if everyone was staring at him, waiting for him to continue. "To start with . . ."

Feeling an itch in his throat, Murphy coughed into his hand. "Excuse me. To begin with, I apologize for any embarrassment I may have caused the agency. It wasn't my intent to cast NASA in a bad light. When I wrote that article, I didn't believe it would be attributed to . . ."

"David . . ." Roger Ordimann regarded him with a paternal smile. "This isn't a formal board of inquiry, let alone an inquisition. We simply want to know . . . well, at least I'd like to know . . . how you drew your conclusions, and why you decided to publish them at this time."

"And who gave you clearance to do so," Morris added, much less warmly.

Murphy glanced across the table at the PAO deputy chief, and that was when he noticed a copy of the February issue of *Analog* resting before him. Not only that, but Ordmann and Cummisky also had copies. The very same science fiction magazine currently on sale in bookstores and newsstands across the country which, along with new stories by Michael F. Flynn, Paul Levinson, and Bud Sparhawk and book reviews by Tom Easton, also featured a nonfiction article by one David Z. Murphy: "How to Travel Through Time (And Not Get Caught)."

"So . . ." Steepling his fingers together, Ordmann leaned back in his chair. "Tell us why you think UFOs may be time machines."

Franc Lu awoke as the lunar shuttle fired its braking thrusters. Feeling the momentary pull of gravity, he pushed off the eyeshades he had donned a couple of hours ago and carefully blinked a few times. The ceiling lights had been turned down, though, so he didn't have to squint; free fall returned after a moment, and he felt his body once more beginning to rise above his seat; he was thankful that he hadn't neglected to check the straps before taking a nap.

Turning his head to the left, he peered out the oval port-hole window next to his seat. Past the port engine nacelle, he caught a brief glimpse of Earth, an enormous, cloud-flecked shield that glided away as the shuttle completed its turnaround maneuver. Unable to make out any major continents through the clouds, he assumed that they must be somewhere over the Pacific. Probably just beyond the visible horizon lay Hong Kong, his ancestral home. Franc smiled at the thought. Someday, he would like to get another chance to visit . . .

"Well. Now there's a pleasant smile." Across the aisle, Lea put down her compad to regard him with mischievous eyes. "Pfennig for your thoughts?"

Franc started to reply, then realized, too late, that she was indulging one of her favorite games. "Caught you!" She playfully wagged a finger at him. "Now, tell me . . ."

"A pfennig is a coin." Franc laid his head back against the seat. "Smallest form of hard currency used in Germany until 2003, when the deutsche mark was replaced by the Eurodollar."

"Very good." Yet she wasn't about to let him get off so easily. "And what does that expression mean, 'pfennig for your thoughts'?"

"That you've made a bad pun. And I was thinking about Hong Kong, if you must know. It might be an interesting place to visit."

"I thought you've already been there. Three years ago, when . . ." Then her elegant eyebrows arched slightly. "Oh. You mean a CRC expedition."

Franc nodded. "Dec 31, 1997. The day Great Britain formally ceded the island to the People's Republic of China. An intriguing period, from what I've read."

She shook her head as she folded shut her compad. "It might be, but it's probably well documented. Nothing of major interest there. You could always file a proposal, of course, but . . ."

"The Board would probably turn it down. You're right." He shrugged, then turned toward the window again. "Just a passing thought."

Earth had completely disappeared; now all he could see was the black expanse of cislunar space. From behind him, he could hear the small handful of fellow passengers beginning to move restlessly in their seats. They had been travelling for a little more than eighteen hours now, following the shuttle's departure from the Mare Imbrium spaceport. A private spacecraft owned and operated by the Chronospace Research Centre, the shuttle didn't have the luxury accommodations afforded by the large commercial moonships. Everyone aboard was a CRC employee; some were returning from furlough, while others like Lea and himself had their homes on the Moon. Yet because commercial craft weren't permitted to dock at Chronos Station, you had to take the CRC shuttle or else try hitching a ride aboard a freighter.

Thinking about their destination, Franc reached to the comp in the seatback in front of him. He ran his forefinger across the index, and the panel changed to display a forward view. Now he could see what the pilots saw from the cockpit: a cruciform-shaped station, each arm comprised of five cylindrical modules, with two spherical spacedocks located at opposite ends of its elongated central core. Within the rectangular bay of the closer dock, Franc could make out tiny spacecraft, while others hovered in parking orbit nearby.

Out of curiosity, Franc touched his finger against the image of the spacedock farther away from the shuttle. As the shuttle completed an orbit around the station, for a brief instant he caught a glimpse of a small, saucer-shaped craft nestled within the hangar bays. Then, just as he expected, the scene was blotted out by a graphic inverted triangle.

*** CLASSIFIED ** CLASSIFIED ***
REMOTE IMAGING NOT
PERMITTED
CRC 103-B
DOWN

The screen wiped clean, to be replaced by the original index bar. "*Verdammt,*" Franc murmured in disgust. It was at times like this when the gentlemen in Security Division took their work a little too seriously. As if no one aboard a CRC shuttle had ever seen a timeship before . . .

Lea chuckled. "You're getting better with your explicatives."

"Cut it out." He cast her a warning look. "I've been studying as hard as I can, and you know it."

Closing her eyes, she laid her head back against the seat.

"I just hope you've learned your history better than your German. You're going to need it."

Franc opened his mouth to object, then thought better of it. There was no sense in arguing with Lea when she was in one of her moods. So he tried to relax, but after a moment he touched the comp again, and passed the remaining minutes of the flight watching the shuttle complete its primary approach.

As the spacedock filled the screen, he reflected that Chronos Station was just over a kilometer in length. It wasn't very large, at least in comparison to some of the colonies in Lagrange orbit, yet it was amazing to think that, almost three hundred years ago, airships nearly this same size had been built—and actually flown!—on Earth.

Franc smiled to himself. In just two days, they would see the *Hindenburg*. Then he'd offer Lea a pfennig for *her* thoughts.

Monday, January 14, 1998: 8:06 A.M.

Like so many physicists, David Zachary Murphy had fallen in love with science by reading science fiction.

His love affair began when he was ten years old and saw *Star Trek* on TV. That sent him straight to his elementary-school library, where in turn he discovered, tucked in among more conventional fare like *The Wind in the Willows* and *Johnny Tremain,* a half dozen lesser-known books: *Rocket Ship Galileo, Attack from Atlantis, Islands in the Sky,* and the Lucky Starr series by someone named Paul French. He read everything in a few weeks, then reread them a couple more times, before finally bicycling to a nearby branch library, where he found more sophisticated fare: *I, Robot; Double Star; Needle in a Timestack; Way Station;* and other classics of the genre.

By the time David Murphy reached the sixth grade, not only was he reading at college freshman level, but he was also taking a sharp interest in science, so much so that he regularly confounded his teachers by asking questions they couldn't answer, such as the definition of a parsec. For Christmas, his bemused yet proud parents gave him a hobby telescope; when he caught a flu after spending one too many winter evenings in the backyard, his mother brought back from the neighborhood drugstore, along with Robitussin and orange juice, a magazine she happened to spot on the rack just below the new issue of *Look:* the January, 1969, issue of *Analog.* It seemed to be just the sort of thing her strange young son would like, and it might help keep him in bed.

David recovered from the flu two days later, but he faked sick for another school day so he could finish reading every story in the magazine. One of them was the first installment of a three-part serial by Gordon R. Dickson, *Wolfling;* for the next two weeks, he haunted the pharmacy newsstand until the February issue finally appeared. Not only did it have the second part of *Wolfling,* but it also contained, as the cover story, a novelette by Anne McCaffrey, "A Womanly Talent." An insightful observer might have noted, in retrospect, that the lissome young lady depicted in Frank Kelly Freas's cover painting for this story bore a strong resemblance to the woman David would eventually marry, yet that may have only been a coincidence.

For the next twenty-nine years of his life, David Murphy remained a devoted reader of *Analog,* seldom missing an issue, never disposing of any after he read them. On occasion he picked up some of the other science fiction magazines—*Galaxy, If, The Magazine of Fantasy & Science Fiction, Vertex*—but it was only in *Analog,* in some indescribable way, that he found the sort of thing he liked to read. He went through high school with a copy tucked in among his textbooks—no small matter, for during the seventies it was far more socially acceptable to smoke pot than to be caught reading science fiction—and when he was in college and faced a choice between a meal or the latest issue, he would sooner go hungry before passing up on what he called "his *Analog* fix." After he met Donna during his third semester of his postgrad tenure at Cornell, on the first night she spent with him she was astonished to find a dozen issues of *Analog* beneath the bed of his small apartment.

She was even more amused the first time he took her home to visit his mother for Christmas, and she found boxes upon boxes of science fiction magazines stacked in the attic.

It was during this time, while he was working on his Ph.D. in astrophysics, that David attempted to write science fiction. It didn't take very long—only a couple of dozen reject slips, garnered not only from *Analog* but also *Asimov's, Omni,* and *F&SF*—for him to realize that, no matter how much he enjoyed reading SF, he had absolutely no talent for creating it. Not that he couldn't write at all—in fact, one of his dissertation advisors, no less than the estimable Carl Sagan, often remarked on his innate writing skills—yet the art of fiction was beyond him; his dialogue was tone-deaf, his characters wooden, his plots contrived and reliant upon unlikely coincidences. This wasn't very heartbreaking; writing was little more than a hobby, and certainly not a passion. Nonetheless, his secret ambition was to have his name appear in the same magazine he had followed since he was a kid. Even after he received his doctorate and was happily married to Donna, with a ten-month-old baby in his arms and a new job at NASA waiting for him, he considered his life to be incomplete until he was published in *Analog.*

Then, late one afternoon while sitting out a Beltway traffic jam with nothing but *All Things Considered* on the radio to keep him company, Murphy had a brainstorm. He may not have much talent as a fiction writer, but he wasn't half-bad at nonfiction. After all, he had already published three articles in major astrophysics journals; it might be possible for him to turn those same skills to writing pop-science articles. Indeed, he knew several working scientists who moonlighted as regular contributors to *Astronomy* and *Discover.* Why couldn't he do the same with *Analog?*

After dinner that evening, Murphy sat down in his study and, very methodically, made a list of ideas for articles he could see himself writing for *Analog.* It was remarkably easy; as a lifelong reader, he had a good grasp of what the magazine published, and as a NASA researcher he was able to keep up with the latest developments in the space science community.

At the top of the list was "Spacewarp Drives—Are They Possible?" This was followed by "Three Ways to Terraform Mars," "Biostasis for Interstellar Travel," "New Space Suit Designs," "How to Grow Tomatoes on the Moon," so forth and so on . . . and at the bottom of the list, added almost as an afterthought, was: "UFOs—A Different Explanation (Time Travel)."

Much to his surprise, *Analog* bought his article about spacewarp drives. The check he received for six weeks of part-time work amounted to a little less than half of his weekly take-home pay from NASA, but that wasn't the point. Nine months later, when the article finally saw print, Murphy blew away the money by getting a baby-sitter to look after Steven and taking Donna to the best five-star restaurant in Georgetown. He proudly showed his advance copy to everyone from the maître'd to the cab driver, and Donna was embarrassed when he got mildly drunk and suggested that they have sex in the ladies room, but it was all worth it. His life was complete. He had been published in *Analog*.

Few of his colleagues saw the article. This didn't surprise Murphy; during the last three years he had learned that all too many NASA employees were civil-service drudges who cared nothing for space and would have gladly gone to work at the Department of Agriculture or the IRS for a few more dollars and a reserved parking space in the garage. Yet a handful of people in the Space Science office were *Analog* readers; they recognized his by-line, and they stopped by his office to offer their compliments. Among them was Harry Cummisky; much to Murphy's surprise, Harry not only liked the piece, but he also gave him permission to do research during office hours, so long as it didn't interfere with his work.

That response, along with favorable letters published

several months later in the magazine, was sufficient en-
couragement to send Murphy back to the keyboard. Over
the course of the next four years, he became a semiregular
contributor to *Analog*. The checks he received were deposited in Steven's college fund, but earning a little extra
cash wasn't the major reason why he wrote. Besides the
satisfaction of the craft itself, on occasion he found himself
exchanging correspondence with science fiction authors
who had read his articles and wanted to ask a few questions
for stories they were developing. Likewise, his stock at
NASA gradually rose. After his article on human biostasis
was published, Harry sent him down to Huntsville to lecture on the subject at the Marshall Space Flight Center; a
few months later he and his family were invited to Cape
Canaveral to watch a shuttle launch from the VIP area. He
became regarded within NASA headquarters as a member
of the brain trust.

Then he wrote an article linking UFOs to time travel,
and that's when the shit hit the fan.

"This is . . . ah, it's an intriguing theory." Roger Ordmann slipped off his wire-frame glasses and pulled a handkerchief from his vest pocket to clean the lenses. "Rather
unorthodox, but intriguing nonetheless."

"And you have evidence for this?" Kent Morris had his
copy of *Analog* open on the boardroom table.

"Well . . . no. But it isn't a theory." Murphy shifted uncomfortably in his seat. "Kind of a thought experiment,
really. This is a science fiction magazine, after all. This
kind of speculation goes on all the . . ."

"I understand that," Morris said impatiently, "but here,
in your footnotes . . ." He peered at the last page of the article. "You've cited a NASA study on wormholes . . ."

"A paper from an academic conference held last spring
on interstellar travel. I found it on the Web."

"I know. I read it after I read your piece." Morris
frowned as he tapped a finger against the magazine. "The
paper says nothing about time travel, let alone any connec-

tion with UFOs. You've drawn upon it to reach some rather far-fetched conclusions."

Out of the corner of his eye, Murphy stole a glance at Cummisky. Harry wasn't looking directly at anyone; his hands were folded together in his lap. He had remained silent so far, offering no comment, and Murphy had gradually come to the realization that Harry's main concern was covering his own ass. There was no way his boss would rise to his defense.

"They're far-fetched, I'll admit," Murphy said, "but they're not inappropriate."

Ordmann looked up sharply, and Morris raised a skeptical eyebrow. Cummisky softly let out his breath. Too late, Murphy realized that he had said the wrong thing. "What I mean is, I don't think . . ."

"Please." Ordmann held up a hand. "Perhaps we should back up a little, summarize what we know so far." He put on his glasses again, picked up his copy of *Analog*. "David, on your own initiative, you've written an article for this . . . uh, sci-fi magazine . . . which claims that the UFOs aren't from another planet, but instead may be time machines."

"I didn't make any such claim, sir. I merely speculated that . . ."

"Let me finish, please. Your main point is that, since there's no feasible way for small spacecraft to cross interstellar distances, and since the star systems most likely to contain planets capable of harboring intelligent life are dozens of light-years from Earth, the only reasonable explanation for UFOs is that they're vehicles somehow capable of generating wormholes, which in turn would enable their passengers to travel backward in time. Therefore, UFOs may have originated on Earth, but from hundreds of years in the future. That's the gist of it, right?"

From across the table, Morris regarded him much as if he was one of the fanatics who haunted Lafayette Park across from the White House, holding up signs demanding the release of the Roswell aliens from Wright-Patterson Air

Force Base. Harry sank lower in his seat, if that was at all possible.

"Yes, sir," Murphy said, "but, like I said, it's an entirely speculative proposition. I mean, I don't think this is what's happening. I'm only suggesting . . . extrapolating, that is, that . . ."

"I understand." Unexpectedly, Ordmann smiled, with no trace of condescension. "As I said, it's an intriguing idea. If someone in Hollywood made a movie out of it, it'd probably be a hit." He chuckled and shook his head. "If I were you, I'd write a screenplay and send it to Steven Spielberg. Maybe he'd buy it for a few million dollars." His smile faded. "But that's not the point. You've written this article as a NASA scientist . . ."

"Pardon me, sir," Murphy interrupted, "but I didn't present my credentials in the article. There's nothing in the piece which states that I work for the agency . . ."

"I understand that," Ordmann said. "Nevertheless, you're a senior NASA scientist. That lends a certain amount of credibility to your theory . . . or speculation, as you call it."

Murphy was about to object, only to be headed off by Morris. "I went back and read your earlier pieces," the Public Affairs chief said. "On two separate occasions, you made mention of the fact that you're a physicist working for NASA. Although you don't present your credentials in this particular article, many of them are bound to remember your affiliation with the agency."

"Right. And there's the problem." Ordmann closed the magazine, placed it on the table. "David, I can take you downstairs to the mailroom and show you how many crackpot letters we receive each month. People claiming the Apollo program was canceled because we found cities on the Moon, that shuttle astronauts have seen flying saucers in orbit, that we're covering up everything from alien invasions to the Kennedy assassination. That sort of thing's been going on since the Mercury days, and hasn't let up since."

The Associate Administrator sighed as he removed his glasses once more. "This is why NASA has no official position on UFOs, other than to state that we're not actively engaged in researching them. Even unofficially, we say that they don't exist. Son, if a flying saucer landed in front of the White House and the *Post* called to ask for my opinion, I'd say it wasn't there. That's how carefully we have to play this sort of thing."

Although he nodded, Murphy remained unconvinced. His previous articles had touched on subjects nearly as far-fetched. Indeed, in his piece on lunar agriculture, he had playfully suggested that marijuana could be potentially useful as a cash crop. No one had complained about that. Yet any public discussion of UFOs appeared to be off-limits.

There was no sense in arguing the point, though. "I see," he said. "I'm sorry if this has embarrassed the agency. That wasn't my intent."

Ordmann smiled. "I'm sure that wasn't the idea, David. And believe me, I don't want to do anything that would stifle your creativity. When Kent brought this to my attention, I asked Harry to let me see some of the other things you've done. You're a pretty good writer." He chuckled a little. "You know, back when I was a kid, I used to read this magazine when it was still called *Astounding.* It was one of the things that got me interested in space. I'm glad to see that one of our people has this connection. It's a good way of touching base with the public."

Then he shook his head. "But I can't let you go off half-cocked like this. Have you done any other articles lately?"

"Is there anything else awaiting publication?" Morris asked more pointedly.

"No, sir," Murphy replied. "I've been a little too busy lately to do much writing." Which was only a half-truth. Although he had been involved with analyzing the data received from the Galileo space probe, he had also been collecting notes on the same for an article he hoped to pitch to

Analog. Perhaps he should come clean. "I've been thinking about doing a piece about Jupiter," he added. "What Galileo tells us about the possibility of life in the Jovian system, that sort of thing."

Morris ran a hand across his brow. There was no mistaking the look on his face: *Christ, here we go again.* Ordmann didn't seem to notice, yet he frowned slightly. "Well, if and when you write that piece . . . or any other articles, for that matter . . . I want you to forward a copy to Kent, just to let him see what you're doing."

"Send it to me *before* you submit." Morris glared across the table at Murphy. "And let me know if it's going anywhere else other than this magazine. Understand?"

Murphy's stomach turned to glass. For him, writing was an intimate experience; he never let anyone, not even Donna, see what he was doing before it was published. Being mandated to show his work to someone before he sent it away was like being told that he had to set up a camcorder in the bedroom. Yet the Associate Administrator had just laid down the law, with no hope of compromise.

"I understand, sir," he said quietly.

Ordmann smiled sympathetically. "David, you're a fine writer. I don't want to do anything that puts a crimp in your creativity. But you've got to contain some of your wilder ideas . . . or at least while you're working for NASA."

And that was the bottom line, wasn't it? For all Roger Ordmann cared, David Zachary Murphy could write that the President was under mind control by aliens from Alpha Centauri and that the Air Force had a fleet of starships hidden at the Nevada Test Range . . . but the moment he did so, he was out on the street. The last thing NASA HQ would tolerate was an in-house crank.

"I understand, sir," Murphy repeated.

Harry exhaled as if he had been underwater for the last five minutes. He wasn't going to lose his job today. Morris looked like a hyena gloating over a giraffe carcass. "Well, then . . . I'm glad we've got this settled." Ordmann pushed back his chair, glanced at his watch. "Now, if you'll excuse me, I'm running late for a budget meeting on the Hill. It's been a pleasure to meet you, Dr. Murphy."

Then he was out the door, where a female aide anxiously waited for him, attaché case in hand. Harry mumbled something about making a phone call, then he hastily stood up and exited the conference room. Out in the hall, Murphy heard him taking the opportunity to shake hands with Ordmann and thank him profusely for his time and patience. Never too late to curry favor, he reflected sourly.

Which left him, for the moment, alone with Morris. At first, the Public Affairs chief studiously avoided meeting his eye as he folded his notebook and gathered his papers. Then he picked up the copy of *Analog* and his gaze lingered on the cover art, a Vincent Di Fate painting of an astronaut spacewalking outside a large spacecraft.

"You really like this sci-fi stuff, don't you?" he asked.

"Been reading it all my life." Murphy kept his voice even. Like most lifelong science fiction fans, he despised the word "sci-fi."

Morris shook his head. "Not for me," he murmured. "Too unbelievable. I prefer real stories." He dropped the magazine on the table. "Kinda like *The X-Files,* though. That's pretty good." He turned toward the door. "Anyway, keep in touch. "

Murphy waited until he was gone, then he picked up the discarded *Analog.* Leafing through the magazine, he noted that several passages of his article had been highlighted with a yellow marker.

For some reason, he found himself oddly flattered. At least Morris had bothered to read the piece. Too bad he hadn't understood a word.

Franc expected to have a meeting with the Commissioner, yet not for several hours. When he arrived at his quarters on Deck 5E to drop off his bag, however, his desk had a message for him: Sanchez wished to see him and Lea as soon as possible.

Lea apparently had received the same message; he found her waiting for him in the central hub corridor, just outside the hatch leading to Arm 5. As a selenian, she could have taken a room on one of the upper levels, but since she was trying to get herself reacclimated to Earth-normal gravity, she had requested a berth on 4E. During the flight up from Tycho, Franc had once again tried to talk her into sharing his quarters on 5E. She had politely turned down his invitation, but it wasn't too late to ask one more time.

"We can still get a room together, you know," he said. "I checked with the AI. It told me there's a double available on my deck, right across from where I am now. I looked at it before I came up here, and it's really quite comfortable. All we have to do is move our stuff over there and . . ."

"Thank you, but no." She favored him with a smile. "I'd prefer to sleep alone, if you don't mind."

"Well . . ." He hesitated. "Yes, I do mind, since you ask. I thought we were partners."

"Oh, come on now." She gave him a admonishing look. "We are partners . . . but I think you're taking this a little too seriously for your own . . . our own good. Keep this up, and the next thing you know, you'll be asking for a contract."

"I never said anything about a contract." Although, in fact, the thought had crossed his mind more than a few times lately. Even a twelve-month MH-2, with a nonexclusionary clause, would do. "I just hate breaking up a good team."

She was about to say something when they were interrupted by a shrill electronic beep. They looked around to see a service bot moving down the corridor, the electrostatic brushes at the ends of its rotating arms sweeping dust from the cylindrical walls. "Move aside, please," it droned as it approached. "Move aside, please."

Irritated, Franc resisted the urge to kick the bot out of the way. That would have been recorded by the bot's camera, though, and then he would have received a warning from the station AI not to interfere with maintenance equipment. He reached up to grasp an overhead handrail, and swung his legs up to let the bot pass. "Thank you for your cooperation," the bot said as it whirred beneath him; its brushes barely missed Lea, who had flattened herself against the wall. "Please do not block the corridor."

"That's the whole point." Lea looked up at Franc while he was still hovering above her. "We're teammates. We've got to work together. Not only that, but we're about to go on another expedition . . ."

"You didn't mind New York."

"That was different." The first time they had slept together, it was while they were researching the causes of the Great Depression of the twentieth century. Three days after the crash of the New York Stock Exchange, it had been easy to get a suite at the Waldorf-Astoria; by then, they wanted some relief from the mass panic that had caused young millionaires to throw themselves through office windows. "That was a Class-3," she added, speaking a little more softly now. "We're about to do a Class-1. You know how dangerous that is."

Franc reluctantly nodded. Like it or not, he had to agree. Class-3 expeditions were relatively low-risk sorties so long as no one interfered with the turn of events. The stock-market crash of 1929 was one of these, as was the *Challenger* disaster of 1985. Class-2 expeditions were more difficult, since they required CRC researchers to be closer to hazardous situations: the Paris student riots of 1968 were an example, as was pre-Renaissance Europe during the Plague. Class-1 missions were those in which the lives of researchers were directly placed in jeopardy. During the entire existence of the Chronospace Research Centre, there had only been two previous Class-1 expeditions: the eruption of Mont Pelée on Martinique in 1902, and the Battle of Gettysburg in 1864. No one had been hurt during the 1902 expedition, mainly because the research team had vacated St. Pierre before the village was destroyed, but during the Gettysburg expedition a CRC historian posing as a contemporary newspaper reporter was shot and killed by a Confederate rifleman while attempting to document Pickett's Charge. His colleagues had been forced to leave his body behind, after first removing his recording equipment. Fortunately, there had been no risk of causing a paradox; so many unidentified corpses had littered the Gettysburg battlefield, the addition of one more made no real difference.

Since then, the Board of Review had been more careful in selecting potential missions. This wasn't a difficult task; because of the inherent limitations posed by chronospace travel, many destinations were already out of the question. For reasons as yet unknown, it was impossible to travel farther back in time than approximately one thousand years. No one knew why, yet all previous attempts to open Morris-Thorne bridges that extended beyond the mid-1300s failed when the tunnels through the spacetime foam collapsed in upon themselves. Although there seemed to be no static cutoff line, the barrier existed nevertheless.

Likewise, although a timeship was able to return to its point of departure—say, from 1902 to Tues, Feb 12, 2313, when the Mont Pelée expedition was sent out—it was impossible to travel past the departure point. Therefore, the future was just as unvisitable as the more distant past. Just as no expeditions would ever be sent to witness the crucifixion of Christ or the destruction of the Library of Alexandria no one from the early twenty-fourth century would ever know what happened even a nanosecond after their departure. Chronospace could be breached, but it would never be conquered.

The *Hindenburg* expedition was dangerous. Franc didn't dispute that. He was about to ask why this made any difference to their relationship when something scuttled across the ceiling past his shoulder. A tail gently flicked the side of his side, then a shrill voice shrieked next to his ear:

"Come now, come now, Franc Lu come to Paolo! Hurry! Come now!"

Franc quickly looked around, saw a blue-skinned lizard clinging to the ceiling rail. About fifteen centimeters in length, it regarded him through doll-like black eyes. When it spoke again, a long red tongue vibrated within its elongated mouth: "Come now! Now! Paolo wants you! Now!"

"Marcel!" Lea had anticipated seeing the little mimosaur again. Before she had boarded the shuttle at Mare Imbrium, she had taken a moment to purchase some cashews from a spaceport vendor. She pulled the bag out of her pocket and ripped open the cellophane. "Here," she said, pushing off from the wall and gliding beneath Franc. "Brought these especially for you."

"*Nuts!* Nuts nuts nuts nuts!" Marcel leaped from the handrail onto Lea's shoulder. She laughed delightedly as the lizard curled its long tail around her neck, then she let the mimosaur thrust its mouth into the bag, gently stroking the fin on the back of its head.

"That's one way of shutting him up," Franc murmured. Personally, he found Marcel a trifle annoying. "He'll make a fine pair of shoes one day."

Mimosaurs were among the more interesting inhabitants of Gliese 876-B, an Earth-like satellite orbiting a gas giant fifteen light-years from Earth. Discovered during one of humankind's first interstellar expeditions, they possessed the ability to learn simple words or phrases and recite them at will, along with an excellent memory for faces and names. Although they weren't much more intelligent than the average house cat, they were far more adaptable to microgravity, which made them the favored pets of deep-space explorers. Paolo Sanchez had brought Marcel home from his last voyage as captain of the *Olaf Stapledon* before taking his present position as CRC's Chief Commissioner. Now the mimosaur served as Sanchez's messenger, running errands for him within Chronos Station.

Lea cast him a hostile glare. "Better be nice, or I'll have him wake you up tomorrow morning." She smiled at Marcel as she fed him the rest of his favorite treat. "Sousa. Do you remember Sousa, Marcel? Dah-dah-dah . . . dum-de-dah-dah-dum-de-dah . . . ?"

On cue, Marcel lifted his head from the bag and began to whistle "The Stars and Stripes Forever," just as Lea had taught him several months ago. That was as much as Franc could stomach. He had a low tolerance for cuteness.

"I get the point." He turned and pushed himself toward Arm 6. "Let's go see what Paolo has to say."

Sixteen letters awaited Murphy when he checked his
morning email. This wasn't unusual; given a choice between picking up the phone or writing a memo, NASA
people tended to opt for the latter. Sometimes his email
came from people in the same building, even just down the
hall. It was more convenient this way, to be sure, especially
since it allowed the sender to attach files without having to
use paper that inevitably would have to be recycled.

Nonetheless, there were times when he wondered whether
email wasn't the largest drawback of the computer revolution. At least three times a day he had to check for new
messages, and every one of them had to be answered, if
only by a short line: "Got it. Thanks. DZM." Government
work used to be a never-ending paper chase; now it was an
electron derby.

Murphy pulled off his snow boots, slipped on a pair of
felt loafers he kept beneath his desk, then settled the keyboard on his lap as he put his feet up on the desktop. Most
of the stuff in queue was fairly routine. A note from one of
his contacts at JPL in Pasadena, answering a couple of
questions he had about Galileo data. Another message from

another JPL scientist, with an attached GIF from Mars Pathfinder. A half dozen news releases from the press office, updates on the next shuttle mission and the current status of the Space Station program. A letter from a friend at Goddard Space Flight Center out in Greenbelt, telling him that he was coming into D.C. on Thursday and asking if he would be free for lunch. A Dilbert strip from last week which he had already read and forgotten, sent via listserv by a pal at Interior who apparently believed the comic strip was the font of all human wisdom; another jester relayed Letterman's Top-Ten list of the come-on lines President Clinton might have tried on Paula Jones, which Murphy deleted without reading.

As he scrolled down the screen, Murphy picked up the chipped Star Wars mug Steven had given him for his birthday a couple of years ago, sipped the lukewarm coffee he had taken from the break room down the hall. Yet even as he skimmed through the email, his mind was elsewhere.

Why would an article in *Analog* garner so much attention from an associate administrator? After all, January was the beginning of the Washington budget season. As always, NASA would not only have to put together a proposal for the White House to take before Congress, but the Office of Space Science would also have to publicly defend its programs from critics on the Hill. So why would Roger Ordmann take an hour from his schedule—indeed, be willing to make himself late for a House subcommittee hearing—just to talk to some junior staffer who had written a piece about UFOs for a science fiction magazine?

And wasn't there something rather unconstitutional about Ordmann's insistence that he submit all future articles to Public Affairs Office? NASA was a civilian agency; although it still maintained ties to the Department of Defense, it had been several years since the last time a military payload had been sent into orbit aboard a shuttle, and now that the Air Force had its own space program, Murphy never heard of any classified projects being undertaken by

NASA. Had Kent Morris, a former Pentagon PAO, simply been overeager? And if so, why would Ordmann mandate a review of any future articles Murphy might write?

Murphy rubbed the bridge of his nose between thumb and forefinger as he glanced out the window. White flakes of snow flurried outside, obscuring the low rooftops that stretched out toward the Potomac. Although he was fortunate enough to have a window office, he didn't rate high enough for a view of the Capitol. He gazed up at the narrow shelf above his desk: loose-leaf report binders, reference texts on astronautics and space physics, a few recent pop-science books about planetary exploration, guarded by the Darth Vader and Luke Skywalker action figures he bought for himself once when he had taken Steven to Toys "R" Us.

"Trust the Force, Luke," he murmured. Yeah, right. And you know what Darth Vader would have said. *The Force is strong with you . . . but you're not a Jedi yet. . . .*

The phone rang, startling him from his reverie. Murphy dropped his feet from the desk, reached forward to pick up the receiver.

"Space Science, Murphy," he said.

For a moment, he heard nothing, making him wonder if someone in the building had dialed the wrong extension. It happened all the time. Then, a male voice:

"Is this Za . . . I mean, David Z. Murphy?"

"Speaking."

"The same David Z. Murphy who writes for *Analog?*"

"Sometimes, yeah." He glanced at the button pad, noted that the call was coming in from the outside line. "Who's calling, please?"

"Dr. Murphy, this is Gregory Benford. I'm a professor of physics at the University of California-Irvine. I also write science fiction on occasion."

Murphy's mouth dropped open. "Yes, of course I've heard of you." He sat up straight in his chair. "I'm a big fan of your work."

Which was the unvarnished truth. One of the SF authors

whom he admired the most was Gregory Benford; not only did he have a superb imagination, but he was also one of the small handful of writers whose novels and stories possessed a high degree of scientific plausibility. When Murphy began writing, one of the authors whose style he had consciously attempted to emulate was Benford's, albeit unsuccessfully.

A dry chuckle from the other end of the line. "Call me Greg, please. And I rather like your stuff, too."

"But I haven't written any . . ." Then he realized Benford wasn't talking about science fiction. "Oh, you mean my *Analog* articles."

"You mean you've been published elsewhere? I haven't seen your by-line except in . . ."

"No, no," Murphy said hastily. "The things I've done for *Analog* are all . . . I mean, y'know, I've tried to write fiction, but they didn't . . . I mean, it just didn't work out."

"That's too bad. Anyway, Dr. Murphy . . ."

"David."

"Sure. Anyway, as I was saying, the reason why I'm calling is that I've just read that article about time travel . . ."

"Really?" Murphy absently picked up a paper clip, tumbled it between his fingers. "Hope you liked it. I mean, I was really out in left field . . ."

"No, no, it was really quite interesting. The premise is a bit radical, to be sure, but you managed to support it quite well. I'm quite intrigued by the idea. In fact, I was hoping we could discuss it further. I have questions I'd like to ask you."

"Certainly. My pleasure." Murphy craned his neck to glance at the wall clock near the door. "I've got a department meeting in about a half hour, but I've got time before then. What do you want to know?"

"Actually, I sort of hoped we could get together for lunch."

Murphy's eyebrows rose. "For lunch? Today?"

"Sure, if it's not too much trouble. I'm in town right

now . . . there was a physics conference in Baltimore last weekend, and I stayed over to visit some friends in the area. I'm catching a flight back to L.A. this afternoon, but I've got some time to kill before then. Since I knew you worked at NASA, I thought I'd give you a buzz and see if you were available for lunch."

Odd. Murphy hadn't heard of any physics conferences being held in Baltimore, and his colleagues at Goddard were usually pretty good about keeping him informed of these things. Yet such conferences were commonplace; this one probably slipped his mind. "No . . . I mean, yes. By all means, I'd love to get together with you. Where are you staying? I'll . . ."

"I was at the Hyatt, but I've already checked out," Benford said. "Actually, I was thinking about dropping by the Air and Space Museum. It's close to you, and I don't want to take up your whole lunch hour, so why don't we meet there?"

"Well . . . sure," Murphy said, a little more reluctantly than he meant to sound. There was a restaurant on the museum's fourth floor, but it wasn't anything special: a cafeteria for tourists, offering little more than cheeseburgers and pizza. If he was going to have lunch with Gregory Benford, he would have preferred a more upscale bistro. There were a half dozen good cafés on Capitol Hill where they could meet. Yet Benford was probably in a hurry; after all, he had a plane to catch later today. "The Air and Space it is. How about twelve noon?"

"That's good for me. I'll meet you . . . how about on the ground floor, in front of the lunar lander? At twelve o'clock?"

"Fine by me. Twelve noon, then."

"Very good, David. I'll see you then."

"It'll be a pleasure, Dr. . . . Greg, I mean."

Another warm chuckle. "The pleasure's all mine. See you at noon. Bye."

Murphy put down the phone, took a deep breath, slowly

let it out as he leaned back in his chair. How strange life could be sometimes. You start the morning getting carpeted by an associate administrator for something you've written, then less than an hour later you receive a call from one of the world's leading SF authors, complimenting you for the same material and requesting your company for lunch.

"Maybe he's right," he muttered. "I ought to be a science fiction writer."

The Chief Commissioner's suite was located on Deck 6A, at the top of Arm 6. Like nearly half of Chronos Station's personnel, Paolo Sanchez had been born and raised on the Moon, and therefore preferred the decks closer to the hub, where the centripedal force was one-sixth Earth-normal. Unlike most other selenians, though, Sanchez had never visited Earth. As a former starship captain who had spent most of his ninety-seven Gregorians aboard ships and orbitals, it was likely that a trip to his ancestral home in Mexico City would be lethal. If high gravity didn't crush his bones or bring about a coronary seizure, then he would soon become fatally ill from any one of thousands of air-borne microorganisms against which his body did not have any natural defenses.

Franc and Lea entered Sanchez's office through an antechamber that briefly subjected them to intense UV radiation. They shut their eyes and covered their faces with their hands until the humming ceased and a bell chimed, then the door slid open. The mimosaur, who had buried its face within Lea's collar during the decontamination procedure, immediately leaped from her shoulder and bounded across the broad, semicircular room.

"Franc here, Lea here!" Marcel's voice was an excited squeal. "Lea give Marcel nuts! Franc say . . ." Its voice changed to a pitch-perfect imitation of Franc's: "That's one way of shutting him up. He'll make a fine pair of shoes one day."

Franc winced. One more reason why he disliked mimosaurs in general, and Marcel in particular: they had a tendency to repeat verbatim everything they heard, particularly when it had to do with themselves. "A joke, sir," he said. "I didn't mean it the way it sounds."

"I certainly hope not," Sanchez replied coldly. "I like my friend just the way he is."

The Commissioner was seated in a wing-back chair, surrounded by the three-dimensional framework of his desk. Writing tables, flatscreens, data units, shelves, and cabinets encompassed him like a cage; when he moved in a certain direction, his chair automatically pivoted upon six major points of axis. As Marcel ran toward him, Sanchez shifted his skeletal body slightly, and the chair rotated him from upside down to an upright position. The blue lizard leaped onto a slender bar holding a flatscreen, then bounced into Sanchez's lap.

"Sing Sousa for Lea!" Marcel yelped as it nuzzled against the long, white-streaked beard flowing down Sanchez's shallow chest. "She like! Sing for you . . . ?" Once again, it began to whistle the archaic marching-band song.

"No, no, Marcel. Thank you, but another time." Sanchez gently stroked the back of the mimosaur's neck with his bony fingers. The mimosaur went quiet, save for a contented reptilian purr. "Hush now. We have many things to discuss."

Having soothed his pet to silence, Sanchez raised dark eyes that vaguely hinted at his Latino bloodline. "Dr.

Oschner, Dr. Lu, *gracias* for coming here on such short notice. I hope your holiday was pleasant."

"Muchas gracias, señor." Franc found a seat in one of the normal-style chairs positioned outside the Commissioner's desk. "It was very pleasant. Thank you for allowing us to take a furlough."

"Sì, señor. Taking a break helped us immensely." Like Franc, Lea addressed the Commissioner in formal Spanish. It wasn't necessary to do so, of course, yet it was common knowledge among CRC researchers that Sanchez was proud of his Mexican ancestry. His office was decorated with murals of nineteenth-century Catholic missions, and a matador's costume and swords, brought back from a CRC expedition to that period, hung within an airtight frame on the wall behind his desk. If Sanchez had been physically capable of leading an expedition himself, it would probably be a Class-1 to the Republic of Texas, so he could witness the Battle of the Alamo firsthand.

"I'm glad to hear that." The Commissioner switched back to colloquial English. "So you're ready for the C120-37?" he added, referring to the upcoming expedition by its serial number. "I take it that you've completed your research."

"Yes, sir," Franc said. "Lea and I finished our work at Tycho College. We've confirmed through contemporary census records that our personae perished aboard the *Hindenburg.* Pending successful extraction by the *Miranda,* we should able to assume their roles with no major problems."

"I'm meeting with the *Miranda* team later in order to work out the final details." Lea raised her left arm, touched her wristcomp. "Here's the preliminary report, as you've requested."

Thank you." The frail fingers of Sanchez's left hand glided across the keypad on his armrest. The chair swiveled to the right and tilted upward slightly, allowing him to gaze at a screen above his head. The two researchers patiently waited while the Commissioner skimmed Lea's report. "And you'll be able to record their vocal patterns?"

"The extraction team will do that before we arrive," Lea said. "The Frankfurter Hof was the favored hotel for American travelers, and the plan is for them to pick up our personae a few hours before our arrival."

"John and Emma Pannes visited the Alte Oper the night before the *Hindenburg* left Frankfurt," Franc added. "That's within walking distance of the opera, so the plan calls for the abduction to take place in a pedestrian mall between those two points."

Sanchez raised an elegantly tufted eyebrow. "And how do you intend to accomplish this, if it's in a public place?"

"Two members of the *Miranda* team will be posing as Gestapo agents, and they'll have rented an automobile for transportation. They'll drive to the curb, stop, get out, and approach Mr. and Mrs. Pannes. After presenting their documents, they'll demand that they accompany them." Franc smiled. "This sort of thing was a common occurrence at this place and time, particularly in regard to foreigners. No one will report it. This was a very paranoid society, after all."

"And the placement of your equipment?"

"Once the Pannes have been spirited away," Lea said, "the team members will return to the Frankfurter Hof, this time dressed as civilians. They'll be carrying our luggage. Once they've checked into the hotel, they will simply take our luggage to the Pannes' room and, after using their room keys to gain entrance, substitute our bags for their bags, replacing tags as necessary. Early the next morning, they'll check out again and return to the safe house in Griesheim."

Sanchez nodded, but didn't say anything as he continued reading the report. Franc was puzzled by his reticence. For a Class-1 briefing, the Commissioner was asking remarkably few questions. When Franc had been on the 1929

New York expedition, Sanchez had peppered his team with dozens of inquiries, and that had only been a Class-3 survey. This trip was not only more dangerous, it was also far more complex. Two timeships working in tandem, with the extraction of two contemporaries from a potentially hostile environment and replacing them with two researchers who would be in situ during a major disaster . . . any one of several dozen things could go wrong at any time. Not only that, but once he and Lea were aboard the *Hindenburg* and it was in flight, there was no way the mission could be aborted.

Nonetheless, Sanchez seemed to be accepting their prognosis at face value. Was the Commissioner becoming complacent? Or, as the thought suddenly occurred to Franc, was he preoccupied with some other matter?

He shifted uncomfortably in his seat. From the corner of his eye, he saw Lea do the same. The mimosaur stood up in Sanchez's lap, yawned and stretched in an oddly feline way, then hopped upon the warm surface of a data unit and curled up to take a nap. After a while, Sanchez grunted with what might have been satisfaction and rotated his chair to face them.

"Your preliminary report appears to cover all the foreseeable factors," he said, "and as you probably expect, I have quite a few questions to ask. But there's something I'd like to bring to your attention first . . . an incident that occurred during our last expedition."

"The last expedition?" Franc glanced at Lea, then back at Sanchez. "If you mean the C320-29, we didn't . . ."

"No, no." Sanchez shook his head. "The C320-29 was flawless. If it hadn't gone well, I would have never approved of the proposal for C120-37." He smiled slightly. "And, yes, Dr. Lu, if this expedition is successful and your team delivers useful new information, I'll consider taking your proposal for the C120-12 to the Board."

Franc took a deep breath. The C120-12 was his dream

mission: an expedition to Southampton, England, in 1912 to place two or more researchers aboard the HMS *Titanic* before it embarked upon its doomed Atlantic crossing. Within the CRC, this was widely considered to be the Mt. Everest of historical surveys, mainly because of the extraordinary risks it presented. In many ways, the C120-37 was a rehearsal for the C120-12; if he and Lea could prove that two CRC researchers could record the *Hindenburg* disaster and survive, then putting historians aboard the *Titanic* would be considered feasible.

"Thank you, sir," he said. "I appreciate your support."

"That's beside the point. I'm referring to the last expedition. The one which returned last week." He peered at him through the bars of his desk. "The C314-65. The *Miranda* expedition to New Mexico. You haven't studied the final report?"

He knew about the mission to which Sanchez was referring, but he was embarrassed to admit that he hadn't been keeping track of it. Lea stepped in to save him. "Many apologies, sir," she said. "We were so involved with our own work, we didn't have a chance to . . ."

"Not acceptable, Dr. Oschner. All researchers are required to read reports from previous expeditions. The objectives may be different, but there's much to learned from . . ." Sanchez sighed, looked away. "I'm sorry. Perhaps I should know better. Thirteenth-century North American history isn't your area, and you've been preoccupied with the C120-37." Then he looked back at them. "You say you haven't spoken with Hans Brech? He was the *Miranda*'s pilot for that mission, and for your own as well." He hesitated. "By the way, Vasili Metz will be your pilot on the *Oberon*. Any objections?"

Franc pursed his lips and hoped that Sanchez wouldn't pick up on his distaste for Metz. He was a good timeship pilot—one of the best, Franc had to reluctantly admit—yet they had worked together during the C320-29, and Franc had found Metz to be insufferable. "No, sir," he said, then he changed the subject. "I haven't spoken with Hans. Did something happen during his last flight?"

Sanchez said nothing for a moment. He settled his wiry frame back in his chair and solemnly regarded them with his unfathomable black eyes.

"Hans says they saw an angel," he said at last.

Monday, January 14, 1998: 11:58 A.M.

A frigid blast of wind followed Murphy through the rear entrance of the National Air and Space Museum. Pausing for a moment by the Robert McCall mural to unbutton his parka, he glanced around the lobby. Save for a boisterous group of elementary-school children on a field trip, the ground floor was uncommonly quiet. A handful of people strolled through the Hall of Flight, pausing now and then to examine the Apollo 11 command module and Alan Shepard's Mercury capsule, while kids in hockey jackets chased each other beneath the Wright Brothers flyer and the Bell X-1. By next spring, the museum would regain its stature as one of Washington's most crowded public sites, yet during winter it was mainly visited by locals taking advantage of the dearth of tourists.

Blowing into the palms of his chilled hands, Murphy quickly walked through the museum, entering the Hall of Astronautics in the building's west wing. He had been here countless times, yet still he hadn't become jaded to the exhibits on this side of the building. A life-size mock-up of the Skylab space station; just beyond it, Apollo and Soyuz spacecraft, permanently docked in low orbit; between them, a small forest of boosters—Scout, Mercury-Redstone, Atlas, Titan II. As often as he had seen these giants, Murphy still found himself slowing his pace to marvel at them, and it was only when he happened to spot the digital clock above the entrance to the IMAX theater that he remembered that he had a lunch date to keep.

At the far end of the hall, symbolically positioned in front of the tall windows overlooking the Capitol Building, rested a full-size mock-up of the Apollo 11 Lunar Module. Schoolchildren impatiently shuffled their feet while a teacher attempted to explain its historical significance; they were more interested in the posters advertising the *Star Wars* exhibit on the third floor. Yet the tall gentleman standing near the red velvet rope seemed fascinated by the spacecraft. As Murphy walked closer, he saw him hunch forward slightly, as if to more closely examine one of the silver Mylar-covered panels on its lower fuselage.

Murphy approached him. "Dr. Benford?"

Startled, the visitor looked around sharply, then turned to face him. "Dr. Murphy, I presume." He pulled a hand from the pocket of his parka. "Greg Benford. Pleased to meet you. Thanks for taking time to . . ."

"No, no, really. The pleasure's all mine." Murphy returned the affable smile as they shook hands. "Like I said on the phone, this is a real surprise. I never expected . . ."

"Any chance I get to come here, I take it." Benford glanced again at the LM. "Always seems a little bigger than you think it is. When you see it in pictures from the Moon, it looks small, but then you get up close . . ."

"I know what you mean, yeah." For once, though, Murphy found himself ignoring the LM. It was an odd experience, meeting someone whose photo he had previously seen on the back flaps of book jackets. Nonetheless, it was the same person: trim gray beard, salted brown hair, calm and studious eyes framed by wire-rim glasses. About his own height, with a middle-age paunch around the waistline. The barest trace of a Southern accent.

So this was Greg Benford. The author of "Doing Lennon," the story which caused him to blow a high-school chemistry exam because he preferred to read it behind his textbook when he should have been paying attention to a review session, and *In the Ocean of Night,* which made him forget that he was supposed to take Karen Dolen to the freshman mixer, and *Artifact,* which he read during his honeymoon vacation in England, and . . .

"It really is an amazing machine." Benford took a final glance at the LM, then he pulled back the sleeve of his L.L. Bean parka, glanced at the Rolex on his left wrist. "But, hey, I don't want to keep you. I know you've got to get back to work soon."

"No problem." Murphy shook his head. "Really. I've done my last meeting for the day, and it isn't like I've got to punch a clock."

"Yeah, but I've still got a plane to catch." Benford nodded toward the nearby staircase. The field trippers were already scurrying upstairs, screaming with adolescent excitement, followed by their exhausted teacher. "We'd better hurry, if don't want to get caught behind the rugrats. After you . . ."

And so they marched up the four flights to the café, carrying on idle conversation until they reached the restaurant. The kids got there first, of course, but they were clustered outside, waiting for the rest of their group. Murphy led his guest past them into the cafeteria, and while they picked up plastic trays and began moving down the serving line, he told Benford about his work at the agency, how he had been hired to write summaries of current NASA science programs and expressing his frustration that it wasn't the basic research for which he had been trained, his hopes that he might one day get transferred to Marshall or Goddard, or maybe even JPL in Pasadena. He even found himself talking about the irritation of having to take the Metro to work today before he realized that this probably wouldn't interest anyone.

For his part, Benford kept his silence, listening attentively yet nonetheless remaining laconic. He said that he was writing a nonfiction book titled *Deep Time,* but he didn't say much of what it was about, and he casually mentioned his involvement in a TV miniseries about a Mars colony, yet he distracted himself by asking for Italian dressing to go with his garden salad when Murphy pressed for details. After a while, Murphy came to the conclusion that Greg was better at listening than talking. So much the better; during his tenure at NASA, he had met far too many egoists who could smother you with their bombast, and with far less justification.

They took their trays to a table near the back of the room, where they hoped to avoid the noise created by forty children piling into the cafeteria. "So," Benford said as he reached for the pepper shaker, "about this UFO article . . . what inspired you to write it?"

Murphy shrugged. "Remember that piece in *Analog* a long time ago, 'How to Build a Flying Saucer'?" Benford thought about it a moment, then shook his head. "Anyway, someone examined the reports about UFOs—their general appearance, how they fly, the electromagnetic disturbances they're supposed to cause, so forth and so on—and wrote an article which explained them, more or less, on the basis of aeronautical science and known physics. I just took it a step further, really. Ask the next question, as Theodore Sturgeon used to say."

Benford speared a cucumber slice with his fork. "And what question was that?"

"If we accept the premise that UFOs exist . . . just for the sake of argument . . . then we've got to ask where they come from." Warming to the subject, Murphy ignored the cheeseburger growing cold on his plate. "The extraterrestrial hypothesis, of course, is the favorite explanation, but that falls apart when you look at it from a logical perspective. There aren't any other planets in our solar system where intelligent life could have evolved, let alone a technologically advanced race. The nearest habitable star systems are dozens of light-years away, so someone out there could conceivably have built starships to visit us, but any ship capable of travelling such enormous distances would have to be very large. The size of a small moon, really, if they're reliant upon sub-c drives . . ."

"Sub-c?" Benford shook his head. "I don't understand."

"Umm . . . y'know. If c is the mathematical constant for the speed of light, then something travelling slower than light-speed is . . ."

"Oh, right. Of course." Benford shook his head. "Sorry. Just a little distracted." He nodded toward the children cavorting nearby. "You were saying . . . ?"

"Right . . . well, if no one has seen a UFO that's the reasonable size of a starship, and if we reject the notion that mother ships are lurking nearby . . . because, y'know, any backyard astronomer with a decent telescope would be able to spot them . . . then we have to discard the idea that they're from space."

"As most scientists already do." Benford used his fork to play with his salad. "Have you read Philip Klass's work? He's been debunking UFO sightings for a long time."

"And I don't argue with any of it." Murphy chuckled. "Believe me, I'm not a UFO buff of any sort. I think Klass is on the right track. If you ask me, ninety-nine percent of UFO sightings are a crock. If they're not hoaxes or optical illusions, then they're cloud formations, airplanes, meteors, hot-air balloons . . . anything but spaceships."

"And the remaining one percent?"

Murphy picked up a couple of fries, daubed them in the tiny cup of ketchup. "The remaining one percent is the stuff no one's been able to adequately explain, or at least without stretching things . . . swamp gas, Venus, all that. That doesn't mean there aren't reasonable explanations. We just haven't learned what they are yet."

"Which brings us to time machines."

"Sort of." Murphy shrugged. "I'm just playing the 'what

if' game. Time travel may not be a reasonable explanation, but it certainly is a rational one. I mean, realistically speaking, an operational time machine would have to perform much like a spacecraft. First, it would have to open a quantum wormhole, and the only place you can safely do that is outside the atmosphere. Second, it would have to be capable of atmospheric flight. A saucer-shaped vehicle could do this. And third, a time traveler would probably want to be secretive, which accounts for why no flying saucers have landed on the White House lawn."

"Sounds like a reasonable line of thought."

"I kind of think so. Maybe it's baloney . . . but like I said, I was just conducting a thought experiment." Realizing that he was hungry, he picked up his cheeseburger. "Hey, apropos of nothing, but . . . if I sent you my copy of *Heart of the Comet,* would you sign it for me?"

"Sure, I'd be happy to."

"That'd be great." Murphy lifted the cheeseburger's bun to make sure that there wasn't a pickle hidden beneath it. "Maybe someday I can get Brin to sign it, too."

"Who?"

"David Brin." Murphy peered at him, but Benford's expression remained neutral. "Your collaborator. The guy who cowrote . . ."

"Oh, yeah. Right." Benford grinned sheepishly. "David, of course." He shook his head. "Sorry. It's been a long weekend." He plunged his fork back into his salad. "It's an interesting theory, but not entirely original. I've seen some New Age books that postulate much the same idea."

"So have I. One guy even went so far as to claim that Einstein was a time traveller. But that's not where I'm coming from. In fact, I don't even believe this myself . . ."

"You don't?" Benford looked up. "But you made a pretty good case, and you supported it with known physics. The idea that wormholes, if they could be artificially created, could serve as gateways through time as well as through space . . . that was very convincing."

"Thanks, but I was only reiterating things Hawking and Thorne have said. You're familiar with their work, of course." Benford gave a noncommittal nod. "Really, I was just doing the same thing that science fiction writers do . . . throwing out ideas, playing with crazy notions. It doesn't necessarily mean that I think UFOs are time machines. It's just . . . well, it's just something to think about."

"It certainly got my attention, that's for sure." Benford reached for the pepper shaker again. "That's why I decided to call you. I read your piece on the plane flight over here, and thought it might be a good premise for a novel."

"Really? I'm flattered."

"Uh-huh." Benford shook some more pepper over his salad. "I've never written a time-machine story, y'know. I figured this might be a good place to start."

Murphy said nothing for a moment. Behind them, the schoolchildren were making a ruckus as they moved through the cafeteria line, fighting over slices of pizza while their harried teachers tried to keep them from turning the restaurant upside-down. Gregory Benford continued to poke at his salad. For the first time during their conversation, it seemed to Murphy as if he was consciously avoiding his gaze.

"Will you excuse me a moment?" he asked.

"Sure." Benford barely looked up from his plate. "Not a problem."

Murphy forced a smile as he pushed back his chair and rose from the table. He looked around for a moment until he found the signs indicating the way to the rest rooms. Trying not to walk too fast, he left the cafeteria.

As he hoped, there was a pay phone on the wall between the men's and ladies' rooms. Picking up the receiver, he shoved a quarter into the slot, then dialed the number for NASA's main switchboard from memory. "Jan Zimmermann, please," he said once the operator answered, and glanced at a nearby ceiling clock. It was almost a quarter to one; he hoped that Jan was still brown-bagging her lunch at her desk.

A short pause, then the phone buzzed twice. It was picked up on the third ring. "Policy and Plans, Janice Zimmermann."

"Jan, it's David Murphy. How'ya doing?"

The voice brightened. "Dave! I read your article in *Analog* this month! Great stuff!"

Murphy smiled despite himself. Although she held a low-level position, Jan Zimmermann was one of NASA's true believers, those who worked for the agency because they fervently supported the idea of space exploration. But more importantly, or at least at this particular moment, she was a science fiction fan.

"Thanks, I appreciate it." Murphy glanced over his shoulder. "Hey, I'm in a little bit of a rush here, but . . ."

"What can I do for you, hon? Did you get my email about the next Disclave?"

A longtime member of the Washington Science Fiction Society, Jan was deeply involved in running the annual SF convention held in Maryland. As head of programming, Jan had been bugging him to be a guest speaker for several years now. He had always turned her down, if only because the thought of sitting on a panel made him uneasy, but now that invitation might work in his favor. . . .

"Sure did," he said. "In fact, that's sort of why I'm calling. I'd like to show up this year, but I'm sort of thinking that I'd like to do a panel with Gregory Benford, if he's going to be there."

"Well, I dunno . . ." Jan sounded reluctant. "He was a Disclave guest several years ago, but he hasn't been back since . . ."

"Do you have his number?" Murphy asked, seeing his opening. "I've been in touch with him recently . . . I mean, he sent me a letter just a little while ago . . . and maybe I could talk him into coming out here for the next convention."

"Really? That would be fantastic! Hold on a sec . . ." There was a short pause, during which Murphy heard a vague rustling in the background; he imagined her searching through the perpetual mess on her desk for an address book. He reached into his shirt pocket, found a Bic pen. After a few moments, her voice came back: "Okay, here it is. It's his office number . . ."

Cradling the receiver against his shoulder, Murphy scribbled down the number on the back of his left hand, then repeated it back to Jan to make sure he had copied it correctly. "Thanks, dear," he said. "I've really got to run. I'll get back to you."

Hoping he wasn't being rude, he hung up, then pulled his wallet from his back pocket. After locating his ATT card, he carefully dialed the number Jan had given him, charging it to his home phone.

Somewhere on the other side of the continent, a phone began to ring. Once, twice, three times . . . Murphy glanced at the clock. It was nearly ten to one; in California, it would be almost ten o'clock. It shouldn't be too early to . . .

The phone was picked up on the fourth ring.

"Hello?" a familiar voice said.

Murphy felt something tickle the nape of his neck.

"Ahh . . . Dr. Gregory Benford, please."

"Speaking."

"Greg Benford?" Murphy flattened the receiver against his ear. "Is this Gregory Benford, the writer?"

"Ahh . . . well, yes, it is, May I ask who's calling?"

The very same voice. From over three thousand miles away.

"I'm . . . I'm . . ." Murphy felt a hot rush through his face. "I'm sorry, sir, but . . . sorry, I think there's been a mistake."

"What? I don't. . . ."

Murphy slammed down the phone, his mind racing as he sought to understand what was happening.

He had just met someone who looked exactly like Gregory Benford, who sounded just like Gregory Benford, but who was not only ignorant of one of the most common mathematical denominators in theoretical physics, but had also forgotten that he had coauthored a best-selling novel with another physicist, David Brin. Sure, all this might be explained by travel fatigue. Yet Gregory Benford would never be amnesiac of the fact that he had written *Timescape,* a novel which was not only regarded as one of his best-known works, and a Nebula Award winner as well . . .

But also a time-machine story.

Yet the Greg Benford with whom he had just shared lunch claimed never to have written a time-machine story.

And now, however briefly, Murphy had spoken with a Gregory Benford whose voice was absolutely identical, yet who was in his office on the other side of the country.

"Son of a . . . !" Murphy slammed his fist against the phone, then turned and stalked back down the hall toward the restaurant. Whoever this guy was, he had just played him like a yo-yo. It was a good impersonation, to be sure. For a little while there, the impostor had actually convinced him that he was the real deal. But just wait until . . .

Murphy stopped at the cafeteria entrance.

Their table was vacant. The chair where the impostor had been seated had been pushed back. Only their cafeteria trays remained in place. Children ran back and forth through the restaurant, but his lunch companion was nowhere to be seen.

Murphy stared at the table, then dashed to the nearby stairwell. Catching himself against the railing, he peered down. Far below, he saw the top of Apollo lunar module, but nothing else. No one was on the stairs.

What the hell was going on here?

Like a scarab caught within a web of electrical lines and mooring cables, the *Oberon* floated in spacedock, its silver hull reflecting the raw sunlight that steamed through the bay doors. Hardsuited space workers moved around the timeship, their tethers uncoiling behind them as they inspected the vehicle's negmass grid and wormhole generators. Standing in an observation cupola overlooking the spherical hangar, Franc watched the activity while he waited for the gangway to mate with the vessel. A foreman at a nearby console studied his screens as he gently coaxed the joystick that maneuvered the gangway into position; when its boxlike airlock was firmly nestled against the *Oberon,* he locked it into place and glanced over his shoulder at Franc.

"All right, Dr. Lu, you can go through now. Vasili's waiting for you aboard."

"Danke shön." He was still practicing his German; the foreman gave him a baffled look in return. Franc slipped his feet from the stirrups on the floor, then pushed himself toward a nearby hatch. It parted in the center with a soft hiss, and he ducked his head as he entered an accordion-

walled tunnel. The gangway was cold, its handholds frigid to the touch; regretting that he had neglected to put on a sweater before coming down here, he moved quickly down the long passageway.

At the end of the tunnel, he reached up and pressed a couple of recessed buttons on the ceiling. A panel flashed from red to green, then the gangway hatch rolled open, revealing the timeship's outer hatch. Much to his irritation, it was still shut. "I'm here, Vasili," he murmured, tapping his headset mike. "You can let me in anytime you're ready."

There was no reply, but a few moments later the hatch irised open. A young man floating upside down within the airlock peered down at him. "Sorry, Franc," he said, giving him a embarrassed grin as he extended a hand. "We didn't hear you coming."

Vasili had doubtless known that he was on his way over; he was just subtly reminding Franc who was in the charge of the timeship, if not the expedition. "Not a problem, Tom." He grasped Hoffman's hand and allowed himself to be pulled up into the narrow compartment. "Everything on schedule?"

"We're finishing the checklist now." Hoffman backed away and nearly banged the back of his head against an open service port in the ceiling. He carefully shut it, mindful not to loosen the color-coded ribbons tied around the snakelike conduits that dangled from within. "Got a few more things to do, but we'll be out of here on time."

Franc nodded as he glanced around the compartment. While in spacedock, the timeship's artificial gravity was neutralized; since its floors and ceilings lacked handrails and foot restraints, slender nylon ropes had been temporarily laid throughout the vessel's four major compartments. He noted that the timeship's EVA suit was barely fastened to the wall; someone had used it recently and hadn't stowed it properly. "Good to hear," he said, reaching over to cinch its straps a little more tightly. "Hey, nice haircut."

"Like it?" The last time Franc had seen Hoffman, he

was still sporting a scalplock. The braid was gone now, replaced by an early-twentieth-century hairstyle: sides and
back trimmed close, slightly longer on top, neatly parted
on the left. "I got it from a picture of Charles Lindbergh,"
he said, running a hand through the bristles on the nape of
his neck. "Think I'll pass?"

"Sure. You look fine." This expedition was going to be
Hoffman's first, and he was understandably self-conscious
about his appearance. "Don't worry about it," Franc added.
"So long as you keep a low profile, nobody'll notice. Is
Vasili in the control room?"

"He's waiting for you." Then he dropped his voice.
"What's going on? I hear you and Lea had a meeting with
Sanchez."

"Just the usual. Nothing to be concerned about." Franc
didn't like lying to a member of his team, but he didn't
want to make Hoffman any more nervous than he already
was. He reached into his shirt pocket, pulled out a library
fiche. "Here," he said, handing the wafer to the mission
specialist, "do me a favor and load this into the pedestal.
Historical appendices for the twentieth century."

"No problem." Pulling himself along a rope, Hoffman
floated through the open hatch into the narrow passageway.
Franc fell in behind him and waited until Hoffman entered
the monitor room at the far end of the corridor before he
entered the open hatch on the right.

Oberon's control room was a wedge-shaped compartment, its longest wall dominated by a horseshoe-shaped
console. Some of the screens displayed diagrams and
rapidly changing text, while others showed only test patterns. Service panels gaped open on the floor and ceiling,
exposing densely packed nanocircuitry and bundled wiring.
Through the single rectangular porthole above the console,
he saw a space worker hovering just outside.

Vasili Metz was seated in the pilot's seat, his head and
shoulders thrust beneath the console. "Hello, Dr. Lu," he
said, not looking up. "You've seen Sanchez, I take it."

"We met with him a couple of hours ago." Pushing himself over to the chair, Franc grasped the seatback and let his feet dangle in the air. "He told us about the *Miranda*. They say they spotted an angel."

"Yep. That's what I've heard from Brech." Beneath the console, Metz's penlight moved back and forth. "It was only for a couple of seconds, but Hans mentioned it in his reports, and I've spoken with him about it. Did Paolo give you my recommendation?"

"Yes, he did. We discussed it for a while, and decided to proceed with the C120-37."

Metz said nothing. Franc waited patiently until the pilot finally backed out from beneath the console and sat up straight in his chair. "You know," he said at last, "I should be surprised, but I'm not. Figures you'd ignore this."

"I'm not ignoring anything. I'm just refusing to be deterred by something we can't explain."

"I can't explain them either." Metz clicked off the penlight, shoved it in the breast pocket of his jumpsuit. "I just know that they show up when something's about to go wrong."

Franc knew all about angels. They had been spotted during two previous CRC expeditions: luminescent, vaguely man-shaped apparitions that suddenly appeared in the close vicinity of timeships, then winked out of sight just as quickly as they had appeared. Each time, only CRC historians or pilots had seen them; they never appeared when locals were present. Although no one knew what they were, several theories had been advanced to explain the sightings, the most popular being that they themselves were chrononauts, yet from farther up the timestream. They had never directly interfered with an expedition or caused any historical disturbances, but timeship pilots in particular regarded them as harbingers of misfortune. This fear wasn't entirely unwarranted; the first time an angel had been spotted, it was during the C119-64, when a historian had been lost during the Battle of Gettysburg, and the second sight-ing was during the C220-63, when two researchers had been inadvertently photographed by contemporary bystanders in Dealy Plaza during the Kennedy assassination.

"But nothing went wrong during the C314-65, did it?" Franc asked. "The *Miranda* came home safely, right? No mishaps, no paradoxes?" Metz reluctantly nodded. "Then don't worry about it. Whatever these things are, it's nothing we should worry about."

Metz seemed unconvinced. "I still don't like it. It's a bad omen. . . ."

"We can always find another pilot, if it makes you that nervous."

Franc tried not to sound too hopeful, but Metz shook his head. "No time to train another pilot. *Miranda* launches at 1800 hours, and *Oberon* follows at 0600 tomorrow." He glanced toward the passageway. "Speaking of which, where's Lea?"

"Up at Artifacts Division, making sure our outfits are ready." Franc gazed around the control room. "Is this tub going to be flightworthy by tomorrow morning?"

"Routine maintenance. I always tear *Oberon* apart before we make a trip." He scowled as he pulled an electric screwdriver from his tool belt. "And don't call my ship a tub," he added. "She'll get us there and back, so treat her with a little respect."

"Right. Sorry." One more reason he didn't much care for Metz: he got along better with machines than people. Franc released the seatback, turned toward the door. "All right, then. I'll see you at 0500 for the prelaunch briefing."

"I'll be there." Metz was already crawling back underneath the console. Franc heard the thin whine of a screwdriver as he loosened another panel. He waited another moment to see if the pilot had anything more to say, but apparently their discussion had come to an end.

Murphy almost collided with a pair of nuns as he flung open the glass front doors of the Air and Space Museum and dashed out onto the broad plaza.

The nuns glared at him as he trotted down the stairs to the sidewalk. He stopped to look first one way, then the next. A couple of teachers sneaking a smoke near the line of yellow school buses idling at the curb, a hot-dog vendor chatting with a police officer next to his pushcart, a homeless man rummaging through a garbage can. The fake Gregory Benford, though, was nowhere in sight.

There was no way he could have disappeared so quickly. He must still be nearby. Neglecting to button his parka, Murphy walked quickly past the school buses, then left the sidewalk and jogged across Independence Avenue to the Mall. Frozen grass below the thin blanket of fresh snow crunched beneath his boots as he jogged down the greenway, his eyes darting back and forth as he searched the faces of pedestrians strolling past the Smithsonian.

A couple of hundred feet away, he spotted a red M-sign: Smithsonian Station, the nearest Metro stop. He must have gone there. Lungs burning with each breath of cold, dry air,

Murphy ran past snow-covered park benches and bare trees until he reached the subway station. Ignoring the slow-moving escalator, he bolted down the stairs, taking the steps three at a time.

He halted on the upper concourse, glanced in all directions. There were a dozen or so people in sight, purchasing farecards from the ticket machines or hurrying through the turnstiles to the lower platform, yet of the impostor there was no sign. A train rumbled into the platform below, and for a moment he fumbled in his pocket for a dollar. If he was fast enough, he could still buy a card and catch the next train. Yet common sense told him that there was no way Benford—or rather, the pseudo-Benford, as he now thought of him—could have reached the Metro before he did.

Gasping for air, Murphy sagged against a newspaper machine. He had guessed wrong. Whichever direction the impostor had taken after leaving the museum, it clearly hadn't been this way.

He waited until he caught his wind, then he stepped onto the escalator and rode it back up to street level. He glanced at his watch: five after one. He could turn around, catch the subway to L'Enfant Plaza, yet there was always the slim chance that he might spot the impostor on the sidewalk. And even if he didn't, he needed time to think. . . .

Why would anyone impersonate a science fiction author just to talk to him? That was the big question, of course, but besides *why?* there was also *how?* The impersonation had been nearly perfect; not only had the impostor looked exactly like Gregory Benford, but—judging from the brief conversation Murphy had with the real Benford on the phone—he sounded like him as well. True, a good actor might be able to don a wig, a false beard, and fake glasses. An even more talented actor could mimic someone's voice . . .

But why go to so much trouble?

Buttoning up his parka against the cold, his head lowered against the wind, Murphy strode down the sidewalk.

As he reached the corner and waited for the green Walk light, another thought occurred to him: hadn't he read somewhere that Gregory Benford had a twin brother?

Yes, he did: James Benford, another physicist, an identical twin who had also written some science fiction, both on his own and in collaboration with his more famous sibling. Could that be the person who . . . ?

No. Murphy shook his head as the light changed and he stepped into the street. That didn't make sense either. For one thing, why would Jim Benford want to impersonate his brother? Perhaps as a practical joke, but what would be the point if the intended victim was a complete stranger? And for another, Jim Benford wouldn't have made the mistakes that had gradually tipped him off: not knowing that *c* was the common variable for the speed of light, for instance, or being unaware that his brother had written a time-machine novel.

He could always call Greg Benford again, once he had returned to the office. Yeah, sure; Murphy could imagine how that conversation would go. *Hello, Dr. Benford? You don't know me, but my name's David Murphy and I work for NASA Headquarters in Washington, and I just had lunch with someone who looks exactly like you . . . well, yes, I know there's a lot of guys who kinda look like you, but this guy said he was you, and . . . anyway, can you tell me where your brother is right now, and if he has a weird sense of humor?* Right. And if he was Greg Benford, he'd call someone at NASA to say that some wacko named Murphy was asking bizarre questions about him and his brother Jim.

The sky had begun to spit snow again. Glancing up, Murphy could make out the Capitol, obscured behind a milk white haze beyond the Reflecting Pool. He lowered his gaze again, began making his way back up Independence toward the Air and Space. No, better leave the real Gregory Benford out of this. Yet whoever the impostor was, he knew enough about Murphy to know that he would have been impressed enough with Benford's reputation to meet with him for lunch to discuss . . .

An article in *Analog* about time travel.

Murphy stopped. That was the crux of the issue, wasn't it? Forget for a moment whom he had met; it was the subject of their conversation that mattered.

This was the second time today that someone had paid undue attention to a piece he had written.

Despite the warmth of his parka, Murphy felt a chill run down his spine. First, a meeting with a senior NASA administrator, who had expressed concern that Murphy might somehow embarrass the agency by writing about UFOs and time travel, and then requested . . . no, mandated, really . . . that any future articles he wrote be submitted in advance to the Public Affairs Office. Then, less than an hour after that meeting, a phone call from someone pretending to be a noted physicist and author, who in turn wanted to know where he had gained the inspiration to write the same article . . .

How much of a coincidence could that be?

Murphy pulled up the parka's hood and tucked his hands deep in its pockets. For some reason, his article had attracted someone's attention. Yet all he had done was taken a few available facts, tied them to possible explanations, and come up with a plausible scenario, however unlikely it might be. Yet his piece hadn't appeared in *Nature* or in the science section of the *New York Times,* but in a science fiction magazine. Hardly a venue guaranteed to gain a lot of attention.

Only . . . hadn't this sort of thing happened once before?

Yes, it had. Back in 1944, at the height of World War II, when a writer . . . who was it again? Digging at his memory, Murphy absently snapped his fingers. Heinlein? Asimov? Maybe Hal Clement or Jack Williamson . . . ?

No. Now he remembered. It was Cleve Cartmell, a

writer almost completely forgotten today were it not for one particular story he had written for *Astounding*.

Titled "Deadline," it was otherwise negligible save for one important detail: in it, Cartmell accurately described an atomic weapon, one which used U-235 as its reactive mass. He even went so far as to say that two such bombs, if dropped on enemy cities, could end the fictional war depicted in his story. An innocuous novelette in the back of a pulp SF magazine, yet within a few days of its publication in *Astounding*, its editor, John W. Campbell, Jr., was visited at his New York office by a military intelligence officer, who inquired who Cartmell was and how he might have come by his information. Yet Cartmell hadn't worked for the Manhattan Project; his bomb was strictly the product of his imagination, his sources no more classified than textbooks found in any well-stocked public library. Nonetheless, he had stumbled upon the closest-kept secret of World War II; little more than eighteen months later, Fat Man and Little Boy were dropped on the cities of Hiroshima and Nagasaki.

If this sort of thing had happened before, why couldn't it happen again?

Murphy found his hands were trembling, but not from the cold.

He glanced over his shoulder, saw someone walking up the sidewalk a couple of dozen feet behind him. He quickened his pace . . . then, on impulse, he crossed the street, putting a little more distance between himself and the man following him. At the end of the block, he turned another corner, taking an unanticipated detour on his route back to the office. When he looked back again, he no longer saw the other pedestrian.

Get a grip, he told himself. *You're jumping at shadows.*

What he had written was fantasy. Sure, it possessed a certain air of verisimilitude—a handful of footnotes, some well-turned bits of technobabble—but it had no more basis in reality than the average *Star Trek* episode. There was no way that UFOs could actually be time machines. . . .

Could they?

Suddenly, it seemed as if the city itself was watching him, the windows of the government office buildings peering down at him like great, unblinking eyes.

He began to walk a little faster.

"Thank you, Traffic. *Oberon* ready for departure." Metz tapped the lobe of his headset, then glanced over his shoulder at Franc. "If you want to take your seat . . ."

"Thanks, but I'd like to watch." Holding on to the back of Vasili's chair, Franc gazed through the control room porthole. "If you don't mind, that is."

Metz seemed ready to object, then he shrugged. "Suit yourself. Just as long as you and your people are strapped down in ten minutes, you can watch all you want." He turned back to his console. "Traffic, take us out, please."

A pair of spiderlike tugs began moving away from the timeship. The slender cables they dragged behind them uncoiled and became taut, then there was an almost imperceptible jolt as they began to haul *Oberon* out of spacedock. Spotlights passed across the timeship's hull as it was slowly pulled toward the hangar door; off to one side, Franc caught a glimpse of a tiny figure in a hardsuit, holding a pair of luminescent wands above his head. The *Oberon* was on full internal power, of course, and capable of leaving spacedock without the assistance, yet for safety reasons it was customary not to activate the negmass drive until the vessel was clear of the station.

There really should be a band playing, Franc mused. Back in the early twentieth century, when a ship left port on a long voyage, it was a ceremonial occasion. A brass band performing "God Save the Queen," colored ribbons tossed from the decks, the bellow of foghorns, cheering crowds gathered on the wharf. Now, there were only images flashing across flatscreens, the faint murmur of voices over the comlink. Logical, perfect, and utterly without soul.

The hangar door disappeared behind them; now they saw the blue-green expanse of Earth's horizon. "All right, we're clear." Metz leaned forward against his straps, began tapping commands into the keypad. "T-minus six minutes to warp. Dr. Lu . . ."

"You don't have to remind me." Yet he lingered for another moment, observing the tugs as they detached their lines and peeled away to either side. In the far distance, above the limb of the earth, he caught a glimpse of a tiny spacecraft: a chase-ship positioned to observe *Oberon*'s passage into chronospace. "You're sure you've got the right coordinates?"

Wrong question. "You want to go back and have the AI rechecked?" Vasili murmured, gesturing to the dense columns of algorithms scrolling down the screens on either side of him. "We can always scrub the launch, if you're not . . ."

" Sorry. Didn't meant to insult you." He pushed himself toward the hatch. "Tell us when you're ready."

"I always do. Just make sure your people are strapped in."

Franc left the flight deck, floated across the passageway to the passenger compartment. As he expected, Lea and Tom were already in their couches, the seats turned so that they could see the broad flatscreen on the far wall. Lea looked up as Franc pulled himself along the ceiling rungs to the middle couch. "Everything set?" she asked.

"Uh-huh. All we have to do is wait." He pushed himself into the vacant couch, then reached for the lap and shoulder straps. Out of the corner of his eye, he noticed that Hoffman was anxiously watching the status panel next to the screen, his hands gripping the armrests of his couch so tightly that his knuckles were white. "Hey, Tom," he said softly, "don't damage the upholstery."

"Sorry." Hoffman managed a nervous smile. "First time."

"Relax." Franc gave him an easy grin as he cinched his straps tight. "It'll be over so quick, you'll barely know it happened."

If the transition into chronospace went well, of course. There was no sense in reminding Hoffman of what would happen if something went wrong. The smallest, most seemingly insignificant miscalculation by *Oberon*'s AI and the wormhole would collapse in upon itself, forming a quantum singularity which would instantly destroy the timeship. If that happened, they'd find out what it was like to be stretched into spaghetti just before they were obliterated. Such catastrophic accidents had never occurred, or at least not to a timeship carrying a human crew, yet everyone in the CRC was aware of the fate suffered by primates aboard test vehicles during the late 2200s.

Now he was spooking himself. Deliberately casting the thought from his mind, Franc turned his attention to the wallscreen. It displayed a rear-view projection behind the *Oberon;* propelled by its negmass drive, the timeship was quickly moving away from Chronos, and now the space station was a small toy receding in the distance. Farther away, a small band of bright stars moved above the limb of the Earth: orbital colonies, solar-power satellites, other spacecraft. Even now, Chronos traffic controllers would be closely monitoring *Oberon*'s flight path, making sure that the sixty-kilometer sphere of space surrounding the timeship was clear of any other vehicles.

"T-minus one minute." Metz's voice in his headset was terse. *"Wormhole generators coming online."*

He felt Lea's hand stray to his lap. He glanced at her, caught the look in her eyes. She wasn't saying anything in front of Tom, but she was nearly as anxious as he was. Franc briefly clasped her hand, gave her a comforting smile. She nodded briefly, then returned her gaze to the status panel. Displayed on a smaller screen was a wire model of Earth's gravity well. *Oberon* was coasting along a steep incline deep within the well; it was here, using the planet's natural perturbation of spacetime, that the timeship's wormhole generators would soon open a tiny orifice in the quantum foam.

"Thirty seconds and counting," Metz said.

Franc closed his eyes, forced himself to relax. Imagine a pinhole in a sheet of tightly stretched rubber, he told himself. You push your finger against the pinhole, and it grows a little larger, dilating outward. You exert a little more pressure, and now the hole expands, large enough for you to stick your finger through. Yet you don't stop there; you keep pushing, and now you can insert your hand . . . now your arm . . . now your entire body . . .

"Ten seconds," Metz said.

He opened his eyes, saw the planet rushing toward him. The timeship was hurtling toward Earth's atmosphere. If it remained on this course for four or five more minutes, the timeship would soon begin entering the ionosphere, and Metz would have to correct its angle of descent to prevent burn-up. The status panel, though, told a different tale: the timeship was rushing down an invisible funnel, the event horizon of the wormhole *Oberon* was beginning to form around itself. Push a finger against a pinhole, and keep pushing until . . .

"Five . . . four . . . three . . ."

"Oh, God . . ." Hoffman whispered.

"Shut your eyes," Franc said, just before he did so himself.

"Two . . . one . . ."

In the next instant, it felt as if reality itself had become that imaginary rubber sheet, stretched to an infinite length, longer than the entire galaxy, longer than the universe itself . . .

Then abruptly snapped.

He slammed back into his couch, so hard that he felt the vertebrae at the base of his neck pop, and at the same instant he heard a distant scream—Tom, or maybe it was Lea—as everything seemed to shake at once. There was a harsh, high-pitched whine that came from everywhere yet nowhere; he smelled something acrid and sickly-sour, and then . . .

"*All right,*" Metz said, "*you can relax now. We're through.*"

Franc opened his eyes.

The first thing he saw was a globular, semiliquid mass floating in midair next to his couch. Mystified, he raised a hand and reached out to touch it . . . then recoiled when he realized what it was. He carefully turned his head to the right, saw Hoffman wiping his mouth with the back of his hand.

Tom caught Franc's scowl, winced with embarrassment. "Sorry . . ."

"Never mind. Happens now and then." *And now you understand why we warned you not to eat breakfast,* he silently added, but there was no sense in pointing that out now. He tried not to smile when Lea ducked away from the globule of vomitus as it floated closer to her. He touched the lobe of his headset. "Vasili, if it's not too much trouble, we could use some gravity in here."

"Just a moment," the pilot said. A bar on the status panel shifted from red to green, and a few seconds later he felt the sudden sensation of falling, as if he were in an elevator that had just dropped a few floors. The globule splattered messily on the deck between their couches. It wasn't pleasant, but at least it was better than having it wandering freely around.

Franc unclasped his lap and shoulder harnesses, rose

unsteadily to his feet. At first glance, the image on the wallscreen seemed unchanged, until he looked a little closer and noticed that they were at a higher altitude. The daylight terminator, too, was in a different place; now it ran across the eastern edge of the Atlantic Ocean, with nighttime falling on the British Isles and Spain.

"Are we in the right frame?" Tom asked.

"The AI says we've hit the correct coordinates," Metz replied. *"May 2, 1937, about 1800 hours GMT. I'd like to get a stellar reading to confirm it, though. Dr. Oschner, can you do that for me, please?"*

"I'm on it." Lea was already out of her couch; shoulders hunched slightly, she staggered to the hatch, opened it, and exited the compartment. In the monitor room, she would be able to access historical star charts from the library and match them against the real-time positions of visible constellations.

Although Hoffman had unbuckled his restraints, the younger man still lay in his couch, his face pale as he stared up at the ceiling. "Are you all right?" Franc asked quietly, and Tom gave him a weak nod. "Good. Take it easy for a minute, but then we've got work to do."

"Yeah . . . okay, sure." Tom took a deep breath, let out a rattling sigh. "It's . . . different from the simulator, isn't it?"

"It's always different in the simulator." He swatted Hoffman's knee. "Cleanup detail is yours. When you're done with that, you can help Lea and me get ready for insertion."

Tom nodded again. Franc walked to the hatch, then silently waited another few moments to see if Hoffman could get up without any further coaxing. When Tom finally stirred, he opened the hatch and headed for the control room.

"Hoffman got sick, didn't he?" Vasili had left his chair; he stood in front of the main engineering panel, running a check on the main systems. "I told Paolo I wanted a more experienced mission specialist for this trip."

"First time for everyone." So far as he understood the *Oberon*'s major control systems, everything looked as it should. "He's a little shaky, but he's getting over it. How's the ship?"

"Fine. Made it through without a problem." Metz turned away from the engineering panel. "Soon as Lea confirms our position, I'll raise the *Miranda,* tell her we're in position."

"Okay." Franc hesitated. "Need any help in here?"

"None, thank you." Metz shot him a dark look as he returned to his seat. "When I need a copilot, Dr. Lu, I'll ask for one."

"Sure." Rebuffed, Franc stepped away. "Pardon me for asking . . ."

"You're pardoned." Metz inched his seat a little closer to the console, began typing commands into the keypad. "If you want to help, you can go see what's taking Lea so long. I should have received those readings five minutes ago."

There were a few choice words Franc had for the pilot, but he resisted the urge to voice them. Indeed, there wasn't much point in saying anything. Leaving Metz to his work, he turned and left the control room. Once in the passageway, he took a few moments to slowly count to ten, then turned and headed for the monitor room.

The screen dominating the far wall of the monitor room displayed a stellar chart, overlaid across a real-time view of the starscape outside the timeship. Lea stood before the pedestal in the center of the compartment; although her hands rested upon its touch pad, she seemed to be intently listening to something through her headset. She didn't notice Franc's presence until he touched her shoulder, and even then she barely looked up at him.

"Metz wants to know . . ."

"We're here," she said, distractedly nodding toward the

wallscreen. "We're where we're supposed to be. Hold on a sec . . ." Lea impatiently ran her fingers across the touch pad, relaying the data to Metz's console. "You've got to hear this."

The compartment was suddenly filled with a strident, somewhat high-pitched male voice. Apparently coming from a ground-based radio source, it was distorted by static. The language was clearly German, though, and the voice steadily rose with intensity.

" I don't have a clear fix, but it seems to originating from Berlin. I'll feed it through the interpreter." Lea tapped another command into the pedestal, and the screen changed to display upward-scrolling bars of text:

I, too, am a child of the people. I do not trace my line from any castle. I come from the workshop. Neither was I a general. I was simply a solider as were millions of others. It is something wonderful that amongst us an unknown from an army of millions of the German people—of workers and soldiers—could rise to be head of the Reich and nation.

"You know who that is?" she whispered. "You know who we were listening to?"

Franc slowly nodded. Almost 377 years in the past, he was hearing the voice of one of the worst figures ever to emerge from human history.

Somewhere down there, speaking into a radio microphone, was the hate-filled monster known as Adolf Hitler.

It wasn't until he heard people in the corridor that Murphy realized that the workday had come to an end. Raising his head from the paperwork in which he had deliberately absorbed himself, he watched as a couple of secretaries marched past the half-open door of his office, pulling on their overcoats as they chatted about a Billy Joel concert they were attending later that evening. Outside the window, night had fallen without his noticing.

Murphy slipped some files into his briefcase, then straightened his desk and switched off the computer. He exchanged his loafers for snow boots, then stood up and gathered his parka. All the while, his gaze kept falling on the phone. For the past several hours, as much as he had tried to distract himself, he had kept expecting it to ring. Yet it never did, not even once, until the prolonged silence became unnerving.

"Cut it out," he said to himself, under his breath. "There's nothing to be afraid of."

Oh, yeah? a small voice in the back of his mind asked. *Then why are you scared to go home?*

No. He wasn't scared to go home. It was leaving the office that bothered him. For the dozenth time this afternoon, he considered calling Donna and asking her to drive into the city to pick him up at the office. Perhaps he could sweeten the deal by suggesting that they go out to dinner. But that would mean she would have to battle rush-hour traffic on the Beltway, and she was undoubtedly already making dinner, and Steven wouldn't get his homework done, and . . .

Nuts. He was taking public transportation, wasn't he? There would be dozens of subway riders around him at all times. He'd never be alone for a minute. And what was he expecting anyway? A couple of guys in trench coats? That was like something from a Robert Ludlum novel. The pseudo-Benford? Okay, if he saw him again, he'd find a pay phone and call the cops. Or maybe the Science Fiction and Fantasy Writers of America . . .

Murphy chuckled as he switched off the lights. No, there was nothing to worry about. He was just spooking himself. Hell, for all he knew, this might be an elaborate practical joke someone was playing on him. Whatever it was, he'd get it straightened out eventually . . .

The snow had continued to fall all afternoon, leaving the sidewalks covered with a layer of fresh white powder, the wind whisking it past streetlights and passing automobiles, giving it the appearance of fairy dust. A yellow snowplow grumbled up E Street, its blade grinding against icy asphalt as it shoved the drifts out of the way. Burying his face within his scarf, Murphy fell in with office workers trudging their way toward L'Enfant Plaza; he paused at the top of the subway escalator to buy the late edition of the *Washington Times,* then descended into the welcome warmth of the Metro station.

Murphy had become spoiled by having a reserved space in the NASA garage. In all the years he had lived in the D.C. area, he had seldom ridden the subway to and from work, preferring to use it on the weekends as a means of taking Steven to ball games at Kennedy Stadium or for

Sunday shopping trips at Eastern Market. So the ride to the Virginia 'burbs took longer than he expected; the train was packed, with every seat taken and people standing in the aisles, gamely clinging to posts and ceiling rails as the car gently swayed back and forth. It was too crowded to open his newspaper, so after glancing at the headlines—the *Times,* in its usual self-righteous indignation, was making the most of the Paula Jones scandal—he tucked it beneath his briefcase and stared straight ahead, silently observing everyone while making eye contact with no one, the customary behavior of straphangers everywhere.

As the train emerged from beneath the Potomac, the crowd began to gradually thin out with each stop. Pentagon, Pentagon City, Crystal City, National Airport, Braddock Road, King Street . . . as the stations went by in turn, a few more people got on while even more got off, until by the time the Yellow Line reached Eisenhower Avenue there was no one left standing and there were empty seats here and there. When the old pensioner who had shared his seat got off at Eisenhower, Murphy was finally able to open his newspaper, yet he didn't bother to do so. The next stop was Huntington, where he had parked his car this morning. Why bother to read when he was getting off soon?

Fatigued, idly hoping that Donna had fixed meat loaf and mashed potatoes for dinner and that Steven wasn't going to be too demanding tonight, he absently gazed around the half-empty train. Across the aisle, a businessman read a John Grisham thriller. A little farther away, a couple of Latino teenagers in hooded sweatshirts muttered to each other in Spanish, loudly laughing every now and then. A middle-aged black woman stared listlessly out the window. A pretty girl with long red hair flowing from beneath her black beret caught his eye; she was easy to look at, and he found himself studying her until she noticed him. She regarded him coolly, her hard eyes challenging his intrusion, and he quickly glanced away, self-consciously shifting his attention to the window beside him.

Murphy might not have noticed the old man sitting in the rear of the train, had he not looked at the window at just that moment. Captured in its dark reflection, three rows back on the other side of the aisle, was a tall, gaunt man. Long brown hair turning gray, white beard covering his face, he wore an Army-surplus parka, its collar zipped up to his neck, a blue Mets baseball cap pulled low over his eyes. Another one of Washington's countless derelicts, easily ignored until they try to beg change from you . . .

Yet, in the instant Murphy spotted him, the bum was staring straight at him. Watching him.

Murphy instinctively glanced away. Then, uneasily, he turned his eyes toward the window once more. The man in the back of the train was still watching him, apparently unaware that he himself was being surreptitiously observed.

No, it wasn't the pseudo-Benford; this guy was a bit shorter, his build less solid. A complete stranger . . . and yet, in some unfathomable way, his face seemed vaguely familiar. If you shaved off the beard, perhaps gave him a haircut . . .

The train lurched, began to slow down. Streetlights swept into view, distorting the window reflection. They were coming into the next station. *"Huntington,"* the recorded voice said from the ceiling speakers. *"Doors opening on the right."*

The businessman put away his paperback, picked up his briefcase. The black lady sighed wearily, shifted her feet as if getting ready to stand. The Latino kids sullenly watched Murphy as he nervously moved his briefcase into his lap. The reflection disappeared behind the jaundiced glare of sodium-vapor streetlights as the train rushed into the elevated station. Through the window, Murphy could see a dozen or so people waiting on the platform, but no sign of a transit cop.

Faking a sudden cough, Murphy raised a hand to his mouth, then stole a glance behind him. The old man hastily looked away, yet he had one foot already in the aisle. Yes, he was planning to get off here.

For an instant, Murphy had an impulse to stay seated. Yet this was where he had parked his car. Unless he wanted to ride the Metro all the way to the end of the line, then buy another farecard and double back again, he had to get off here.

It's only some wino, he told himself. Some poor homeless bastard. Maybe a little crazy. Likes to watch people on the train, that's all. . . .

The train trundled to a stop. The businessman and the black lady stood up, moved toward the door. Murphy hesitated a moment longer, then as the doors slid open, he quickly rose from his seat, rushed down the aisle. The black lady stared at him in mute surprise as he pushed past her, and the businessman muttered an obscenity at his back when their shoulders briefly collided. Then he was off the train, walking as fast as he could for the platform exit.

At the top of the stairs, he stopped briefly to peer over his shoulder. He couldn't see the bum, yet the crowd was so dense, it was impossible to tell for certain. Holding on to the handrail, Murphy turned and began jogging down the stairs.

Just beyond the turnstiles, past the gated steel-mesh fence, lay the parking lot.

At first the city could not be seen, its environs hidden by
a dense blanket of rain-swollen clouds, then the *Oberon*
penetrated the overcast and suddenly Frankfurt appeared as
a sprawl of urban light, its luminescence divided into un-
equal halves by the serpentine trail of the River Main. The
infrared scopes picked out the most prominent landmarks:
the high Gothic spire of St. Batholomäus Dom, the banks
and office buildings of the central financial district, the immense shell of the Hauptbahnhof train station.

"Over there." Standing next to Metz in the control room,
Franc pointed to a small, irregular blotch of darkness just
northwest of the Cityring, the narrow greenway that surrounded the oldest part of the city. "Near the Alte Oper . . .
see it? That's the Rothschild estate. Put us down there."

The pilot peered at the screen. "No way. Too small, and
way too close." He pointed to a larger park several kilometers farther away, at the edge of the city just north of the
Goethe-Universität. "I'd rather set down there. Less chance
of being spotted."

"That's the botanical garden. You know how far we'd
have to hike to get from there to the Frankfurter Hof?"

Franc shook his head. "Don't worry about it. So long as we're in chameleon mode, no one's going to see us. The streets are nearly vacant this time of night."

"So you take a long walk." Metz remained unconvinced. "An old man like you needs the exercise."

Franc scowled. He was still getting used to his changed appearance. Now the apparent age of sixty, he had thinning gray hair and a slight paunch around the middle, along with an unaccustomed set of wrinkles around his eyes and mouth. Although his nanoskin disguise wasn't uncomfortable—it was his own epidermis, after all, reshaped at the microscopic level to provide a living mask—the period outfit he wore was nearly unbearable: a stiff black tuxedo with archaic tails over a cotton dress shirt and white tie. The sort of thing a gentleman would wear to the Sunday night opera in a European city. For all intents and purposes, he now resembled John Pannes, the American business-man whose place he would soon take aboard the *Hindenburg*.

"The farther we have to walk, the more likely we are to get into trouble. Just put us down there, all right?"

"Well, but . . ." Metz shrugged. "Whatever you say."

"Good." Despite his anxiety, he found himself eager to leave the *Oberon*. He was getting tired of quarreling with the pilot. "Give us about ten minutes. I'll go check on Lea."

He left the flight deck, walked down the passageway to the monitor room. The hatch was shut; he slid it open, and was immediately greeted by an outraged scream:.

"Franc! Knock first, for God's sake!"

"Entschuldigen," he murmured, grinning despite him-self. Lea had apparently just emerged from the replication cell. The cylinder rested on one side of the compartment, steam rising from its open hood. "Didn't mean to intrude."

"Sorry. I just don't . . . like the way I look, that's all."

No wonder Lea was embarrassed; although he had seen her nude many times, as the forty-five-year-old Emma

Pannes she looked completely different. The replication cell had added about ten kilos of artificial flesh to her body, giving her larger breasts, broader hips, a little more round-ness to her tummy and thighs. Emma Pannes wasn't an un-pleasant-looking woman, but she certainly didn't possess Lea's svelte figure.

"You better get used to this," he added as he gallantly turned his back. "We're an old married couple from Long Island, remember?"

"Never mind." Behind him, he heard the rustle of fabric as she began to get dressed. "Have we made contact with the *Miranda*?"

"Vasili spoke with Hans about ten minutes ago." Although Franc kept his back to her, from the corner of his eye he could see her figure half-reflected on the wallscreen, like a ghost superimposed above the nightscape of Frankfurt-Am-Main. "The advance team picked up the Pannes about an hour and half ago, shortly after they left the Frankfurter Hof on their way to the opera. They were alone, and no-body saw them. They're at the safe house in Griesheim, and Hans will pick them up outside town tomorrow night after the *Hindenburg* departs from the aerodrome."

"And our bags?"

"They're on the way right now. Oh, and one more thing . . ." He reached to the high collar of his shirt, pressed his thumb and forefingers against his throat to activate the subcutaneous mimics implanted within his vocal cords. When he spoke again, his voice was gravelly and lower-pitched, with a distinct American accent. "We've received the voice patterns from the extraction team," he said, and watched when she jerked her head in surprise. "I've already downloaded mine from the AI. Remember to get yours."

"I won't forget." She let out her breath with relief. If one of the most risky parts of the mission had been the extrica-tion of John and Emma Pannes from the city, then success-fully obtaining their vocal patterns had been one of the most delicate. "So where's Vasili going to put us down?"

"He wanted to put us down in the Botanischer Garten, but I held out for the Rothschild estate." When the German members of the Rothschild family fled the country earlier this year, the grounds of their Frankfurt home had been claimed by the Nazi government; already it had been turned into a public park. "It's much smaller, but we shouldn't have any trouble."

"No radar, and this side of the city isn't known for its night life." An irritated sigh. "Button me up, will you? I can't reach behind me."

She was wearing an ankle-length white evening gown of the late-1930s style. Artifacts Division had done their usual thorough job of researching contemporary fashions and tailoring authentic replicas, but he hoped that this style was close to what Emma Pannes had worn when she and her husband had left the Frankfurter Hof earlier this evening. Franc buttoned up the back of her dress, and she turned around to face him.

"How do I look?"

"Like my wife." He couldn't help but grin.

"Give up." But she smiled when she said that, and it was a testament of the effectiveness of her nanosurgical treatment that her cheeks reddened slightly. "Get through this, and I might reconsider your proposal."

"I'll remember that." She gave him a quick kiss on the cheek. "Ready?" he asked, and she nodded as she picked up her overcoat. "All right, then . . . let's go."

They joined Hoffman in the passenger compartment and watched on the wallscreen as the *Oberon* fell toward the city. Metz brought the timeship down until it was two thousand meters directly above Rothschild Park, then paused to sweep the area with its infrared scopes. It was a drizzly Sunday night; as they anticipated, few people were on the streets, and the park was deserted.

Only the gentle stirring of tree limbs signaled the *Oberon*'s silent descent upon a broad clearing in the park's center. Its hull now matte black, the timeship was virtually invisible to the naked eye. A few seconds before touchdown, its landing flanges spread open. The negmass drive whisked dead leaves aside as the saucer settled down, then everything was still.

As Hoffman opened the airlock hatch, Franc hastily turned off the interior lights. "Just to be on the safe side," he murmured before he climbed down the ladder to the ground. He waited until Lea had come down the ladder, then he looked back up at Hoffman. "See you in New Jersey," he added.

"I'll be waiting. Good luck." Hoffman gave him a quick thumbs-up, then the hatch irised shut.

Franc took Lea's arm as they trotted away from the timeship. Once they were clear of the landing site, they turned and watched as the *Oberon* lifted off. The timeship was little more than an oval shadow as it silently ascended into the overcast sky; for a few moments, they heard the muted hum of its negmass drive, then even that disappeared.

The night was cool, the crisp air redolent of pine and oak, the grass moist with dew. A short distance away, from the top of a low rise, rose an ancient stone tower, a solitary remnant of the battlements that once surrounded the city in medieval times. Beyond the trees bordering the park, lights glimmered within the windows of nearby houses. All was dark and quiet.

"Let's get out here." Lea shivered within her coat, pulled it more tightly around her. "This place makes me nervous."

If he had time, Franc would have lingered here for a little while longer. So much space, so many trees. On the Moon, nature was a luxury deliberately cultivated within subsurface habitats. Here, on Earth at this time, it could be found everywhere, even in the largest of cities. And the night was so full of secrets . . .

Yet Lea was right. The opera would be ending soon. Like the last act of any great drama, timing was everything.

"Very well," he said. His eyes now accustomed to the gloom, he spotted a nearby gravel path. "This way, I think."

Together, they walked out of the park, at last finding an open gate in the high stone fence surrounding the former estate. Stepping out into the mellow glow of a streetlamp, they found themselves on the sidewalk of the Bockenheimer Antge, across the street from the Alte Oper. The opera house loomed before them as a massive Gothic edifice, a grotesque wedding cake made of marble and white granite. Lights gleamed from within high-arched windows, illuminating the statues on its gabled rooftops and the classical bas-relief on its ornate walls. From somewhere deep within the building, they could hear the muted, melodic rumble of an orchestra reaching its crescendo. Wagner, perhaps . . .

"It's . . ." Fascinated by the sight of the Alte Oper, Lea searched for the right words. "Beautiful, but in an ugly sort of way."

"Something like that, yes." Franc stepped off the curb, then hastily retreated as an automobile's headlights caught him in their glare. Its horn bleeped a shrill protest, then a sedan swept past them. He caught a glimpse of a woman's face stoically regarding them from the passenger side, and he quickly looked away.

"Come on," he murmured, taking her arm again. "We're beginning to look like tourists."

Lea smiled at him. "Well, that's what we are, aren't we?"

"Perhaps, but this isn't a good time or place to be a foreigner." He cautiously looked up and down the street. Now the music had stopped, and he could make out the staccato clatter of applause. "Come on . . . it's letting out."

They crossed the Bockenheimer Antge just as the first members of the audience emerged from the Alte Oper's vaulted entrance. Although a few were plainly dressed, most were decked out in formal evening attire. Franc and

Lea melded with the crowd as it spilled out onto the broad
plaza in front of the opera house. Deliberately maintaining
a casual pace, they sauntered past the central fountain and,
ignoring the taxis parked alongside the Oper Platz, headed
for the Cityring.

In the Middle Ages, Frankfurt had been surrounded by a
broad moat flooded by waters diverted from the Main;
within the moat were the walls which further protected the
city from invading armies. During the eighteenth century,
such fortifications were deemed no longer necessary, so the
walls were torn down and the moat was filled. Now Frankfurt's old city was encircled by a narrow park thick with
trees, bordered on either side by motorways.

Arm in arm, Franc and Lea strolled down the cobble-
stone walkways leading through the center of the mall. The
park was dark and densely wooded, its paths illuminated
only by the occasional lamp. Every now and then someone
quickly walked past, barely acknowledging their presence
with a perfunctory nod and the murmured *hallo* or *guten
Abend,* but otherwise the Cityring was almost completely
deserted.

But not quite. As the path turned to the left, they came
upon a couple of teenagers sitting on a stone bench beneath
an old bronze water fountain, their arms wrapped around
one another, their faces buried together. They could have
been young lovers from any place and any time, except that
the boy wore the brown uniform of Hitler Youth, and beneath her overcoat the girl wore the white blouse, blue
skirt, and severe black shoes of the *Jungmaedel,* the Young
Maidens. They looked up in alarm as Franc and Lea approached, then got up and guiltily scurried away, vanishing
into the night like criminals.

"'In the fields and on the heath,'" Lea murmured as she
watched them go, "'I lose Strength Through Joy.'"

"What?"

"Nothing. A takeoff on a propaganda song." She gazed
sadly after the young couple, then at the small handful of

automobiles passing along the nearby Taunusanlage. "How empty this place is. For a late-spring night, you'd think there would be more people."

Franc nodded. The silence was unnerving, as if an unofficial curfew had been declared. Above the trees, he could see the top floors of offices, banks, and apartment buildings across the adjacent avenues. Almost all the lights had been extinguished, giving them the appearance of cold stone hulks. There was a forlorn, almost dismal quality to the city, as if all humor and life had been drained from it.

"I don't think it's a good idea to be here," he said softly. "We'd better hurry."

A little more quickly now, they strolled down the path, following the mall as it led them closer toward the city center. Soon the path ended where a street bisected the park. A sign beneath a lamp identified the avenue as the Kaiserstrasse. To the right, a half block down the sidewalk, just past a large statue, lay the Taunusanlage, and across the intersection was the Dresdener Bank.

Franc stopped, looked both ways in confusion. He had studied this area thoroughly, committing historical street maps to memory, yet all of a sudden he found himself disoriented. Memorizing map coordinates was one thing; being in the actual location was another.

"Do you remember which way we turn?" he asked.

Lea raised an eyebrow. "I thought you knew."

"I thought I did, but ... ." Everything looks different on a map, he started to add, but that would only get her started. Right now, he didn't need to have her needling him. On impulse, he turned to the right, strode down the sidewalk toward the intersection. He was positive that they were only two or three blocks from the Frankfurter Hof, and that the Kaiserstrasse would take them there ... but two or three blocks in which direction?

He stopped again at the corner, turned around, looked at the statue. "Goethe," he murmured as Lea joined him, nodding toward the twice-life-size figure of the German philosopher. "I didn't read anything about passing this land-mark, so maybe we're . . ."

"Shh!" she suddenly whispered. "Walk the other way, John."

John? He looked around, saw her beginning to walk away. "Lea, what . . . ?"

"Halten!" a voice shouted. *"Wohin gehen sie?"*

Franc froze. A few steps ahead, Lea did the same. Reluctantly, he slowly turned to face the person she had spotted before Franc had become aware of his presence.

The stocky figure approaching them wore a brown uniform shirt with a red swastika armband, dark brown jodhpurs tucked into knee-high leather jackboots; suspended from his belt was a ceremonial dagger. The short bill of his uniform cap, emblazoned with the Nazi eagle, shadowed a broad, beefy face. Most menacing of all, in his right hand he held a long, black-painted wooden baton, its handle wrapped with strips of leather. The baton's surface was faintly scarred, as if it had recently seen heavy use.

One of the *Sturmabteilung,* the so-called brown shirts with whom the Nazi Party had effectively taken control over all of Germany. Street brawlers and thugs from the beer gardens where they had been recruited, they roamed the streets at will, a paramilitary force whose authority superseded that of the local *Polizei.* This one looked as if he had just come from a nearby tavern; his red tie was loosened and slightly askew, his shirttails wadded around his belt.

"Wohin gehen sie?" he repeated. As he came closer, Franc could smell the schnapps on his breath. He thrust out his hand. *"Wo sind sie Urkunde?"* he demanded, looking past Franc at Lea as he impatiently snapped his fingers at her. *"Geben sie mir Urkunde! Schnell!"*

The subcutaneous translator beneath Franc's left ear interpreted his demands—*Where are you going? Where are your documents? Give them to me, quickly!*—but there was no point in pretending to be a German native. *"Wie bitte,"* he said, a little more hesitantly than necessary, pretending not to speak the language as well as he actually did. *"Ich sprech kaum Deutsch . . . sphrechen sie Englisch?"*

The brown shirt's eyebrows raised a little. *"Amerikaner?"* he asked, and smirked with contempt when Franc nodded. *"Amerikan Juden?"*

"Nein, mein Herr," Lea said stiffly, then she resorted to English. "We're not Jews. We're tourists. We've just come from the opera."

"Ja. Der Oper, ja." The Nazi regarded them stoically for a few moments, his hand still thrust forward. "I speak some English," he said at last, slowly and carefully. "Show me your papers, please."

Franc dug into the pocket of his covercoat, pulled out his American passport and German visa. Lea did the same, but the brown shirt ignored her while he opened Franc's passport and unfolded his visa. He stared at the passport photo, then held it up against Franc's face. Franc waited patiently. Both were immaculate forgeries, courtesy of the Artifacts Division; they could easily pass close inspection by German customs officials and *Schutzstaffel,* let alone the bleary-eyed scrutiny of a drunk barbarian. Yet this oaf was clearly looking for trouble, and Franc was aware that the S.A needed no reason to arrest or detain them; they were foreigners, and therefore deemed worthy of suspicion.

"Wo ist . . ." he started, then belched sourly and began again. "Where are you staying, *Herr* Pannes?"

"The Frankfurter Hof." Franc shrugged sheepishly. "I'm afraid we got a little lost . . ."

"Lost?" The brown shirt looked up sharply. *"Was bedeutet das?"*

"We don't know where we are," Franc said. Yes, the Nazi spoke English, but not very much, nor very well. "Can you tell us how to get to the Frankfurter Hof?"

"Ah! Lost. *Ja."* He closed John's passport and visa, but didn't return them immediately. "It is down the street. A short distance." He nodded past them, in the direction they had been taking on Kaiserstrasse before he stopped them. "You should be more careful, *Herr* Pannes. Frankfurt is a large city. Easy to get lost."

"I understand, yes. Thank you for your assistance."

The brown shirt nodded, then almost reluctantly he handed back Franc's papers. "You may go. *Auf wiedersehen.*"

"*Danke schön. Auf wiedersehen.*"

"*Heil Hitler,*" the brown shirt muttered, almost as an afterthought, as he turned around and began staggering back the way he came.

Lea slowly let out her breath. "He didn't even bother to check my papers," she murmured, tucking her visa and passport back in her coat. "Not much regard for women, I see."

Franc shook his head. "He wasn't interested in you. He only wanted to harass me. Maybe I reminded him of someone he dislikes." He smiled at her. "Nice move, speaking to him in English. They're still giving Americans a wide berth, I think."

"Not for very much longer."

They continued down Kaiserstrasse, leaving the Cityring behind as they entered a long, narrow stretch of closed storefronts. Here and there, they spotted Nazi posters plastered to walls: recruitment propaganda for Nazi Youth, slogans for Strength Through Joy, heroic pictures of Adolf Hitler gazing down upon happy, industrious German workers. They came upon a tailor shop whose windows had been painted with a Star of David and the word *Juden*. Lea paused to regard it disdainfully; she was about to say something when Franc spotted someone walking down the opposite side of the street. He prodded her elbow, and she wisely kept her mouth shut as they hurried away.

Two blocks later, the Kaiserstrasse ended in a large plaza, and there they found the Frankfurter Hof. The city's largest grand hotel, it sprawled across a city block on one side of the Kaiserplatz, its name inscribed above the

Romanesque-columned archway between the five-story wings surrounding a central courtyard. Crossing the plaza, Franc and Lea strode through the archway and entered the courtyard; glancing up, he noticed the four carved Titans between the balconies of the fourth-floor rooms, their backs bowed as they held up the roof.

The uniformed doorman bowed gracefully as they walked through the front entrance, then helped Lea remove her coat. Taking off his own overcoat, Franc took a moment to glance around. The lobby was warm after the unseasonable coolness of the night, and it looked much the same as it did from the historical photos he had studied: velvet-upholstered chairs and sofas, with a grand piano in one corner and framed prints of country scenes on the papered walls. If his research was correct, then the registration desk would be through that archway to the left, with the elevators located only a short way from . . .

"Pannes! Hey, John!"

The voice was English-accented, and it came from the direction of the bar at the far end of the lobby. Looking around, Franc spotted several men seated around a low table. One, a ruddy-faced man in his mid-sixties, had raised his arm to gesture to him. "Come over here, man, and have a drink with us."

"Be right there," he called back, then he glanced at Lea. She gave him a wary smile; apparently his disguise was working. "I think some of the chaps want to see me," he said. "Be a good girl, will you, and get our key from the front desk?"

"I'd be delighted to," she said formally. She understood the protocol; in this age, proper ladies were not invited to share a nightcap with the gentlemen. "I'll be up in the room."

"Thank you, dear. I'll come up soon." He gave her a good-night kiss, then he folded his coat over his arm and marched across the lobby and up a short flight of polished oak steps to the hotel bar.

The bar was small and dimly lit, serenely masculine in the old European style: glass-fronted bookcases along dark oak-paneled walls, blue leather-backed chairs surrounding low tables, a long bar in front of mirror-backed shelves holding rows of liquor bottles. This time of night, it was nearly empty, save for the handful of men seated around a table beneath a classical painting. The barkeep, a stoical young man wearing a service tuxedo, studied Franc as he washed glasses in the sink behind the counter.

"John. Come over and sit down." The oldest gentleman at the table, an Englishman about the same age as John Pannes, motioned to a vacant chair. "How was the opera?"

"It was . . . very German," Franc said drily as he took a seat, and the other men chuckled knowingly. "It's really much more Emma's sort of thing. I only went along because she insisted."

The other man smiled as he reached for a pack of Dunhills next to his drink. Franc recognized him immediately: George Grant, an assistant manager for the London office of the Hamburg American Line. Since John Pannes worked for the same company, they knew each other as business associates. "I've never followed it myself," he admitted as he shuffled a cigarette from the pack. "By the way, have you met these fellows? They're sharing our flight with us tomorrow . . . well, most of them, at any rate."

Two of the others introduced themselves with cordial handshakes. Franc pretended not to know them, although he was all too familiar with them. Edward Douglas, in his late thirties, was an advertising executive from New Jersey. Although it was now a secret, history would later record that, while in Germany doing marketing research on behalf of his company's chief client, General Motors, Douglas had also been covertly gathering information for the U.S. Navy on German manufacturing capability. Yet the Gestapo had recently become aware of his espionage activities, and now he was fleeing Germany before he could be arrested as a spy. Dolan Curtis, on the other hand, was nothing more nor less than the president of a perfume-importing company in Chicago; like Pannes himself, he had been visiting Germany on business, and now was heading home to America.

The fourth man at the table, though, was an unfamiliar face: prematurely balding, with a trim mustache, his wire-rim glasses framed a pair of inquisitive eyes. As he bent across the table to pick up a briar pipe from the cut-glass ashtray, he offered his right hand to Franc. "Bill Shirer," he said mildly. "Pleased to meet you, Mr. Pannes."

Franc was barely able to conceal his astonishment. Too late, Shirer noticed the look of recognition on his face. "Bill Shirer?" he said as they shook hands. "Not the columnist William Shirer . . . ?"

Douglas laughed out loud as Shirer smiled indifferently. "Bill, you're becoming famous," he said, giving the journalist a slap on the knee. "Now even John's heard of you, and he hardly ever reads the papers."

"I pick it up on occasion," Franc said, recovering quickly. Yet in the years to come, William L. Shirer's reputation would outgrow his present job as a European correspondent for the Universal Press Syndicate. As an eyewitness to the events leading to World War II, he would later write several books about the Nazi regime, including its definitive history, *The Rise and Fall of the Third Reich.* Indeed, Franc had studied that same book while preparing himself for this expedition. Shirer's presence here, though, was a surprise. "I thought you were based in Berlin, Mr. Shirer."

"Bill, please." Shirer settled back in his chair as he lit a match and held it to the bowl of his pipe. "I still am, but I've just taken a new job. Radio correspondent for the Columbia Broadcasting System. I'm down here doing a little research for a story."

"And here I thought you were going to take us up on our offer." Grant gave Shirer a sly wink. "We can still get you a ticket, if you care to change your mind. The flight's not even half-booked."

Franc was about to inquire what they were talking about, but decided to remain quiet. If it involved Hamburg American Lines, then John Pannes would have probably been privy to it. Fortunately, Dolan Curtis raised the question. "George offered you a ticket on the *Hindenburg?*" he asked, and Shirer nodded as he sucked on his pipe. "Why didn't you take him up on it?"

"Entschuldigen sie?" Douglas raised his hand, signaling the barkeep. *"Konnen sie mir helfen, bitte?"*

"I would have liked to," Shirer said, as the barkeep walked over, carrying his service tray, "but I have to turn it down. My editors didn't want me to leave Berlin just now." He shrugged. "I can see their point. A couple years ago, the *Hindenburg* was major news, but now another flight to New York . . . well . . ."

"Old hat. I suppose you're right." Grant turned to the barkeep and pointed to the empty glasses on the table. "Another round for all of us, please." Apparently the waiter understood English, for he nodded. Grant looked at Franc. "What will you have, John. Your usual?"

Franc had no idea what John Pannes usually drank. "Nothing for me, thank you," he said, then he turned back to Shirer. "I'm sorry you're not coming along," he said, which was only half a lie; although he would have enjoyed the opportunity to spend more time with this soon-to-be-legendary writer, history might have suffered a terrible loss if William Shirer had been aboard the *Hindenburg*. "So what story are you covering down here?"

Shirer pretended not to hear. Stoking his pipe, he glanced away, as if casually studying the books on the wall. No one else spoke, and for a few moments there was an uncomfortable silence at the table. The barkeep took his time gathering their glasses, then he returned to the bar and busied himself preparing their drinks. When he was gone, Shirer bent over the table. "Sorry about that," he said quietly. "The walls have ears, you know."

"He means that you have to be careful these days." Douglas cast a meaningful glance at the barkeep. "You never know who's an S.D. informant. And our friend here has been keeping the bar open for us a little longer than usual."

Franc nodded. The *Sicherheitdienst,* the internal security directorate allied with the Gestapo, had infiltrated every aspect of daily life in Nazi Germany during this time. At one point, they employed nearly a hundred thousand people to eavesdrop upon their fellow citizens and report any anti-National Socialist activities to the secret police. Nonetheless, Franc couldn't help but wonder whether Shirer's visit to Frankfurt had anything to do with his own research.

"It doesn't have anything to do with the *Hindenburg,* does it?" he asked, keeping his voice low.

Shirer raised a curious eyebrow. "No. I'm just talking to some Catholic clergymen who are disturbed about recent events." His eyes narrowed behind his glasses. "Why, is there something about the *Hindenburg* I should know?"

Franc wondered how Shirer would react if he told him, even in private, that the S.S. had heard rumors—and even a letter from an alleged psychic in Milwaukee, sent last month to the German embassy in Washington, D.C.—that a bomb was going to be placed aboard the airship. Yet there was no way he could let the journalist know this. History had to be allowed to take its course.

"No," he said. "Just a thought."

Shirer nodded, yet his piercing blue eyes remained locked on Franc through the pale smoke rising from his pipe. Somehow, in those intangible, almost telepathic ways a good journalist develops over years of experience, Shirer knew that John Pannes was lying. And Franc, playing the role of John Pannes, wondered if Shirer would recall this conversation four nights later, when he would be informed that the *Hindenburg* had mysteriously exploded while landing in Lakehurst, New Jersey.

But, of course, by then John and Emma Pannes would be dead. . . .

There was a clink of glasses from behind them. The barkeep was returning to their table, his tray laden with schnapps, vodka, and bourbon. As he set down the drinks, Franc made a pretense of checking his watch. "Gentlemen, it's getting a little late for me," he said. "Emma's probably wondering where I am by now." He pushed back his chair, stood up. "If you'll excuse me. . . ."

"By all means."

"Of course."

"See you tomorrow, John."

"A pleasure to make your acquaintance, Mr. Pannes." William Shirer stood, offered his hand once more. "Next time you're in the country, look me up."

"I'd be delighted to, Bill," Franc said, as they shook hands for the last time.

Monday, January 14, 1998: 6:02 P.M.

The parking lot outside the Metro station was well-lighted, yet not bright enough to put Murphy's mind at ease. Long stretches of darkness lay between the evenly spaced lampposts, and the long ranks of snow-covered automobiles held many shadows.

He had walked about halfway down the center row, glancing over his shoulder now and then to see if he was being followed, before he realized that he couldn't recall exactly where he had parked his car this morning. Somewhere toward the back of the lot; he had driven down the length of one row, then doubled back and driven all the way up another before he had found an empty space, which he vaguely remembered as being close to the fence. In his haste to catch the next train, though, he hadn't taken note of the row number; all he had done was lock the door, shove the keys in his pocket, and dash to the platform.

Christ. For a guy with a Ph.D. in astrophysics, sometimes he could be the dumbest guy on the planet. For the first time in several hours, irritation replaced fear. The wind had picked up again, and now it blew glistening sheets of snow off the hoods of the cars parked around him. He pulled the hood of his parka up around his head as he marched through the icy fog, and wished again that he had held out for a NASA job in Alabama or Texas.

Somewhere close behind him, he heard ice being crunched underfoot.

Murphy stopped, then quickly looked around. Only a dozen yards away, someone was walking down the row behind him: a tall figure wearing a parka and a baseball cap, his right hand thrust in his coat pocket.

In that instant, Murphy was sure that it was the homeless man he had seen on the train. He glanced about, but there was no one else in sight. In the far distance, beyond the tops of dozens of cars, he could make out the squat box of the tollbooth. It was at least a hundred feet away, on the other side of a maze of automobiles, but there would be someone in there. A bored lot attendant, no doubt leafing through *People* magazine and listening to hip-hop on a ghetto-blaster as he warmed his feet next to a space heater. But he would have a phone, and . . .

Then the figure stopped in front of a Nissan Pathfinder, and his hand came out of his pocket. There was a shrill *bwoop! bwoop!* and the Pathfinder's headlights flashed. The man walked to his utility vehicle and began dusting a patina of snow off the windshield.

Murphy relaxed. "Idiot," he muttered as he turned around again. "You're getting wound up over nothing."

He reached the end of the row. Okay, he was at the back of the lot, and there was the fence. His wheels had to be somewhere nearby. Turning his face into the wind, he raised his hand against his face to shield his eyes against the blown snow as he trudged down the cross lane. Goddammit, did everyone in Arlington drive a Ford Escort? His old Volvo had once had a Grateful Dead sticker on the rear bumper—it made his car a little easier to identify, or at least until all the yuppies started sporting skull-and-lightning-bolt decals on their BMWs—but now he had something a little more distinctive. If he looked hard enough . . .

And there it was: a five-year-old forest green Escort, blanketed with snow but the white-and-blue sticker on its rear bumper clearly visible in the light cast by the nearby lamppost: *I Want To Go—National Space Society 202/593-1900.* Perhaps half of the cars in the NASA garage had this same sticker, but here in Huntington park 'n' ride lot it stood out like a beacon. Murphy grinned, and decided this alone was good reason to renew his NSS membership.

Setting his briefcase down on the hood, he fumbled in his coat pockets until he found his key ring. He unlocked the driver's side door, pulled it open, then leaned inside and found the long-handled ice scraper he kept beneath the passenger seat. Closing the door once again, he used its brush to clear off the windshield and side windows, then he began chipping at the thin layer of ice frozen to the glass. Yes, it was definitely time to consider moving to Houston. Next year, the shuttles would start sending up the first American modules of the new space station. Maybe he could get transferred to Johnson. They might need a new . . .

A man-shaped shadow fell across the Escort's hood. Someone else searching for their car? Lost in dreams of Texas, he didn't look up until he detected a vague motion just behind him.

"Dr. Murphy?"

The voice was old, harsh with age, yet oddly familiar.

Still bent over the car hood, Murphy half turned to see the old man from the train standing next to the Ford's rear bumper.

His face was shaded by the baseball cap and shrouded by dense gray beard, yet nonetheless it seemed as if Murphy had seen it before. And there was something in his right hand, something that he held like a pistol, but not quite like a gun.

Murphy slowly raised himself from the hood. He lifted

the ice scraper, defensively held it in front of him. The old man shifted uneasily; the weapon came up a little more, and now Murphy could see that its barrel formed a blunt, holeless shape. Absurdly, it resembled a Lazer Tag gun, like the ones he had seen at Toys "R" Us.

"Yeah," he said. "Who are you?"

The old man hesitated. Although Murphy couldn't clearly see his eyes beneath the bill of his ball cap, they seemed to shift from left to right, as if making sure that they were alone. Murphy was all too aware that they were.

"What do you want?" he demanded. "Why are you following me?"

"I'm sorry," the stranger murmured. "I'm so sorry."

He lifted the weapon, pointed it straight at Murphy.

"What . . . ?"

The last thing Murphy felt was a white-hot charge of electricity surging through his body. He didn't have a chance to scream before his body was flung backward into the space between the parked cars.

The old man regarded Murphy for a moment, his steamy breath rising from within his coarse beard. Then he thrust the weapon back into his pocket and, with a final look around, knelt over Murphy and picked up his ankles.

Dragging him through the snow, the stranger dropped him next to the driver's door; he opened it, then hoisted Murphy by the shoulders and shoved him into the car. After setting him upright in the passenger seat, the old man searched Murphy's pockets until he located his key ring and wallet. He retrieved Murphy's briefcase from the hood of his car; after throwing it into the rear seat, he climbed into the Ford, settling behind the wheel before he shut the door behind him.

It took only a few seconds for him to locate the lot ticket; it was tucked into the pocket of the sun visor. He pulled a twenty-dollar bill from Murphy's wallet and clenched it between his teeth, then he inserted the Ford key

into the ignition. The cold engine clunked a little as it
turned over, but start it did.

The old man smiled, checked Murphy again to make
sure that he looked as if he was only dozing in the passenger seat, then he carefully backed out of the space.

It had rained all day in southern Germany, yet the rain had lapsed into a light drizzle by the time the buses carrying the *Hindenburg* passengers from the Frankfurter Hof arrived at the aerodrome on the other side of the Main. Their luggage had been freighted out to the aerodrome earlier that afternoon, but not before every bag, suitcase, steamer trunk, and shipping crate had been opened and thoroughly searched in the hotel lobby by uniformed Gestapo officers. The few passengers who came to the airfield from other locations also had their baggage opened and searched. As a routine precaution taken before every zeppelin flight, every matchbox and cigarette lighter was confiscated from the passengers, yet few were aware that the Gestapo were going through the baggage not in search of contraband, but for the explosive devices.

Finally, the passengers were allowed to leave the waiting room within the enormous hangar. The airship had already been towed out onto the field, and a uniformed band stood nearby, performing German folk ballads on brass instruments. As Franc and Lea strolled out of the hangar, a steward fell into step next to Lea to hold an umbrella over her head. Franc was just as happy the same courtesy was not afforded him; he wanted to look at the airship without something obscuring his vision.

He had studied the *Hindenburg* for nearly a year, was as familiar with every detail as its own crew; if asked, he could have recited its vital statistics from memory. Yet studying archival blueprints, photographs, and film clips was one thing; seeing the LZ-129 for himself was quite another. It loomed above them as a massive silver ellipse, as large as any interplanetary spacecraft that had ever been built in the lunar shipyards, so huge that, walking toward its bow, he couldn't see its broad stabilizers at the stern. He stopped for a moment, not only to allow the nanorecorders concealed within the buttons of his overcoat to capture the image, but to drink in the sight himself.

"Magnificent," he murmured. "Absolutely incredible . . ."

"Come along, John." Lea stopped next to him; the steward patiently halted beside her, still carrying the umbrella. "You've seen this before," she added, with just the right tartness in her voice. "It's nothing new."

She was right. John Pannes would be jaded by the sight of German airships; this wasn't the first time he had boarded the *Hindenburg*. He shouldn't be gawking at it now. "Of course, dear," he said, reluctantly lowering his gaze. "I just can never get over it, that's all."

"Neither can I, *Herr* Pannes." The steward might have only been being polite, but Franc sensed that he was also genuinely proud of his ship. "If you'll come this way, please . . ."

As they walked toward the gangway stairs, the band began playing the *"Horst Wessel Lied."* A contingent of Hitler Youth emerged from behind the hangar and began goose-stepping in formation toward the airship, their leader carrying the Nazi flag. Seeing this, Franc was suddenly glad to be leaving Germany. Glancing over his shoulder, he noted the carefully guarded expressions on the faces of many of the other passengers. Although the owners of the Zeppelin

Corporation were trying to keep the Nazi Party at arm's length—Hugo Eckener, its president, was profoundly opposed to the National Socialists to the point of refusing to christen the LZ-129 in Hitler's honor—the *Hindenburg* had nonetheless been constructed with Nazi funds. Indeed, the *Hindenburg,* along with its smaller sister ship, the *Graf Zeppelin,* had already been used to drop Nazi leaflets on crowds during rallies in Nuremburg and Berlin. Conceived and built for less loathsome purposes, the *Hindenburg* had nonetheless become a major symbol of Nazi power.

Which was the very reason why the nascent German resistance movement had sought to place a bomb aboard. For all their ruthless authority, the Gestapo had been helpless to prevent this. The bomb was already concealed next to a gas bag in the airship's aft section, just beneath the swastika painted on its upper vertical stabilizer. And three days from now, it would detonate, killing thirty-seven passengers and crew . . .

Franc felt something clutch his stomach. For an instant he had the urge to walk away from the *Hindenburg* as fast as he could. Lea must have noticed the look on his face, for she peered at him closely. "Something wrong, dear?" she murmured.

"Just a touch of indigestion." This wasn't a good time to contemplate history. "I'll be better once we reach our cabin."

They joined the line of passengers making their way up the gangways folded down from the airship's belly. Franc didn't allow himself another moment of hesitancy; he followed Lea up the stairs.They passed B Deck, which contained the crew quarters and galley, and emerged on the landing of A Deck, where another steward met them just in front of the bronze bust of Marshal von Hindenburg.

"*Herr* Pannes, *Frau* Pannes, welcome aboard." He turned to lead them down a narrow corridor running amidships along the keel. "You're in Cabin 12. This way, please . . ."

Their cabin was surprisingly small: a pair of double-decker bunks, a compact aluminum desk and a miniature sink which folded down from the bulkhead, a little closet in which their baggage had already been stowed. Somehow, Franc had expected something a little more spacious; the *Oberon*'s passenger compartment was larger than this. The steward showed them where everything was, told them that the lavatories were located below them on B Deck, and sternly reminded them that *rauchen* was *verboten* outside the smoking room. Then he wished them a good flight, and left them in privacy.

Franc climbed the aluminum ladder to the upper bunk, sat down on its thin mattress, patted its handkerchief-size pillow. When he tried to sit up straight, his head touched the ceiling. He looked down at Lea and grinned. "I think we're going to have to invent some new positions," he said.

"Think of something else." She gave him a brief scowl as she opened the cabin door. "They're going to raise ship anytime now. I don't want to miss this."

The promenade on A Deck was crowded by the time they got there. A steward handed them glasses of champagne, then they found a vacant place near the starboard windows. On the ground below, they could see men holding on to the taut mooring cables. Twilight was beginning to set over the airfield; the rain had stopped, and rays of green-hued sunlight were slanting down through the heavy clouds.

The band struck up *"Deutschland Uber Alles,"* and after seemingly endless recitals of its refrain, the ground crew released the cables, then rushed forward to push away the control car. And then—slowly, ever so ponderously—the *Hindenburg* began to rise from the airfield.

Franc put his right arm around Lea's waist. After a moment, she nestled her head against his shoulder. "We're on our way," she said softly, as they watched Germany fall below them. "Next stop, New Jersey."

He nodded, then ducked his head to give her a kiss on the cheek. "The next stop is history," he whispered in her ear.

He didn't mean his remark to be ominous, yet she took it as such. He knew she did, for he felt her tremble.

PART 2

" . . . Where Angels Fear to Tread"

When the Center Hill Lake affair was over, after all the reports were filed with the appropriate agencies and various subcommittees had held closed-door hearings, when everyone with proper clearance had been reassured that the situation, although not completely resolved, at least was no longer critical . . . only then, looking back on the course of events, did Murphy come to realize that it really started the night before, in the Bullfinch on Pennsylvania Avenue.

The Bullfinch was a venerable Capitol Hill watering hole, located about three blocks from the Rayburn Building in one direction and within walking distance of one of Washington's more crime-ridden neighborhoods in the other. It was a favorite lunch spot for congressional aides and journalists who invaded it during happy hour, but by evening it became the after-hours hangout of federal employees from a dozen different departments and agencies. Coming off twelve-hour workdays, their shirts stained with sweat, their guts full of junk food, they emerged from Commerce and Agriculture and Justice and made their way to the Bullfinch for a few rounds with the boys before stumbling to Capitol South station to catch the next Metro out to the Maryland and Virginia suburbs.

Thursday was beer night for the Office of Paranormal Sciences. Murphy skipped these bull sessions more often than not, preferring to spend his evenings at home in Arlington with his wife and son. Donna was still mourning her mother's death just before Christmas, though, and Steve seemed to be more interested these days in Magic cards than his father, so when Harry Cummisky tapped on his door shortly after eight and asked if he wanted to grab a couple of brewskis with the boys, Murphy decided to go along. It had been a long time since he had given himself a break; if he came home an hour late with Budweiser on his breath, then so be it. Donna would burrow into her side of the bed anyway, and Steven wouldn't care so long as Dad took him to the comics shop on Saturday.

So he shut down the computer, locked up his office, and joined Harry and Kent Morris on a five-block trudge through sleet and slush to the Bullfinch. They were the last of the OPS regulars to arrive; several tables had already been pushed together in the back room, and an overworked waitress had already set the group up with pitchers of beer and bowls of popcorn. Although everyone was mildly surprised to see him, they quickly made room at the table. Murphy was aware of his button-down rep; he loosened his tie, admonished a wide-eyed Yale intern to stop addressing him as Sir and call him Zack instead, and poured the first of what he initially promised himself would be only two beers. A couple of drinks with the gang, a few laughs, then he would head home.

But that was not to be. It was a cold, damp night, and he was in a warm, dry bar. Gas flames hissed beneath fake logs in the nearby hearth, and firelight reflected off the panes of framed sports photos on the wood-paneled walls. Conversation was light, ranging from next week's Super

Bowl to current movies to the latest Hill gossip. The waitress's name was Cindy, and although she wore an engagement ring she seemed to enjoy flirting with the OPS guys. Every time his mug was half-empty, Kent or Harry or someone else would quickly top it off. After his second trip to the john, Zack stepped into a phone booth and called home to tell Donna not to wait up for him. No, he wasn't drunk; just a little tired, that's all. No, he wouldn't drive; he'd leave his car in the garage and take a cab. Yes, dear. No, dear. I love you, too. Sweet dreams, good night. And then he sailed back to the table, where Orson was regaling Cindy with the joke about the Texas senator, the prostitute, and the longhorn steer.

Before he realized it, the hour was late and the barroom was half-empty. One by one, the chairs had been vacated as the boys polished off their drinks, shrugged into their parkas and overcoats, and moseyed back out into the clammy night. Where there had once been nearly a dozen, now there were only three—Kent, Harry, and himself—teetering on that uncertain precipice between insobriety and inarticulate stupor. Cindy had long since ceased being amused and was now merely disgusted; she cleared away the empty mugs, delivered a pitcher that she firmly told them would be their last, and asked who needed a cab. Murphy managed to tell her that, yes ma'am, a cab would be a mighty fine idea, thank you very much, before he returned to the discussion at hand. Which, coincidentally enough, happened to be time travel.

Perhaps it wasn't so odd. Although time travel was a subject usually addressed in the more obscure books on theoretical physics, OPS people were acutely interested in the bizarre; they had to be, for that was the nature of their business. So it didn't seem strange that Murphy would find himself discussing something like this with Kent and Harry; it was late, they were drunk, and that was all there was to it.

"So imagine . . ." Harry belched into his fist. "'S'cuse me, sorry . . . well, imagine if time travel was possible. I mean, le's say it's possible to go past to the past, y'know . . ."

"You can't do it," Kent said flatly.

"Sure, sure, I know." Harry waved his hand back and forth. "I know it can't be done, I know that, okay? But le's jus' pretend . . ."

"You can't do it, I'm tellin' ya. It can't be done. I've read the same books, too, y'know, and I'm tellin' ya it's impossible. Nobody can do it. Nobody has the technology . . ."

"I'm not talkin' 'bout *now,* dammit. I'm talkin' 'bout sometime in the *future.* Couple'a hundred thousand years from now, thass what I'm . . . that's what I'm tryin' to get at, y'know."

"Somebody from the future, coming back here for a visit. That it?" Murphy had read a lot of science fiction when he was a kid, and time travel was a big subject in those stories. He even had a few beat-up old Ace Doubles stashed away in his attic, although he'd never admit that to these guys. Science fiction wasn't well respected at OPS, unless it was *The X-Files.*

"Thass it." Harry nodded vigorously. "Thass what I'm talkin' 'bout. Somebody from the future comin' back here for a visit."

"Can't be done," Kent insisted. "Not in a hundred million years."

"Yeah, well, maybe not," Murphy said, "but just for the sake of argument, okay. Le's pretend someone from the future . . ."

"Not just someone." Harry reached for the half-empty pitcher, sloshed some more beer into his mug. "A lotta someones . . . a lot of people, comin' back from the . . . y'know, the future."

"Yeah, right, okay." Kent eyed the pitcher with avarice; as soon as Harry put it down, he picked it up and poured much of the rest into his own mug, leaving a half inch at the bottom of the pitcher. "Simon sez le's pretend. So where are they?"

"Tha's it. Tha's the' point. Tha's what summa the phizachists . . . phizzakists . . ."

"Physicists," Murphy said. "What I am. I yam what I yam, and that's all that I . . ."

Harry ignored him. "If you can go back in time in the future, come back to here . . ." He jabbed a finger against the table. ". . . then where *are* they? That's what one of the Brits . . . the guy in the wheelchair, whassisname . . ."

"Hawking."

"Right, Hawking. Anyway, that's what he says . . . if time travel is possible, then where're the time travellers?"

"Yeah, but didn't somebody say that about aliens?" Kent raised an eyebrow; for an instant, he almost looked sober again. "That other guy . . . whatchamacallit, the Italian, Fermi . . . once said the same thing about aliens. Luggit what we do now . . . look for aliens!"

Murphy was about to add that, out of all the UFO sightings and abductions he had investigated in ten years with the OPS, he had yet to find one which panned out in terms of hard evidence. He had interviewed dozens of people who claimed to be have been taken aboard extraterrestrial spacecraft, and he'd collected enough out-of-focus photos of disc-shaped objects to fill a file cabinet, yet after a decade of government service, he had never found an alien or an alien spacecraft. He let it pass, though; this was not the time or place to be questioning his agency's mission or methods, nor were these the people to whom he should be expressing his doubts.

"Not the same thing, man. Not the same thing." Although there was still some beer left in his mug, Harry reached for the pitcher, but Kent snagged it first. "If'n there was time travellers, they'd sway . . . stay hidden. Nobody would know they were there. They'd do it for their own good. Right?"

Kent barked laughter as he poured the last dregs into his mug. "Yeah, sure. Like we got people from the future all 'round us now . . ."

"Well, shit, we *might*." Harry turned toward some guys seated nearby. "Hey, any of you fuggers from the future?"

They glared at him, but said nothing. Cindy was wiping tables and putting up chairs; she shot them a dark look. It was getting close to last call; she didn't seem to be happy to have garrulous drunks harassing her last remaining customers. "You wanna cool it?" Kent murmured. "Geez, I didn't meanta make it a federal case . . ."

"Hey, it *is* a federal case, man! Thass what we do, izzn'it? I say we bust this place for acceptin' time travellers withoutta . . . withoutta . . . fuck, I dunno, a green card?"

Harry reached into his suit pocket, pulled out his badge holder with the OPS seal engraved on its leatherette cover, started to push back his chair. That was enough for Murphy; he grabbed Harry's wrist before he could stand up. "Hey, hey, take it easy . . ."

Harry started to pull his hand free, but Murphy hung on. Out of the corner of his eye, he saw Cindy giving the bartender a discreet hand signal; they were about a second away from being thrown out. "Calm down," he murmured. "Keep this up and we're going to land in jail."

Harry glowered at him, and for a moment Murphy wondered if he was going to throw a punch. Then he grinned and dropped back into his chair. The badge folder slipped from his hand and fell onto the table. "Shit, man . . . I was just kidding, thass all. Jus' makin' a point, y'know."

"Yeah, that's right." Murphy relaxed, pulled his hand away. "I know. You're just kidding."

"Thass right. Y'know an' I know . . . ain' no such thing as . . . geez, whatchamacallit . . ."

"I know, I know. We got the point . . ."

And that was it. Murphy hung around long enough to make sure that Harry had a cab ride and that he wouldn't cause any more trouble, then he pulled on his parka and headed for the door, pausing at the bar to guiltily slip a five-spot into Cindy's tip glass. The sidewalk was empty; the night frigid and silent. Pale exhaust fumes from the waiting taxi lingered above the curb like pallid ghosts; he climbed in, gave the driver directions to his place in Arlington, then settled back against the duct-taped seat and gazed out the frosted windows as they passed the floodlighted dome of the Capitol Building.

Time travel. Jesus. What a stupid idea.

Thursday, May 6, 1937: 7:04 P.M.

The leviathan descended from the slate gray sky. At first it was a silver ovoid, but as it turned northeast, it gradually expanded in size and shape, taking on the dimensions of a vast pumpkin seed. As the drone of its four diesel engines reached the crowd gathered in the New Jersey meadow, Navy seamen in white caps jogged toward an iron mooring mast positioned in the center of the landing field. Everyone else stared up at the behemoth as it cruised six hundred feet overhead, its great shadow passing across their faces as it began making a sharp turn to the west. Now they could clearly see the swastikas on its vertical stabilizers, the Olympic rings on the fuselage above the passenger windows, and—above its control gondola, just aft of its blunt prow, painted in enormous Gothic letters—the giant's name.

Within the airship, passengers stood at titled cellon windows on A Deck's promenade, watching as the *Hindenburg* made its final approach to Lakehurst Naval Air Station. They were arriving thirteen hours late, because of high headwinds over the Atlantic and an additional delay while a thunderstorm swept out to sea, but few people cared; dur-

ing the last few hours, they had gazed down upon the spire
of the Empire State Building, caused a Dodgers game to
grind to a halt as they passed over Ebbets Field, and
watched whitecaps breaking on the Jersey shore. Stewards
had already carried their baggage to the gangway stairs aft
of the staterooms, where it now lay piled beneath the
bronze bust of Marshal von Hindenburg. It had been a wonderful trip: three days aboard the world's largest and most
glamorous airship, a flying hotel where mornings began
with breakfast in the dining room and evenings ended with
brandy and cigars in the smoking room.

Now the voyage was over, though, and everyone wanted
to get their feet on the ground again. For the Americans, it
was homecoming; in a few minutes, they'd be reunited
with family and friends waiting for them at the aerodrome.
For the sixty-one crew members, it was the *Hindenburg*'s
seventh flight to the United States, the first this year. For a
couple of German Jews, it was escape from the harsh
regime that had taken control of their native country. For
three Luftwaffe intelligence officers posing as tourists, it
was a temporary layover in a decadent nation of mongrels.

For the passengers listed on the manifest as John and
Emma Pannes, it was the beginning of the final countdown.

Franc Lu raised a hand from the promenade rail to his
spectacles, gently tapped their wire frame as if absently adjusting them. A readout appeared on the inside of the right
lens: *19:11:31/—13:41(?)*

"Thirteen minutes," he murmured.

Lea Oschner said nothing, but gripped the rail a little
harder. Around them, passengers were chatting, laughing,
pointing at baffled cows in the pastures far below. The airship's faint shadow was larger now, and moving closer; according to history, the *Hindenburg* would drop to 120
meters as it turned eastward again, heading back toward the
mooring mast. The passenger decks were soundproof, so
they couldn't hear the engines, but Captain Pruss should
now be ordering the engines reduced to idle-ahead; in an-

other minute, they would be reversed to brake the airship for its docking maneuver.

"Relax," he whispered. "Nothing's going to happen yet."

Lea forced a smile, but furtively clasped the back of his hand. Everyone around them was having a wonderful time; it was important that she and Franc appear just as carefree. They were John and Emma Pannes, from Manhasset, Long Island. John Pannes was the passenger manager for Hamburg-American German Lloyd Lines, the company that was the American representative for the Zeppelin airship fleet. Emma Pannes, fifteen years younger than her husband, was originally from Illinois. She had followed John's job from Philadelphia to New York, and now they were returning from another business trip to Germany.

Nice, quiet, middle-aged people who wouldn't be at all nervous about being aboard the *Hindenburg* despite the fact that thirteen . . . no, make that twelve . . . minutes from now, they were destined to die.

Yet John and Emma Pannes wouldn't perish in the coming inferno. In fact, they were very much alive, well, and living somewhere in the twenty-fourth century. The CRC advance team had quietly abducted them while they were walking from their hotel to the opera on the evening of May 2, 1937, and delivered them safely to its safe house outside Frankfurt; by now they should have been picked up by the *Miranda* and transported to A.D. 2314. Franc hoped that the real John Pannes wouldn't object too strongly to being kidnapped; given the alternative, though, he rather doubted that he would, once the facts were explained to him and his wife.

Now Franc was a sixty-year-old American businessman, and Lea was forty-five instead of twenty-nine. Their appearance had been altered so convincingly that, two nights earlier, they were able to share a table in the salon with the Pannes' old friend, Ernst Lehmann, the dirigible captain who was aboard the *Hindenburg* to observe Captain Pruss on his first transatlantic flight. They had dinner with Lehmann without the captain noticing any difference, yet they carefully remained aloof during most of the trip, preferring to stay in their cabin. The less interaction they had with the passengers and crew, the less chance of them inadvertently influencing history.

There had been a close moment yesterday, though, when they'd joined a tour of the ship.

The tour was necessary. John and Emma had toured the airship, so they had to follow the course of history. Yet, more importantly, it gave the researchers an opportunity to fulfill the primary objective of their mission: delivering an eyewitness account of the *Hindenburg*'s last voyage, and documenting the reason why the LZ-129 had been destroyed. So while the passengers marched single file along the keel catwalk, gaping at the vast hydrogen cells within the giant duraluminum rings, Franc and Lea paused now and then to stick adhesive divots, each no larger than the rivets they resembled, to girders and conduits. They had artfully scattered the divots everywhere aboard the airship; the divots transmitted sights and sounds to the recorders concealed within Franc's cigarette case and Lea's makeup compact, both of which had evaded discovery by the Gestapo agents who inspected everything carried aboard the *Hindenburg* by its passengers before they left the Frankfurter Hof the morning of the flight. Of course, the Nazis had been searching for a bomb, not for surveillance equipment so microscopic that it could be hidden within commonplace items of the early twentieth century.

The incident occurred when the tour reached the airship's stern, just below the place where the bomb was carefully sewn into the canvas liner beneath Cell Number 4. Kurt Ruediger, the ship's doctor who was conducting the tour, had paused to point out the landing-gear well in the lower vertical stabilizer when they heard footfalls descending a ladder above them. A few seconds later, a rigger appeared from the darkness, stepping off the ladder to head forward toward the nose.

When he came into the half-light cast by the electric lamps strung along the catwalk, Franc and Lea recognized him at once: Eric Spehl, whom history would cast as the man who had planted the bomb that would destroy the *Hindenburg*. He didn't look much like a saboteur, although he was within sight of the tiny package he had hidden in the gas cell while the ship was hangared at Friedrichshafen. Indeed, he seemed little more than an overworked rigger: a tall, blond man in drab cotton coveralls and rubber-soled shoes. As the passengers stepped aside to let him pass, though, Lea hesitated on the narrow catwalk. The necklace around her throat held a nanocam; this was her only chance to record Spehl's image.

The heel of her left shoe caught on the aluminum-mesh floor, though, and she tripped and staggered backward, her hands blindly groping for the railing. The airship's taut canvas skin lay only thirty feet below the catwalk; past that was a three-hundred-meter plummet into the frigid waters of the North Atlantic. Franc reached out to catch her, but Spehl was closer. He grabbed her by the shoulders and steadied her, then he smiled politely and said something about being careful, *Fraulein.* Then he turned and walked away.

A small occurrence, over and done within a few seconds, yet the significance of such incidents had long been a matter of debate within the Chronospace Research Centre. Some researchers argued that worldlines were so rigid that even the slightest disturbance could have vast ramifications; look what had almost happened when the CRC placed someone in a parking lot behind a high fence near Dealy Plaza in Dallas on November 22, 1963. Others contended that chronospace was more flexible than anyone believed; minor accidents were allowable during expeditions because history was already in motion. It didn't matter how many butterflies one crushed underfoot during the Pleistocene; the dinosaurs would die anyway.

Nonetheless, once Franc and Lea returned to their cabin, they had quietly fretted over whether the incident would cause a paradox. Yet history apparently hadn't been disturbed. Monitoring the airship from their cabin the following morning, as the *Hindenburg* approached the American coast, they watched as Spehl walked down the keel catwalk, furtively looked either way, then climbed the ladder to Cell Number 4. The divot Franc placed at the bottom of the ladder couldn't make him out in the visible spectrum, but his thermographic image showed him clinging to the ladder beneath the cell as he set the photographer's timer that would send an electric current from two dry-cell batteries into a small phosphorous charge.

At 7:25 P.M. local, plus an indeterminate number of seconds, 203,760 cubic meters of hydrogen would be ignited. Thirty-seven seconds later, the *Hindenburg* would hit the ground as 241 tons of flaming mass.

Now the mighty airship was slowing down. Through the promenade windows, they saw the crackerbox shape of the hangar, the skeletal mooring mast surrounded by tiny figures in white caps. Franc tapped his glasses again: *19:17:31/–08.29(?)* In a few seconds, the aft water ballast tanks would be released, the bowlines dropped.

It wasn't the next eight minutes that bothered him, though; it was the thirty-seven-plus seconds that would follow the explosion. He and Lea had had little trouble getting aboard the *Hindenburg*. Now they had to see if they could get off again.

One of the most interesting things about the early 20th century, Vasili Metz concluded, was the way Earth looked from space.

It wasn't just the relative smallness of its cities, or the clarity of the skies above them, or the subtle differences of the coastlines. It was surprising to see New York City when its skyline was new and not half-submerged, but even that was to be expected. This was his third mission as the *Oberon*'s pilot, and he had become accustomed to such changes. What struck him as unreal was the emptiness of near-Earth space. No powersats, no colonies, no shuttles. Chronos Station was nowhere to be seen. There wasn't even any space debris; the first satellite wouldn't be launched for forty years, and another thirty years would pass before free-falling junk would pose a navigational hazard.

On the other hand, it would be another ten years before anyone ever reported having seen a flying saucer. And it would remain that way if he had any say in the matter.

For the past three days, after a brief visit to Earth to drop off Lu and Oschner within Frankfurt, then a suborbital jaunt to deposit Tom Hoffman in New Jersey, Metz had held station in geosynchronous orbit above the Garden State. Except for when he monitored the *Miranda*'s departure, when it opened the wormhole that would send the support team, plus two nice people named John and Emma Pannes, back to Chronos Station, he had been almost alone.

Three hours earlier, *Oberon* had descended to a new orbit 289 kilometers above New Jersey, and Metz had suddenly become quite busy. Maintaining the proper balance between the timeship's negmass drive and Earth's gravity, while simultaneously compensating for the planet's rotation, was difficult enough; he also had to remain in contact with Hoffman. With no comsats available to assist them, and Tom unable to throw up a transceiver dish, they had to relay on old-fashioned ELF bands that wouldn't likely be intercepted by ham radio operators of this period.

"Oberon, this is Lakehurst Base." Hoffman's voice came over Metz's headset. *"Do you copy? Over."*

Metz prodded his throat mike. "We copy, Lakehurst. What's the mission status?"

"Status good. Hindenburg's at the tower. Water ballast down, bowlines have just been dropped. Holding steady at about ninety-one meters. Event minus three minutes, sixteen seconds, and counting."

Hoffman was trying to remain professionally detached, but Metz could hear the excitement in his voice. Nor could he blame him; the mission specialist was about to witness one of the classic technodisasters of this century, one which would put an end to commercial airship travel for the next nine decades. It was probably all Tom could do to remain seated within the automobile he had rented a couple of days earlier; however, it wouldn't do for him to be seen lugging a comlink case around the aerodrome.

"Copy that, Lakehurst." A flatscreen below the porthole displayed a false-color radar image of the *Hindenburg* floating above Lakehurst Naval Air Station. The dirigible was a light blue bullet-shaped blip surrounded by hundreds of tiny white gnats. Above the image was the mission timer: *5.07.37/19.22.05/E—02.45(?)*. "Holding station, ready for pickup on your mark."

"Very good, Oberon. I'm about . . ." The rest was lost in a wave of static. Metz's hands moved across his console, correcting the timeship's position; the static cleared and Hoffman's voice came back: *". . . is huge. You wouldn't believe how big it is. Almost the size of an asteroid freighter. It's . . ."*

"Keep your mind on the job."

"The motor's running. I'm ready to go." Another pause. *"Can you believe people actually used these things to get around? They smell awful."*

"I know. Stay focused." Metz glanced at the mission chronometer again. Two minutes, eleven seconds and counting, plus or minus a few seconds given the inexactness of contemporary records. Those few seconds were going to be the tricky part of this operation.

"All right, Franc," he murmured. "Don't screw up now."

Thursday, May 6, 1937: 7:23 P.M.

An odd stillness had fallen over the airfield. The light
drizzle had let up for a moment as dull gray clouds
parted here and there, allowing sunlight to lance down
upon the aerodrome and reflect greenish twilight off the
Hindenburg's silver skin. The Navy men had the zeppelin's
mooring lines in their hands; they dug in their heels, playing tug-of-war with the leviathan looming three hundred
feet above their heads. On the outskirts of the crowd, a radio newsman from Chicago delivered a breathless report of
the airship's arrival into a portable dictaphone machine.

Glancing around the promenade, Franc realized that he
was surrounded by dead people. Fritz Erdmann, the Luftwaffe colonel who had been trying to ferret out a saboteur
among his fellow passengers, but failed to notice Eric
Spehl; he would soon be crushed by a flaming girder. Her-
mann Doehner and his lovely teenage daughter Irene, taking a family vacation to America: they were doomed as
well. Moritz Feibusch, the sweet man whom the stewards
had segregated from other German passengers simply
because he was a Jew; he would soon perish. Edward
Douglas, the General Motors businessman the Gestapo be-

lieved was an American spy, whom Erdmann had dogged during the entire flight; he, too, was living his last minutes.

And so were John and Emma Pannes. At least, this was how history would record their fate.

Although the clothes he and Lea had put on this morning appeared to be made of contemporary wool and cotton, they were woven from flame-resistant fabrics unknown in this century. The handkerchiefs in their pockets, once unfolded and placed over their mouths, contained two-minute supplies of molecular oxygen. They had left nothing in their baggage which had been made in the twenty-fourth century; the divots they had scattered throughout the airship would dissolve when the ambient air temperature reached 96 Celsius. When no one recovered their bodies from the wreckage, it would be presumed that their corpses had been incinerated by the inferno. This wasn't too far from the mark; some of the bodies recovered from the disaster had only been identifiable by wedding bands or engraved watches.

"Time," Lea whispered.

Franc prodded his glasses again. "Sixty-five seconds, plus or minus a few." Then he took off the spectacles and slipped them into a vest pocket. She nodded and returned her hand to the railing.

There was a sudden rush of cool air. A few feet down the promenade, someone had cranked open a window. A woman waved to a man with a bulky motion-picture camera on the ground far below. Ghosts. He was surrounded by ghosts.

In the breast pocket of his jacket, Franc carried the one personal souvenir of this trip he had permitted himself: a folded sheet of paper, engraved with the *Hindenburg*'s name and picture, upon which were printed the airship's passenger list. This wasn't for the CRC; when he got home, he would frame it on the wall of his Tycho City apartment. Lea had nagged him about taking it, until he pointed out that it would be destroyed anyway; he later pretended not to notice when she tucked a teaspoon into the garter belt of her stockings. Little things like that wouldn't be missed. He just wished he could save the two caged dogs back in the baggage compartment. Dogs were so scarce where they came from, and he hated to think what would happen to them when . . .

Franc took a deep breath. Calm down, calm down. You're going to get through this. Just don't lose your head now . . .

They had deliberately placed themselves on the starboard promenade of Deck B, not far from the gangway stairs. Many of the survivors had lived simply because they were here and not on the port promenade of the same deck, where others would be pinned down by dining-room furniture. The original John Pannes died because he left the promenade just before the crash to see about Emma, who had remained in their cabin for unknown reasons. Airsickness? A premonition, perhaps? History hadn't recorded the exact reasons why the Pannes had died, but he and Lea wouldn't make the same fatal error.

The airship's stern would hit the ground first. Although the aluminum grand piano at the far end of the promenade worried them, they had already agreed to rush the gangway as soon as they felt that first, fateful jerk that everyone would initially assume to be a mooring rope snapping. Down the stairs past the Deck A landing, then down another flight of stairs to the passenger hatch . . . by the time they got that far, the airship would be almost on the ground. They shouldn't have to jump more than four meters.

Thirty-seven seconds. From the instant when the first flame appeared on the upper aft fuselage to the moment the *Hindenburg* was a flaming skeleton, only thirty-seven seconds would elapse. Time enough to cheat history . . .

Or time enough to lose the bet.

Franc felt Lea slide against him. "If we don't . . ."

"We will."

Her head nodded against his shoulder. "But if we don't . . ."

"Don't tell me you love me."

Her laughter was nervous and dry. "Stop flattering yourself."

He managed to chuckle, and her hand briefly squeezed his arm before it returned to the railing. Franc glanced to his left, saw the dirigible's shadow gliding closer to the mooring mast. "Hang on . . . any second now . . ."

The airship drifted back, forward, back again. The ground crew fought the wind as they hauled the behemoth toward the iron tripod. The two ground shadows converged, became as one.

Franc clung to the railing, felt it dig into his palms. Okay, okay . . . when is it going to happen?

A sudden, hard jolt ran through the ship.

He grabbed Lea's shoulders, turned her toward the door heading to the gangway. "Okay, let's go!" he snapped. "Move, move . . . !"

Lea took a step, then stopped. He slammed into her back.

"Wait a minute . . ." she whispered.

"Move!" He shoved at her. "We don't have . . . !"

Then he stopped, and listened.

The deck was stable. It wasn't tilting beneath their feet.

No screams. No shouting. The chairs and tables remained where they were.

Passengers gaped at them with baffled amusement. Edward Douglas chuckled and turned to say something behind his hand to his wife. Moritz Feibusch gave him a look of sympathy. Irene Doehner enjoyed a brief moment of teenage condescension. Colonel Erdmann sneered at him.

Then one of the stewards strolled down the promenade, announcing that the *Hindenburg* had arrived and that all passengers were to make way to gangway stairs. Please do not forget your baggage. Please proceed directly to American customs.

Franc looked down at Lea. Her face was pale; she trembled against him.

"What went wrong?" she whispered.

Friday, January 16, 1998: 8:12 A.M.

Murphy didn't hear the phone when it rang; he was in the bathroom, using a styptic pen on the cuts his razor had made against his chin and neck. Lately he had been keeping the razor beneath a little glass pyramid that his wife had given him for Christmas, but it wasn't preserving the blade's sharpness the way its brochure claimed it would. Either that, or the brutal hangover he suffered this morning had made him sloppy while shaving.

At any rate, he wasn't aware that someone was calling for him until Donna knocked on the door. *Office,* she mouthed silently as she extended the cordless to him, and Murphy winced. He was already running late, thanks to the blinding headache he'd woken up with; there must be some eight o'clock meeting he had forgotten, and someone at OPS had phoned to find out what was keeping him. Donna hadn't been pleased when he'd come home drunk in a cab, and the prospect of having to give him a lift to the office wasn't helping her forgive him. She gave him another withering look as he took the phone, then went back to watching the morning horoscope on TV.

"This is Zack." He tucked the phone under his chin as he reached for the deodorant stick.

"Zack, it's Roger Ordmann . . ."

The phone almost fell into the sink. Roger Ordmann was the agency's Chief Administrator. Murphy had spoken with him exactly three times during his tenure at OPS; the first time was when he had been hired, the other two during social occasions. Roger Ordmann was the man the President called when Mary Lincoln's ghost was seen roaming the second floor of the White House.

"Yes, sir, Mr. Ordmann. Sorry I'm running late, but the car battery died this morning. My wife's about ready to bring me in, though, so . . ."

"That's okay, Dr. Murphy. Perfectly understandable. We have a small problem here that we need to discuss."

The bathroom tiles suddenly felt much colder beneath his bare feet. Oh, God, it's something to do with last night. Harry got in a fight at the bar and was taken downtown. Or Kent cracked up his car while trying to drive home. The police got involved and his name came out. "A problem, sir?"

"Are you on a secure line?"

A moment of puzzlement. What was Ordmann asking? Then he remembered that he was on a cordless phone. "Umm . . . no, sir. Do you want me to . . . ?"

"Please."

"Just a moment, sir . . ." Murphy fumbled with the phone until he found the *Hold* button, then he stalked across the house to the little office next to the den. Donna barely glanced up as he shut the door behind him; the TV volume was up, which meant that she shouldn't be able to hear what he was saying. The forecaster was explaining why this was a good day for Capricorns to renew old friendships, particularly with Scorpios.

Murphy sat down at the desk, picked up the hardwired phone, switched off the cordless. "I'm here, sir. Sorry to . . ."

"Is this a secure line?"

What was this? "I'm on another extension, yes sir, if that's what you're asking. I was in the bathroom, speaking on a cordless. Just got out of the . . ." Realizing that he was starting to babble, Murphy stopped himself. "Yes, sir, it's secure."

A pause, then: "There's been a wreck."

Oh, Jesus! One of the guys did try to drive home drunk! Kent or Harry—probably Harry, he had been the most inebriated—climbed behind the wheel, and then he . . .

Then Murphy remembered with whom he was speaking, and why it might be so important that they'd want to have a phone conversation on a line that couldn't be casually monitored, and what this particular phrase signified in a different context.

"Yes sir, I understand." His mind was already racing. "Where did it happen?"

"Tennessee. About sixty miles east of Nashville. About an hour and a half ago."

"I see . . ." Murphy glanced around the office, trying to spot his road atlas, before he remembered where he had seen it last: in Steven's room, where he had taken it for a homework assignment. Forget it. "Has anyone . . . I mean, has anyone found the car? "

"We've located the vehicle, but no one's looked inside yet. An ambulance is being sent to check it out. Can you be ready to go in ten minutes?"

Something cold raced up his back. "Ten . . . ? Mr. Ordmann, I haven't even left the . . ."

"We've sent a car to pick you up. A plane's waiting at Dulles, and we've got the rest of the team assembled. You'll be briefed on the way. Can you be ready in ten minutes?"

Murphy was in his robe. His suit was still on the hanger and could probably use a pass with a lint brush; he hadn't even picked out a tie. But an old Adidas gym bag in his closet had some clean clothes left over from last fall's hunting trip, and it would only take a moment for him to pack up his laptop. "I'll be ready."

"Very good. You've got the ball, Dr. Murphy. Don't drop it."

"I won't, sir," he said, managing for the moment to sound much more confident than he felt. "We'll be in touch."

"Good karma," Ordmann said, then he hung up.

Murphy gently placed the receiver in its cradle, sat back in his chair, and let out his breath. Sometime during the night, a light snow had fallen on Arlington. Through the office window, he could see where it had frosted Donna's backyard garden and laid a white skein over the swing set Steve no longer used. It looked cold and lonely out there. He wondered if it was any warmer in Tennessee.

He sighed, then stood up and went to tell Donna that he was going away on a business trip.

Thursday, May 5, 1937: 8:00 P.M.

Thirty-five minutes after the *Hindenburg* docked at Lake-hurst Naval Air Station, an explosion in one of the aft gas cells destroyed the airship.

No one was aboard when the fire ripped through the di-rigible. All the passengers and crew members had disem-barked by then, and even the ground crew managed to dash to safety before the burning airship hit the ground, taking out the mooring mast with it. A newsreel cameraman caught the conflagration on film; it was later remarked how fortunate it had been that the *Hindenburg* hadn't exploded while still in the air, or otherwise an untold number of lives might have been lost.

Franc and Lea watched the fire from the safety of Tom's rented Ford sedan, which he had driven to the outskirts of the aerodrome and pulled over on the shoulder. They had quietly collected their bags and walked down the gangway stairs; a stunned shuffle through customs, where officials stamped the Pannes' passports and welcomed them back to America, then Hoffman met them just outside the receiving area. He instantly started to ask questions, but they signaled him to stay silent until they were out of earshot of the other passengers.

As they walked out to the car, Franc spotted Eric Spehl, still wearing his flight coveralls, climbing into the back of a checker cab. Unnoticed by either his fellow zeppelin men or the Luftwaffe intelligence officers, the rigger made his getaway. Fifteen minutes later, the bomb went off.

As clanging fire trucks raced down the road toward the inferno, the three of them looked at one another. "Well," Tom said, "at least we haven't created a paradox. We're still here."

Franc stared at the blazing airship. "The hell we haven't!"

"We don't know that yet," Lea said from the backseat. "There's been an anomaly. A serious one, to be sure, but it's still only an anomaly."

"Some anomaly." Franc nodded toward the burning ship. "This isn't like someone in Dallas noticing a couple of our people behind a fence during the Kennedy shooting. That didn't change the course of history. *This* . . ."

"*Oberon*'s still there." Tom cocked his head toward the uplink case where it lay open next to Lea; she had just used it to contact the timeship. "If this was a paradox, Vasili shouldn't be up there and we would have disappeared. Right?"

"Define paradox," Franc said angrily. "Tell me exactly what happens during a spatiotemporal paradox."

"I don't . . ."

"Come on, tell me precisely *how* a spatiotemporal paradox would affect a contemporary worldline . . ."

"Cut it out." Lea snapped the case shut. "We can figure it out after we get to the rendezvous point."

So they drove away from Lakehurst, heading southwest down lonely country roads into the cool New Jersey night. Deep within the Pine Barrens, house lights gradually became farther apart until they disappeared altogether. A low fog had settled upon the marshlands; the sedan's tires beat against frost heaves in the weathered blacktop. Lea moved the case to the floor and lay down in the backseat; she remarked how incredibly large automobiles had been during this period, and Tom responded by observing how much gasoline they consumed in order to move this much mass. Franc, sullen and impatient, switched on the dashboard radio and turned the knob from one end of the dial to another, picking up AM-band stations out of Trenton, Philadelphia, and New York. Ballroom jazz, comedy shows, crime melodramas: he roamed back and forth, searching for something that might explain what had just happened.

Just as they turned off the highway onto a narrow trip of dirt road, a variety show out of New York was interrupted by a news flash. The German airship *Hindenburg,* which had mysteriously exploded an hour and fifteen minutes ago just after it had arrived in New Jersey, had been destroyed by an act of deliberate sabotage. An unsigned communiqué received by the station only a few minutes earlier stated that an underground organization in Germany was claiming responsibility for the act. The note stated that a bomb had been placed aboard the airship to awaken the world to the atrocities being committed by the Nazi government, and to send a clear signal to the German people that Adolf Hitler could yet be overthrown.

Franc switched off the radio. There was a long silence in the car. "That's what I define as a paradox," he said at last.

"We're still here," Tom said softly.

"Which only means that we've survived our own disturbance."

"Who says it's *our* fault?" Lea was sitting up again. "No one knows why Spehl's bomb went off when it did. Maybe the timer was faulty, and it was supposed to go off at eight o'clock."

"Or maybe he went back and reset it," Tom said.

Franc nodded. "Sure. He ran into Emma Pannes the day

before and decided that he didn't want to sacrifice a beautiful *fraulein* to the flames."

"So it's *my* fault?" Lea gaped at him. "I can't believe you . . . !"

"I'm joking."

"That's not very funny. I don't even think you're . . ."

"Will both of you just shut up?" Tom gripped the wheel more tightly as he strained to make out the primitive road through the fog. "We can't do anything about it now, so just . . ."

Lea wasn't through. "Do you think this is funny?"

"No, I don't. But it's a possible hypothesis for how . . ."

"Shut up!" Tom yelled. "Goddammit, both of you, just shut up!"

Once again, there was cold and awful silence in the car.

The road finally opened onto a broad clearing where a farmhouse had once stood some ten years before, until it had been destroyed by one of the brushfires that periodically raged through the Pine Barrens. Only a half-collapsed brick chimney remained; the rest was rotted cinders, old cedar stumps, and high grass, damp with rain and age.

Tom stopped the car and switched off the headlights; a chorus of bullfrogs and crickets greeted them when they opened the doors. Lea shivered and drew her overcoat more closely around her as she instinctively stepped closer to Franc. She had been born and raised on the Moon; nature sounds made her nervous. Franc put his arm around her as he stared up at the overcast sky. A westerly breeze was blowing the clouds away, revealing crisp bright stars in the moonless sky.

"You gave Vasili the correct coordinates, didn't you?" he asked, then saw the expression on her face. "Sorry. Only asking."

Tom pulled the uplink case out of the backseat, carried it a few feet away, and set it down. He returned to the car, clicked on the dome light, briefly inspected the car's interior. No, there was nothing here that shouldn't be left behind; Franc's and Lea's bags were stowed in the trunk, and they had all their documents and recording equipment with them. He pulled a small gold box out of his breast pocket, thumbed a recessed switch on the side, carefully placed it on the wheel well in the backseat. Five minutes after they departed, the Hertz company would be mysteriously deprived of one Ford sedan, or at least until some hunter chanced upon its charred wreckage.

When he joined Franc and Lea again, he saw that they were staring up at the sky. Looking up, he saw nothing for a moment. Then a small black shape moved past the Big Dipper, a circular patch slightly darker than the night sky. "Better get out the way," he murmured. "Grab the case."

The three of them hurried to the edge of the clearing. When they turned and looked up again, the shape had expanded into a broad opaque spot that grew larger as it blotted out the stars. Metz had the *Oberon* in chameleon mode; it was now nearly invisible to the naked eye. Even if radar had been in widespread use at this time, the timeship wouldn't have appeared on any screens; the beams would have been deflected by its fuselage. Only the negmass grid on the craft's underside could be detected, and that operated in near-total silence. It wasn't until they heard a low hum and the wet grass of the clearing began to flatten out that they knew the *Oberon* was at treetop level.

The humming grew louder, then the timeship suddenly appeared just above them. Deliberately designed to resemble a classic sombrero-shaped flying saucer, it could have appeared on the cover of a late-twentieth-century UFO magazine; indeed, it had, for an alien-abduction story debunked by most contemporary experts. Light gleamed from its single porthole as landing gear opened like flower petals from its flat underside between the hemispherical pods of its wormhole generators. *Oberon* seemed to hesitate for just a moment, then the humming of its negmass drive sharply diminished, and the timeship settled to the ground.

The research team was jogging toward the craft when a hatch above one of the flanges irised open. Metz appeared as a silhouette at the top of the ladder. "What are you waiting for?" he shouted. "We gotta get out of here! Go, go, go!"

Franc was the first to reach the ladder. "Not so fast," he said, hoisting the uplink case above his head. "We need to see what's been done here. There might be something we don't . . ."

"What, you mean you're not through *yet?*" Metz reached down, grabbed the case's handle, and snatched it out of Franc's hand. "Maybe we should drop by Washington on the way up, let you assassinate Teddy Roosevelt . . ."

"It's Franklin, not Teddy . . ."

"Who cares? You're done." Metz deposited the case behind him. "I just hope you haven't screwed things up so much that we can't get out of here."

"Dammit, Vasili, it's not our fault!" Lea's voice was outraged. "We don't know what happened, but it's . . . we didn't. . . ."

"Save it for the Commissioner, Oschner. We're on our way up." Metz disappeared from the hatch. "Get aboard or stay behind. We're out of here in sixty."

"Vasili, wait!" Franc scrambled up the ladder and pulled himself up through the hatch into *Oberon*'s airlock. Contrasted with the cool New Jersey night, the wedge-shaped compartment was uncomfortably warm. The helmet of the EVA hardsuit lashed against the bulkhead reflected his face like a fun-house mirror. Franc took a moment to pull Lea the rest of the way up the ladder, then he darted through the inner hatch and followed the pilot down the narrow midships passageway to the control room. "Calm down. We've got to talk about . . ."

"There's nothing to discuss, Doctor." Metz entered the compartment, dropped into his seat and ran his palms across the console, clearing the timeship's system for new programming. "And don't tell me to calm down. Not after *this*. Now get your people strapped down. We're lifting."

"Okay, all right." Franc raised his hands. "Get us out of here. Take us to orbit. But don't open a bridge until we've assessed the situation and at least tried to determine what caused this in the . . ."

Metz swung around in his chair to jab a finger at Franc. "Look, Dr. Lu, don't make me give you a remedial lecture in chronospace theory. Causality. Inconsistency paradoxes. The care and feeding of Morris-Thorne bridges. Remember?"

"All I'm saying is, we need to slow down, try to study what . . ."

"Study my ass. I'm making a hole while I can still can." Metz swung back around, began stabbing at the console. Lights flashed orange, green, blue, and red; screens arrayed around the horseshoe displayed ship status, local topography, orbital maps, projected spacetime vectors. Metz glanced over his shoulder as he pulled on his headset. "Sorry, Franc, but you're overruled. I'm the pilot, so what I say, goes. I say we make an emergency launch, so we're going. Now get your team in their seats, because it's going to be a fast ride to Chronos."

There was no point in arguing. CRC protocols were strict on this point. Franc was in charge of the expedition's research team, but timeship pilots had final say over what happened once its members were back aboard ship. And Metz was playing the situation by the book.

Franc turned and stalked out of the control room. When the hatch slid shut behind him, he slammed his fist against it in frustration. "Jerk!" he yelled.

Then he stepped across the passageway to the passenger compartment. Hoffman was already strapped into one of the three acceleration couches. "She's in the monitor room," he said before Franc could ask. "I think she's . . ."

"I'll get her. Stay put. Vasili wants to get us out of here."

Franc retreated from the hatch and turned toward the last of the timeship's major compartments, located at the opposite end of the passageway from the ready room. "Lea! Vasili's . . . !"

"I know. I heard." Lea had already discarded her costume and had put on a skinsuit. Franc regretted the change; until Lea shed her disguise, the form-fitting bodysuit didn't flatter her middle-aged appearance. He couldn't blame her, though; once they got a chance, he would do the same. Sweat made these period clothes feel sticky. She stood at the pedestal in the middle of the compartment, her fingers dashing across its panel as she opened the library subsystem. "Just give me a minute. I want to see if I can access something from the mission recorders."

"We don't have a minute. Vasili's going for an emergency launch."

"Shut up and give me your cigarette case." Lea had already hardwired her makeup compact to the pedestal; she held out her palm without looking at him. "Hurry."

"We don't have time for this," he repeated, but he dug into his jacket and pulled out the cigarette case. Lea snatched it from his hand, impatiently shook out the unsmoked cigarettes, and ran a cord from the pedestal to the tiny dataport concealed in the bottom of the case. She tapped her fingers at the pedestal, then glanced up at the wallscreen. A red bar crept across the screen; the library subsystem was downloading everything the divots had collected aboard the *Hindenburg*.

"All right, we've got everything," she murmured. "Now let's see what happened in Cell Number Four just before . . ."

"Never mind that now. We've got to get strapped down." Franc grabbed her by the wrist and hauled her away from the pedestal; she managed to grab the recorders before he propelled her through the hatch toward the passenger compartment. He got her inside just before the hatch sphinctered shut.

They were barely in their couches when the timeship begin to rise. Franc glanced at the status panel, and saw that Metz had switched off *Oberon*'s chameleon and gravity screen in order to divert power to the negmass drive. His lips tightened as he silently swore at the pilot. They were in for a rough ride . . .

Then they were shoved back in their seats as the timeship shot upward into the night. A wallscreen displayed a departure-angle view from beneath the saucer; the lights of the Jersey shore and New York City briefly appeared below them before they were obscured by high cloudbanks, then the *Oberon* punched through the clouds as it headed for space.

Too much, too fast. Franc clenched the armrests as pressure mounted on his chest. They shouldn't be doing it this way. His vision was blurred, but he could make out Lea from the corner of his eye; she looked just as angry as he felt. Damn it, she was *right*. They still didn't understand what had happened down there. He started to raise a leaden hand, then remembered that he had neglected to put on a headset. He couldn't talk to Metz.

Earth's horizon appeared on the wallscreen as a vast dark curve, highlighted by a thin luminescent band of blue. Stars appeared above the blue line at the same instant he felt his body begin to rise from the seat cushion. They had achieved escape velocity; Metz was throttling back the negmass drive. But they had to stop. They had to abort to low orbit. They needed time to study what had happened aboard the *Hindenburg* before . . .

And then the timeship's wormhole generators went on-line.

Oberon's AI discovered a quantum irregularity in Earth's gravity well; exotic matter contained within the pods beneath the saucer enlarged the subatomic rift into a funnel large enough for the timeship to pass through, and laced the funnel's mouth with energy fields that would keep the wormhole temporarily stable. Within moments, a small area of spacetime was warped into something that resembled a four-dimensional ram's horn: a closed-time-like circle. Relentlessly attracted by the wormhole it had just created, the timeship plummeted into the closed-time circle.

Then something that felt like the hand of God slapped the timeship and sent it careening . . . elsewhere.

The jet was a fifteen-year-old Grumman Gulfstream II, a relic from the days when the government was still able to purchase civilian aircraft manufactured in the United States. On the inside, it only looked ten years old, which was a little better than the last ride on a Boeing 727 Murphy had taken. Yet the seats were threadbare, the overhead compartments smudged with handprints; there had been some turbulence when the jet had taken off from Dulles that had caused the fuselage to creak a bit and gave the woman sitting on the other side of the aisle reason to recite her mantra in a low, tense voice.

Once the jet leveled off at thirty-three thousand feet and the pilot switched off the seat-belt lights, an Army lieutenant walked down the aisle to ask if anyone aboard wanted refreshments before the briefing started. Murphy settled for coffee and a bagel with cream cheese. The woman demanded to know whether the bagels were kosher, the cream cheese was low-fat, and the coffee was from Guatemala. She was miffed when the lieutenant politely informed her that the bagels were frozen and that he didn't know about the fat content of the cheese nor where the coffee beans had come from; she settled for hot tea and scrutinized the label on the tea bag before she dipped it in her mug.

There were five passengers aboard the Gulfstream, including Murphy himself. The humorless lady was also from OPS, but he didn't know her name; he recognized her only from having passed her in office corridors, so he assumed she belonged to another division. The two military officers were in civilian clothes; so was the FBI man, but he was the only one besides Murphy who was dressed for the outdoors. He sat in the back of the plane, speaking on a phone while he worked on a laptop computer. When Murphy got up from his seat and went aft in search of a bathroom, the FBI man turned aside and cupped his hand over the phone as Murphy went past.

Weird. But not half as weird when, a half hour after takeoff, the senior military officer started the briefing.

"Gentlemen, ma'am," he began once his aide had helped everyone swivel their chairs around so that they faced the table behind which he stood, "thank you for being here on such short notice. Your government appreciates your willingness to be summoned to duty so quickly, and I hope it hasn't caused you any undue embarrassment."

He then introduced himself as Colonel Baird Ogilvy; with him was Lieutenant Scott Crawford, also from U.S. Army Intelligence. The FBI agent's name was Ray Sanchez; he was here principally to facilitate matters with local law-enforcement officials and to act as an official observer. Ogilvy seemed pleasant enough, a gray-haired gentleman in his mid-fifties who would have been at home in a golf cart; his aide was younger and a bit more intense, but he managed a brief smile when he was introduced. Sanchez, who put down his phone only reluctantly, looked as if he were carrying a glass suppository; he frowned when Ogilvy called him by name, but said nothing. Murphy decided at once to give him a wide berth if he could help it. Most of the guys he had met from the Bureau were decent enough chaps, but Sanchez was one of those who had seen too many Steven Seagal movies.

After the colonel introduced Murphy himself, identifying him as the OPS lead investigator for this mission, he went on to name the last two people on the plane. Murphy put a hand over his mouth when Ogilvy introduced the woman as Meredith Cynthia Luna. Lean and fox-faced, her brown hair styled in a rigid coif, she looked like a real-estate broker who had dropped acid and seen the face of the Almighty in a breakfast croissant. Murphy knew Luna only by reputation; a psychic from Remote Sensing Division, she was supposedly difficult to work with, apparently believing that she possessed a sixth-sense hot line to another dimension. She preened when Ogilvy mentioned her ES-Per abilities, and Murphy wondered if she would demonstrate her talents by proclaiming that they would soon be flying over water.

Not for the first time, Murphy wondered why he was working for the Office of Paranormal Sciences; not for the first time, he remembered the reasons. NASA was dead, salary jobs at the National Science Foundation were vanishing faster than humpback whales, and far more astrologers were gainfully employed these days than astrophysicists. So Murphy did the best he could, trying to be a voice of reason among spoon-benders and firewalkers, and when he found himself contemplating resignation, he reminded himself that there was a mortgage that needed to be paid and a son who had to be sent to college, and thanked God that Carl Sagan was no longer alive so he wouldn't have to tell his old Cornell prof what he was now doing for a living.

As Colonel Ogilvy continued, Crawford began passing out blue folders with eyes-only strips across the covers. "At 6:42 A.M. Eastern this morning, two F-15C fighters from Sewert Air Force Base outside Nashville were on a training sortie over the Cumberland Plateau sixty-eight miles east-southeast of base when they encountered an unidentified object." Ogilvy's eyes occasionally darted to his folder. "The planes were at 30,500 feet at this time, and the object was on a due-east heading above them, altitude approximately 45,000 feet when first sighted, approximately 10 to 15 miles distant from the planes' position. It appeared to be entering the atmosphere at a sharp downward angle of approximately 47 degrees, at an airspeed in excess of Mach 2. Although the object wasn't detected by radar either from the planes or by military or civilian air-traffic control, both pilots reported clear visual confirmation of the object."

Ogilvy flipped to another page. "Upon receiving clearance from base, both planes moved to intercept the object. Upon close approach at 34,000 feet, they described the object as a flying saucer approximately 65 feet in diameter and 20 feet high—about the size of their own aircraft—which flew without any visible means of propulsion. At the front of the object's upper hull was a single window."

Meredith Cynthia Luna held up a hand; Ogilvy acknowledged her with a brief nod. "Did the pilots see any aliens within the spacecraft?"

"No, ma'am, the pilots didn't spot any occupants. They were doing the best they could just to match the object's course and speed."

"Did the pilots report receiving any psychic transmissions?"

"Ma'am, the pilots attempted to contact the craft by radio, on both LF and HF bands. They received no transmissions, radio or otherwise." Was Murphy imagining things, or was Ogilvy trying to keep a straight face?

"But it seemed as if the object had entered the atmosphere. Is that correct?"

"Given the fact that it was first spotted in the upper atmosphere and was descending at supersonic speed, that's the impression they had, yes ma'am." Ogilvy held up his hand. "Please let me finish the briefing, then I'll take your questions."

The colonel consulted his notes again. "When they

failed to establish radio communication with the craft, both pilots maneuvered their aircraft so they could get a closer look at the object. By this point the craft had decelerated to sub-Mach velocity, and it appeared to be leveling off its approach as it passed an altitude of 29,000 feet. One pilot, Capt. Henry G. O'Donnell, took up position 700 feet from the craft's starboard side, while his wingman, Capt. Lawrence H. Binder, attempted to fly closer to the object in order to inspect it. Binder was passing beneath the object's underside when his jet apparently lost electrical power."

"Lost power?" Murphy raised a hand; the colonel nodded in his direction. "You mean, he . . . his jet failed to respond to his controls?"

"I mean, Dr. Murphy, Capt. Binder's aircraft lost *all* electrical power. Avionics, propulsion, telemetry, the works. He said it was as if someone had pulled the plug. His plane went into a flat spin, and Binder was forced to eject manually from the cockpit."

"I've heard of this happening before," Meredith Cynthia Luna murmured. "A police officer in Florida had his car lose power when he encountered a spacecraft."

"Did he eject?" Lieutenant Crawford asked.

Murphy slapped a hand over his mouth. Oh God, don't laugh, don't laugh . . . then he saw Ogilvy forcing a cough into his fist as he shot a look at his aide, and realized that he wasn't the only rational person aboard this plane.

"It's not funny!" Luna's face was red with righteous indignation. "The poor officer suffered a terrible ordeal! He was held captive for twelve hours!" Then she turned to the colonel. "Tell me . . . did the pilot receive any psychic impressions when this occurred?"

Murphy jotted down a note in the margins of his binder: *100% loss of F-15 elec.—EMP?*

Ogilvy ignored her. "Captain O'Donnell, upon seeing his wingman lose control of his craft while in close proximity of the object, decided that hostile action had been taken by the object. Following Air Force rules of engagement, he fell back one thousand feet, then locked his AIM-9 Sidewinder missile onto the object."

Luna was horrified. "Oh, no! He didn't . . ."

"Yes, ma'am. After attempting one last time to establish radio contact with the object, Captain O'Donnell launched his missile."

"Hang on!" Metz shouted.

Franc barely had time to grab the armrest of the pilot's chair before the timeship violently pitched sideways. Even so, he was hurled across the control room; his left shoulder slammed against a bulkhead, and he slid to the deck.

"Did it hit?" he yelled.

"Detonated in the negmass field." Metz was still buckled in his seat, hauling against the stick as he fought for control. He glanced up at the ship-status screen. "No hull damage. We're lucky. But we're still going down."

Ignoring his bruised shoulder, Franc struggled to his hands and knees, crawled upward along the deck toward Metz's chair. In the last moments before the timeship plunged into Earth's atmosphere, the pilot had managed to reactivate *Oberon*'s gravity screen. If he hadn't, the missile's shock wave would have pulverized him against the bulkhead.

A small blessing. *Oberon* was plummeting through Earth's lower atmosphere, less than nine thousand meters above the ground. They didn't know when or where they were, or even how they got there, save that the wormhole had thrown them back toward Earth so quickly that the timeship's negmass drive had drained most of its energy in order to make a safe reentry. The AI had stabilized the ship just enough to keep the crew from being roasted alive, yet the effort had severely drained its fusion cells.

If that wasn't bad enough, two contemporary aircraft had spotted the timeship during its atmospheric entry. One made the mistake of flying within the electromagnetic field cast by *Oberon*'s drive, causing the jet to lose power. Although its pilot had managed to escape, his partner apparently misinterpreted the accident as hostile action.

"Can you get us out of here?" The deck was tilting less sharply now as Metz began to level off the timeship. Grasping the armrest, Franc painfully clambered to his knees. "Maybe we can outrun that thing."

"Any other time, no problem." Clutching the stick, Metz stabbed at the console with his free hand. "But power's down 47 percent and dropping, and the field's getting weaker. If that jet launches another missile . . ."

"Understood." The negmass field had effectively shielded the timeship from the missile, but they couldn't count on the same luck again if the jet launched another one. "Hole generators?"

"Sure, I can open a hole." Metz scowled as he punched at the flatpanels, trying to reroute more power to the drive. "If you want to blow an eighty-klick crater in the ground below us. That'll screw up the worldline nice and proper, won't it?"

"Forget I asked." Stupid question; this was the very reason why timeships always departed from orbit. Franc glanced at a screen. The remaining jet had fallen back a little, but it was still dogging their every move. He tapped the mike he had snagged on his way out of the passenger compartment. "Lea? Got anything on that aircraft yet?"

Her voice came through his earpiece. *"Library identifies it as a F-15C Eagle, circa late twentieth century U.S. Air Force."* She began reading data from the library pedestal.

"Single-seater ... maximum speed Mach 2.5 ... ceiling 18,288 meters ... range about 5,600 kilometers ... armament includes 20-mm cannon, air-to-air and air-to-ground missiles ..."

"Forget that! How do we dodge the thing?"

"Dammit, Franc, how should I know?"

"Tom," Metz snapped, "what's going on back there?"

"I'm working on it!" The last time Franc had seen Hoffman, the mission spec was on his hands and knees in the passenger compartment, his arms thrust deep into a service bay beneath the deck plates. *"I've rerouted the gravity subsystem to the negmass, but I can't access the main bus without ... shit!"*

The deck buffeted violently as the timeship hit heavy turbulence. Through the headset, Franc heard Hoffman curse as he pitched sideways once more; true to his word, he had cut off the gravity screen. Hanging on to the armrest, Franc glanced again at the porthole. The last skeins of cirrus clouds dissipated like smoke, revealing a countryside of rolling hills shadowed by the early-morning sun. High country, dotted here and there by white spots and tiny irregular grids, sprawled below them: houses, small towns, farm fields. According to Lea, they were somewhere over Tennessee. . . .

Franc glimpsed something that looked like two parallel black ribbons running through the hills—a highway, perhaps—then an irregular silver-blue surface swam into view. A large lake, its channels meandering past miles of sharp ridgetops . . .

"We can't do this much longer," Metz murmured. "I'm trying to lose that thing, but it's . . ."

"Put it down," he said softly.

"What?" Metz glanced over his shoulder at him, then followed his gaze to the porthole. "Down *there?*"

"Yeah, down there. Is the chameleon still operational?"

Metz glanced at his board. "If I divert ten percent power, sure, but it won't work unless we're hugging the ground."

"Not the ground. The lake." Franc reached forward, punched up a close-up shot of the lake below them; two more taps on the panel projected a thermographic false-image. "There's the deep end," he said, pointing at a dark blue splotch within the lake's widest area. "If you can get down there, do a water landing, maybe we can submerge, lose that thing once and for all."

The pilot's eyes widened. "Are you out of your mind?"

"Probably, but you got a better idea? Maybe you can find a nice little airport. We can always tell the locals we're from Mars." He nodded toward the flatscreen; the jet continued to follow them like an angry terrier. "Or we can let our friend lob another missile at us. Maybe he'll get lucky this time."

Metz's eyes raced from the porthole to the flatscreen to his status board: the lake, the jet, the uncertain status of his craft. Any way you added it up, it was a losing equation.

"Okay, all right. I'll take us down." The deck canted again as Metz pulled the stick to one side; this time, Franc hung on for dear life. "Now get back to your seat and buckle in. Whatever happens, it's going to be rough."

"Good luck." Franc slapped the pilot's shoulder, then let go of the armrest and flung himself toward the hatch behind him.

He nearly collided with Lea in the passageway; she opened her mouth to speak, but he shoved her into the passenger compartment before him. Hoffman was struggling back onto his knees; the tools from the fixit kit were skittering every which way across the deck, and he had only barely managed to shove the access panel shut.

"What's going on?" he shouted. "What are we doing?"

"Landing in a lake! Hang on, going to be rough!"

Another violent swerve, and Franc fell headfirst into a couch. He managed to wrench its belly strap around himself just as the craft yawed once more.

"Going evasive!" Metz's voice yelled in his headset.

Lea grabbed his thigh and clung to him as he grabbed

her by the shoulders, but Tom was flung backward against a bulkhead. He slid down the wall, his arms limp at his sides.

"Tom!" Lea started to crawl toward the unconscious man.

"Strap down!" Franc yelled at her, then he flung her toward the adjacent couch. Lea hit the seat hard, but somehow she managed to land in it, not next to it. Dazed, she started pulling the straps around herself.

Franc glanced at Tom; there was nothing he could do for him. The timeship was probably working on 50 percent power or less; Metz was trying to dredge what little energy remained in *Oberon*'s cells for a controlled crash landing. Safely strapped down, Lea was shouting at Hoffman again, but he couldn't answer; the mission specialist was out cold.

His throat gnarled with fear, his fingers digging into the armrests, Franc stared at the wallscreen. A rippling blue-green surface scudded past them only a hundred meters below, its edges marked by tall limestone bluffs. A trestle bridge shot beneath them with less than ten meters to spare, then it vanished, and they were going down, down, down . . .

"Tom, get up!" Lea was screaming at the top of her lungs. "Tom, wake up, wake up, oh God, we're going to . . . !"

And then they hit the water.

From the Air Force chopper, Center Hill Lake looked cold and gray. High clouds reflected dully off its meandering channels and tributaries, where the Caney Fork River flowed into deep valleys inundated long ago by a flood-control dam. At midwinter, the waterline was at its lowest level; when the UH-60 Blackhawk dropped to about two hundred feet, the noisy clatter of its rotors reverberated off high bluffs as the chopper flew past densely wooded ridges and hilltops.

From his seat behind the cockpit, Murphy studied Center Hill Lake with curiosity. Although most of the surrounding hills were filled were summer homes, a few of them almost mansions, none were on the shoreline itself; most of them looked closed for the winter. Colonel Ogilvy, who turned out to be a native Tennessean, told him on the flight out from Sewert AFB that the Army Corps of Engineers, which had erected the dam in the early fifties and maintained it today, had strict regulations against anyone building within five hundred feet of the shore. The few boathouses were ones protected by a grandfather clause in the regulations; most of the summer residents docked their boats at commercial marinas scattered along the lake. The regulations probably seemed draconian to the wealthy Nashville doctors, lawyers, and country musicians who kept summer getaways out here, but the trade-off was one of the most underdeveloped lakes Murphy had ever seen. He gazed down at the bare-branched woods and wondered how many deer he might bag during hunting season.

Then the Blackhawk swept around a bend, and the main channel opened before them: a vast expanse of water stretching several miles from shore to shore, with a tall road bridge towering above a bottleneck at the eastern end of the channel. The pilot brought the helicopter down lower as he banked to the left, and Murphy saw a sandy beach within a shallow lagoon on the opposite side of the channel. The beach belonged to a picnic area; as the chopper came closer, he saw that it had been invaded by the U.S. Army. A large tent had already been erected in the nearby picnic area; a couple of dozen figures, most wearing military fatigues, moved around the tent and the olive trucks parked nearby.

Even then, the helicopter didn't immediately head for the beach. Instead, it veered toward the middle of the channel. From his seat next to him, Colonel Ogilvy unlatched his seat belt and leaned across Murphy to point at something through the window.

"Down there!" he yelled. "Can you see it?"

Murphy pushed aside the right cup of his ear protector as he looked where the colonel was pointing. At first, he couldn't see anything; then he spotted a tiny island, not much larger than one of the summer houses surrounding the lake. Not an island, really, but rather a large sandbar; a couple of hardy oak trees had managed to survive the lake's seasonal rise and fall, but he doubted that anything more than a few wood ducks lived out there.

Yet he didn't see anything peculiar, save for several small plastic buoys forming a half circle around one side of the island. "See what?" he shouted back, shouting against the prop noise. "I don't see anything!"

Across the narrow cabin, Meredith Cynthia Luna had her eyes tightly closed; she took deep breaths as her hands fondled a pair of animal energy stones: an armadillo for protection and safety, a butterfly for balance and grace. She had been airsick once already, shortly after the Blackhawk lifted off from Sewert AFB; apparently her painted pebbles didn't work for nausea. Lieutenant Crawford sat next to her, relief bag in hand just in case she needed it. Her hair remained perfect.

"I can't see anything either!" Agent Sanchez had taken another window and was staring downward. "Where are you looking?"

"Gotta look close!" Ogilvy jabbed a finger at the sandbar. "See that distortion? Like a warped mirror or something?"

Murphy peered out the window . . . and yes, now that the colonel mentioned it, he could detect an odd, semicircular object shimmering in the shallow water within the buoys. At first glance, it was undetectable, melding almost perfectly with the tiny island and the lake surrounding it. Then the helicopter passed over the object, and he was startled to see its shadow bulge outward slightly, as if reflected by an invisible convex surface.

"That's it!" the colonel shouted. "That's the yew-foh!"

"What's making it do that?"

"Damn if I know! That's why we called you!" Ogilvy reached forward to prod the pilot's shoulder. "Okay, Captain, put us on the ground! We've got work to do!"

White sand kicked up as the copter settled down on a concrete boat ramp within the lagoon; the pilot waited just long enough for his passengers to get clear of his aircraft, then he took it back up into the sky. Now that he was closer, Murphy noticed that the soldiers wore black tabs over the division patches on the shoulders of their parkas: Rangers from the 101st Airborne at Fort Campbell, Kentucky. All wore helmets and sidearms; a few carried M-16s on shoulder straps. Murphy noticed several soldiers using entrenchment tools to fill burlap bags with sand, while others lugged them to shallow foxholes scattered along the beach. One contained a canvas-covered machine gun. The military wasn't taking any chances.

A lieutenant hurried over to Ogilvy, saluted, and began to speak to him in a low voice. Sanchez headed straight for a concrete picnic table, where two other civilians had spread out topographic maps; the FBI had already gotten the state police to seal off all roads and highways leading to the lake, under the veiled pretense that a top-secret experimental jet had crashed here. Meredith Cynthia Luna walked on stiff legs to a picnic table, where she sat and tucked her head between her knees.

That left Murphy alone, at least for the moment. Unnoticed by anyone, his hiking boots scuffing against the frozen sand, he sauntered past the soldiers, the sandbag emplacements, the trucks, and the FBI men until he reached the water's edge. Now there was nothing between him and the tiny island; it lay about half a mile across the channel, clearly visible by its lonely stand of oak trees. Yet the crashed UFO was invisible; only the buoys gently bobbing in the water marked its whereabouts.

What allowed it to camouflage itself like that? An energy field of some sort? That was his first guess, considering what happened to the jet that had flown too close to it. The pilot of the second F-15 claimed that his missile exploded before it reached its target, yet he also said that the object nearly disappeared when it got close to the lake; he had been able to follow it only by the shadow it cast against the lake, and he didn't see clearly it again until it skipped across the lake's surface like a flat rock before running aground on the sandbar. So if it was a field, perhaps it wasn't completely impenetrable. It might be able to ward off kinetic-energy sources, like an incoming missile, but was useless against inert matter like . . .

"Find anything interesting, Dr. Murphy?"

Startled by Ogilvy's voice, Murphy turned around so quickly that he almost lost balance. "Oh shit, don't do that! You . . ."

"Sorry." The colonel was faintly amused. "Didn't realize you were so nervous."

"I'm not." Not really. Murphy let out his breath, nodded toward the sandbar. "Just trying to figure out what . . . um, what makes it go away like that."

"From what I've been told, nobody knows." Ogilvy pointed farther down the beach; a pair of inflated rubber boats lay on the shore. "Six men paddled out there about a half hour ago. They approached within thirty feet of the sandbar, but couldn't make out anything except that shimmer we saw from the air."

"Did they . . . ?"

"No. They were under orders to only recon the area and drop buoys. One man said that he felt his paddle hit something under the water, like a smooth surface, but they didn't see anything when they looked down. It spooked them, so they skedaddled."

A smooth, invisible surface just under the water. "How deep is it out there, Colonel?"

"Maximum depth is about fifty feet. Around the sandbar, only ten to fifteen where the dinghy was. Five or less at the waterline."

Damn! They were right on top of the thing, and still couldn't see it. "This used to be farm country before the dam was built," Ogilvy was saying, "so that's probably the top of a low hill. The yew-foh might have sunk completely if it hadn't hit it."

"Maybe that's what it was trying to do."

"Maybe. But why would it want to do that?"

"Well, it was being chased by a fighter, so . . ." Murphy shrugged. "I don't know. Still trying to figure that part out. When I know more, I'll tell you."

Ogilvy nodded, but didn't say anything for a few moments. "Y'know, Dr. Murphy," he said quietly, "you seem to have your head screwed on tight. For an OPS guy, that is."

"How's that, Colonel?" he asked warily.

"Call me Baird . . ."

"I'm Zack."

"Zack." They shook hands. "You're a normal scientist, aren't you?"

Normal scientist. Like there was another kind . . . "Astrophysicist, if that's what you're asking."

"I can tell. You're asking questions, not assuming anything. You're not jumping to conclusions, then trying to make the facts fit the answers you've already figured out. Ms. Luna, on the other hand . . ."

He didn't finish, but stepped aside to let Murphy see for himself. Meredith Cynthia Luna had recovered her poise; she had now taken a lotus position at the picnic table, palms spread upward on her knees, head tilted back on her neck, eyes tightly closed. A handful of soldiers had paused to watch her, until an officer walked by and told them to get back to work.

"Asked her what she was doing," Ogilvy murmured, "and she said she was trying to establish communion. Not communication . . . communion."

On top of everything else, she was a Strieber believer. Lord . . . "She's not in my division. If she wants anything, give it to her. I don't care, just keep her out of my way."

"So you don't think she's . . . ?"

"Got anything to contribute? Not really. But I can't get rid of her either."

"Sort of figured as much." Ogilvy paused, then went on in a low voice. " Frankly, my people don't have much respect for your people. Cashews and pistachios, we tend to call 'em. But you've got a good rep. Word up is that you're probably the most reliable person at OPS. If you think you've got a lock on this situation . . ."

"I'm flattered, but I don't."

"This is new to all of us, but you're the nearest thing

we've got to an expert." Ogilvy took a deep breath. "Look, Zack, we're making it up as we go along. Mr. Sanchez is working with the locals to keep a lid on this thing as long as we can. We've been lucky so far . . . hardly anyone saw this thing go down, and we've got the area bottled up. But that dog won't hunt much longer."

"How much longer?"

"Six, twelve hours. Twenty-four, tops. My people are ready to fly in more people and equipment, but we need to know what we're dealing with first. Think you can do it, Dr. Murphy?"

Ogilvy posed this as a question, but it really wasn't one. They both had higher authorities to whom they had to answer, and nobody upstairs was going to accept no for an answer.

"Yeah, I can do it," Murphy said.

"I'm sorry, Tom."

Franc gently folded Hoffman's hands together on his chest, then pulled a blanket over the body. He spent another moment with the mission specialist, then carefully stood up and made his way upward along the precariously slanted deck to the hatch.

He had just left the passenger compartment when something thumped against *Oberon*'s hull. Bracing himself against a bulkhead, he listened carefully, but didn't hear anything until Metz's voice rang out from the control room.

"Lu! Get in here! We've got a problem!"

Like they didn't have enough already. Franc pitched himself down the dark passageway until he reached the ajar hatch to the control room, then dropped to his hands and knees and crawled into the compartment. Seated at his station, Metz was a shadow against the luminescent band of emergency lamps. Most of the screens glowed with status reports; one, however, displayed a camera view from outside the timeship.

"Oh, no," Franc murmured. "Where did they come from?"

Just outside *Oberon,* three soldiers in a rubber boat. One

cradled an archaic rifle in his arms; the second had an old-fashioned film camera aimed straight at them; the third gently guided the boat with a long plastic paddle. The first two were looking back at the oarsman, who gazed uncertainly into the water just beneath the boat.

"I didn't see them coming," Metz said in a low voice, as if afraid the intruders could hear them. "I had my head under the console, didn't know they were out there until . . ."

"I know. I heard it, too." They were floating just above the submerged end of the ship; the guy in the rear must have hit the hull with his paddle. "Is the chameleon functional?"

Metz glanced at one of the displays. "Still working. They can't see us. But if they get much closer . . ."

He didn't finish his thought. It hardly mattered. The soldiers knew they were here. The first vehicles had arrived on the nearby shore little more than an hour after *Oberon*'s crash landing, and although the chameleon hid the timeship from direct view, a vague outline of its hull could be detected from certain angles in midday sunlight. Helicopters had circled low over the sandbar several times already, but this was the closest any of the locals had dared to venture.

At least the airlock hatch was underwater. In fact, judging from the position of the raft, it was directly beneath the soldiers. The locals would have to send out divers to find it. Judging from the amount of activity on the shore, though, it wouldn't be long before it occurred to them to do so.

They watched as the men in the boat took a few more pictures—at such close range, they were probably photographing distorted reflections of themselves—before they hastily paddled away again. Metz let out his breath. "Close one. Worse than Dallas."

"Far worse than Dallas," Franc said, but not accusingly. Recrimination was pointless by now; whatever happened in 1937, they were foiled but good. One expedition member was dead, his neck broken during that first violent impact with the lake. The timeship was down, its operational condition uncertain. Contemporaries had discovered their whereabouts, and these weren't aborigines who would leave little more record of their brief passage than a few legends and some mysterious cave drawings.

Worst of all, they were shipwrecked in the late twentieth century. The most dangerous era in the history of humankind.

"They're cautious now, but they'll be back." Franc clambered forward to peer at the screens. "How's it coming so far?"

"Do you want the good news first, or . . . ?" Metz caught Franc's stern look. "Never mind. I've been working my way through the system to the primary drive. It's still down, but the AI's located the major problem. Main bus is damaged, a few boards are shot. I've retasked some repair nannies and sent them in, so they should complete their work in about an hour or so. Backup's fully operational, though, so I'm . . ."

Franc impatiently twirled a finger, and Metz got to the point. "Pods are still intact. The drive can be fixed, although the grid's flooded and it won't work at optimal levels until we've been airborne for at least sixty seconds."

"So we can get out of here. Right?"

Metz didn't reply.

"Come on, Vasili. We can or we can't. Which is it?"

"Two problems. The first, you know about already. Energy reserve's down to 15 percent, just enough to keep the chameleon operational and the AI alive. I've got the cells on full recharge. Fortunately, we can electrolyze all the hydrogen we need from the water around us . . . one good thing about crashing in a lake. AI estimate is that we'll be able to lift off again within six hours, less if we reserve internal power as much as we can."

"Including low-orbit escape and wormhole entry?" Franc asked. Metz nodded, but he wasn't smiling. He looked even more tense than usual. "So what's the second problem?"

The pilot let out his breath. "We don't know when we

are. Where, that's certain . . . the AI established a fix on our coordinates before we crashed. Tennessee, Cumberland Plateau, Center Hill Lake . . . the numbers are safely stored away. And judging from what we've seen so far, we're in the late twentieth. Probably in the 1990s, but . . ."

"What year?"

"Can't tell you that." Metz shook his head. "That's the problem. Primary telemetry grid is down, so we can't pull in outside feed. No way to lock onto the local net. I might have been able to get a lock before we crashed, but I didn't have to chance to . . ."

"I understand." Under the circumstances, Vasili had done the best he could just to get them safely to the ground. However, lacking a precise fix on when they were, *Oberon's* AI was unable to accurately plot a CTC return trajectory. This was something that couldn't be guesstimated; the AI had to know exactly when and where in chronospace the timeship now existed. Spatial coordinates were estimated, but temporal weren't; the most vital factor of the four-dimensional equation was missing.

"Sorry, Franc." For once, Metz had put his arrogance in a drawer. "I wish I could give you better news, but . . ."

"Any idea what caused this? The paradox . . . the anomaly, I mean . . ."

"Lea's still working on it. You might want to check with her." Then he turned back to his console and didn't look up again until Franc left the control room.

He found Lea at the library, running through the footage their divots had captured from the *Hindenburg*. Like Franc, she had taken a few minutes in the replication cell to change her appearance back to normal; her long black hair was pulled back in a ponytail that fell over her broad shoulders as she braced herself against the pedestal. She didn't look up when he entered the compartment.

"Find anything?"

"Yes, I have," she said. "I think I've isolated the divergence point."

Franc propped himself against the pedestal as Lea typed a command into its keypad. "There was a lot of sift through, so I concentrated on the last three hours before we landed. We passed over Lakehurst at four o'clock, but had to divert because of wind gusts and high cumulus clouds at the field."

"Uh-huh, I remember."

"We flew south along the Jersey shore to ride it out. An hour and a half later, according to the historical record, Captain Pruss received a telegraph message from the field, stating that the weather conditions were still bad and recommending that he not attempt a landing until later. He wired back a message, stating that he wouldn't return to Lakehurst until we was given clearance. That message was sent at 5:35 P.M. local. Now watch . . ."

She pressed the PLAY button on the pedestal. The wallscreen displayed the vast interior of the *Hindenburg*'s envelope. Franc recognized the angle immediately; it was the catwalk beneath Cell Number 4, where he had placed a divot during their tour of the airship. The digital readout at the bottom of the screen read *5.6.37: 1741:29* when a lone figure walked past the divot. As he paused at the bottom of the ladder to quickly glance both ways, his face became visible for a brief instant. It was Eric Spehl, the rigger who had placed the bomb.

Spehl ascended the ladder, then passed out of camera range. "He's gone about six minutes," Lea said, tapping the pedestal again to skip forward, "and then . . ."

At *5.6.37: 1747:52,* Spehl reappeared on the ladder, climbing back down from Cell Number 4. Once again, he hastily glanced again, then walked back up the catwalk, heading toward airship's bow. "I checked the record from this divot again," Lea said, "both before and after *Hindenburg* landed. He didn't come back here again."

"He came back and reset the bomb. I'll be damned."

"That's a good way of putting it, yes. And he did it just

after the second time Captain Pruss postponed the landing."

"But why didn't he do this earlier?" Franc rubbed his chin thoughtfully; it felt good to feel his own flesh again. "Why the sudden change of mind?"

Lea let out her breath. "Maybe you were right. Perhaps he remembered the woman he encountered at this same spot . . ." She pointed at the frozen image of the empty catwalk . . . "the day before, and decided that he didn't want to be responsible for her death. So he came back and reset the timer so that the bomb wouldn't detonate until exactly eight o'clock, by which time he was certain the ship would be safely moored and all the passengers disembarked."

Franc wanted to tell her that she was wrong, that she was blaming herself needlessly for what had happened. The evidence wasn't inarguable; he wasn't convinced. He couldn't believe that history had been changed only because the two of them had been aboard the *Hindenburg*.

"So we created an alternate worldline," he said.

"Right. The airship was destroyed anyway, but this time the German resistance movement was able to claim credit for what Spehl had done."

"We heard that much on the car radio. What sort of difference did it make?"

"That's the question." She drummed a pensive fingertip against the pedestal. "Suppose, just for the sake of argument, that Spehl accomplished what he had intended. The *Hindenburg* was the very symbol of Nazi power. Assume that its destruction was the first act of open dissent that finally led to Hitler being ousted from power. Perhaps one of the subsequent assassination attempts was successful . . ."

"Come on . . . that's one assumption too many."

"Perhaps, but . . ." She hesitated. "Well, there's one more thing. It's not much, but . . ."

"Let's have it."

She turned back to the pedestal, began tapping in another set of commands. "Remember when the jets intercepted us after *Oberon* entered the atmosphere? When they tried to radio us?" He raised an eyebrow, but said nothing. "I searched the flight recorder, full AV mode, then had the library backtrack historical sources. Here's what I found."

The two jets appeared on-screen as a pair of angular dots racing ahead of vapor trails; there was no digital readout at the bottom of the screen. As the dots began closing on the camera, they heard a static-filled radio voice:

"Sewert Tower, this is Wildcat One, we've got a confirmed bogey at . . ."

Lea froze the image, then gently moved a forefinger across the touchpad until a tiny square appeared over the nearest of the two jets. She then enhanced the image until it was magnified several hundred times; a window opened on the screen, showing the aircraft in greater detail. Another couple of keystrokes, and a wire-frame composite appeared next to the photographic image.

"The library positively identified this as an F-15C Eagle," she went on. "A one-seat jet fighter used by the United States Air Force from the late 1970s through the early 1990s, when it was later replaced by an updated version of the same jet, the two-seat F-15E. We know that they had to be F-15C's because only one pilot bailed out of the Eagle that flew through our negmass field."

"So?"

"During radio communications between the jets and their home base, you can clearly hear the base being referred to as Sewert Tower. I checked with the library system, and it turns out Sewert Air Force Base was decommissioned in the late 1960s. It shouldn't be there, let alone sending up fighters not put in service until ten years later."

Franc stared long and hard at the split image on the wallscreen. "All right," he murmured. "You've convinced me. We're in an alternate worldline . . ."

"An alternate worldline we inadvertently created. And when we tried to return from 1937 to our own future, we ran into a rift in chronospace . . . a divergent loop in a closed-timelike circle. We're lucky that we weren't destroyed completely. As it was, we were dumped out here . . ."

"In a parallel universe," Metz said.

Franc and Lea looked around to find the pilot leaning against the hatch. How long he had been there, they couldn't know; he had probably heard most of the discussion. Just as well, Franc thought. It would save them the trouble of reiterating everything Lea had learned.

"Don't bother." Metz held up a hand. "I know. I screwed up. If we had remained in '37, studied this a little longer, we might have seen this coming. I'm sorry. It's my fault."

"No, Vasili. It's everyone's fault." Holding herself up against the pedestal, Lea turned toward him. "Paradoxes like this had been postulated for a long time. Previous expeditions have been lucky until now. We were stupid to think our luck would hold out."

"Forget it," Franc said. "Point is, how do we get out of here?"

No one said anything for a moment. Metz finally cleared his throat.

"First thing," he said softly, "we have to find out what time it is."

The second time the Rangers visited the sandbar, they approached the saucer from the opposite side of the tiny island, with four men in each of the two inflatable boats. They rowed slowly enough as not to cause any ripples when they dipped their oars in the water, and they observed strict silence during the journey, using hand signals to communicate. They went armed, with two of the soldiers carrying 35mm cameras and camcorders.

Colonel Ogilvy placed Lieutenant Crawford in charge of the operation; Murphy accompanied the landing party in the role of a civilian advisor. Not surprisingly, Meredith Cynthia Luna objected to being left behind. After two hours of psychic meditation, she declared that the UFO was inhabited by aliens from a planet located somewhere in the Crab Nebula; on the eve of the third millennium, they had come to invite Earth into the Galactic Federation. Ogilvy heard her out, then handed her an M-16 and asked if she need a refresher course in how to use it. It was a good ploy; she dropped the unloaded rifle as if it was a medium-rare steak, and although she bitched about approaching peaceful emissaries from another star system with weapons, the argument was effectively ended.

Murphy felt the bottom of his boat slide over the sandy shallows a few feet from the island. Crawford pointed to the sandbar, then balled a fist and pumped it down twice. The two Rangers at either end of the raft hopped out; their boots had barely splashed into the freezing water before they grabbed guy ropes and started hauling the boat ashore. About twenty feet away, the four soldiers in the second raft were doing the same. Everyone crouched low, rifles in hand, yet the Rangers were so quiet that a handful of ducks lounging in high weeds at the tip of the sandbar hardly noticed their presence.

It wasn't until the troops had taken positions behind the two oaks that Crawford signaled Murphy to get out of the raft. The sandbar was littered with beer cans, washed-up sandwich wrappers, and lost fishing lures. Between the two trees was a small circle of blackened rock, a rudimentary fireplace left by boat bums. The tree trunks were carved with initials; as Murphy knelt behind one of the oaks, something jabbed against his knee. He looked down, spied a tiny hand sticking out of the soil, and reached down to pull up a sand-crusted Darth Vader action figure. A toy left here last summer by some child; the irony was inescapable. He smiled and tucked it into a breast pocket of his parka; perhaps Steven would like to have it.

Past the trees, though, there was nothing to be seen on the other side of the island. At least nothing that looked like an alien spacecraft, from the Crab Nebula or otherwise. Yet, as he looked closer, it seemed as if the waterline was distorted in a strange way, the late-afternoon sun casting weird, inconsistent shadows upon the beach. If he could only get a little closer . . .

Murphy glanced one way, then another. The Rangers lay on their bellies on either side of him, nervously peering over their rifles as if expecting some monster from a fifties sci-fi flick suddenly to come roaring out of the water. Crawford tapped him on the shoulder, raised a level palm, lowered it the ground, then pointed toward the opposite side of the sandbar. What the hell did he expect him to do, crawl across the island?

"Aw, nuts," Murphy said aloud. "This is silly." Then, before Crawford could stop him, he stood up and started walking toward the area of distortion.

The lieutenant called his name, the Rangers looked up at him in shocked confusion, but Murphy didn't stop. Moving one step at a time, he raised his hands to shoulder height, hands out flat. His heart trip-hammered against his chest, his parka felt a little too warm; suddenly, he wondered if this wasn't such a good idea after all. Yet there was no backing down; if he retreated now, Crawford would probably have him hog-tied and rowed back to the campground. And he was already past the trees, only a few yards from the waterline.

The area of distortion had a rounded look to it. As he drew closer, an image of himself abruptly appeared before him, flattened out as if in a translucent fun-house mirror. He reached out his right hand to touch the reflection . . .

His fingers met a cool, invisible surface. He was so surprised that his hand involuntarily jerked back. "Hey!" he yelled. "I found something!"

"Dr. Murphy, get back here!" Crawford shouted.

Murphy ignored him. He laid both palms against the surface, gently moved them across back and forth. He'd rather expected a tingle, and was mildly astonished not to receive it. Whatever was causing the invisibility effect, it wasn't an energy field. He glanced at his wristwatch and observed that the second hand was still moving. If an electromagnetic source of some sort had disabled one F-15 and detonated the missile of a second, it wasn't active now.

Behind him, he heard soldiers scuttling closer. Crawford was on the radio: "Grumpy to Stepsister One, Grumpy to Stepsister One. Snow White has approached bogey, established presence. Dwarves in position. Please advise. Over . . ."

He glided his hands across sloping surface, carefully exploring it as he established a mental map of the object. It seemed to go all the way down to his ankles, then it abruptly stopped, as if he had reached an edge of some sort. His reflection became sharper when he got closer, warped when he got farther away. Fascinated, he carefully lifted his right leg and braced his knee against the surface. Yes, it was definitely a metal hull of some sort. Putting his full weight against it, he gradually inched forward on his hands and knees . . .

He almost laughed out loud when he realized what he must seem to be doing: crawling in midair, at least five feet above sand and water. Somewhere behind him, he heard the soft whir-and-click of an automatic shutter. One of the soldiers handling the camera record was taking pictures of him. Murphy was just enough of a ham that he didn't want to miss the opportunity. Careful to not lose his balance, he shifted his center of gravity to his haunches, rested the soles of his boots against the invisible surface, then slowly stood up. Good grief, he was . . .

At that instant, the UFO materialized.

One moment, it wasn't there. The next, it was: an enormous silver bowl turned upside down and cast up against the sandbar, with almost half of it submerged beneath the water.

Startled, Murphy turned around too quickly; his feet lost their purchase and he fell down against the side of the saucer. The breath was almost knocked out of him; he slid halfway down the hull before he threw out his hands and braked his fall by sheer friction. As he fell, his head jerked up and . . .

At the top of the craft was a large, round turret, much like the crown of a hat. In the center of the turret was a small, square porthole. As Murphy slid down the saucer, an exterior shutter whisked sideways across the window, closing so quickly that he barely saw it before it molded so perfectly with the rest of the hull that it was impossible to tell it had ever been there at all.

Even so, in that briefest fraction of a second, Murphy caught a glimpse of something peering out at him. No . . . not something, but someone.

A human being.

The amber haze of winter sun briefly set the lake on fire before it set behind the hills, yet the darkness wasn't complete. The timeship gleamed brightly within the halo of portable floodlights set up along the sandbar; tiny figures moved along the tiny island, some moving equipment into place, others standing guard with weapons in hand. Rubber boats shuttled back and forth across the channel; helicopters orbited almost constantly, their searchlights skimming across the dark waters.

Franc waited until night had completely fallen before he emerged from hiding. He had crouched in the shallows at the farthest end of the lagoon for the past half hour, raising his head above the surface only when he thought the darkness would conceal the bulge of the EVA suit's helmet. The camp was little more than fifty meters from his position, yet never once had anyone ventured over here. So long as he remained quiet, no one would know he was nearby.

It was a dangerous scheme, to be sure, but so far it had worked well. The moment he exited the timeship, Metz switched off *Oberon*'s chameleon. Its abrupt appearance so thoroughly rattled the soldiers who had just invaded the island that no one noticed the telltale air bubbles caused by the opening airlock. Franc had fallen less than three meters before his boots sank into the muddy silt; he waited a few minutes, peering upward through the water to see if anyone had detected his presence, then he began his long hike across the lake bottom.

It had taken nearly two hours to reach the end of the lagoon. He didn't switch on the helmet lamps until he was twenty feet below the surface; by then, he had already paused to allow for pressure equalization. Lea had programmed the heads-up display with a map of the lake, but it could only show what lay above the water, not below it. The lake bottom was covered with man-made debris of every shape and size: rusting soda cans, coolers filled with muck, shapeless pieces of painted wood, fiberglass, and metal, broken fishing poles, even an ancient automobile that had loomed out of the brown limbo like a dinosaur carcass. Artifacts from an age of negligence.

The hardsuit would only be the latest addition to the lake's collection. When he was out of the water, safe within the woods along the shore, Franc lay on his back and struggled out of its ceramic carapace. The wool suit he had worn on the *Hindenburg* offered scant protection against the chill night air, but it would have to do; it was the only twentieth-century clothing he had saved from 1937. He took a few minutes to drag the EVA armor back to the lakeshore and shove it into the shallows; he heard a soft gulp as it swallowed water, then it disappeared from sight. With luck, it wouldn't be found for another dozen years or so, if ever.

Franc pulled up the coat lapels and tucked his hands beneath his armpits. He felt the tiny square of the compad in his shirt pocket, and briefly considered using it to contact the *Oberon*. No, that was a bad idea; the locals might be scanning carrier frequencies, including microwave. Better not tip his hand until he was good and ready. Lea and Vasili would just have to sweat a while longer. At least they were warm enough to sweat. . . .

Trying not to think about the cold, Franc began making his way through the dense thicket, careful not to step on any frozen branches underfoot. He heard the muted voices of soldiers on the nearby beach; when he paused to look back, he could just make out the lights encircling the *Oberon*. He regarded the distant timeship for a moment, just long enough to make him wonder at the lunacy of his own idea, then he turned and began trudging up the wooded slope.

Dozens of houses surrounded him, on the hillsides above the lake, but he could see lights from none of them. He briefly considered breaking into one, but decided to hold that only as a last resort. Even if they were presently unoccupied, these homes might have intruder alarms; he didn't possess the tools necessary to circumvent them.

Besides, his task was relatively simple from here on. All he had to do was locate a public telephone. If he could just make his way to a paved road, he knew that a phone wouldn't be distant. This was late-twentieth-century North America, after all. The locals loved telephones.

Road. Phone. Information. What could be more easy?

Wondering why Lea couldn't have done this instead, Franc fought his way through the dark and frigid night.

Dinner was a brown vinyl bag containing an MRE: a Meal Ready to Eat or a Meal Rejected by Ethiopians, depending which definition one wished to accept. Inside were green foil wrappers containing diced cold turkey in gooey brown gravy, a tasteless potato patty, a handful of crackers, a packet of instant coffee, and some wispy blue tissue that Murphy first assumed was a napkin until he was informed that it was toilet paper. Eating at a picnic table by lanternlight, he managed to choke down half of the MRE before he took the rest to a garbage can. He should have been ravenous, but the events of the last couple or hours had left him without much of an appetite.

Shortly after he and Crawford returned from the sandbar, Colonel Ogilvy had held a briefing for the civilian advisors in the command tent. The facts themselves were clear: although the saucer inexplicably became visible at 1505, it had remained silent since then. Listening equipment set up around the craft hadn't disclosed any new information, no hatches had been discovered, and aside from what Murphy alone had seen in that brief instant before its single porthole closed, the craft's occupants hadn't chosen to reveal themselves.

Meredith Cynthia Luna remained adamant that the craft was an alien spaceship from a distant star system, and insisted that it contained emissaries from an interstellar federation. The possibility that these travelers might be human, or at least humanlike, only helped her embroider her revelation a little more: the human form wasn't unique only to the planet Earth, but is widespread throughout the universe, and these "parahumans" were deliberately seeking out others of their own kind. We shouldn't be confronting them with weapons, she charged, but had to find a more peaceful means of communication. She suggested that all the Rangers should immediately withdraw from the sandbar and allow her and several other OPS psychics to congregate on the island to attempt telepathic communication.

That was when Ogilvy laid down his cards. Since the Pentagon believed that the object posed a possible threat to national security, it had been decided that an attempt would be made to force entry. Metal-cutting torches used by the Navy for submarine rescue work were being flown in from Groton, Connecticut, along with technicians trained in their use. At 2400 hours, they would be deployed on the sandbar, where they would attempt to penetrate the object's hull.

Luna objected, and for once Murphy found himself in agreement, albeit for different reasons. They didn't know what was out there, but the fact that it had deliberately dropped its cloak tended to argue that the craft's occupants meant no harm. He needed more time to study the object; perhaps it hadn't come from the Crab Nebula, but neither was it from Tennessee.

Ogilvy had held firm: there would be no further debate on this point. This mission was under Defense Department auspices, and his orders had come from the highest levels. The colonel ended the briefing by telling everyone that chow would soon be served at the roach wagon, and then he closed his notebook and walked away.

Sanchez collared Murphy just before he went in search of a hot and tasty MRE. Although the military was handling the investigation, the FBI had jurisdiction over civilians working on this incident; this meant OPS was now working for the Bureau. Because Murphy hadn't yet received Top Secret security clearance, he would have to sign a document that would ensure that he wouldn't disclose anything he had heard or seen to anyone who didn't have similar clearance. So far as the public was concerned, the incident at Center Hill Lake never happened.

The document would soon be faxed to Sanchez. Once he received it, he would bring it to Murphy for his signature. One look at the agent's face told Murphy that there was no question whether he would sign it. Not unless he wanted to risk losing his job, let alone being sent to prison.

So dinner had been indigestible and the company worse, and Murphy found himself alone once more. The night was cold, the wind rising now that the sun was down. He pulled up his parka's hood and looked for a place to hide. The command tent had been taken over by Ogilvy and Sanchez, and he didn't want to see them right now. He briefly considered taking a quick nap in one of the Army trucks, but realized that he wasn't tired anyway. His eyes roamed to the distant sandbar, and the silver saucer captured within a circle of floodlights. All things considered, he was tired of looking at the bloody thing; just for a little while, he wanted to get away from all this.

So he decided to take a walk.

It was surprisingly easy to leave camp. No one had placed a guard on him, after all, and he didn't tell anyone that he was going away. A narrow paved road led uphill from the entrance to the picnic area; although a lone soldier stood watch at its gate, he didn't object when Murphy told him that he wanted to take a short stroll and would be back soon. The sentry was there to keep people from sneaking in; since Murphy only wanted to stretch his legs, where was the harm? The sergeant informed him that there was a campground store a half mile up the road, near the top of the hill. It was closed down, of course, but there was a Coke machine out front. Would Murphy mind bringing back a soda for him? Murphy didn't mind: one ice-cold Dr Pepper, coming up.

The breeze seemed to let up a bit once he was away from the water, but it rattled the bare branches around him. He tasted the scent of winter pine as the night closed in around him; the lights behind him vanished entirely, and he threw back his head to check out the constellations. It would have been a rare treat, since light pollution in the D.C. area forbade any decent stargazing, yet the sky was still overcast. A dark night; even after his eyes adjusted to the gloom, he could barely see his own hand when he held it at arm's length. Too bad.

Before he knew it, he reached the top of the road, where the mellow glow of a forty-watt bulb faintly illuminated a crossroad nestled in a saddleback between two short hills. There was a small general store at the junction, one which undoubtedly offered minnows, Moon Pies, and Orange Crush during season. The windows were shuttered, its door locked, but the porch light had been left on, illuminating the battered Coca-Cola machine between an empty bait tank and a pay phone.

Someone was using the pay phone.

At first he thought it was one of the soldiers, perhaps sneaking a call home to a wife or girlfriend, but when Murphy got closer he saw that the figure wasn't wearing military gear. Indeed, he seemed to be underdressed for the weather: a dark wool suit and nothing more, not even an overcoat. His back was turned, but even from a distance Murphy could tell that he was shivering in the cold.

Strange. Maybe he was a hitchhiker who had lost his way. Yet all the roads leading to this area had been blocked by state police; even then, the nearest highway was several miles away. Murphy studied the man at the phone as he walked toward the porch. Perhaps he was from one of the lakeside houses; Ogilvy had told them that they were summer homes, but maybe one of them was occupied year-round. Yet if that was the case, why would a permanent resident be using a pay phone to . . . ?

"Thank you . . . yes, that would be most helpful."

In the stillness of the night, Murphy heard the stranger's voice clearly. It held an odd accent that he couldn't quite place: British-American, yet with an faint Asian inflection.

"Yes, operator, would you be so kind as to tell me the exact date? Yes, ma'am . . . today's date. And the year, please."

The date? The year? What, he didn't have a calendar?

The porch steps creaked when Murphy put his weight on them. Startled by his sudden appearance, the stranger looked up sharply, all but dropping the receiver from his hand.

"Sorry," Murphy said automatically. "Didn't mean to interrupt."

The man at the phone looked vaguely Eurasian. He stared at Murphy through wire-rim glasses, then seemed to remember what he had been doing a moment earlier. He raised the receiver again. "I'm sorry, ma'am . . . could you repeat that, please?"

Murphy walked over to the Coke machine, dug into his trouser pockets for change. He felt the stranger's eyes upon him as he found a couple of quarters and fed them into the slot. He had to be a vagrant; his clothes were so old-fashioned, they had to have come from the Salvation Army. Yet even the most destitute homeless men he had seen huddled on steam grates in downtown D.C. wore cast-off down coats or old baseball jackets. The last time Murphy had seen men's clothing of this style was in old photos of his grandfather as a young man.

"Thank you, ma'am. You've been very helpful." The stranger prodded the rim of his glasses as if adjusting them, then hung up the phone. He blew into his hands, cast a furtive glance at Murphy, then started to walk toward the steps.

"Cold night," Murphy said.

The stranger hesitated. "Pardon me?"

"Cold night." Murphy pushed the Dr Pepper button; there was a heavy clunk deep within the vending machine, then a can rattled down the chute. "At least twenty."

"Twenty what?"

"Twenty degrees. The temperature."

"Oh . . . well . . ." Drawing his coat lapels more closely around him, the man nodded in the general direction of the road behind him. "It doesn't bother me. I don't live far away. Just down the road. Came down to use the road . . . the phone, I mean."

Was it his imagination, or did his voice sound a bit different now? Murphy bent to pick up the can of soda, and the stranger hurried past him. "I didn't know anyone lived here year-round," Murphy added. "I thought all these places belonged to summer people."

"A few of us stay through the winter." The other man took off his glasses, carefully folded them, placed them into his coat pocket. "Excuse me, but I . . ."

"Want to get home. Sure." Murphy slipped the unopened soda into a pocket of his parka. "Take it easy."

"Yes . . . uh, yeah." He trotted down the porch steps. "I'll take it easy. You take it easy, too."

Murphy watched the stranger huddle into himself and quickly walk away, moving out of the faint glow of the porch light as he began marching up the road leading to the top of the nearest hill. Poor bastard probably lives in a trailer, he mused. Can't afford a phone of his own, so he has to hike down here when he wants to make a call. Hope he's got a good space heater or something to keep him warm. . . .

But why would anyone call an operator to find out today's date?

Crazy people. Crazy people in Washington, crazy people in Tennessee. Crazy people still working for OPS even though they knew better. Murphy shrugged, then went down the steps. He'd better get back to camp before Ogilvy or Sanchez or someone else missed him. The sergeant minding the checkpoint was probably thirsty for his Dr Pepper.

He had only walked a short distance before he realized that he could use a soda himself. No sense in going back with only one soft drink; it was going to be a long night. Might as well grab another one for the road. So he turned around and jogged back to the lonesome Coke machine.

When he searched his pockets, though, he discovered that he only had a quarter. Tough luck . . . then he glanced at the adjacent pay phone, and realized that the guy he just met had been talking to an operator.

Why would anyone walk all this way just to . . . ?

Never mind. Point was, he hadn't retrieved his change from the return slot. Probably too cold to remember that he had money coming back to him. And since the phone took twenty-five cents, there might be enough left in there for Murphy to buy himself a Sprite.

Murphy stepped over to the phone and poked an inquisitive finger into its tiny drawer. Sure enough, two dimes and a nickel. He dug them out, jingled them in his fist, then walked over to the Coke machine. He slipped his quarter into the slot and was about to slide home one of the dimes when he did a double take.

It was a Mercury dime.

He hadn't seen a Mercury dime since he was in grade school.

Then he opened his palm and saw another Mercury dime and a buffalo nickel.

What were the chances of this occurring by accident? So far beyond the odds of probability that Murphy instantly rejected it as an explanation. And these coins looked good as new.

Okay, so maybe the stranger was a rare coin collector. Yeah, right. A rare coin collector who couldn't afford decent winter clothes, but drops spotless Mercury dimes and buffalo nickels into pay phones. Well, maybe he was an absentminded collector who used rare coins to call operators on pay phones to ask them what time . . .

And just then, something Harry Cummisky said last night at the Bullfinch came back to him.

Careful not to switch it off, Franc folded the compad and thrust it into his pocket, then pulled the jacket more tightly around himself. The wind at the top of the hill was fierce and bone-chilling; his legs shook involuntarily, and he had to clench his jaw to keep his teeth from chattering. He stamped his feet against the blacktop in a vain effort to warm his frozen toes.

"Hurry up," he whispered, glancing up at the opaque sky. "Hurry up, hurry up, hurry up . . ."

It wasn't only the cold that made him impatient. The chance encounter with the local had unnerved him to the point that he had almost forgotten his errand; it had taken a conscious effort to store the exact date and time in the memory of his faux spectacles. The man who had come to use the vending machine had been more than casually interested in his presence at the pay phone, and it wasn't merely late-twentieth-century snoopiness. He might have been from one of the nearby homes, but Franc suspected otherwise.

Well, it didn't matter much now. Metz was probably lifting off even now; once aloft, he'd find Franc by homing in on the signal from his still-active compad. He looked up again, although he knew Metz had probably reactivated the chameleon and that he wouldn't be able to see the timeship until it was . . .

"Okay . . . who are you . . . anyway?"

The voice from the darkness was strained and out of breath, but familiar nonetheless. Franc whirled around, searching the road behind him.

"I said . . . who are you?"

The man from the store.

Franc finally made him out. Only a few meters away, struggling up the hill toward him.

"Nobody you would know, sir," he replied. "I just live around here."

"I . . . kinda doubt that." The stranger stopped; he bent over and rested his hands on his knees, gasping for breath. He must have run all this way. "Nobody . . . lives around here . . . in winter. If they did, they'd . . . they'd . . . have their own phone."

"I don't." Franc's mind raced. The *Oberon* would be here any minute; he couldn't allow his departure to be witnessed by a local. "I just use the pay phone to save money."

"Yeah . . . right." A soft jingle of loose change. "Money like this?"

Franc's blood froze. Just the sort of anachronistic mistake the CRC trained its researchers to avoid committing; he had left 1937 currency in a 1998 pay phone.

"I think I forgot that, yes," he said cautiously. "Thanks for bringing it back." He held out his hand. "If you'll let me have it, I'll . . ."

"Go home . . . sure. That's what you said. " The stranger didn't come any closer. "Which gets back to . . . to my question. Who are you?"

"John Pannes." The reply came automatically, as if he was again being queried by the Nazi brown-shirt on the street in Frankfurt.

"Okay . . . and where are you from, Mr. Pannes?"

"Sir, I don't believe that's any of your business." Aware that the stranger's night vision was probably as good as his own, Franc fought an impulse to glance up at the sky. "Now, if you'll excuse me . . . ?"

"Don't think . . . I don't think you're telling the truth." The other man stood up straight, took a deep breath. "Not from around here, and don't think you're . . ."

He coughed hard, bringing up phlegm. "Not from this time," he said finally. "Are you, Mister Pannes?"

Franc felt blood rush from his face. Whoever this person was—although it was almost certain that he was with the soldiers camped nearby—he had surmised far too much. Whatever happened, he couldn't be allowed to witness the *Oberon*'s touchdown. Yet he was out of wind from running all the way up the hill, and Franc had darkness on his side. If he was quick enough . . .

"You could be right," Franc carefully replied. "Of course, it's a little difficult for me to answer, considering that I don't know you."

"Name's Murphy . . . Dr. Zack Murphy." The stranger seemed to relax a bit. "Astrophysicist. Office of Paranormal Sciences, United States government."

A scientist. However, despite his extensive research of the twentieth century, Franc had never heard of the Office of Paranormal Sciences. A manifestation of this new worldline? No time to wonder about that now.

"Pleasure to meet you, Dr. Murphy," he said, taking a cautious step forward as he held out his hand. "I assume you've been looking for me?"

"Well, not really, but . . ." Murphy raised a hand, started toward him. "You still haven't told me . . ."

He hesitated just then, and for an instant Franc wondered if Murphy had a glimmer of his intentions. Then he audibly gasped, and even in the darkness Franc could tell that he was staring upward at something in the sky above.

"What the hell is . . . ?"

That was the break he needed. Ducking his head, thrusting his arms and shoulders forward, Franc rushed Murphy.

He cleared the distance in a few quick steps. Distracted, the astrophysicist was caught entirely off guard. Two fast, hard blows to the stomach, and he doubled over. Franc heard the breath whuff painfully from his lungs, then Murphy stumbled against him; his hands clawed at Franc's clothes, either in a feeble effort to fight back or simply to keep from falling.

Franc wasn't about to let him do either; he slammed a fist straight into Murphy's jaw. There was the angry sound of tearing fabric as the other man toppled backward, and he felt cold air against his chest. Then the scientist hit the asphalt and lay still.

Now the limbs of the surrounding trees were whipping back and forth as if caught in a supernatural gale. A loud hum surrounded him, then Franc was pinned by a bright shaft of light. For an instant, he caught a glimpse of Murphy's face—he didn't seem much older than Franc himself—then he turned to see a broad, black oval hovering only a few meters above the ground.

Metz was in a hurry; he hadn't lowered the landing flanges, and he hadn't switched off the chameleon again. The light was from the open airlock hatch; Lea knelt in the hatch, extending her arm downward.

"Move it! We've got to get out of there!"

The wind whipped at his ripped coat; Murphy had managed to tear it when he went down. In a panic, he felt at coat pockets; the glasses still there. But he wasn't done here yet . . .

"Hold on!" he shouted, then he stole a moment to kneel beside Murphy. Not completely unconscious, the scientist groaned softly as Franc rolled him over, but he was too groggy to offer any resistance. Franc pawed at his parka until he felt coins and heard the soft jingle of loose change. He reached into a pocket, retrieved the two dimes and one nickel that he had thoughtlessly left in the pay phone. Now the scientist had no tangible proof that he had ever encountered a chrononaut.

He started to stand up when he heard Murphy whisper something to him:

"Does . . . it . . . get any better?"

Franc knew what he meant.

"Depends what you do, my friend," he murmured. Then he leaped up and dashed toward the waiting timeship.

Headlights were already racing up the hill when Metz took the *Oberon* back into the sky. Minutes later, the timeship pierced the dense cloud layer above the Tennessee countryside. This time, there were no hostile aircraft in the sky, only the thinnest reaches of the stratosphere and, far above, the twinkling stars.

By then, Lea had taken Franc's glasses to the library pedestal, where she downloaded the chronological figures gathered by its nanochip into the AI. She and Franc hurried into the control room and held their breath until Metz informed them that the parameters for a successful crosstime jaunt had been established. *Oberon* was still wounded, but it was healing rapidly; a few orbits, and it would be capable of opening a tunnel.

"But we can't go home." Metz's fingers nervously tapped the console beneath a flatscreen image of two parallel closed-time circles. "We'll get back to our year, no question about that. But we'll still be in a different continuum."

"So Chronos Station won't be there." Lea's voice was flat, nearly hopeless.

"Maybe it will. Maybe it won't." The pilot shrugged.

"We'll have no idea until we get there. But we can't stay here, and don't even consider returning to 1937 . . ."

"I know," Franc said. "We can't change what we've already done. Not without creating another paradox, at least."

"Sorry, but no." Metz shook his head. "What's done is done. We're stuck with the results, whatever they may be." He looked over his shoulder. "On the other hand, we could always go back to some point before 1937. Find a place to settle down in the past. A little farm in Kansas, circa 1890? A chateau in southern France around 1700? A modest vineyard in ancient Greece . . . ?"

"Not tempting in the very least." Franc smiled. "It's a new universe, to be sure, but I don't think it'll be all that different." His smile became a broad grin. "In fact, we may find it surprisingly similar."

Metz's face was unapologetically skeptical, but Lea stared at him. "What makes you think that?"

Franc absently played with the torn lining of his coat. "Only a hunch."

"And you didn't see the guy who hit you?"

"Not clearly, no." Seated on the front bumper of the Hummer, Murphy leaned back against the grill. "I mean, it's pretty dark. . . ."

"I got that, but I still don't understand why he'd just attack you." Illuminated by the headlights, Ogilvy crouched on the road before him. "Neither do I understand what you were doing all the way up here. The sergeant at the checkpoint said you had just gone to the store for a soda. That's a quarter mile down the road from here."

Murphy gently touched the bruise on his forehead. It wasn't very sore, but the motion helped hide his face. "Only wanted to stretch my legs a bit more before heading back to camp, that's all. I hope I didn't get your man in any trouble."

"He'll live." Ogilvy glanced over his shoulder at the two soldiers searching the roadside with flashlights. "Let's try it again. You walk all the way up here, just to stretch your legs, and when we find you, you're beat-up and lying here in the road. You say it's because some total stranger stepped out of the woods and asked you for some spare change, and when you told him you didn't have any, he attacked you. Then he vanishes, just like that. Have I got everything?"

"I don't have an explanation, either." Murphy looked the colonel straight in the eye. "Maybe he was just . . . I dunno. Some crazy hitchhiker. Things happen like that."

"Right." The colonel slowly nodded. "Why do I get the feeling you're not telling me the truth?"

"That's all there is. Honest."

Ogilvy sighed as he stood up. "Well, whatever happened up here, it made you miss all the excitement. The yew-foh vanished. We think it lifted off."

"Oh, shit! Really?" It was all Murphy could do to feign astonishment. "You mean it's gone?"

"Happened about ten, fifteen minutes ago. First, it went invisible again, right under the eyes of the guys we left on the island. We heard a loud hum, then all the lights and electronic equipment went dead. Water shot up into the air where the saucer had been resting, and then . . . well, it was gone."

"And you didn't see anything?"

"Just a black shape taking off, but it was gone before we could track it." Ogilvy tucked his hands in the pockets of his parka. "That's when we discovered you were AWOL. It'll be sweet bringing you back. When she found out you were missing, Ms. Luna claimed she received a psychic impression that you'd been taken by her aliens."

Murphy laughed out loud, but not for reasons the colonel probably thought he did. For once, Meredith Cynthia Luna had come close to making the right guess. "I'm sure she's been wrong before."

"Yeah, well . . ." Ogilvy looked around again. "Go on, get in the vehicle. It's warmer in there. I'm going to give my guys a few more minutes to find your mysterious friend, then we'll go back and start breaking down camp. I don't imagine we'll find anything else, do you?"

"No, I doubt it." Wincing from the bruises on his stomach, Murphy stood up from the bumper. "We might check the island again, just to be safe, but you're probably right."

He let Ogilvy open the Hummer's passenger door, and waited in the shotgun seat until the colonel walked away to see whether the soldiers had discovered anything. When he was finally alone, he pulled a crumpled sheet of paper out of his pocket.

The paper had come from the stranger's inside coat pocket, in that half instant when Murphy had grabbed at him during their fight and torn it. Murphy had only the vaguest recollection of the other man whispering something as he knelt over him; the two dimes and the nickel were missing when he regained consciousness, but this single sheet of paper was still clenched in his fist, along with a shred of dark fabric.

Murphy gently uncrumpled the paper and studied it under the dim glow of the dashboard. At the top of the page was a stylized dirigible flanked by olive branches; a scroll beneath the airship declared it to be the LZ-129 *Hindenburg*.

Below the picture of the airship was a list of names: a passenger manifest. Halfway down the list, two names caught his eye: Mr. and Mrs. John and Emma Pannes, of Manhasset, Long Island.

Murphy looked up, saw the colonel walking back to the vehicle, followed by the two soldiers. He had just tucked the paper into an inner pocket when Ogilvy opened the right rear passenger door.

"We're not going to find anything," Ogilvy muttered as he settled into the backseat. "No need to rush, though. We've got until morning till we have to be out of here."

"Yeah. No need to hurry." Murphy turned his head to gaze out the window. The clouds were beginning to dissipate; for the first time tonight, he could make out a few stars. "'Fools rush in . . .'"

One of the Rangers opened the driver's door to climb behind the wheel. "Pardon me, sir?" the soldier asked. "Did you say something?"

"Hmm? Oh, nothing." Murphy smiled at his half reflection in the window. "Just thinking."

PART 3

FREE WILL

Against the darkness of space, from literally out of nowhere, there was the brilliant flash of defocused light as, for the barest fraction of a second, a tunnel opened within spacetime: a wormhole momentarily stabilized by exotic matter formed from vacuum fluctuations. In that sliver of an instant, the *Oberon* plunged out of chronospace.

The last tremors of the timeship's passage had barely subsided when Franc heard the warble of the master alarm. Dazed, his eyes shut as he gripped the armrests of his acceleration couch, at first he thought the sound was imagined. Then he was thrown against his harness as the *Oberon* suddenly rolled to starboard, and it was at that moment he realized they were in trouble.

"Franc! What . . . ?"

His eyes snapped open as Lea screamed, and the first thing he saw was the wallscreen. Earth lay several hundred kilometers below; sunlight reflecting off the tops of dense white clouds hid the ground from sight. Even without checking the chronometer, he knew that they were no longer in 1998, for the last things he had seen before Metz activated the wormhole generators were the nighttime lights of North America. Yet that wasn't what he noticed.

Far above Earth, a vast gray wall stretched across space.

Terrifyingly enormous, apparently solid yet somehow oddly granular, it curved around the planet until it disappeared beyond the horizon, casting a broad shadow across the cloud tops. Somehow, it looked like . . .

"That's impossible." Lea's voice was no more than an awestruck whisper, barely audible beneath the alarm. She stared at the screen, her mouth agape. "Please tell me it isn't there."

"It's there. I see it, too." Franc fumbled at his seat harness, finally locating the buckles and releasing them. His body started to float upward; he hastily grabbed the armrest to keep himself in his seat. With his free hand, he slapped the lobe of his headset. "Vasili!" he shouted. "Give us some gravity! And kill the alarm!"

The pilot didn't respond, but the alarm abruptly went silent. Franc let out his breath, then glanced to his right. Tom Hoffman's body was still securely strapped in the third couch, his corpse wrapped in a blanket. At least the sudden maneuvers hadn't dislodged him, and so long as *Oberon* itself was still in good condition . . .

Franc turned his head to check the status panel next to the wallscreen. The bar graphs for all the major systems were still in the green, and there were no red warning lights. So what triggered the master alarm? He was about to shout for Metz again when his gaze fell on the real-time chronometer.

The readout was 16.10.2314/0601:06.06.

The *Oberon* had returned from the past. In fact, it had reliably emerged from chronospace less than a second into the future after its relative time of entry, with the remaining sixty-six seconds accounted for by the events of the past minute and few seconds. Indeed, they should be directly above the same point on Earth where the timeship had opened its wormhole to May 2, 1937. Therefore, if they were back in their own time, nothing should be different.

Suddenly gaining weight, his body fell back into the couch. The ship's localized gravity field had been restored. A moment later, he heard Vasili's voice in his headset.

"You guys better get up here," he said. "Something's wrong."

Franc nearly laughed out of loud. "Something's . . . ?" He pointed at the gray shape on the wallscreen. "Do you see that?" he demanded, forgetting that the pilot wasn't in the same compartment. "That's a *ring!* That's a goddamn *planet ring!*"

"I know." Vasili's voice was subdued. "We almost collided with it when we came out of chronospace. We got lucky . . . when the AI detected it, it went into autopilot mode and put us into lower orbit." There was a pause. "Never mind that now. Just get up here. That's not the worst of it."

Lea was already unbuckling her harness. She hesitated as her eyes met Franc's, then she prodded her headset. "What aren't you telling us? Have you tried to raise Chronos?"

Another pause. "Chronos isn't there. Nothing's there. The orbitals, the Lagrange colonies . . . they're all gone."

"What do you mean, gone?" Franc snapped. "They're not responding?"

"No, I mean they're *gone*. They're simply not there."

"What about Tycho?" Lea demanded. "Can you raise Tycho? Someone there should . . ."

"Lea," Vasili said, ever so quietly, "the Moon is gone, too."

Saturday, January 17, 1998: 2:30 A.M.

The Gulfstream II was still parked in front of a hangar at Sewert Air Force Base, right where Zack Murphy had last seen it only this morning . . . yesterday morning, he reminded himself, although it was difficult to remember that fact. In the predawn darkness, a brittle wind whipped across the airfield, tugging at the hood of his parka as he marched toward the waiting aircraft.

The Ranger team was still breaking camp at Center Hill Lake when Colonel Ogilvy began gathering the OPS team for the helicopter ride back to Sewert. Meredith Cynthia Luna had refused to leave, though; stubbornly insistent that the spacecraft belonged to alien emissaries, she wanted to remain behind for a little while longer, to "gather residual psychic impressions" from the crash site. Although Murphy secretly believed that she simply didn't want to share company with him and Ogilvy, he wasn't about to argue to the contrary. Much to his surprise, though, Ogilvy agreed to let her stay with the troops, so long as she caught a commercial flight back to Washington within the next twenty-four hours. Perhaps he was trying to appease OPS, or maybe he was just as sick of her as everyone else was;

whatever the reason, after Ogilvy placed her in the care of Lieutenant Crawford—who didn't seem thrilled by the prospect of baby-sitting the psychic—he herded Murphy and Ray Sanchez aboard the Blackhawk.

So now they were back where they had started. Chilled to the bone, exhausted beyond all meaning of the word, Murphy pulled his parka a little more tightly around himself as he shuffled toward the jet. With any luck, he might be able to grab a few winks before the plane landed at Dulles. The flight would take about two hours; factoring in the one-hour time difference, that meant they'd arrive in Virginia at about 5:30 A.M. An hour or so after that, and he'd be walking through his front door. Donna would still be asleep, but Steven would probably be up already, watching cartoons in the living room. Murphy absently patted the jacket pocket where he had tucked the little Darth Vader action figure he had found on the island beach. When he got a chance, he'd rinse the sand off it in the airplane's washroom and give it to his son as a travelling present . . . and then he'd take the phone off the hook, climb into bed next to his wife, and sleep until well into the afternoon.

And after that?

Although he was too tired to think straight, Murphy knew that nothing would ever be the same again. After all, he had just met a time traveller. You don't go to Disneyland after something like this . . .

Forget it, he told himself. Figure it out later.

Just ahead of him, a pair of Air Force officers in flight gear were standing next to the Gulfstream's lowered stairway. Murphy assumed that they were the aircraft's pilots. Ogilvy and Sanchez had stopped to speak with them; the four men were huddled together tightly, their shoulders hunched against the wind. As Murphy approached, they fell silent.

Murphy halted next to the stairs. "Anything wrong?" he asked. "Is there something I can do?"

He caught a sullen glare from Sanchez, but the FBI

agent said nothing as he turned away. Ogilvy mustered an easy smile. "Don't worry about it," he said, then cocked a thumb toward the plane. "Go ahead, get aboard. I'll tell you about it later."

In that instant, Murphy had the premonition that he wasn't going to get any sleep during the flight back to Washington. Yet there wasn't much he could do about it now, so he trotted up the stairs and found a seat in the back of the plane. When he took off his parka, he made sure that he kept it folded in his lap, where he could keep his hands on it at all times. Through the window, he could see Ogilvy and Sanchez still talking to the pilots. As he watched, they turned and headed toward the stairs. A moment later, the pilots emerged through the hatch, followed by the colonel and the FBI agent. The pilots walked into the cockpit and shut the door behind them as Ogilvy and Sanchez took their seats near the front of the plane. Ogilvy propped his feet upon a vacant seat and lay his head back, while Sanchez placed his laptop computer on a table and opened it. Neither of them looked his way; after a few moments, Murphy cranked back his seat, pulled his coat up around his shoulders, and closed his eyes.

The Gulfstream had been airborne for a little less than fifteen minutes, just enough time for Murphy to doze off, when he heard someone settle into the seat next to him. "Zack?" Ogilvy said, insistent but not unkindly. "Wake up, son. We need to talk."

Reluctantly, Murphy opened his eyes. The colonel had brought two foam cups of black coffee from the galley. "Do me a favor and fold down the table, will you?" he asked, nodding toward the seatback in front of him. "My hands are full."

"Hmm . . . ? Oh, sure." Murphy reached out from beneath the parka, pulled down the tray table. "None for me, thanks," he said as Ogilvy gently set down the coffee. "I'd like to get some sleep sometime before we land."

"Sure. We've all had a hard day." The colonel shook his

head apologetically. "But I can't let you do that just yet. We've got some loose ends to tie up first." Picking up his coffee, he looked toward the front of the plane. "Agent Sanchez, would you like to join us?"

As if waiting for his cue, Sanchez moved down the aisle. Instead of taking the vacant seat on the other side of the aisle, though, he rested his elbows on the seatback. He gazed down at Murphy with cool dark eyes, but didn't say anything.

"Is this about the nondisclosure agreement?" Murphy picked up the other coffee, took a tentative sip. Caffeinated or not, its warmth was welcome after the chill of the night. "I said I'd sign whatever you want me to, if that's what's bothering you."

"Glad to hear it, Dr. Murphy. I'm pleased to know that you're willing to cooperate with us. But that's not what I . . . what we want to discuss with you." Turning half-around in his seat, Ogilvy folded his hands together on the armrest. "Let's cut to the chase, shall we? What happened to you on the road just before we found you?"

Oh, hell . . . "Nothing happened," he said, looking the colonel straight in the eye. "I took a walk up the road, that's all. Just catching some air. And when I got to the top of the hill, some guy came out of the woods, asked me what time it was . . ."

"You said earlier that he asked you for spare change."

"Well . . . yeah, I mean, he asked me for some change, and then he . . ."

"Roughed you up, right. That's what you said." Ogilvy reached up the ceiling panel above Murphy's seat, clicked on the reading lamp. The sudden glare made him wince. "Y'know, for someone who's been punched around," Ogilvy said as he peered closely at Murphy, "you look like you're in pretty good shape."

"I got a good punch in the face. After that he hit me in the gut, then he threw me down and . . ."

"Threw you down on the road?" Ogilvy asked, and

Murphy nodded. "The road was paved, so you should have some asphalt burns on your hands, maybe some scrapes on your coat." He studied Murphy's hands, then the back of his parka. "I don't see any marks."

"I didn't . . . I mean, I didn't hit the ground all that hard."

"C'mon, Zack. I didn't buy it back then, so why would I buy it now?" Ogilvy frowned, shook his head. "Something else happened up there. I know it, and you know it, so why don't you just make things easier and come clean?"

"I really don't know what you're talking about," Murphy said quietly.

Baird Ogilvy regarded him silently for a few moments, then slowly let out his breath as an exasperated sigh. "Agent Sanchez, you want to help me out here, please?"

"Dr. Murphy," Sanchez said, "right now this plane is circling above the Kentucky state line, its pilots awaiting my instructions as to its next destination. If you don't agree to render us your full cooperation, the plane will divert to Fort Campbell, where a military escort will meet us at the airfield. They will then drive you to the federal penitentiary in Marion, Illinois, where you'll be placed in their custody under maximum . . ."

"What?"

"You will placed in their custody under maximum security conditions until appropriate federal charges can be levied against you." Sanchez's voice never rose, his eyes never blinking once. "During this time, you will not be permitted to have any contact with the outside world. You will not be allowed to contact an attorney, or speak with your family, or . . ."

"You can't do that!" Livid with anger, Murphy began to rise from his seat. "That's illegal! You can't . . . !"

The .45 automatic appeared so fast, he barely saw Sanchez's hands move.

Murphy froze. From somewhere many miles away, he

felt the liquid warmth of spilled coffee seeping through his right knee of his trousers.

"Please sit down, Dr. Murphy," Sanchez said, his voice remaining even. "Any further action on your part will be considered a threat to . . ."

"Relax, please. Both of you." Ogilvy placed a hand on Murphy's shoulder, easing him back down. "Calm down, Zack. No one's going to prison today." Then he looked up at Sanchez. "Ray, please lower your weapon. That's not necessary."

The FBI agent hesitated, then withdrew his finger from the trigger and returned the .45 to the belt holster behind his back. Murphy's heart galloped as he fell back into his seat. No one had ever pointed a gun at him in his entire life. For as long as he lived, he hoped it would never happen again.

"You . . ." he started, and realized his mouth was too dry to speak. He swallowed a hard lump in his throat. "You're serious. You'd do this, wouldn't you?"

"I'm sorry, but . . . yes, I would." In the heat of the moment, Murphy hadn't noticed that he had knocked over Ogilvy's coffee as well. The colonel set the empty cup upright, then pulled a handkerchief from his shirt pocket and used it to sponge up the coffee. "Try to look at this my way," he continued. "An alien spacecraft . . . or at least what appears to be an alien spacecraft . . . crash-lands in a rural lake after an encounter with two military jets, one of which is forced down for unknown reasons. After being surrounded by army troops and remaining silent for over half a day, the craft inexplicably takes off again, becoming radar-invisible within moments of departure. I don't know about you, but anything that demonstrates that sort of capability scares the cookies out of me."

Ogilvy wadded up the wet handkerchief and dropped in the vacant seat on the other side of the aisle. "Then the senior OPS consultant charged with investigating this event is found on a nearby road. He claims to have been mugged . . . in the middle of the night, out in the middle of nowhere . . . but all evidence points to the contrary. Kind of suspicious, don't you think?"

"I think . . ." Murphy hesitated, then looked away. "Nothing. I've got nothing to say."

Ogilvy shook his head in disappointment. "Dr. Murphy, believe me, this isn't a bluff. You're hiding facts regarding a possible threat to national security. I know you're in this way out of your depth, and I'm sorry that it has to be this way, because you seem to be a nice guy. But I'm telling you right now, if you don't start talking, you're going to be seeing the inside of a prison cell before the sun comes up."

"If you do cooperate," Sanchez added, his voice quietly persuasive, "everything that just happened here stays here, on the plane. I won't file a report about this discussion, and neither will the colonel. Your record remains clean."

"That's right." Ogilvy nodded in agreement. "No one at OPS will know, and neither will your family or colleagues. It'll be classified at the highest levels." Then he let out his breath. "But if you don't cooperate . . ."

"I think I get the picture." Nervously running his fingers through his hair, Murphy gazed out the window. Through a thin skein of clouds, he could see the lights of a large town passing beneath the strobes at the ends of the jet's left wing. If they were above the Kentucky border, then it was probably Fort Campbell. If that was the case, the Gulfstream could be on the ground in five minutes. Military police were probably already waiting at the airstrip, ready to bundle him into a car for a quick ride up I-24 to Marion, Illinois.

He remembered the Darth Vader figure in his coat pocket. He had been looking forward to giving it to Steven when he got home. Sure, the kid probably had one already—Murphy had lost track of all the toys in his collection—but the look on his face would be priceless.

Yet there was something else in his parka, wasn't there?

He glanced down at his coat; it had fallen to the floor when he tried to get up, and it still lay there, rumpled around his feet. He had meant to protect the mysterious thing that he had found, keep it his own private secret, yet that no longer seemed to be an option. It would be found eventually, once his clothes were taken away and he was given a prison track suit . . .

"Your call, Dr. Murphy," Sanchez said. "The clock's ticking."

Murphy slowly let out his breath. "All right," he said, "you've got me." He hesitated, then bent forward to pick up the parka. "There's something here you need to see."

Seen from geosynchronous orbit, just above the plane of the equator, the changeling Earth was a thing of vast and frightening beauty.

The innermost rings, buff-colored swatches of fine dust less than a meter in depth, lay in low orbit only a few hundred kilometers above the planet. Rotating most rapidly of all, they were also in the slow process of disintegration; the night skies past the daylight terminator were constantly lit by the firefly sparks of micrometeorites flaming out in the upper atmosphere. Past a narrow, translucent gap lay the broad, charcoal-colored bands of middle rings; here, the rocky debris ranged in size from pebbles to small boulders, nearly a half kilometer in depth and extending for thousands of kilometers. Beyond them was another, slightly wider gap, and finally there were the outer rings, nearly as fragile as the inner rings yet having a higher albedo than their closer cousins.

The rings were all that remained of the Moon. Obliterated by forces beyond human comprehension, Earth's former companion had betrayed it, become its murderer. The rings cast an elongated shadow upon the southern hemisphere over five hundred kilometers in width; at high noon, everything from the tip of Central America through the Caribbean to Africa's western coast lay within a perpetual eclipse zone that changed only with the passing of the seasons. Worse, without the Moon's gravity to moderate the ocean tides and wind patterns, coastal areas had disappeared beneath the oceans while windstorms perpetually raged inland.

Yet, the heaviest toll had been taken by the asteroid-size chunks of the Moon's mantle and core that had rained down upon the planet's surface. Seen through occasional breaks in the global cloud cover were vast stretches of scorched and cratered terrain. Where there had once been cities were now ruins, and what had once been plains and forests were now blackened wastelands.

Regardless of whatever had caused this planetary catastrophe or when it had occurred, its devastation was as merciless as it was complete. It was impossible for anything to have remained alive down there. Earth was dead.

"I'm not picking up anything." His voice barely more than a whisper, Metz ran his hand across the com panel, searching every available frequency. "No radio, no cybernet, no microwave transmissions . . . nothing. Not a single source."

"Have you tried . . . ?" Franc started to say, then stopped. He was about to ask if there were any satellite uplinks, but that was unlikely; the rings would have wiped out anything orbiting the planet.

"Have you received anything from the colonies?" Standing beside him, Lea trembled against his shoulder. "It's been over an hour. You should have heard something from Mars at least."

"There wasn't anything the last time I checked, but . . ." Metz tapped a button on the panel, listened intently for a few moments, then shook his head. "Nothing. Not even a tachyon pulse." He frowned. "You'd think we'd get some sort of space traffic, though, or least an answer from Deimos Port. But I'm not even receiving word from Ceres."

Franc's throat tightened. Earth and the Moon, wiped out . . . that much was hard to accept. Yet there were nearly fifty million people scattered across the solar system, from the Aresian settlements to the asteroid colonies, and even farther, to the Jovian and Saturnine moons. "I . . . I really can't believe this," he murmured. "I mean . . . every place in the system . . ."

"No . . . no, I don't think so." Lea's eyes were red-rimmed and swollen, her voice a dry rasp. For a short time she had been on the verge of hysteria, yet she was beginning to pull herself together again. "Even if the major colonies had been destroyed, there's too many places for people to hide out there."

"Then maybe . . ." Metz thought about it a moment. "They might have evacuated everyone from the system. Picked up survivors, taken them . . ."

"No. Too many people for that." Removing herself from the comfort of Franc's arm, Lea stepped closer to the porthole, staring through it as if searching for answers in the obscene rings which encircled the planet. "They couldn't get everyone aboard starships, even if they packed them in like . . ."

Her voice trailed off as her mouth slowly fell open. "Damn," she whispered. "We're forgetting something."

"What's going on?" Franc asked. "Lea, what are we forgetting?"

"This isn't our worldline," she said. "This isn't the place we left."

"But we came back to the same time . . ." Metz began.

"The same time, yes . . . but not the same place." Lea continued to stare at the rings. "We changed history in 1937, right? That means our worldline changed. When we tried to return to 2314, we got dumped out into 1998, but it was the 1998 of another worldline. So it stands to reason that, when we left 1998, we would continue to follow this worldline to 2314 . . ."

"So it's not our 2314," Franc said.

"Right." Lea pointed to the com panel. "That's why we're not picking up any transmissions from the colonies . . . because there never *were* any colonies, on Mars or Ceres or anywhere else. Maybe not even on the Moon."

"Wait a minute. Hold on . . ." Turning around in his chair, Metz touched a different panel. Horizontal patterns appeared on a flatscreen; the pilot examined them closely, then pointed at the broadest group. "Look here. The inferometer doesn't pick up any man-made metals in the ring debris, but there should be tons of it floating around out there, from all the orbitals . . ."

"That's because there weren't any orbitals. Chronos Station wasn't destroyed because there never was a Chronos Station. Not in this worldline, at least." Lea gestured at the porthole. "And that didn't happen yesterday, or even last year. I don't know much about planetary physics, but those rings aren't new. They took time to form."

"Three hundred sixteen years?" Franc was skeptical. "That isn't my area either, but . . ."

"You've got another theory?" Lea shot him a hard look, then bent over the console and pointed toward the image of the ring-plane on another screen. "Vasili, can you get us a little closer to the center ring? If we can get a good sensor lock on one of those boulders, maybe the AI can run an analysis, tell us how long ago this happened."

"Sure, I can get us closer, but I don't know . . ."

"Good. I'll be in the monitor room, setting up the program." She turned so quickly that she almost collided with Franc. "You want to help me, or . . . ?"

"No, no. You know what you're doing." Franc hastily stepped aside, and Lea brushed past him without another word. He waited until she had left the flight deck before he dared let out his breath. "She's upset," he said softly.

"You mean you're not?" Metz was already entering the

new trajectory into the flight computer. "Maybe it's not our worldline, Dr. Lu, but in case you haven't noticed . . ."

"I know. Sorry." Everything was still sinking in. There was a certain sense of surrealness to all this, as if he was living in a nightmare. Perhaps it was only the lack of sleep; the last time he had closed his eyes, it was while he was aboard the *Hindenburg,* somewhere above the Atlantic. He glanced down at himself, grimaced in disgust. Although he had long since discarded his nanoskin, he still wore his 1937 clothes, donned again during his foray into 1998. The cuffs of his trousers were caked with dried mud over three and a half centuries old. "I think I'll change, if you don't mind," he murmured, turning away from the console. "Might make me . . ."

"I'm getting something!" Metz snapped.

"What?" Franc looked around, saw that the pilot had his hands clasped over his headset. "What . . . you mean, a signal? Where . . . ?"

"I don't know! It just . . . !"

"Franc! Get in here!"

Hearing Lea, Franc bolted for the hatch. "Get a fix on that!" he yelled at the pilot as he dashed out of the control room. "Don't lose it!"

Lea stood in front of the library pedestal, her hands locked onto the platform as she stared straight ahead "Vasili just received a transmission!" Franc shouted as he charged into the compartment. "He's trying to . . . !"

"I know," she whispered, and pointed at the wallscreen. "Look."

Franc skidded to a halt, almost fell against her. Displayed across the screen, in characters the size of his hand, was a message:

OBERON
COME HERE
72° 35' N 42° 39' W
ALL WILL BE EXPLAINED

"Franc!" Vasili's voice was loud in his headset. "I've got a fix on the signal! It's coming from . . ."

"I know. It fed a message through the AI. We've got it on the screen." All at once, Franc's fatigue evaporated. "Seventy-two degrees, thirty minutes north, forty-two degrees, thirty-nine minutes west." He was already entering the coordinates into the pedestal. "Sounds like it's somewhere in North America. Go ahead and lay in a landing trajectory. I'll figure out exactly where that is."

"You're not seriously thinking of going down there, are you?" Lea stared at him in astonishment. "You don't know who sent that."

"No . . . but they obviously know who we are." Franc tapped the pedestal's touch pad, and waited while the map formed on the screen. "Besides, it's rude to ignore an invitation."

The conference room was located on the second floor of the Capitol, just a few steps down the hall from the Senate cloakroom. Normally used for budget reviews and parliamentary sessions, on certain occasions it also served as a quiet, private place for closed-door hearings. This morning, a Capitol Hill police officer stood guard outside; so far since the meeting had begun, three senators, four aides, and two pages had paused to ask what was going on within, only to be given a wordless shrug in response.

The emptiness of the room made Murphy nervous. Whenever he glanced over his shoulder, all he saw were rows of vacant chairs. Off to one side sat the only spectator, a uniformed U.S. Army lieutenant, her gaze focused upon some distant place as her fingers danced across the keyboard of a portable stenograph. To his left, almost unrecognizable in his braided and service-striped dress uniform, sat Colonel Ogilvy, his papers spread out across the witness table. And directly in front of them, flanked on either side by three senior senators, was no less than the Vice President of the United States.

There was a long, silence as the Vice President studied

the photocopy in his hands. No one said anything for a long time. Colonel Ogilvy had opened the hearing by making his statement; Murphy followed with his testimony. Although the men seated on the dais remained quiet, Murphy was acutely aware of every small sound in the room: the restless shifting of feet, the occasional phlegmy cough from the flu-stricken senator from Vermont, the gentle tinkle of cracked ice as the senator from California poured water into a glass from the pitcher on her desk. His wool suit, comfortable when he put it on this morning, was now unbearably warm, yet he dared not loosen his tie, and he was reluctant to even mop the sweat from his brow until Ogilvy, sliding his hand beneath the table, surreptitiously placed one of his ever-present handkerchiefs in his lap.

The Vice President gazed at the facsimile for another few moments, then raised his questioning eyes. "So, Dr. Murphy," he said, "I take it that this . . ." He raised the photocopy. ". . . is your only evidence that you've encountered someone from the future."

"Uh . . . yes sir." Murphy had trouble finding his voice; he covered his mouth and cleared his throat. "Sorry . . . yes sir, Mr. Vice President. The only tangible evidence, that is. As I've told you, it was recovered only by accident, during my . . . uh, encounter . . . on the road outside the campground."

"We have the original, Mr. Vice President, if you care to inspect it." Ogilvy picked up the *Hindenburg* passenger manifest. Mounted on a piece of cardboard and sealed within a polyurethane wrapper with a red Top-Secret strip across its upper edge, it less resembled a historic artifact than evidence gathered from a crime scene. "I've brought it to show you and the other members of the committee that it's not a forgery, but an authentic item."

The Vice President was unimpressed. "I don't doubt its authenticity, Colonel, yet this is the sort of thing one could find in any private collection."

"We've got antique stores in my state where you could

easily find something like this." The senator from Vermont rubbed his nose in the paper tissue, then reached for the pint carton of orange juice on his desk. "In fact, just a few years ago, a dealer opened the back of a framed painting he had purchased in an estate auction and discovered a copy of the Declaration of Independence. A passenger list from a German airship . . ."

"With all due respect, Senator," Ogilvy interrupted, "any document that old would show signs of aging. The paper would be brittle, the ink faded." He gently laid the manifest on the table, then opened the report which lay before him. "If you'll read page nineteen of our summary, you'll find that we submitted this document to the FBI Crime Lab for analysis. They determined that it was printed no more than two weeks ago, on a type of industrial-grade paper that hasn't been manufactured in Germany since the end of the Hitler regime. It's brand-new, sir. It can't possibly be a forgery."

The senator from Vermont scowled at Ogilvy, then opened his unread copy of the report to the appropriate page. The Vice President, though, remained stoical. "Thank you for clarifying that point, Colonel, but the question was addressed to Dr. Murphy. Aside from this, what proof do you have of your allegation?"

Murphy knew that he had to be careful. Before he became the President's running mate in the '92 election, the Vice President had served as chairman of the Senate Science and Technology Committee, the same position now held by the senator from Vermont. Although the committee approved the annual OPS budget, the VP, no friend to mind readers or spoon-benders, was known to be profoundly skeptical of the agency's purpose. Convincing him would be the toughest task of all.

"Mister Vice President," he started, "regardless of the conclusions made by my agency, I believe that the origin of the . . . uh, the Center Hill Lake anomaly . . . wasn't extraterrestrial . . ."

The senator from California raised a hand, politely interrupting him. "Excuse me, Dr. Murphy, but I wish to clarify this particular point. Although you're a senior OPS investigator, you're presenting testimony which runs contrary to your agency's official findings. May I ask why?"

Again, he had to be careful, although for different reasons. Unlike the Vice President, the senator from California was a major supporter of the Office of Paranormal Sciences; no surprise, since she was known to employ psychics during her reelection campaigns. Murphy was about to reply, but Ogilvy beat him to it. "With respect to OPS, ma'am, Dr. Murphy is here today without his agency's knowledge or approval. He has agreed to offer his testimony on behalf of the Defense Department, under the condition that whatever he says remains classified."

And besides, Murphy thought sourly, *it beats hell out of sitting in prison.* Yet they were far past that point by now. He and Ogilvy had long since reached their peace. Now they had an entirely different agenda.

"Please let Dr. Murphy answer for himself, Colonel." The senator returned her attention to Murphy. "The OPS report unequivocally states that the object which crashed in Tennessee was an alien spacecraft. The other OPS investigator, Ms. Luna, is convinced of this, as is your Chief Administrator, Mr. Ordmann. You, on the other hand, seem to be jumping ship. May I ask why?"

Murphy let out his breath. "Ms. Luna reached that conclusion even before we reached the crash site. She based her opinion on . . . well, personal convictions, rather than the evidence of her own eyes. I can't speak for the Chief Administrator, since I haven't yet personally discussed the matter with him, but I'm basing my conclusion on the evidence of my own eyes . . . along with the document we've shown you."

"Which brings us back to the original question," the Vice President said. "What other proof do you have?"

"When I climbed aboard the . . . uh, time machine, for

lack of any better term . . . I briefly caught sight a human being behind its single porthole. That was my first indication that the craft wasn't extraterrestrial. Later, when I first encountered the unknown party at a nearby camp store, he left behind three coins in the pay phone he was using. The coins were two Mercury dimes and a buffalo nickel, all in mint condition. That made me curious, so I followed him up the road, which is where he attacked me . . ."

"And this is where the . . . as you say, the time machine . . . landed to pick him up." This from the senator from Arizona, who had remained quiet until now. A staunch Republican, he was here because of his chairmanship of the Senate Armed Services Committee, but judging from his bemused expression, Murphy had little doubt that he wouldn't have believed Earth was round if a Democrat told him it was.

"Yes, sir," Murphy continued, "but just before the craft landed, after he knocked me to the ground, he took pains to recover the coins from my pocket. He didn't realize that, during our fight, I had ripped the *Hindenburg* manifest from his pocket. If he had, I'm sure he would have taken that away from me as well. In hindsight, I believe he was trying to remove all evidence of his visit."

"And why would he want to do that?"

Now they were stepping onto thin ice. "I'm not sure, Senator, but I believe that the craft's arrival was entirely accidental. Judging from the man's style of clothing, the change in his pocket, and the manifest I took from him . . . I think the craft was returning from 1937 when it crashed in our time. Why, I don't know, but nonetheless it happened."

"And this leads you to believe that the craft wasn't from outer space," said the senator from California.

Murphy shook his head. "No, ma'am, I think it came from space, all right. I just don't think it originated there. It makes more sense to conclude that it came from somewhere . . . some *time,* rather . . . in the future."

There was a long silence in the conference room. The

senators jotted down notes, shifted in their seats, cleared their throats. The Vice President glanced at his watch, then leafed again through their report. Off to the side, the Air Force stenographer briefly rested her hands next to her keyboard. Murphy glanced at the pitcher of ice water on the table between him and Ogilvy. His throat was parched, but he dared not reach for it. Don't look scared, he told himself. They can smell fear.

"Colonel Ogilvy," the Vice President said at last, and the colonel sat up a little straighter, "on page thirty-two of your report, you state that this affair constitutes a scientific crisis of the highest order. Would you mind telling us why?"

"Mr. Vice President," Ogilvy said, "we have here evidence that we've been visited by individuals from the future." The senator from Arizona rolled his eyes in disbelief, but the colonel chose to ignore him. "Whether or not this visitation was deliberate or accidental is almost a moot point, for the fact remains that time travel is possible. Furthermore, these visitors have displayed the ability to cloak their craft to the point of near-total invisibility, thus allowing them to penetrate American airspace. Their ships are capable of disabling F-15 warplanes without firing a shot themselves, and operate by means of propulsion systems far beyond our current technology."

The senator from Arizona stopped smiling. He leaned forward in his chair, his hands clasped together on his desk. "Do you think this constitutes a threat, Colonel?"

"It very well may," Ogilvy replied. "I've discussed this incident with a couple of a senior colleagues at the Pentagon, and they concur with my belief that this presents a possible threat to national security. Yet even if that isn't the case, then there's another consideration . . . if time travel is possible, then when was it invented?"

The senator from Vermont lowered the wad of tissue paper from his face. "I'm sorry, Colonel, but I don't follow you. Why does that matter?"

"May I?" Murphy glanced at Ogilvy, and Baird nodded.

"What the colonel means is, if some means of time travel was . . . or rather, will be . . . invented in the future, then when did this effort begin? We don't know where . . . *when,* I mean . . . the ship came from. It could have come from two or three hundred years in the future, but it's also possible that time travel was developed even sooner than that. Albert Einstein postulated that it was feasible when he devised his general theory of relativity over eighty years ago. Since then, several leading physicists have refined Einstein's work to the point that many agree that the only real barriers to this sort of thing are technological."

He hesitated. "This all sounds very wild-eyed, to be sure, and I may be stepping out on a limb here . . . but I think it can be done. Perhaps even sooner than we think."

The senator from Arizona raised an cynical eyebrow. The senator from Vermont regarded him with eyes as stony as New England granite. The senator from California absently ran a hand through her hair. For just an instant, even the stenographer seemed to react; she blinked, and her fingers paused on the keyboard. Next to him, Baird Ogilvy allowed himself a slight smile, which he quickly covered with the back of his hand.

Yet Murphy knew he had made his point when he saw the Vice President, just for an instant, nod in agreement.

Mt. Sugarloaf rose from the middle of the Frontier Valley of the eastern Berkshires as a talon-shaped rock, its steep granite bluffs looming above the Connecticut River. During the twentieth century, the Commonwealth of Massachusetts had taken possession of the mountain and set it aside as a nature reserve; a winding asphalt road led up its rounded western side to its craggy summit, where a fieldstone observation tower had been erected as a scenic overlook. From here the entire valley could be seen, from the Holyoke Range at its southern end to the foothills of Vermont's Green Mountains in the north, with the river cutting straight through the flatlands spread across the valley floor.

At least, that was how it must have appeared three hundred years ago. As the *Oberon* cruised over the Pioneer Valley, Franc, Lea, and Vasili saw that even this placid corner of New England hadn't survived the catastrophe that had wiped out all life on Earth. The Connecticut River was covered with a thick sheet of ice; with the average global temperature now five degrees below normal, this place hadn't experienced summer for almost three centuries. Uncontrolled fires had ravaged the dense forests of the surrounding mountains, and acid rain had sterilized farm fields where corn, squash, and potatoes had once been cultivated in abundance. As the timeship closed in upon Mt. Sugarloaf, it passed over the burnt-out and lifeless ruins of nearby Amherst; the skyscrapers of the University of Massachusetts library and dormitories, oddly misplaced in the countryside, now rose above the decaying campus like soot-blackened tombstones.

The coordinates specified in the transmission they had received pinpointed Mt. Sugarloaf as the rendezvous site. Although Vasili and Lea agreed that there was no real reason to cloak the timeship, Franc decided to err on the side of caution; after all, they didn't know who might be down there, or what they wanted. So Metz reluctantly activated the *Oberon*'s chameleon, yet they were almost a half kilometer from the mountain when they discovered that subterfuge wasn't necessary.

"Smoke," Lea said softly, pointing toward the summit. "There. See it?"

Franc leaned over the back of Vasili's chair to peer through the porthole. A wavering brown plume spiraled upward from the mountaintop. "Could be a forest fire," he murmured. "Maybe lightning struck there recently."

"No, I don't think so." Vasili nodded toward one of the screens above his console, where a tiny, irregular blotch of light glowed on the radar-topography map. "I'm picking up an isolated IR trace. Too small to be from a natural source." He looked up at Franc. "Someone's down there. They've set a signal fire."

"I think we're expected." Lea glanced uncertainly at Franc. "You want to go down now, or do you want to hold back a little longer?"

Franc hesitated. "No . . . no, let's find out what this is all about." He tapped Metz on the shoulder. "Deactivate the chameleon, then bring us in. Set down near the fire if you can."

The pilot nodded, then he took *Oberon* out of chameleon mode. As the timeship closed in upon the mountain, they could see that the smoke rose from a rocky spur near the base of the observation tower. "We're going to have trouble finding a place to land," he murmured. "I don't see any level . . ."

"Over there." Franc pointed to a small clearing within the burnt-out remains of the woods just below the summit. "That looks flat enough."

As the *Oberon* began to descend upon the mountain, the timeship was abruptly buffeted by crosswinds. As Lea grabbed the edge of the console for support; she happened to glance through the porthole. "Someone's down there!" she snapped. "See him? Look . . . !"

One of the screens above the porthole displayed a close-up of the summit. Just as Lea said, a lone figure stood near the fire, watching the timeship as it approached. He raised his arms over his head and began to wave them back and forth.

"I see him." Franc grabbed the back of Metz's chair as the timeship was once again violently shaken by the wind. "How could anyone have lived through this?"

"We'll find out soon enough." Gripping the yoke within his fists, Metz carefully moved it back and forth as he fought for control. "Hang on, this might be a little rough."

Metz waited until almost the last moment before he lowered the landing gear; despite his caution, the wind caught the flanges. Franc was nearly thrown off his feet as the deck tilted beneath him, and Lea yelled as she fell against the console. Then the flanges connected with hard surface and *Oberon* was down. Metz quickly shut down the negmass drive, then slowly let out his breath. "Sorry about that," he murmured. "This just isn't my day."

Franc smiled to himself, then glanced at Lea and found

that she was grinning as well. Perhaps it was only fatigue, but Vasili was beginning to show a little humility. "You did fine," Franc said, patting the pilot's shoulder. "We're in one piece, that's all that counts."

"Yes, well, that's only half of it." Lea picked herself off the console, headed for the hatch. "Let's go see who's out there."

"Better put something on," Vasili called after them as Franc moved to follow her. "Temperature gauge says it's just above freezing out there."

The *Oberon* didn't carry any survival gear, so they had to make do with the clothes they had worn in 1937. However, Franc found a stun gun in one of the equipment lockers; he had nearly forgotten that it was there, although it was standard equipment for timeships, just in case a research team encountered hostile contemporaries. He contemplated the weapon for a moment, then shoved it into his coat pocket while Lea's back was turned to him. She probably would have objected to him carrying it, and under any other circumstances he might have left it behind, yet nonetheless he felt marginally safer for taking precautions.

The *Oberon* had landed in what appeared to have once been a small parking lot. Once upon a time, visitors to the overlook had parked their cars here, but now the asphalt was weather-beaten and broken, with weeds rising from its cracks. The air was brittle at the bottom of the ladder, the wind mournful as it groaned through the branches of dead trees. A short path led them past the blackened remains of a picnic shelter to the summit's barren crown, where the ruins of the observation tower loomed against the hostile sky. The gray clouds had parted somewhat, allowing the cold rays of the midafternoon sun to bathe the mountaintop with its sullen light. As they reached the base of the tower, they saw Earth's rings rising high above the distant mountains like a stone-colored rainbow.

The bonfire was a little larger than Franc expected, and

the man who tended it said nothing as he and Lea cautiously approached him. Hands shoved in the pockets of what appeared to be a military-issue parka from the late twentieth century, he wore a dark blue baseball cap embroidered with the intertwined letters NY. The chill wind caught his brown-gray hair and blew it past his stooped shoulders, and his white beard smothered his mouth.

The old man barely glanced at Lea, but he regarded Franc with puzzlement which slowly turned to recognition.

"I . . . I know you," he said, his voice a quiet stammer.

Franc stared back at him. "Have we met?" he asked. "I don't . . ."

"You don't remember me? It's been nearly twenty-five years, but . . ."

"Twenty-five years?" Lea asked. "How would you know him from . . . ?"

"I only sort of remember your face." Ignoring Lea, he pulled a hand from his pocket, pointed a trembling finger at Franc. "But your coat . . . that's what I remember the most. It didn't look right, even back then. That's the first thing that tipped me off . . ."

His coat? Franc self-consciously looked down at himself. He was wearing the same wool suit coat he had worn aboard the *Hindenburg* . . . yet hadn't he worn it a second time? Only a few hours ago, in Tennessee . . . ?

"Oh, my God," he whispered.

"Your name is . . ." The old man shut his eyes. "John Pannes. We met a long time ago, in a place in . . ."

"You're the man on the road," Franc said. "The person I met when I . . ."

"When you made the phone call, yes." The old man raised his eyes, took a deep breath. "My name is Zack Murphy . . . Dr. David Zachery Murphy. I've been brought here to meet you."

Franc found himself unable to speak. "Brought here?" Lea asked. "By whom?"

For the first time, Murphy seemed to notice her. He opened his mouth and was about to answer when, out of the corner of his eye, Franc caught a sudden flash of light.

He turned around, looked at the observation tower. At its top, a luminescent halo had appeared: a corona of light, brighter than either the autumn sun or the bonfire beside which they stood. Within its nucleus, suspended within the phosphorescent glare, hovered a figure, featureless yet vaguely humanlike, save for the broad, wing-shaped appendages that spread outward from behind its back.

An angel.

"That's what brought me here," Murphy said, his voice shaking. "It . . . it brought me here because . . ."

He suddenly stopped, glancing to one side as if he had just heard something. When he looked back at them again, his face was ashen.

"It tells me we're responsible for the end of the world."

"You're sure no one's going to find this place?" Murphy gazed at the towers of the University of Massachusetts as they drove past the campus on Route 116. "We're pretty close to town."

"Right on the Amherst line, to be exact." Baird Ogilvy kept his left hand on the wheel as he reached for the cell phone tucked beneath the Blazer's dashboard. "It's actually in Sunderland, but that's not much of a difference. Sure, someone's bound to notice. There's not too many places left where you can put something like this . . . at least, not unless you want to move out to the desert, and that's more trouble than it's worth, believe me."

"Then why here?"

"The trick is to hide in plain sight. Now pay attention. This is how you get in." Turning on the phone, the colonel switched to hands-off mode, then pressed a couple of digits on the keypad. The dial tone was replaced by the swift electronic beeping of a number being dialed, then the phone on the other end of the line buzzed three times before it was picked up. "ICR, may I help you?" a woman's voice asked.

"Extension 121, please," Ogilvy said.

"One moment, I'll connect you." Ambient music drifted over the speakerphone for a few moments, then the other line was picked up again. "Shipping, Roucheau speaking," a man's voice said.

"Hi, is Gary in?" Ogilvy asked, giving Murphy a sly wink.

"Sorry, he's out sick today." The voice sounded bored. "Wanna leave a message?"

"Thanks. Just tell him Jeff called, okay?"

"Jeff called. Right. Will do."

"Thanks, bye." The line was hung up, and Ogilvy reached over to switch off the cell phone. "Got that? As you're coming in, you call this number—555-8602—and ask for extension 121, then ask whoever picks up for Gary. He's always going to be sick or out to lunch . . . unless there's a site emergency, then he'll be out of town. Understand?"

"Right. Ask for Gary, tell 'em Jeff called." Murphy was admiring the countryside. Woods, farmland, mountains on all four sides. The foothills of the Berkshires. Deer season was pretty good around here, or at least so he had been told, although he had a feeling he wouldn't get a chance to do much hunting. "What happens if there's an emergency?"

"Drive past. Go straight home and wait for someone to call you." Baird shook his head. "Don't worry, it's just a precaution. We're not anticipating any problems."

Murphy nodded. Although this part of western Massachusetts was as rural as you could get, they weren't exactly in the middle of nowhere. On the right, they passed a convenience store and log-cabin barbecue shack; on the left, a farm-equipment supplier and a vegetable stand. Hidden in plain sight, he reminded himself. "What does ICR stand for, anyway?"

"Doesn't stand for anything." The colonel smiled at him from behind his sunglasses. After seven months of working together in the Pentagon, Murphy was still getting used to seeing him in civilian clothes again. "Three letters a DOD computer selected at random. If anyone asks, though, we make precision machine parts for offshore oil rigs. Hope you like being a company VP."

"It's a promotion," Murphy said sourly. Although he was glad to get out of Washington, Donna had been upset when he resigned from OPS to take an unglamorous job in the private sector, until he pointed out that his annual salary would be three times that which he earned as a government employee and that Steven would be able to attend public schools where they wouldn't have to worry about him getting harassed by street gangs. And the place they were buying in Deerfield was a bargain: a refurbished turn-of-the-century farmhouse on two acres, with a clear view of Mt. Sugarloaf from the kitchen window. For the first time in years, they wouldn't have to worry much about traffic, crime, or smog. They would even be able to give Steven the dog he wanted so much. Life was looking up. . . .

So long as he continued to lie to his family about what he was really doing out here, and pretend that the words *Blue Plate* only referred to a restaurant dinner special.

"Here we are." Ogilvy slowed down, clicked the turn indicator downward as he turned left into a paved driveway. "Your new lab."

It didn't look anything like a government research facility: a large, flat-roofed factory building, the letters ICR painted across one panel of its beige aluminum-sided walls. Although a ten-foot chain-link fence surrounded the premises, there was no gatehouse, no armed guards patrolling the perimeter. Three sixteen-wheel trucks, each stenciled with the ICR logo, were parked beside the loading dock; Murphy spotted several men hauling crates from the trailers, some large enough to require forklifts. A black man riding a mower looked up as they pulled into the parking lot, then went back to cutting the grass. Everything was as boring as boring can be.

As Murphy and Ogilvy opened the Blazer's doors and climbed out, a young man wearing a long-sleeved flannel shirt pulled out over a T-shirt and a pair of jeans sauntered toward them. He glanced at Murphy, then raised a hand to Ogilvy. "Hi, Jeff!" he called out.

"Hi, Gary," Ogilvy said, returning the friendly gesture. "Hey, lemme introduce you to my friend Zack. Zack, this is Gary. Gary, Zack Murphy."

"Hi, Gary," Murphy said, offering his hand. "Pleased to meet you."

"Likewise." The young man shook Murphy's hand, then he strolled away. "Have a nice day."

Ogilvy moved a little closer to Murphy. "U.S. Marine," he murmured. "He's stationed out here to greet everyone who arrives. I've just introduced you, so he'll remember your face from now on."

Murphy stared at the young man. "Is he armed?" he asked quietly.

"Of course, though I bet you can't figure out where he hides his weapon." Ogilvy nodded toward the man on the riding mower. "So is he, and so's the guy out back. They're all named Gary, and so are their reliefs. We've got three guards on active duty at all times. When you see them, call them Gary after they call you Jeff. That's the password."

"Gary. Jeff. Got it." Murphy watched Gary as he stopped, casually looked around, spit on the asphalt, and began moseying his way back across the parking lot. "Hard to believe that's a Marine," he said quietly.

"You're telling me." Ogilvy shook his head as he escorted Murphy toward the front door. "You don't know what it took to get those guys to stop saluting every time they saw me."

They walked into the building through the front entrance, where a nice-looking young woman sat behind a reception desk decorated with Beanie Babies and framed snapshots of children. "Hi, Jeff!" she said as they approached her desk. "Who's your friend?"

"Lucy, this is Zack Murphy, our new VP. Zack, Lucy." Ogilvy nodded toward the door behind her. "Is Doug in?"

"Yes, sir, he . . ."

"Don't call me sir," Ogilvy said, very softly. Lucy blanched as she hastily nodded. "Don't do that again, okay?"

"Okay." Embarrassed, Lucy reached into her desk drawer, pulled out a pair of laminated ID badges. "Doug's in. Right that way."

"Thanks, Lucy. Right this way, Zack." Ogilvy led Murphy through the door behind Lucy's desk, then sighed as it closed behind them. "That's the third time I've had to tell her that."

"So what does Lucy do, besides give us these?" He clipped the badge to his shirt pocket and flicked it with his finger.

"She's the gatekeeper. When I called in, she was the one who answered the phone, so she knew we were coming. Remember, you have to do that every time before you arrive." They began walking down a narrow corridor whose walls were decorated with framed photos of offshore oil rigs. "Other than that, she handles the public. When someone comes looking for a job, she tells them we're not hiring. When the Girl Scouts drop in, she buys some cookies. When a reporter from the local paper wants to meet the company president, she arranges for an interview . . ."

"We've got a company president?"

"Sure. Doug reports to work every day." Ogilvy grinned. "And before you ask, we really do ship machine parts out of here. They're actually made in Taiwan, but you wouldn't know unless you checked the serial numbers. We bring them in, put them in our own crates, load 'em on the trucks, send 'em to a warehouse in New Jersey, recrate them, and send 'em back here again, complete with new truck manifests for the interstate weigh stations. A never-ending cycle."

Murphy was impressed. "You've got everything covered, don't you?"

"Not yet. We still haven't invented a time machine."

The elevator at the end of the hall didn't open until both Ogilvy and Murphy passed the bar codes on the back of their badges across its concealed scanner, then it took them upstairs, where the real offices were located. Here, everything was as busy as downstairs was quiet; the hallway was filled with stacked boxes and open shipping crates, and men were setting up computer terminals and phones on government-issue desks. "The first members of your team begin arriving next week," Ogilvy said as they strolled down the corridor. "We hope to get everything up and running by Labor Day."

"Three weeks?" Murphy raised an eyebrow. "That's pretty short, isn't it?"

Ogilvy shrugged. "For the main research center, sure, but we'll be doing work elsewhere. One of the reasons why we've established operations in New England is because we're close to MIT and Cornell . . ."

"And Washington, of course."

"The Senate committee insisted upon that." Ogilvy clasped his hands behind his back. "We may see some of them from time to time, but overall I think they're going to . . . ah, check this out."

They stopped in front of a large windowless room whose open door was a little thicker than the others. Coils of thick black cable lay scattered across the floor; several men in overalls stood on stepladders below open ceiling tiles or squatted beside floor panels, consulting wiring charts as they installed nests of electrical line. "This is where the supercomputer will go," Ogilvy said. "It may take a little longer before it goes online, but the schedule calls for it to be operational by the end of November."

Murphy was beginning to feel like a kid on Christmas Eve. "And the main lab? Where's that going to be?"

Ogilvy smiled and crooked a finger, silently beckoning him to follow. They walked to the end of the corridor, and the colonel paused before a pair of wood-paneled doors on either side of the hallway. "My office is here," he said, pointing to the left: a strip of masking tape on the door read *Ogilvy—MD*. "And here's yours. After you."

The door to the right was marked *Murphy—SD*. Military Director and Scientific Director, respectively. Murphy opened it and stepped into an office a little larger than the others down the hall. The furniture was still covered with plastic, the walls as yet unpainted; among the cardboard boxes stacked in the far corner, Murphy recognized some as the ones he had packed during his last days at OPS three weeks ago.

One wall of the office was dominated by a broad pane-glass window overlooking what had once been a factory floor. The building that Blue Plate now occupied was formerly owned by an industrial ceramics company that had folded two years earlier; its machinery had been removed, and now the main floor was being converted into a high-energy physics research lab. From this vantage point, Murphy could see a couple of dozen workmen preparing for installation of the equipment that would soon go here: parallel-processing computers, control consoles, ruby lasers, a lead-lined radioactive materials storage vault, the tall steel cylinder of a vacuum experiment chamber.

Forget Christmas, Murphy thought. *This is Creation itself. . . .*

"Just don't blow us up, okay?" Ogilvy said quietly. "You wouldn't believe how many strings we had to pull to get funding for this."

"I can believe it. Black budget, right?"

"Zack, the budget for this isn't black . . . it's ultraviolet." The expression on the colonel's face was as hard as his voice was soft. "The most ambitious scientific program in over fifty years. Nobody's undertaken anything like this since the Manhattan Project. Nine months ago, I would have said it was impossible." His reflection studied Murphy's in the window. "I know what you've told the committee, Doc, but that's Washington and this is here. So tell me the truth . . . you really think we can do this?"

Good question. He had been losing sleep over it for months now. In fact, the last time Murphy remembered having a good night's rest was sometime last January, just before a UFO had crashed in Tennessee. Ever since then, the last words of the mysterious stranger he had encountered at Center Hill Lake had haunted him:

Depends what you do, my friend.

"Someone in the future did it," he replied. "That much we know for certain. Which means they had to get started sometime in their past." He looked straight at Ogilvy. "Yeah, we can do this. In fact, I'd say it's a matter of predestination."

Ogilvy didn't respond. Instead, he rested his elbows on the windowsill as he contemplated the activity on the lab floor. "You know," he said at last, "I was raised Lutheran. Religion never really took with me, but I remember some of it, and the idea of predestination was one of those things I remember being taught in Sunday school."

Murphy put his hands in his pockets. He had never been particularly religious either, yet he felt even less comfortable talking about his beliefs than others. "Yeah? So?"

The colonel shrugged. "Well, you tell me that we're predestined to do this, and on the face of it I'm not going to argue with you. As you say, someone managed time travel in the future, so it's only logical that they . . . or, I guess, we . . . started here and now." He hesitated. "But personally, I was always something of a Sunday school heretic. I happen to believe in free will."

"And . . . ?"

"And . . ." Ogilvy appeared as if he was ready to say something before he thought better of it. "Never mind," he finished, turning away from the window. "Just a thought. C'mon, let me show you the rest of the setup."

And you say you began researching time travel in 1998?"
Franc stared at Murphy in disbelief.

"That's when the lab was built. We didn't actually . . ."
Murphy paused. He held his head a little to the right as if
listening to something none of the others seated around the
bonfire could hear. "I'm . . . I'm told that there's other
things you should know first," he said. Noticing the curious
expressions on the faces of the others, he shrugged in baf-
flement. "I don't know how, but every now and then I hear
a voice in my head. I was unconscious for some time before I woke up here, so maybe . . . perhaps it implanted
something in my head."

"I rather doubt that," Franc said. "You don't show any
signs of surgery." He peered up at the top of the nearby observation tower. The "angel" had vanished almost as
quickly as it had appeared, yet nonetheless he had the eerie
feeling that it hadn't gone very far away. "Telepathic link?"
he asked quietly, glancing at Lea. "It might be using him as
a conduit."

"It's possible. Right now, it's as good an explanation as

any." She looked back at Murphy. "But why doesn't it want to reveal itself?"

"Where were you before you woke up?" Metz asked. He had left the *Oberon* and joined the others by the fire. "Did the angel . . . ?"

"Wait, please." Murphy shook his head, held up his hands "I realize you've got a lot of questions, but you've got to believe me when I say I don't know all the answers." Shivering against the late-afternoon wind, he tucked his hands within his armpits for warmth. "I'm just as confused about this as you are. The last time I clearly remember anything, it was . . ."

Once again, he abruptly fell silent, his eyes half-closing as his head tilted slightly forward. "I'm told," he said at last, "that we've got to take this one step at a time, or otherwise you won't understand anything. Does that make sense to you?"

"Sort of," Franc said. Apparently, for reasons as yet unknown, Murphy was acting as a spokesman for the entity they had glimpsed at the top of the tower. "All right, we'll take this bit by bit. What does it want us to know first?"

Frowning with concentration, Murphy stared into the fire. "Your history . . . your past . . . is somehow different from mine," he said slowly. "The *Hindenburg* explosion . . . that's when everything changed."

"Yes, we know that," Lea said. "We had gone back to 1937 to research its causes, and . . ." She glanced uncertainly at Franc, and he silently nodded. "Well, somehow we made a mistake that caused history to be changed, so that when we tried to return to our future . . ."

"You crashed in 1998," Murphy said, "but now it was a different worldline than the one you left behind." Again, the attentive pause, but this time his mouth dropped open in surprise. "There was a major war in the middle of the twentieth century, wasn't there? Between Germany and the rest of Europe, with the United States, Russia, and Japan eventually becoming involved. Right?"

"That's correct," Franc said. "You mean that didn't happen in your worldline?"

Murphy shook his head. "Germany annexed Austria in 1938, but that was as far as it went. The destruction of the *Hindenburg* was the turning point for the Nazi regime. After that, the German resistance movement rose against the Nazis, and it wasn't long before the Vatican began secretly funneling aid to a Catholic underground organization known as White Rose."

Hearing this, Franc felt a chill run down his back. Suddenly, he recalled the conversation he'd had with William Shirer in the bar at the Frankfurter Hof. The journalist had mentioned something about meeting with Catholic clergymen who were . . . how had he put it? . . . concerned about recent events. "Were they successful? White Rose, I mean."

"Yeah, sure. It's in all the history books . . . or at least, the ones I read. A few days after Germany took over Austria, the resistance staged a mass protest in Berlin. When the Gestapo arrested their leaders and publicly executed them, it touched off riots all across Germany. Nazi headquarters in major cities were torched, prominent party members were shot in their homes . . . overnight, the whole country turned against the Nazis. It ended when Adolf Hitler was assassinated by a conspiracy of his own generals, and after that the government fell apart pretty quickly. Their leaders were rounded up, or at least the ones who didn't escape the country, and most of them put on trial and hanged or imprisoned. By then, the German army had retreated from Austria, and by 1940 it was all over." Murphy seemed mildly surprised. "You mean it didn't happen that way in your worldline?"

"No Second World War." Lea was incredulous. "That means . . . no development of rocketry, no invention of the atomic bomb . . ."

"Sure, we got those," Murphy said. "The U.S. tested the first atomic bomb in 1945. It was supposed to be dropped on Japan during the Pacific War, but President Truman opted for invasion instead. Russia sent the first satellite into orbit in 1960, and we launched ours a few months later. In 1976, America, Germany, and England sent a five-man expedition to the Moon, but that was the only time we . . ."

"When was the first computer invented?" Vasili asked.

"If you mean the very first one, that was designed by Charles Babbage sometime in the 1820s, but it was never actually . . ."

"No, I mean the ones that caused an information revolution in the late twentieth century."

"Desktop computers?" Murphy shrugged. "I bought mine in '91. A DEC Spectrum. One of the first on the market. Why?"

"I'm beginning to see a pattern." Franc picked up a branch, fed it into the bonfire. "With the exception of the atomic bomb, there wasn't major technological progress during the 1940s. Without World War II, there wasn't an urgent need for the V-2 rocket or the Enigma codebreaker. Manned spaceflight and microelectronics were eventually developed, but at a much slower pace."

"You mean, it happened sooner than that?" Murphy was outright astonished, and just a little envious. "If your worldline is that different, you must have had people living on the Moon by the end of the twentieth century."

"Well, not really," Lea said. "We didn't build the first lunar colony until . . ."

"Never mind that now." Franc didn't want to get sidetracked. "When I met you . . . when I first met you, I mean . . . you mentioned something about an Office of Paranormal Sciences. What's that?"

"OPS? It's . . ." Again, there was an abrupt silence as Murphy listened to the voice in his head. "They . . . the ones you call angels, I mean . . . say that's important. They don't say why, but I guess this is another point where the worldlines diverge."

"Go on." Franc struggled to remain patient. "What's different?"

Murphy stared into the fire for a few moments before he answered. "I think . . . I mean, I think it has to do with something that happened while I was in college. Sort of a social trend or a fad or whatever you want to call it, but in the seventies and eighties a lot of people started getting interested in psuedoscience. Astrology, ESP, channeling, dowsing, all that stuff . . ."

"UFOs?" Metz asked, giving a meaningful glance at the others.

"UFOs, sure. Seemed like everyone you knew had seen one, or at least knew someone who had seen one." Murphy glanced in the direction of the *Oberon*. "Guess they weren't that far off. But the biggest part of it was what people called lost German science . . . the crap a lot of the Nazis believed in."

"I don't understand." Lea shook her head.

"Ariosophy, the hollow earth theory, using pendulums for decision-making, the world ice doctrine . . ." Murphy picked up a stick, prodded the bonfire's embers. "It was all bullshit, of course, but a couple of best-sellers were published which claimed that the Nazis achieved scientific breakthroughs that were deliberately suppressed after the fall of the Hitler regime."

"Makes sense." Lea absently rubbed a forefinger across her lips. "Without a major European war or the Holocaust, the Nazis might not have been as stigmatized in the West as they were in our worldline. Some of the things they believed in might have been romanticized."

"That's what happened, exactly." Murphy nodded. "Psuedoscience became popular, and it led people in the United States to demand that the government do more to investigate . . . y'know, that sort of thing." His expression became grim. " So while NASA was being cannibalized and the National Academy of Sciences was begging for chump change, Congress founded OPS. I took a job with them because it was either that or flip burgers at McDonald's."

He shook his head at the memory. "The irony of all this was that, while Americans were going nuts over Nazi pseudoscience, the Germans themselves were racing ahead of us in terms of technological progress. So was England, France, Italy . . . first it started with basic research, then it went to product development, and finally it reached consumer goods. Got to the point that if you wanted a half-decent car, you had to buy European. Good ol' Yankee know-how became knowing how to get the best deal from an Audi or BMW salesman . . . and then you guys crashed in '98, and that changed the ball game."

"That's the part I don't understand," Franc said. "If the U.S. had fallen so far behind, how were you able to develop time travel?"

"Blue Plate was . . . well, it was done on the bootstrap principle." Murphy picked up a branch, broke it over his knee, tossed the short end into the fire, and used the long end to poke at the embers. "You know the idea of someone trying to jump up by pulling at his bootstraps? No? Well, it's sort of the same thing . . . if you can do it, you've taught yourself a new trick. The final objective of Blue Plate was figuring out time travel . . . because, y'know, if y'all were able to accomplish it, then that meant it must be possible . . . but the point was using this as a means of developing new technologies that would once again put the U.S. ahead of Europe. We needed a goal, and being the first country to accomplish time travel was it. Like the Manhattan Project all over again, only this time we didn't have to worry about nuking anyone. War without casualties."

"So Blue Plate was a crash program," Vasili said.

"It started out that way, but it turned into a long-term effort. Theory is one thing. Putting it into actual practice is another." Murphy tossed the stick into the flames. "Still, we didn't do too badly. The underlying principles were well established, of course, and many physicists had already spent considerable effort refining Einstein's work. It was mainly a matter of figuring out how to implement them, and then developing the hardware. We were ready for our first full-out test by . . ."

He suddenly stopped as if he had just heard something, then his face changed. "Oh, my God," he whispered, his voice quiet with horror. "I didn't know . . ."

"Know what?" Franc reached forward to grasp his arm. "What didn't you know?"

"We were too early," Murphy said. "We were much, much too early . . ."

Cold night lay across the Nevada desert. Pale moonlight glazed the distant slopes of the Papoosa Mountains, and an occasional errant breeze kicked up sand from the dry lake bed. A good night for secrets, for impossible things to become reality.

Standing at the edge of the long desert airstrip, Murphy sipped black coffee from a foam cup as he watched helicopters make a final low-level sweep across the foothills northeast of Groom Lake, their searchlights prowling the boulders and crevices of what had become unofficially named Freedom Ridge. UFO buffs had discovered the ridge about thirty years ago when it still lay in the no-man's-land bordering the Nellis Test Range and used it as a vantage point for observing activity at this remote Air Force test site. After too many people began coming out here, the Air Force managed to persuade various congressional committees to expand the test range to include Freedom Ridge. The flying-saucer groupies retreated to Tikaboo Peak, yet that lay twenty-five miles from Groom Lake, too far for any meaningful observation, and even the most inquisitive of them no longer dared to hike into the restricted area. Nonetheless, the military always took the precaution of making sure that the adjacent hills were deserted before any test flights; there was no telling who might be camped out there, crouched beneath camouflage tarps with high-power telescopes and tripod-mounted cameras.

Murphy smiled at the thought. If so, he wished them luck. If there was anyone lurking on Freedom Ridge tonight, they were about to witness history being made, for not since the first prototype stealth aircraft had been developed had anything like this flown out of Area 51.

He turned to gaze upon the complex sprawled across the southeast side of the dry lake. Sodium-vapor lights illuminated a collection of low-built concrete office buildings, military barracks, machine shops, radar dishes, and fuel depots, all surrounding several aircraft hangars, the largest of them spacious enough to hold a C-5A Galaxy. As he watched, its doors were being slowly rolled open, revealing the massive black shape within.

"Time to rock," he murmured.

Murphy took a last sip from his coffee, then tossed out its lukewarm remains and began sauntering back toward the hangar. The wind chose that moment to snatch at his baseball cap; he managed to grab it before it went dancing off across the desert, yet not before his hair, which he had allowed to grow out in the last few years, was blown from beneath its cover. Steven had given him the cap last summer when he had gone down to Brooklyn to visit him and his family. Murphy wasn't much of a baseball fan, truth be told, but he had let Stevie take him to a Mets game if only to make up for all the times he had ducked Little League playoffs and day-trips to Boston to catch the Red Sox.

He scowled as he pulled the hood of his old Army parka over his head to keep the wind at bay. It was only slightly less cold than Donna's voice the terrible night she demanded a divorce, barely more than fourteen months after they moved to Massachusetts. She took Steven with her when she moved back to upstate New York, and it was nearly two years before the court granted him full visitation rights; by then, his son had become alienated from his father, his ex-wife little more than a ghost seen through the living-room window of her second husband's house in Syracuse. During the entire time, he had never been able to tell either one of them what he was really doing during all those eighteen-hour, seven-day work weeks he spent at ICR. No wonder she had left him; he couldn't blame her for doing so. Yet losing Donna hadn't been nearly as painful as the distance he had placed between him and Steven. Twenty-six years later, and the only tangible evidence he had that his son hadn't utterly disowned him was a Mets cap . . .

God, he silently prayed, *please don't let tonight's test be a washout. I've sacrificed far too much already.*

Although a small crowd of military officials and civilian scientists had gathered outside the hangar, no one noticed Murphy until a soldier in desert camies spotted him strolling toward them. Murphy had partly unzipped his parka and was still groping for his ID badge when an Air Force general walked over to intervene.

"At ease, Sergeant," he said. "He's one of us." The soldier cast Murphy a look of silent admonishment, then released his hand from his holstered sidearm, saluted the general, and walked away. The officer watched him go, then turned to Murphy. "Didn't I tell you to keep your badge in plain sight at all times?"

"Sorry, Jake," he murmured. "Just went out to see if I could spot any UFOs." He gave him a wry grin. "Say, you don't have any hidden around here, do you? I read this book once that said . . ."

"Cut it out." The general wasn't amused. "This is a high-security area. You can't just wander off without letting anyone know where you're going."

"I'll keep that in mind," Murphy said. "My apologies. I'll ask permission next time."

As he closed his parka once more, he sourly reflected upon the fact that his relationship with Jake Leclede was nowhere near as informal as the one he had enjoyed with his predecessor. It had been almost three years since Baird Ogilvy had suffered a fatal stroke while playing golf in Florida, but Murphy still mourned his late friend as if he had only passed away last week. General Leclede had taken over as Blue Plate's military director shortly thereafter; he had kept the project going, a remarkable feat considering that it had already cost the taxpayers nearly $60 billion and its original timetable had long since been thrown out the window, yet never once in those three years had he and Murphy ever gone out for beer and barbecue, as Murphy had frequently done with Baird. Indeed, it had taken two months before Murphy felt comfortable addressing the younger man by his first name.

"Please see that you do." Then Leclede relented a little. "There's your baby," he said, nodding toward the aircraft being towed out of the hangar. "Ready for the big moment?"

Murphy didn't answer immediately. It was difficult to find the right words, although "baby" wouldn't have been one of them.

The SR-75 Penetrator was a sleek black condor, its titanium fuselage just over 160 feet in length, the span of its delta-shaped wings 97 feet from the sharp edges of its upward-canted winglets. Retractable canards folded outward from either side of its three-seater cockpit; the airscoops of its turbo-ramjets were large enough to swallow a man whole. Formerly code-named Aurora, the SR-75 had been a highly classified military secret, its test flights from Area 51 responsible for many of the UFO sightings from Freedom Ridge, until its existence had been reluctantly acknowledged shortly after the turn of the century when it flew reconnaissance missions during the Russian conflict.

Even then, only one of the massive planes had ever been built; although capable of achieving hypersonic velocities in excess of Mach 3.5, its intense infrared signature and the noise it made at cruise speed made it easily detectable by ground forces.

Yet it wasn't the SR-75 that attracted Murphy's attention, but the smaller aircraft riding piggyback on a saddle-like pylon atop its upper fuselage. An unmanned lifting body 42 feet long, it vaguely resembled a silver manta ray, yet it lacked engines and, despite the oval porthole at its tapering prow, a cockpit capable of carrying a pilot. Nonetheless, it could have been any sort of experimental aircraft, save for the three small humps just aft of the cockpit.

The Pentagon had code-named the second craft Jade Lantern, yet Murphy and everyone else intimately associated with Blue Plate, with the sole exception of General Leclede, referred to their creation by a simpler name: Herbert. Herbert as in Herbert George Wells, the author of a novella that had given rise to the entire notion of time travel almost exactly a century before Blue Plate had been set into motion. Murphy had reread *The Time Machine* at least a dozen times during the last twenty-six years; more than once, lying awake at night, he had shared imaginary conversations with Mr. Wells. The military could call his creation Daffy Duck for all he cared; for him, Jade Lantern was Herbert, plain and simple.

"Yeah," he said, "I'm ready."

They watched as a yellow tractor towed the SR-75 across the concrete apron to edge of the airstrip. The runway lights came on, a double row of red lamps receding for three miles in either direction, as the tractor released the plane from its yoke. There was a loud whine as the pilot powered up the turbines, then the Penetrator began to taxi toward the southern end of the airstrip. From his briefing, Murphy knew that the enormous plane would need every inch of the six-mile runway in order to achieve takeoff.

"Okay, time to head in." Leclede prodded Murphy's arm. "We can watch from inside."

"Why can't we stay out here?" Murphy looked around, saw that most of the onlookers were heading toward the nearby operations building. "Is this dangerous or something?"

"Only to your ears. See those guys?" He pointed to a handful of jumpsuited ground crew standing near a candy-striped rescue vehicle. They were fitting ear protectors over their caps. "When this thing takes off, it's like standing next to a space shuttle during launch. If you don't want to lip-read for the next few days . . ."

"Right." At age 66, Murphy was proud of the fact that he hadn't yet lost his sense of hearing.

He followed Leclede through the security door, then climbed the stairs to an observation room on the second floor. Everyone who had been on the apron was now gathered in front of a row of plate-glass windows. The inside lights had been turned off, and it took a moment for his eyes to adjust to the gloom, but the airstrip was clearly visible by its runway lamps. The voices of the tower controller and the SR-75 pilot came through speakers in the ceiling:

"Runway check, Farm."

"Runway clear, Janet Two."

A pause, then: *"All systems green-for-go, Farm. Request permission for takeoff."*

"You have permission, Janet Two. Happy trails."

"Thank you, Farm. We're rolling."

For nearly half a minute, Murphy couldn't see anything from the southern end of the runway. Then he began to hear a thin, high-pitched whine which quickly escalated into a howl as, all of a sudden, the SR-75 raced out of the darkness, its tricycle landing gear barely touching the ground as it hurtled past them. At that instant the whine dopplered into a thunderous roar that shook the window and made him instinctively cup his ears. He caught a fleeting glimpse of the flickering red torchlight of its afterburners, then the massive aircraft disappeared from sight.

"Wheels up, Farm."

"Farm, we've started the clocks," a new voice said. "Both are synched and running."

"Copy that, Janet Two."

Leclede unclasped his ears as he turned to him. "They're away. All right, Zack, it's your show now."

"Thank you, sir," Murphy muttered. He wondered how long that state of affairs would last. Not very much longer, if the test was a success . . .

They trotted back down the stairs, then crossed the operations building to an unmarked door guarded by an Air Force sergeant in camo gear. The general flashed his ID at the sentry; he saluted, then stood aside to let them pass. The room resembled a miniature version of Mission Control at Johnson Space Center; wide and dimly lit, the only light came from ostrich-neck lamps over the workstations arranged across the floor, its consoles winking with diodes, the CRTs casting a blue glow across the faces of the half dozen men and women seated at the carrels. The room was made more crowded by the military men gathered in the rear; Murphy had to push past a couple of Air Force officers just to get to his station.

"How're we looking, Ev?" he murmured as he pulled off his parka and took his seat.

"So far, we're golden." Everett Backofen, the bearded young black man on his left, pointed with his pen toward a computer screen. It displayed a row of multicolored vertical bars, each pulsing slightly beneath a horizontal row of numbers that changed slightly with each passing moment. "We had a little spike about a minute ago, but I think that was just caused by g-force during takeoff. Otherwise, everything's nominal. Herb's staying within his parameters."

"Good deal." Murphy turned to the prim middle-aged woman sitting to his right. "Dorie, how's telemetry?"

"We're getting downlink now." Doris Gofurther gently massaged her console's trackball, and a tiny arrow leaped across her screen to a miniature pair of video images, both depicted in ghostly monochromatic shades of gray and black. She clicked once, and the one on the left expanded to show a vague form crossed by flickering lines of static. "There's the rear-cockpit view," she murmured. "I think I can clean it up a bit."

"Do that, please. This looks like its coming from Mars." Murphy studied the TV image of Herbert as seen from the backward-facing third seat of the SR-75. Even aided by starlight enhancement, it was difficult to make out the drone. "Ev, keep an eye on Herbert and tell me if he spikes again." He allowed himself a smile. "And whatever you do, agree on which direction you want to go."

Everett scowled as Doris chuckled under her breath, but no one else overheard the private joke. Which was just as well. Murphy had worked with Everett and Doris on Blue Plate for several months before he recognized the puns inherent in their last names. It was ironic that two of the physicists involved in the first attempt to penetrate chronospace would be named Gofurther and Backofen, but Murphy had long since decided to accept it as a good omen.

Pulling on a headset, Murphy opened the spiral notebook in front of him and ran his finger down the checklist. He studied the plan for a couple of minutes, listening to the reports coming from the other controllers in the room, then he glanced up at the pair of digital chronometers positioned on the far wall of the room, just below the strategic display of the SR-75's flight plan. The clock on the left showed elapsed mission time as recorded by the SR-75; at this instant, it read 00:10:47:02. The one on the right, which showed the elapsed mission time as independently recorded by Herbert's onboard computer, gave an identical reading. Both clocks had been synchronized to a tenth of a second, and both were set to begin recording the moment they were triggered by the mission specialist in the rear-facing backseat of the SR-75. Redundant recording systems had been built into both the Penetrator and Herbert, yet this was the one he and his team would monitor during the course of the experiment.

A faint rumble passed through the walls of the room. Murphy looked again from his notebook as the floor trembled beneath his feet. "Janet's gone Mach," an Air Force lieutenant seated at the carrel in front of Everett reported, his right hand clasped over his headset as he studied the radar panel before him. "Altitude 22,000 feet, range 10 miles."

Murphy nodded. Like a hawk rising on desert thermals, the SR-75 was ascending in the steep gyre which would keep it above Area 51 even as it headed for the the stratosphere. Through his headset, he periodically heard the pilot's terse voice as he communicated with the tower. The men in the back of the room murmured to one another, and Murphy was all too aware of General Leclede standing directly behind him, watching his every move. Murphy wished he could rid the room of all of them, Leclede included, but since there was no way he could do that, he nervously tapped his pen against an armrest and waited.

Eight minutes later, they heard the pilot's voice again: *"Farm, this is Janet Two. Angels one hundred and holding position. Waiting for your word, over."*

"We copy, Janet. Transferring com to Barn."

"Janet, this is Barn," the lieutenant said. "Stand by for preliminary test, over."

"Roger that, Barn, we copy."

"Okay, we're on," Murphy said. "Doris, how are we looking?"

"Good visual contact." The TV monitor clearly showed Herbert reflecting the moonlight as it rode its saddlelike pylon on the back of the mother ship. Murphy smiled with satisfaction; they had deliberately picked this night for the test to take advantage of the full moon. "Activating onboard cameras," she added as she flipped toggle switches on her console. A moment later, a second monitor lit, revealing the SR-75's forward fuselage as seen from Herbert's nose. "Flight recorders running, we've got good downlink."

"Very well." Murphy turned a page of his checklist, took a deep breath. "Everett, bring the SDM online up to fifty percent, then hold for check."

Everett said nothing, but Murphy noticed that he quickly wiped his palms across his jeans before he laid his hands on the slidebars of his console. "SDM up to fifty," he said softly as he gently raised the power levels of the spacetime displacement module within Herbert's fuselage. The bar graphs on his screen rose halfway up the screen, then obediently stopped. "Fifty and holding," he murmured. "All levels within safe parameters."

They spent the next few minutes conducting a last-minute diagnostic check of all of Herbert's major systems. Finding no problems at their end, they waited another minute for the SR-75's crew to conduct their own checks. "All right," Murphy said at last. "Gentlemen, ladies . . . if you're ready?"

Everett gave his board a final lookover, then nodded. Doris slowly let out her breath, then gave him a thumbs-up. They were even more anxious than he was, if such a thing were possible. He glanced over his shoulder at Leclede, but received no solace from the general's stoical expression. "All right," he said, turning back to his console. "Lieutenant, tell them we're ready for the drop."

"Janet Two, we're ready for deployment," the lieutenant said tersely into his mike. A moment passed. "Commencing countdown . . . ten . . . nine . . . eight . . ."

At zero, there was a brief flash of pyros as Herbert was detached from the back of the SR-75. Murphy heard mild applause from behind him as the drone lifted away from the Penetrator. Its wings waggled briefly as it caught the larger aircraft's slipstream, then the screen on the left went dark while the right showed the vague image of the black ship peeling away.

"Janet Two moving to safe distance," the lieutenant reported. "Herbert at 100,000 feet and holding altitude, eight miles downrange."

For the next few moments, the drone would remain at its present altitude, gliding at the edge of the stratosphere a little more than sixteen nautical miles above the desert, before it began its long plunge back to the ground below. Which was exactly what they wanted: a high-velocity fall toward a large gravitational mass.

"Everett, bring the SDM up to 100 percent," Murphy said. "Arm master program, execute on my mark.

Backofen's hands flew across his console. "SDM at 100 percent, master program loaded and armed, waiting your mark."

"Doris . . . ?"

"Telemetry locked, clear fix, recorders running."

"Lieutenant?"

"Janet Two reports safe distance at 90,000 feet, two miles west from Herbert. They say they can see it clearly. Ground radar tracking both bodies."

"Commence countdown on my mark." Shoving back his chair, Murphy quickly moved to the lieutenant's side. Leaning over him, he saw two distinct blips on the screen: Herbert in the center, the SR-75 just below it. He felt men pushing against his back as they tried to get closer, but he paid no attention to them. He glanced at the twin mission clocks on the wall. Both read the same: 00:23:18:46. He waited until they were at ten seconds short of the minute . . .

"Mark!" he snapped.

"Go on mark!" Backofen jabbed switches on his console. "T-minus ten . . . nine . . . eight . . ."

Murphy checked the mission clocks one more time, then he pointed his finger at a blank area on the radar screen, directly to the right of Herbert's blip. "Watch that," he whispered to the lieutenant. "Don't blink, not even for a second . . ."

"I'm watching it, sir," the lieutenant murmured. His right hand was clasped over his headset, listening to the voices from the SR-75.

"Five . . . four . . . three . . ."

"I'm getting a corona!" Gofurther yelled.

Murphy kept his eyes locked on the radar screen. "C'mon, sweetheart . . ." he whispered.

"Two . . . one . . . !"

"There it is!" Doris shouted.

At that instant, a third blip appeared near the right edge of the radar screen, directly behind the drone.

"Zero!"

Herbert's blip suddenly vanished . . . but the one behind it remained.

"It went through!" the lieutenant yelled.

"I saw it!" Doris pointed at her TV screen. "It vanished! It disappeared, then it . . . Zack, I saw it!"

The SR-75 pilot was saying something, but his voice was lost in the uproar that swept through the control room. Murphy stared at the radar, watching as the new blip traced a solitary trajectory across the scope, while the men around him shouted in astonishment, cheered, clapped him on the back. It was then, and only then, that he raised his eyes to the mission clocks.

The one on the left, displaying the time as perceived by the SR-75, was 00:24:03:24. Yet the one on the right, which relayed the time as transmitted from Herbert, was 00:24:02:24.

For an instant barely longer than a human heartbeat, Herbert had caused a wormhole to open around itself, then slipped back in time . . . for one second.

In that single second, there had been two Herberts: the one about to disappear into chronospace, and the one that had appeared out of nowhere some distance behind it.

When that happened, the ground radar had briefly captured both of them as two distinct blips.

Not only that, but Herbert's nose camera had picked up an image of itself . . . as seen from behind.

"Jesus . . ." Feeling his knees beginning to buckle, Murphy sagged against the lieutenant's console. He made himself take deep breaths; for a moment he thought he was going to faint. All around him, Air Force officers were shouting at one another as Doris and Everett hugged each other. He looked around, caught the expression on General Leclede's face. It was nauseatingly smug, and Murphy had little doubt that, when he made his final report, he would claim most of the credit for the success of Blue Plate.

All of a sudden, the one thing he wanted most in the world was to get a breath of fresh air.

"Save the data," he said to Everett, "and transfer control to the tower for the flyback phase." Then, muttering apologies no one seemed to hear, Murphy grabbed his parka and began pushing through the crowd. Leclede called after him, but he pretended not to hear as he headed for the door.

The chill desert air was a relief after the closeness of the control room. The wind had died down, so he pulled his Mets cap out of his pocket and put it on. The ground crew was gathered at the edge of the airstrip, waiting for Herbert to make its remote-controlled landing. Murphy hoped he would get a chance to inspect the drone for himself before it was spirited away into one of the hangars. However, now that the Air Force knew the secret to temporal transit, everyone involved in Blue Plate—or at least the civilian R&D staff—would be retired. Herbert had just become a military asset.

Now he knew how J. Robert Oppenheimer must have felt . . .

The hell with it. Thrusting his hands in his jacket pockets, Murphy strolled away from the operations building. Perhaps it was just as well. He had never intended to let Blue Plate consume nearly one-third of his life. All he had ever wanted to do was figure out how someone with a handful of archaic pocket change and a passenger manifest for the *Hindenburg* could wind up in 1998.

"So now you know," he murmured to himself. "Happy?"

Well, at least he had a military pension coming to him. The mortgage was paid off, and he had come to enjoy living in New England. Perhaps he could see Steven a little more often, and take in a few ball games at Shea Stadium . . .

Suddenly, everything around him seemed a little brighter, like the first light of dawn breaking over the secret airstrip.

Murphy was looking at the ground when it happened. He saw his own shadow stretching out before him, much as if a great floodlight had abruptly been switched on the night sky. Then he heard men shouting behind him . . .

"Hey, what . . : ?"

"Holy shit, it's . . . !"

"Nuke!"

Murphy whipped around, stared upward. For an instant, he, too, believed that the nuclear bomb had exploded far above the desert. He instinctively covered his eyes with his hands, yet there was no sound, no concussion, only a hellishly bright glare from high in the night sky, as if a miniature supernova had suddenly erupted far out in space . . .

"Oh, my God!" someone yelled. *"Look at the Moon!"*

Lowering his hands, Murphy gaped at the sky. The source of the glare was coming from where he had seen the Moon only a few moments ago . . .

He was still staring at the white-hot orb in the sky when something flashed directly behind him.

At first, he thought it the high beams of a nearby truck. He couldn't take his eyes off the sky, and so he ignored it, but then the illumination grew brighter, overwhelming even the distant cataclysm, and suddenly he was aware of nearby men pointing his way, shouting in horror . . .

Murphy turned, found himself standing at the edge of a

ball of light that had materialized directly behind him. Within the center of the aura was a vaguely man-shaped form, yet with wings that rose above its head.

Raising his hands against the blinding glare, Murphy started to step back, yet any thoughts of escape came much too late. The corona stretched out to envelop him, the figure within its nucleus reaching toward him . . .

The taloned hands that grasped his arms weren't human.

"You say you saw it?" Lea asked. "The angel, I mean . . . you got a close look at it?"

"Only for a second." Murphy shrugged as he continued to gaze into the remains of the bonfire, as if summoning memories from its dying embers. "I'm not sure what happened then, except that I blacked out. When I woke up, I was here." He gestured toward the fire. "I guess it left that to keep me warm. I don't why or how, but I knew that you were coming, so I just waited until . . ."

"Tell us about the angel," Lea said quietly. "What did it look like?"

Murphy shivered. "Lady, whatever it was, it was no angel. More like a reptile on two legs, with a face that would give you nightmares." His brow furrowed as he thought about it. "About seven, eight feet tall, with long fins coming from its back. Leathery brown skin, long bony skull, black eyes. Evil-looking, but . . ."

He said nothing for a moment, then he shook his head. "But they're not evil. At least, that's what it's telling me now. It says it's deliberately hiding its appearance because we associate ugliness with evil, and it's aware that we'd consider it repulsive." A corner of his mouth inched up-ward. "I can't fault its reasoning. From the brief glimpse I got of the one who brought me here, it's about the worst thing I can imagine."

The sun was starting to set behind the western side of the valley. With twilight closing in, the rings in the sky were beginning to change color, assuming muted shades of orange and red which vaguely resembled the autumn fo-liage that once graced New England at this time of year. "But these . . . this race, I mean . . . weren't they the ones who destroyed the Moon?" Franc picked his words care-fully, mindful that someone or something else was eaves-dropping on their conversation. "That led to the destruction of our planet and everyone on it. Why shouldn't we regard them as evil?"

Again, Murphy shut his eyes and lowered his head, as-suming the posture of someone listening carefully to an un-seen voice. "It insists that it's . . . I mean, they . . . that they're not evil," he said at last, speaking haltingly. "It's speaking about its race. It claims that they're destroying our satellite . . . the Moon, I mean . . . was necessary in or-der to prevent us from damaging spacetime any further. If they hadn't done so, we would have caused more para-doxes to occur, until . . ."

"So they snuff out five billion people?" Metz hurled a stick into the fire as he angrily rose to his feet. "You just can't . . . I mean, who the hell elected them God? They're . . ."

"For chrissakes, shut up!" Hands clamped over his ears, Murphy bent forward as if in physical pain. "I didn't . . . I can't . . . !"

"Vasili, sit down, please." Lea moved closer to Murphy, wrapped an arm around him. "Take it easy," she whispered. "It's all right. Don't rush, just take it easy . . ."

She shared a meaningful look with Franc. Like him, she was concerned about the precarious state of the scientist's sanity. No wonder he was frightened; for the last couple of hours, he had been forced to act as a telepathic channel between them and the . . . whatever it was. Indeed, watching Murphy lay his head against Lea's shoulder like a frightened child, Franc wondered whether he wasn't close to snapping.

Metz regarded Murphy with disgust and loathing. "Sure," he muttered. "Take it easy. We've got all the time in the world . . ."

"Be quiet." Franc locked eyes with the timeship pilot. "And if you can't be quiet, then go back to the *Oberon*." Perhaps there was some sort of washover effect associated with the telepathic link; whenever any one of them—particularly Vasili, the most irritable of all—had become emotionally aroused, Murphy had reacted accordingly. He returned his attention to the old man cradled in Lea's arms. "Dr. Murphy," he said as quietly as he could, "if you need some rest, we can continue this later."

Like it or not, he had to admit that Metz was right on one point: they did have all the time in world. Indeed, time was the only thing Earth had left. . . .

Murphy surprised him by shaking his head. "No, no . . . this is too important. I just . . ." Opening his eyes, he sighed as he sat up straight. "I'm sorry, it's just that . . . when I woke up this morning, it was 2024, and everyone I knew was still alive. And now . . ."

"We understand," Lea said. "If it makes any difference, it hasn't been easy on us, either."

Daylight was beginning to fade, the fire quickly dying out. Franc found another branch behind him; he broke it in half, fed it into the low flames. "So tell us everything you know," he said quietly, giving Metz an admonishing look. "We won't interrupt again, I promise."

"Everything I know. Sure . . ." Murphy pulled off his baseball cap, absently ran his fingers across its embroidered logo. "Okay, for what it's worth, here goes . . ."

Again, a reticent moment. "The angels . . . the aliens, or whatever you want to call them . . . are an old race. I mean, very old . . . they were technologically sophisticated when we were still in the Stone Age. They won't tell me what they called themselves, or where their home world is . . . *was,* I mean . . . located, because they wish to keep that secret. However, they will tell me that, for about a thousand years . . . our years, I think . . . they dominated a quadrant of our galaxy nearly two hundred light-years in diameter, and had explored most of the rest."

"So they were conquerors," Metz said flatly.

Franc shot him another look, but Murphy didn't seem to mind. "At first they were, yeah, but as time went on they abandoned their ambitions for empire. I guess you could say they grew up. They realized it wasn't much fun being the toughest kid on the block, because then nobody wants to play with you." He smiled. "Those are my words, not theirs, but you get the point."

"We do," Franc said. "Go on, please."

"There's lots of intelligent races out there . . . no surprise, I guess we knew that all along . . . but very few reach the point of achieving space travel, and even fewer learn how to construct wormholes. The ones that do, though, soon discover that if they're able to bridge space, they're also able to bridge time. If you're able to accomplish one, then the other comes naturally. Follow me so far?"

"Sure. That's the way it happened with us," Franc said. Lea shook her head at him, but he ignored her. At this juncture, there was no sense in hiding anything from Murphy; his future was their past, even if on different worldlines, and right now none of them had anything left to lose. "Where we came from, humankind launched the first hyperspace starship in 2257. We started exploring chronospace about twenty-five years later. And you're right . . . we've found plenty of eetees, but none of them are capable of space travel, let alone time travel. So far, at least."

Murphy nodded. "Well, they're out there . . . or at least, the ones that survived. Apparently, time travel is the most dangerous thing an intelligent race can discover, because a civilization capable of exploring its own history is likewise capable of changing it. When that happens, more often than not they destroy themselves . . . and sometimes they take other races with them."

He paused to heave a deep sigh. "That's what happened to the angels. First they began to explore chronospace, and then they began to change history. They caused paradoxes which eventually destroyed not only their own home world, but also those of all the worlds within their dominium, until virtually none of their kind were left. The handful that remain alive have taken it upon themselves to make sure that this sort of thing never happens again."

"So they're . . . what? Time policemen?" Metz was skeptical. "Who appointed them?"

Murphy raised his shoulders in an empty shrug. "If you want to call them that, sure. They seem to see themselves as sentries. As for who appointed them . . . I guess you could say they appointed themselves." He smiled slightly. "Maybe you can argue with that idea, but I don't think they'd listen."

"Well, if they're listening right now, I've got two words for them . . ."

"Metz, just shut up, all right?" Franc glared at Vasili until he pointedly turned away, then he turned back to Murphy. "So they see themselves as sentries. You mean they monitor other races who are capable of time travel?"

"Exactly, yes. When they detect disturbances in space-time, they investigate the source, and if it turns out that they're being caused by the creation of artificial wormholes, then they observe the race that constructed them to see if they're using them to travel back in time. If that's the case, and if they believe that race is acting irresponsibly then they . . . well, they intervene."

"That explains the other sightings." Lea hugged her knees as she stared into the fire. "The angels other CRC expeditions reported . . . those were angels observing us, trying to determine what we were doing." She looked at

Murphy. "We've seen them before, but we didn't know what they were."

"So now you know." Murphy picked his cap, pulled it back on his head. "When you went back to 1937, you caused a paradox that changed history and created a new worldline, and when you crashed in 1998, you caused yet another paradox which compounded the mistake. . . .

"Which, in turn, led to humankind developing time travel two hundred years earlier than it originally had," Lea finished.

"Right, and the angels couldn't let that happen. They . . ." Murphy closed his eyes, his mouth pursing in concentration. "They say that . . . a race that values free will as strongly as we do . . . cannot be allowed to pursue time travel. We simply aren't mature enough to understand the full consequences of our actions. This was why we had to be stopped."

"Even at the cost of our world," Franc said softly.

"Yes. Better the destruction of one world than many others." When he raised his head once more, there were tears at the corners of his eyes. "They waited until we tested Herbert, and then they obliterated the Moon. Most of the human race perished virtually overnight when its larger fragments rained down on Earth. The survivors held on for a few more years, but by then the global climate had been damaged beyond the point of recovery. I'm . . . I'm the only person from my time to survive, and that's only because the . . . I can't call them angels, sorry . . . they brought me here, to tell you these things."

"And that's it?" Metz swung around to face him. "That's all? 'Hey, we blew up the Moon and killed everyone on your planet . . . sorry, but it's your fault'?" He gestured to the nearby bluff. "Give me one good reason why I shouldn't pitch you over."

"It's not his fault!" Franc scrambled to his feet.

"Stop it, both of you!" Lea yelled. "Vasili, he didn't . . . !"

"No," Murphy said quietly. "He's right. It is my fault."

Remaining seated on the ground, he gazed into the amber coals. "I shouldn't have kept that piece of paper," he continued, "but I did, and I shouldn't have let myself be forced into telling anyone else where I thought it came from, but I did, and I shouldn't have spent the next twenty-six years developing Herbert, but . . ."

He let out his breath, wiped tears from his face with the back of his hand. "Well, you know the rest. Maybe you guys made a mistake in 1937, but five billion people died because of mine." He nodded toward the desolate valley spread out below them. "The folks who lived down there used to be my neighbors. Believe me, I'm tempted to jump myself. If it wasn't because of . . ."

He stopped, listening for a few moments, then he looked up at them again. "But the aliens didn't bring me here just to fill you in. They say this is just a warning . . ."

"A *what?*" Metz demanded.

"Yeah, I know . . . some warning, huh?" Murphy smiled bitterly. "But they say that we can still undo everything, if we're willing to do so."

He clambered to his feet, brushed off the back of his trousers. "I'm not hearing any more voices, but I think I can figure out the rest. This is only one worldline, right? That means there's others. Other possible futures, I mean." He glanced in the direction of the *Oberon,* then looked at Franc. "If I'm not mistaken, then that thing can still go back in time, right?"

"Sure. Of course it can," Franc said. "It's a little damaged, but it's still flightworthy." He turned toward Metz. "You can finish the repairs, can't you?"

The pilot slowly let out his breath, scratched the back of his head. "Well, I don't have . . ." Then he nodded. "Sure, I can do it. Give me a few hours, and we'll be ready to go. What are you getting at, Lu?"

Franc didn't reply at once. Stepping away from the fire,

he looked at the obscene rings rising above the distant mountains. The last light of day was upon them, the cold wind beginning to rise once more.

"We made a mistake back there," he said at last. "Now we're going to undo it."

Thursday, May 6, 1937: 6:43 P.M.

Twilight was settling upon the New Jersey coast, the last light of day gilding the breakers as they crashed against the beach. A pair of children building a sand castle at the edge of the surf heard the growl of engines just before an immense shadow passed over them. Looking up, they gaped in astonishment, then leaped to their feet and screamed in delight as a great silver ellipse cruised overhead.

The *Hindenburg* had been following the Jersey shoreline for nearly three hours now, its arrival at Lakehurst Naval Air Station delayed until weather conditions at the landing field improved. Yet now, just as the giant airship was approaching the town of Forked River, its radio operator received word that visibility was up to five miles and the winds had fallen to twenty knots. Captain Pruss told the pilots to set course for Lakehurst.

On the beach far below, one of the children watching the LZ-129 noticed a brief shimmer in the air just above the dirigible's upper fin. Mystified, he raised a hand to shade his eyes against the sun, yet as the enormous craft slowed to make a northwest turn, the odd illusion was lost to sight. The boy decided his eyes were playing tricks; he grinned as the zeppelin gradually swung around. One day, he silently swore to himself, he was going to ride in one of those things. . . .

"We're almost in position," Metz's voice murmured in Franc's headset. *"Ready back there?"*

Sitting in the open airlock hatch, his feet dangling over empty space, Franc watched as the *Hindenburg* grew steadily closer. Although invisible, the *Oberon* still cast a shadow across the dirigible; the timeship hovered barely thirty meters above the airship, and now he could clearly see the ribbing beneath its taut canvas skin.

"Ready," he said. The palms of his hands were slick with sweat; he wiped them across his trousers, and tried not to think too much about what he was about to do. "Just get me above the aft flue vents."

The *Hindenburg* swelled in size. Now he couldn't see the ground anymore, only a vast expanse of silver-painted fabric. There was a limit to how close Metz could dare to bring the *Oberon* before the electromagnetic field of its negmass drive began to interfere with the dirigible's diesel engines, yet he also had to take advantage of those few precious minutes over the town of Forked River when the airship made its turn toward Lakehurst, during which time it would be moving just slowly enough for Franc to safely board her.

At least, so he hoped. . . .

"Ready for the ladder?" Murphy squatted on the other side of the hatch, clutching a floor bracket as he held onto a rolled-up fire ladder with the other. The ladder, along with the crowbar Franc had slipped into his belt, had come from the ruins of a hardware store just outside Amherst. Franc nodded, and Murphy tossed the ladder through the hatch. Its stainless-steel links rattled as it fell, then it snapped tight against the bracket.

Murphy leaned over the hatch and peered downward, then looked up again. "You're about five feet short," he shouted, trying to make himself heard over the keening whistle of the wind. "Can we get any closer?"

Franc glanced over his shoulder at Lea. Squatting on the deck behind him, her face pale, she shook her head. He looked down just as the rectangular slotted panels of the flues came into sight. They were almost on top of the airship. He reached forward, grabbed the top rung of the ladder

"I'm over the vents!" Metz yelled. *"Go now!"*

He felt Lea's hand on his shoulder, as if she was trying to hold him back. Yet he couldn't allow himself the luxury of hesitation. Franc sucked in his breath, then gently pushed himself off the deck and through the hatch.

There was a terrifying instant when, as he put his weight on the ladder, the rungs gave a few centimeters of slack. He fell backward, yet he held on, and then the ladder took his weight and stopped his plunge. The wind ripped at his clothes and threatened to tear him off; he felt a surge of panic, and for a few moments all he wanted to do was cling to the rungs until Lea and Murphy hauled him back to safety. . . .

"Franc, you can do this." Lea's voice was calm presence in his headset. *"You can do this. Don't look down. Just take it one step at a time, and don't look down."*

"Right . . . okay." Franc carefully lowered his right foot, blindly searched for the next rung down until the toe of his shoe found it. He reluctantly released his hand from the top rung, then reached down to grab the one below it. "Got it."

"That's it," Lea gently coaxed him onward. *"You're doing fine. Now the next rung . . ."*

Step by step, one rung at a time, Franc made his way down the ladder. It seemed to get easier the farther down he went; although he dared not look down, he could hear the roar of the *Hindenburg*'s engines from far below. He glanced up, and almost laughed at what he saw: a square-shaped hole in the cloudy sky, with Murphy and Lea staring down at him. Incredibly, they were nearly twenty meters away.

"You're almost there," Lea said. *"C'mon, you can do it. . . ."*

'Franc, you're going to have to hurry." Metz's voice came over the comlink. "They've completed the turn-around, and they're throttling up the engines."

Now the ladder was swaying like a pendulum. Metz was trying to keep up with the *Hindenburg.* Disregarding Lea's admonition, Franc looked down. Six more rungs to go, but the bottom of the ladder was still two meters above the top of the dirigible. Worse, the leading edge of the vertical stabilizer was less than thirty meters away. If the ladder swung any closer to it, he would be hurled against the huge fin.

"Franc, hurry!"

No time. Franc scrambled down the remaining rungs, until his feet had nowhere left to go. He took a deep breath, hesitated for a second, then released the ladder.

Much to his surprise, he managed to land on all fours. The envelope sagged beneath him, the rough canvas burning the palms of his hands. The slipstream threatened to grab his body and pitch him over the side. Franc flattened himself against the envelope, then began to crawl forward on his stomach, making his way toward the twin flue vents rising from the top of the airship.

The hinged wooden cover of the left vent was frozen shut. Still hugging the airship, he pulled the crowbar out of his belt and shoved the narrow end forward, wedging it between its cover's lower slats. Bracing his feet against a rib and rising on his knees as high as he dared, he leaned against the crowbar, putting his weight upon it. The cover creaked in protest, then popped open, exposing the dark shaft below it.

Franc tucked the crowbar back into his belt, then crawled to the open flue, straightening up just long enough to swing his legs over the opening. As anticipated, the shaft's interior was lined with ladder rungs. He swung himself over the side, relieved to get out of the wind.

"Okay, I'm in." He glanced at the Rolex watch he had borrowed from Murphy; it read 6:55. "By my reckoning, I've got thirty minutes."

"You don't have that long," Metz said.

"I know. Hang on as long as you can."

The flue shafts were designed to vent hot air from the airship's interior, but the *Hindenburg*'s riggers also used them to inspect and repair the hydrogen gas cells. As Franc hastily climbed down the narrow shaft, he listened for sounds from the catwalk below. He heard no one, but that was to be expected; the crewmen would be at their landing stations by now, either in the airship's nose or in the small auxiliary control compartment located in the bottom of the lower stabilizer.

The shaft intersected the middle catwalk leading through the axial center of the ship. Franc carefully opened the hatch, peered first one way and then another, before creeping out onto the triangular gangway. All around him, enormous gas cells made of hand-stitched lengths of sheep gut gently groaned like the lungs of a leviathan, held in place by skeletal duraluminum rings and weblike strands of cable. Franc jogged down the catwalk, heading for the stern. He prayed that his footsteps wouldn't be heard by anyone below, yet there wasn't enough time for stealth.

He found the narrow ladder leading upward along the side of Cell Number Four. Somewhere up there was the place where the rigger had hidden his bomb. He dug into his trouser pocket, found the miniature electromagnetic sensor Metz had given him. It came from *Oberon*'s repair kit; Vasili used it to detect faulty wiring, and now Franc hoped that it would help him pinpoint the location of the explosive device concealed within the hydrogen cell.

Yet he didn't need the sensor after all. Halfway up the ladder, he heard the gentle rustle of loose fabric. Clutching the sensor between his teeth, Franc scaled the last few rungs until he found the place where Spehl had used a knife to slice open the canvas outer envelope of the cell. He had stitched shut the opening, but the flap had come loose; as Franc gently prized it open, he found the bomb taped within.

It was a crude device: a small cotton bag filled with phosphorus, with wires leading into it from four flashlight batteries, which in turn were rigged to a Swiss nautical watch. "I've found it," Franc said as he carefully inspected the bomb.

"You've got nineteen minutes." Metz's voice was terse. *"Franc . . ."*

"Shut up. I'm working." Disarming the bomb without knowing exactly what he was doing would probably be a lethal mistake, but that wasn't his intention. Peering closer at the watch face, he observed that its bevel was set at eight o'clock. The bevel must be the timer; when the minute hand touched its red index, the positive and negative wires connected to them would touch, and an electrical charge would be sent into the phosphorus charge. He reached into the gas bag and, ever so carefully, turned the bevel counterclockwise until the index rested above 7:25.

He slowly let out his breath. Regardless of his reasons for doing so, he had just condemned thirty-five people to death. On the other side of the airship, he and Lea would be standing on the Deck A promenade, watching through the windows as the *Hindenburg* coasted across New Jersey farmland toward Lakehurst. This time, though, they would get what they had come here for . . .

"Okay, it's set," he said as he closed the flap.

"Hindenburg's dropping altitude," Metz said. *"I can't stay here much longer."*

Franc checked his own watch: 7:07. Only eighteen minutes left. He swore under his breath as he began to scurry back down the ladder. Eighteen minutes. Perhaps there was marginally enough time for him to get back to the flue vent and climb back up to the top of the airship before the bomb went off, yet if he tried to board the *Oberon* while it was within sight of the airfield, it was almost certain that some-one on the ground would spot him. Although the timeship was cloaked, he wasn't; eyewitnesses would later report, and newsreel cameras would verify, the strange sight of a man climbing a ladder into thin air.

"Get out here," he said. "I'll find another way off."

"Are you out of your . . . ?"

"Don't argue. I'll signal when I get away. You can pick me up somewhere else." He was at the bottom of the ladder now. He looked both ways, but no one else was on the cat-walk. "Signing off now. If you don't hear from me again . . . well, get Lea to figure it out. She'll know what to do."

Metz was saying something, but Franc didn't have time to listen. He pulled off the headset and shoved it in his pocket, then began jogging down the catwalk, heading for the bow.

When the *Hindenburg* crashed, it went down fast. Thirty-seven seconds after the explosion, it was . . . *would* be-come . . . a flaming heap of collapsing metal. Although the stern hit ground first, most the survivors had been in the front of the ship, save for a handful of crewmen stationed in the lower rudder who managed to escape before they were burned or crushed to death. So his best chance of survival was to reach the lower decks at the front of the ship. How-ever, he couldn't allow himself to be seen in the passenger compartments, and too many crewmen would be in their quarters behind B Deck.

If he correctly remembered the ship's layout, though, there was an airshaft between Cells Twelve and Thirteen which led down the lower catwalk forward of B Deck, just aft of the freight and mail rooms behind the control car. Two cargo hatches were located there; if he could get that far, he might be able to hide just long enough to wait out the explosion.

Franc was three-quarters of the way down the catwalk, just past the airshaft between Cells Ten and Eleven, when he heard German voices echoing from somewhere close by.

He stopped, breathing hard as his eyes sought movement within the dimness of the envelope. He couldn't see anything, but now he could hear footsteps against metal. There was someone—two engineers, probably—on the middle catwalk just ahead of him.

Franc turned, walked as quickly and quietly as he could back to the airshaft he had just passed. With a final glance over his shoulder, he opened its hatch, then ducked inside, pausing on the ladder just long enough to close the hatch behind him.

The shaft thrummed loudly with the muffled noise of the nearby engines; the ladder vibrated beneath the palms of his hands as he climbed downward. If his memory didn't betray him, this shaft would take him to the lower catwalk running along the keel, just aft of the crew quarters. Yet there were no cargo hatches in this part of the ship's underbelly, and he didn't dare enter the forward engine cars, where engineers would be stationed during landing operations.

Like it or not, he'd have to make his way through the crew quarters to B Deck of the passenger compartment.

Reaching the bottom of the airshaft, he placed his ear against the hatch, yet the engine noise made it impossible for him to hear anything. Time was running out; he'd have to take a risk. Franc started to open the hatch, then he felt a familiar weight against his thigh. Looking down, he saw the crowbar he had taken with him from the *Oberon,* still dangling by its crook from his belt. Useless now, and an unexplainable liability if he was caught with it. Franc pulled it out of his belt, hung it from a ladder rung, then opened the hatch.

The keel catwalk was deserted. On either side of its triangular framework were the massive horizontal cylinders of fuel and water tanks; directly ahead lay a duraluminum bulkhead, with a closed door leading into the compartment beyond. Franc shut the airshaft hatch, then walked quickly past the tanks to the door. From somewhere far above, he could hear the indistinct voices of the engineers he had managed to avoid. He hesitated at the door, his right hand on the knob, then he turned it and pushed open the door.

The warmth of the crew quarters was welcome after the unheated chill of the envelope. Franc quietly shut the door, then put his back against the plaster wall, straining to listen for human sounds from the narrow passageway that lay before him. Just ahead, he heard vague movement within a cabin to the right; as he crept closer, he saw that its door was open. The crew quarters were almost empty, but not quite.

Holding his breath, walking on the balls of his feet, Franc stole toward the cabin door. Peering through the jamb, he spotted a young, dark-haired man bending over an open suitcase. Franc recognized him as one of the dining-room stewards; indeed, it was the same one who had escorted him and Lea to the *Hindenburg* when it left Frankfurt. With the ship coming into Lakehurst, his job was done, and now he was packing for a weekend layover in New York. Humming to himself, he turned toward the closet, and Franc took the moment to tiptoe past his cabin. *Auf wiedersehen, mein freund,* he thought. *Hope you get out alive.*

At the end of the passageway was another door. Franc carefully opened it, then slipped through into the corridor that lay beyond. He immediately recognized his surroundings; he was on B Deck, across from the keel corridor which ran through the lower deck of the passenger compartment. Just ahead was the landing that led to the stairs to A Deck; just around the corridor behind them, below his feet, were the twin gangways, still folded up within the airship's belly.

He sighed with relief as he sagged against the bulkhead. Perfect. All he had to do was remain hidden for . . . how long? Realizing that he hadn't checked the time in at least fifteen minutes, he raised his wrist, glanced at Murphy's watch.

It read 7:23. Two minutes, perhaps less. The *Hinden-*

burg should be hovering directly over the landing field by now, slowly easing its way toward the mooring tower.

Just enough time to make contact with the *Oberon*. He pulled the headset from his trouser pocket, clasped it against his face. "*Oberon*, do you copy?" he said softly.

A few precious moments passed, then he heard Lea's voice. *"Franc, where are you?"*

"B Deck, near the gangway," he whispered. "Where are you?"

From down the corridor, he could hear the clatter of cookware in the galley; somewhere above, the faint voices of passengers watching from the A Deck promenade as the Navy ground crew ran to grab the ropes that had just been dropped. Up there, he would be touching the rim of his glasses, surreptitiously checking the time, murmuring something to Lea about getting ready. . . .

"We've landed at the northern edge of the airfield," Lea said. *"Zack's coming to . . ."*

From the other side of the stairs, he heard a commode flush. A second later, the door to the nearest of the three toilets on B Deck swung open, and a passenger stepped out into the corridor: a tall, gray-haired man, instinctively looking down to check the fly of his trousers.

Franc whipped the headset from his face, shoved it back in his pocket as he glanced first one way, then the other. There was no place for him to hide. All he could do was stay still, hope that he wouldn't be noticed.

Then the passenger turned to walk toward him, and Franc suddenly felt an icy chasm open in the pit of his stomach.

It was John Pannes.

For an instant, he believed it was he himself: the other version of Franc Lu, disguised to resemble one of the ill-fated passengers. Yet as the other man came closer, his eyes met Franc's, and there was no hint of recognition, no shock of seeing oneself. Pannes merely looked at him oddly, as if spotting a fellow passenger who had somehow escaped his notice during the past three days, then turned toward the stairs leading to A Deck.

As he put a foot on the first riser, though, Pannes paused to look back at Franc. "Can I help you, young man?" he asked politely.

"No . . . no, sir," Franc stammered. "Just . . . I'm just waiting, that's all."

Pannes nodded curtly. "One bathroom's as good as the next," he murmured, then he continued climbing the stairs.

Franc felt himself trembling as he watched Pannes disappear from sight. No doubt about it: that was the real John Pannes, the one who should now be in the twenty-fourth century, not taking a last-minute run to the toilet before the *Hindenburg* landed. Which meant that, one way or another, Franc wasn't aboard, nor was Lea . . .

"Oh, my God," he whispered. "What went. . . . ?"

There was a loud, hard thump from somewhere above and behind him, as if a great weight had suddenly landed on the back of the airship.

An instant later, the deck pitched violently beneath his feet, and Franc was hurled face forward. His breath was knocked from his lungs as he hit the carpeted floor, and for a moment he lay dazed and confused. Then he heard men and women screaming in terror as the airship made a sickening lurch and the deck tilted farther forward, throwing him against the floor even as he tried to clamber to his knees.

He managed to twist to one side just before he hit the bulkhead below the stairs. A sharp pain in his left shoulder; he ignored it as he grabbed a railing and staggered to his feet. Now he could feel heat against the back of his neck—something above him was burning—and all around him he heard heavy objects crashing against walls. From down the corridor behind him, men were shouting in German.

Another lurch, and now the airship plummeted downward. He grabbed a post next to the gangway stairs, clung to it with both hands as the ceiling behind him caved in.

Through the cellon windows on the other side of the lower promenade, he caught a brief glimpse of the ground rushing toward him; he turned away just as the windows shattered.

Glass lacerated the side of his face, ripped skin from the backs of his hands. He was deafened by an infernal roar: burning hydrogen, groaning metal, voices raised in horror. Somehow, though, the gangway remained intact; dislodged by the impact, it gaped open, an exit from hell barely discernible through walls of acrid smoke.

Franc released the post, covered his face with his arms, charged headfirst down the gangway, Flaming debris rained down around him as his feet touched the ground; through heavy smoke, he caught glimpses of men and women running for their lives.

Hands above his head, gagging and coughing against fumes that threatened to fill his lungs, he lurched away from the flaming wreckage, ignoring the hands of the sailors who sought to rescue him.

He was safe. He had escaped. The *Hindenburg* had exploded, just as history had predicated it would. . . .

And just as before, something had gone horribly wrong.

"And you're sure it was him?"

"Of course, I'm sure," Franc insisted. "I wore his face for four days, didn't I? And he was so close I could have . . . *ow!*"

"Sorry." Lea withdrew the antiseptic spray, carefully examined the burns across his shoulders and back. Stripped to his briefs, his twentieth-century outfit now tattered rags heaped on the floor, Franc sat on one of the couches in *Oberon*'s passenger compartment, leaning forward on his elbows as Lea tended to his injuries. "Hold still," she said. "I haven't gotten to your legs yet."

Franc grimaced, but obediently stretched out his legs as she bent down next to him. "I wouldn't complain if I were you," Murphy said. "You're lucky to have gotten out of there at all. That thing went up like a furnace."

Lea nodded, but avoided looking his way. The scientist was sitting on the couch formerly occupied by Tom Hoffman. Although she had balked at leaving his body behind, Vasili had pointed out that, if Murphy was going with them, there wasn't room for Tom's body aboard the timeship. In the end, they had buried him on the summit of Mt. Sugarloaf, near the base of the ruined observation tower.

"You should have been inside," Franc hissed between his teeth as Lea sprayed the backs of his thighs and knees. He hadn't even realized that he had suffered first-degree burns until he made it back to the *Oberon*. He looked down at Lea, then reached forth his hand to gently stroke her hair. She looked up sharply, and he smiled at her. "I'm glad it didn't work out the first time," he said softly. "I don't think . . . I'm not sure we would have escaped."

For a moment it seemed as if she was repressing a shudder, then she deliberately looked away. "Pass me that, will you?" she said to Murphy, pointing to the open med kit on the floor. Murphy leaned and pushed the box toward her. "So you don't think the Pannes got away? You said he was on the stairs to A Deck when the bomb went off."

"It's possible, but . . ." Franc shook his head. "If this is the way it happened . . . the way it should have happened, I mean . . . then they didn't escape. According to the historical record, he remained aboard to find his wife, and neither of them got out in time." He looked down at the floor. "It's too bad, really," he added quietly. "I only met him for a moment, but he seemed like a good man."

"Then consider yourself lucky," Murphy said.

Franc nodded. He knew that he had been lucky, in more ways than one. Knowing that Franc was in serious trouble, Metz had gambled that *Oberon*'s chameleon would render it invisible to everyone at the naval station, and touched down at the edge of the landing field only a few hundred meters from the mooring tower. Since their attention had been focused entirely upon the *Hindenburg,* though, no one noticed the slight disturbance it made during touchdown. As soon as Franc was away from the crash scene, Murphy exited the *Oberon,* found him at the edge of the crowd, and, under the cover of twilight, guided him back to the timeship. Once they were both safely aboard, Metz lifted off again.

As makeshift rescue operations went, this one had gone off without a hitch. Yet every time Franc permitted himself to think about it, whenever he allowed his mind to reach back to those terrifying seconds—although they seemed like much longer: minutes, even hours—it all came rushing back. The hollow thud of the explosion, the violent plunge, the falling debris, the screams . . .

"Just be still," Lea murmured. "This should only tickle." She had pulled on a pair of thin plastic gloves, and now she was carefully opening a small, hermetically sealed canister. She noticed Murphy's curious gaze and held it up for him to examine. "Naderm-310 . . . nanocellular epidermal restorative. It's like a lotion. We, uh, put it on, and it . . ."

"Repairs the skin, using microscopic nanites." Absently stroking his beard, Murphy inched a little closer as he studied the canister with fascination. "C'mon . . . it's not like I'm a caveman, you know."

"You had this?" she asked, raising a skeptical eyebrow.

"Not yet, but an Italian biotech firm was supposed to be working on it." Murphy watched as Lea carefully poured a little of the lotion onto Franc's back. "Where did this stuff come from?"

"I don't know. The Moon, probably." Lea began massaging the Naderm into the red and blistered parts of Franc's skin. "So let's try to figure this out. If you saw John Pannes on the *Hindenburg,* then that means you and I never got aboard. Right?"

"That's the way it seems to me." Franc scowled as he resisted the urge to reach back and scratch at himself. She was wrong; the lotion didn't tickle, it itched, like a bad case of poison ivy. "And that shouldn't have happened, if we've returned to our original worldline . . . that is, the worldline we left in 1937."

"No, that would have been the changed worldline." Murphy raised a finger. "The way you've explained it to me, in Worldline A, the *Hindenburg* explodes on schedule, killing John and Emma Pannes along with a couple of dozen other people." He raised another finger. "And in Worldline B, the changed worldline, the two of you are on board instead of the Pannes, but screw things up so that history is altered and this new worldline is created . . . the one I'm from. Have I got it right so far?" Franc nodded. "So this shouldn't be Worldline B, because you went back and changed things back to the way they should be, in Worldline A."

"Yes, but when we boarded the *Hindenburg,* we were in Worldline A." Lea finished spreading the lotion on Franc's back and moved to his legs. "The night before we left Frankfurt, we arranged for the Pannes to be abducted on their way to the opera. We wouldn't . . . we couldn't have boarded the airship if that hadn't succeeded."

"So now we're in Worldline C . . . a completely new worldline?" Franc suddenly felt hollow inside. "Then all this has been for nothing."

"No . . . no, not necessarily." Murphy stood up and walked to the wallscreen. It displayed Earth from low orbit, where Franc had taken the *Oberon* after leaving New Jersey. The elderly scientist had relished the ride into space; now he gazed down upon Earth, marshaling his thoughts. "You say you reset the bomb from eight o'clock to seven-twenty-five, right? It may have been that the bomb was set for eight o'clock all along, but the timer simply malfunctioned and it detonated prematurely. The fact that Lea encountered this Spehl guy may have been totally coincidental."

"That doesn't work," Lea said. "When we checked the recordings made by the divots we placed in the envelope, we saw Spehl go back to Cell Number Four shortly before the *Hindenburg* reached Lakehurst."

"Yes, but did you actually *see* him reset the timer? Or was he simply checking to make sure the bomb hadn't been discovered?"

"That . . . seemed to be the logical assumption," Franc said reluctantly.

Murphy smiled and shook his head. "Never assume anything . . . and that includes the notion that Worldline A has been altered because of events that occurred prior to today."

Lea's mouth fell open; for a moment she stared at Murphy. Then, without bothering to put away the Naderm, she got up from the floor. "Is there something wrong?" Franc asked.

"No. Stay here. I'll be right back." She left the compartment, heading in the direction of the monitor room.

"Nice lady," Murphy said once she was out of earshot. He returned to his seat and sat down. "Your girlfriend?"

"No . . . not really." Franc impulsively reached down to scratch at his legs, then thought better of it and removed his hand. The nanites were rebuilding his burned flesh; the pain had disappeared, but the constant itch threatened to drive him out of his mind. "What gives you that idea?"

"She was worried sick about you while you were aboard the *Hindenburg*. I thought she was going to tear your pilot's head off when he told you that he couldn't maintain position any longer." Murphy's eyes crinkled with amusement. "Maybe it's none of my business, but I think she cares a lot for you. If you don't know that . . . well, like my generation used to say, you need to get a clue."

Franc felt his face growing warm. "Let's get back to what we were talking about before," he said, deliberately changing the subject. "What did you mean by that?"

"What I meant was, you're working under the assumption that this worldline may have altered solely because of actions you may or may not have taken before this date. Given the nature of your previous visit, I don't blame you for reaching that conclusion." Murphy shook his head. "But you're forgetting that nearly three hundred years have gone by since 1937 and 2314. In other words, something in the future may prevent you from coming back here. And that . . ."

"Would you two mind keeping quiet? I can hear you all the way across the ship."

They looked up, saw Metz standing in the doorway. Pleading exhaustion, the pilot had chased everyone from the control room shortly after the *Oberon* had achieved orbit, then shut the door to get some sleep. Now he stood just outside the passenger compartment, bleary-eyed and slump-shouldered, plainly irritated at having been wakened.

"Sorry, Vasili," Franc said. "We didn't know we were keeping you awake."

"You are," Metz grumbled. "If you're going to talk, at least . . ." Then he looked aside. "Hey, what's the . . . ?"

"Excuse me." Lea pushed Metz aside and stuck her head through the door. "I've found something in the library you need to see," she said to the other two. "I think it's important."

As they entered the monitor room, Murphy was the first to react to the person whose image was displayed on the wallscreen. "Hey, that's me!" he exclaimed, then he peered a little closer. "At least I think that's me. I've never worn a mustache."

"No, that's definitely you." Lea squeezed between him and Metz to take her place at the pedestal. "Just on the chance that I might find something, I entered your name into the library system. There was nothing under Zack Murphy, but then I tried David Zachary Murphy, and . . ."

"Man, I'm so young." Murphy walked around the pedestal, stared at the archival still photo. The image was of a youngish-looking man in his early forties, wearing a black turtleneck under a tweed sports coat, casually leaning against a bookshelf. "Where did this picture come from? I mean . . . do you know when it was taken?"

"According to the file on you, it was taken in 2001." Lea ran her hands across the pedestal keypad, and the photo diminished slightly in size as a horizontal bar of text appeared on the right side of the screen. "It comes from the dust jacket of the novel you . . . or rather, David Z. Murphy . . . published that year. *Time Loves A Hero,* it was called."

"I . . . I published a . . . ?"

"No," Lea said, "*he* published a novel. David Z. Murphy, the man you became in Worldline A." She scrolled down the text, reciting the vital statistics as they appeared. "Dr. David Z. Murphy was a NASA astrophysicist until 1998, when he left the space agency to become a freelance writer. He wrote nonfiction articles for various magazines until, in 2001, he published his first work of fiction, *Time Loves A Hero,* a science fiction novel . . .'"

"Wow," Murphy breathed. "I used to love science fiction." He grinned at Franc and Vasili. "They hated the stuff at OPS, but I . . ."

"Wait a minute," Lea interrupted. "It becomes more interesting. *Time Loves A Hero* was acclaimed as a major work of . . . get this . . . time-travel literature, in which the existence of UFOs was interpreted as being timeships from the distant future."

Murphy's expression changed from pride to horror. "Oh, no."

"The novel was well received," Lea continued, "and when interviewed by a science fiction fanzine . . . I have no idea what that term means . . . Murphy claimed that it was inspired by things he observed while working for NASA. In fact, he first delineated his theories regarding a possible connection between UFO sightings and time travel in an article published in 1998, in a magazine called *Analog* . . ."

"I used to read that when I was a kid." Murphy shook his head in puzzlement. "But this is too weird to be a coincidence. A science fiction novel about timeships . . ."

"Hold on. It gets even more weird than that." Lea touched the pedestal again and the screen changed; now it displayed a photograph of an athletic-looking man of indeterminate age, wearing a laboratory coat and standing near a large cylindrical machine. Although taller and with curly blond hair, his face bore a striking resemblance to Murphy's.

Lea didn't say anything for a moment. She watched Murphy as he studied the man on the screen. For a few seconds, he didn't seem to recognize him . . . then his mouth fell open in astonishment.

"That's Steven," he whispered. "My son."

"Yes, it is," she said quietly. "Steven David Murphy . . . or rather, Dr. Steven D. Murphy, Ph.D., associate director of the Hawking High-Energy Physics Laboratory. Your son, Zack . . . or rather, your son in this worldline."

"Steven became a physicist?" Murphy laughed out loud. "But he didn't . . . I mean, he couldn't . . . Christ, I love my boy, but he can't balance his checkbook, let alone an equation. In fact, he has no interest in science at all. Where I come from, he's a truck driver in New York . . ."

"In this worldline, it appears things went a bit differently." Lea shrank the photo, adding text to the right side of the screen. "According to CRC historical data, Steven Murphy was inspired by his father's writings to pursue a career in the sciences, particularly high-energy physics. After receiving his doctorate from Princeton, he went to work at Lawrence Livermore National Laboratory, then moved to Hawking Station when it was built on the Moon in 2047 . . ."

"That's . . . c'mon, there must be a mistake!" Murphy pointed a shaking finger at the screen. "Steven . . . at least my Steven . . . was born in 1989! If that picture was taken in 2047 . . ."

"Actually, it was taken in 2049, two years after he became its associate director." Lea smiled at him. "And you're correct . . . according to his biographical records, he was born in 1989 in this worldline as well." She glanced over her shoulder at Franc. "Do you want to explain this, or shall I?"

"There's been no mistake." Franc glided up behind Murphy, lay a comforting hand on his arm. "Beginning in the early twenty-first century, considerable progress was made toward increasing human longevity. Eradication of major diseases, cellular rejuvenation, gene therapy . . . it's a bit too long to explain. Trust me . . . he may not look it, but your son is sixty years old in that picture."

"In fact, he didn't die until 2152, at the age of 163," Lea said. "But that's not the point. According to CRC data, Dr. Steven Murphy was . . . pardon me, will become . . . one of the major theorists responsible for the practical development of time travel. His work at Hawking is directly connected to the invention of the wormhole generators."

No one spoke. The room went quiet as Zack Murphy stared at the image of the man who, following in his father's footsteps, would make profound discoveries that would inevitably lead to the development of time travel. His son, yet not quite his son, nonetheless responsible for a long train of events that, in the long run, would cause a paradox that would bring about the destruction of Earth itself.

"I'm . . . I think I'm. . . ." Murphy abruptly turned away, lurched to the side of the room. His face was ashen as he collapsed against the bulkhead; for a second it seemed as if he would retch, then his legs seemed to collapse beneath him.

Franc rushed to his side. "Easy," he murmured as he caught the old man by the shoulders, helped him slide down onto the floor. "Don't worry. It's going to be all right . . ."

"I don't see how." Silent until now, Metz nodded toward the screen. "Not if his son's one of the main people behind the discovery of time travel."

"But he didn't!" Lea turned toward him. "Don't you see? If John and Emma Pannes died on the *Hindenburg,* then that means Franc and I never got aboard, and the only way that could have happened is if we never left 2314! That must mean time travel was never developed in the first place!"

"So why are we here at all?"

"I don't know. I can't answer that." Lea raised her hands

in a helpless shrug. "I don't think anyone could. Maybe it's because of the laws of conservation of matter and energy, the fact that matter can neither be created nor destroyed. Even though there's been another paradox, we don't simply disappear because . . . well, because we're already here. Yet something must have happened . . . something *will* happen . . . which will prevent Steven Murphy from becoming the scientist who makes the conceptual breakthroughs that will lead to time travel."

"You might have something there." Franc stroked his chin as he regarded the image on the wallscreen. "You know," he said slowly, "there may be a common thread here." Turning around, he looked down at Murphy. Huddled on the floor of the compartment, his arms wrapped around his knees, the scientist once more looked as distraught as when they found him in 2314. "Zack, in your worldline—Worldline B, in 1998—you began work on a project that led to the development of time travel. That happened because you encountered us and therefore discovered that time travel was possible."

"That's . . . yeah, I follow you." Murphy seemed to stir himself from his misery. "I think I do, at least . . ."

"Stay with me. In this worldline—Worldline A, in 1998, the very same year—your counterpart also began work on time travel, although in an indirect way . . . he wrote a magazine article postulating that UFOs might be timeships. This, in turn, inspired your son . . . *his* son, I mean . . ."

"I prefer to think that's my son, thank you." Murphy smiled despite himself. "Stevie's a good kid, but his idea of intellectual discourse is comparing batting averages."

"What's a . . . ? Oh, right. Baseball." Franc waved it off. "Never mind. What I'm trying to say is, the point of conjunction between these two worldlines may not be the *Hindenburg* disaster, but rather you yourself."

Murphy raised an incredulous eyebrow. "Me? But haven't we already decided that the *Hindenburg* was . . . ?"

"No," Lea interrupted. "That was what we assumed,

certainly, but it may be that the different outcomes of the *Hindenburg* disaster were only a consequence of the paradox. The true cause may well be something different. Both you and David Murphy did things that resulted in . . ."

"Wait a minute. Hold on." Metz broke into the conversation. "Look, I'm not sure I'm following all of this, but aren't you missing something? If Murphy . . . the other Murphy, I mean . . . wrote an article about timeships being mistaken for UFOs, then where did he get the idea?" He looked at Murphy. "If he's as smart as you are, then something must have given him a clue . . . right?"

For the first time in several minutes, no one said anything. Lea fell silent as she turned back toward the pedestal, and Murphy stared up the photo of his alternative-worldline son. Franc finally let out his breath.

"I think we all know where this is going," he said quietly. "Whatever the reason, we're going to have to pay another visit to 1998 . . . *this* 1998, that is." He glanced at Metz. "Can we do that? Without crashing this time, I mean?"

"Sure." The pilot gave a weary shrug. "Why not? The coordinates are still entered, so we shouldn't have any problems."

"And what do you propose we do when we get there?" Murphy asked.

"We're going to have a little chat with you," Franc replied.

Murphy had just bought a hot dog from the pushcart vendor and was about to cross Independence to have lunch on a park bench in the Mall when he heard someone running down the front steps of the National Air and Space Museum.

He turned just in time to see Dr. David Z. Murphy come to a stop on the sidewalk only a dozen feet away. Behind him, a pair of nuns near the glass doors were glaring at him; a few feet away, the Washington police officer who had been carrying on a bull session with the vendor gave him a curious eye.

As David looked his way, Murphy stepped behind the hood of one of the school buses parked at the curb, ducking his head to avoid being spotted. Neither of the teachers taking a cigarette break in front of the bus noticed him, nor did the cop or the homeless man rooting through a nearby garbage can.

Murphy waited a few moments, then he cautiously emerged from hiding. He observed the younger version of himself striding the opposite way down the sidewalk; once past the last school buses, he dashed across Independence. Careful to remain out of direct line of sight, Murphy followed him across the street, and watched from a discreet distance as David began jogging down the Mall, heading in the direction of the M station.

For a moment, he had an impulse to follow him. It was a strange thing to see himself as others must have seen him twenty-six years ago: a time-dilated mirror image, observed from afar. So far as he could tell, there was no significant physical difference; indeed, he had recognized himself immediately. He would have liked to continue spying upon himself, yet at the same time, the eeriness of the situation left a cold sensation in his stomach.

Finding that he had lost his appetite, Murphy walked back to the Air and Space Museum and offered his hot dog to the homeless man, who regarded it with suspicion for a second before taking it from him with mumbled thanks. He reflected that he probably looked only a little less shabby: old Army parka, battered Mets cap, sleepless eyes. Probably just as well; it might help him fade into the background.

Yet that wasn't his immediate concern. Shoving his hands into his pockets, he walked up the front steps of the museum, then loitered just outside the front entrance. He didn't have long to wait; less than a minute later, Franc came out of the building.

The traveller pushed open the glass door carefully, glancing both ways. Once again, Murphy found himself marvelling at his changed appearance; when Franc had emerged from *Oberon*'s replication cell, Murphy couldn't quite believe this was the same man he had seen climb into the cylinder only thirty minutes earlier. True, he wasn't a perfect physical match for the author Gregory Benford— they had been forced to rely upon the biographical information in the timeship's library, which fortunately included a digital recording of the real Benford's voice along with a full-body photograph—but it was enough to fool anyone whom, they presumed, had never actually met the man. Yet one look at Franc's—or rather, Benford's—face told him that something had gone wrong.

"Which way did he go?" Franc asked quietly as he joined Murphy.

"That way." He nodded in the direction David had taken. "He ran out about two or three minutes ago, looked around, then took off down the Mall. He looked rather upset."

"That way?" Franc asked, and Murphy nodded again. "All right, let's walk the other way. Better hurry . . . he might be back any minute."

Zipping up the parka Murphy had purchased for him yesterday, Franc trotted down the steps. Murphy fell in beside him as he began marching up the sidewalk toward the Capitol. "What happened?"

"I'm not sure," Franc murmured. "He believed I was Benford when we met. I'd even say he was a bit awestruck, although he tried to hide it. We went to lunch, had a long conversation, and then . . ." He shook his head. "He made some references to Benford's work, and I think I gave the wrong answers."

"I was afraid that might happen." The biographical information had covered Benford's contributions as a physicist, but hadn't gone in great detail into his dual role as a science fiction author; Murphy had noticed the gaps when he and Franc were studying his background. Yet since the strategy had been for David Murphy to be interviewed by someone he would immediately recognize and trust, yet was unlikely ever to see again, Gregory Benford had been the best possible candidate, and Franc had undertaken the mission with the foreknowledge that a certain element of risk was involved. "He got suspicious, right?"

"It seems that way." Franc furtively glanced over his shoulder, then began walking a little faster. "He excused himself to visit the men's room and left the restaurant. I followed him, stayed back so he wouldn't see me, and saw him go to a phone and make a call. I decided that he might be trying to check up on me, so I waited until his back was turned, then I sneaked down the stairs."

"And he didn't see you?" *I would have,* Murphy silently added.

Franc shook his head. "No. I hid behind a post on the second floor and waited until he left the restaurant and ran back down to the first floor, then I came out behind him."

"You're lucky he didn't search the whole museum." Murphy smiled to himself. "I must be a little dumber in this worldline," he murmured.

Franc shrugged. "It's a big place. He wouldn't have found me." Then he sighed. "We can't afford for him to see me again, or at least in this persona. If he's discovered that I'm not Benford . . ."

"The way he flew out of there, I'd say it's a pretty good chance he has." Just ahead, on the other side of the street, lay the Capitol Reflecting Pool, its waters covered with a thin sheet of milky ice. Office workers and bureaucrats strode past it, the collars of their overcoats turned up against the brisk wind. "So what did you find out? Has there been another paradox?"

"No. Of that, I'm certain." Franc waited until a cab trundled past, throwing icy slush onto the curb, then he stepped off the sidewalk and crossed the street, heading for the broad terrace surrounding the pool. "He made it all up. It was a good guess, but nothing more than that. He hasn't seen any timeships, that's the main thing."

"That means we're in the clear."

"No, not quite. It only means that he doesn't know anything . . . or at least not yet. But I'm afraid this incident may lead him to investigate further, and if that's the case, it may lead him to conclusions that we don't want him to make." Franc shoved his hands deeper within the pockets of his parka. "We can't let that happen," he added quietly, looking down at the snow-covered ground.

Hearing this, Murphy stopped. Lost in his own thoughts, Franc walked a few more steps before he noticed that Murphy was no longer with him. He halted, turned around, gazed back at him. He didn't say anything, but simply waited.

"Are you saying what I think you're saying?" Murphy asked.

"I don't know," Franc replied. "What do you think I'm saying?"

"If you're saying what I think you're saying," Murphy said, "then this is where we part company. No thanks, I'm getting off here." He took a step back, half-intending to walk away as fast as he could.

"And where do you plan to go?" Franc pulled off his fake glasses and put them in his pocket. "You're a man who's already here. If you've got any identification, it's from twenty-six years in the future. I hope you're not planning on using it, because no one will ever honor it, let alone believe your story."

"I'll get by," Murphy said. "I've done well so far."

And indeed he had. After the *Oberon* landed the day before out on the outskirts of suburban Virginia, Murphy had left the timeship, taking with him the remaining reserves of 1937 American dollars and German marks left over from the *Hindenburg* expedition. After hitchhiking into downtown Washington, he visited a succession of rare-coin dealers until he found one willing to purchase his cache without asking many embarrassing questions. The currency was counterfeit, of course, but Franc had assured him that it was as authentic in appearance as the CRC's Artifacts Division could make it. After acquiring nearly $500 in trade, he visited a second-rate car-rental place and, using a photo-laminated credit card from his wallet to prove his identity, managed to lease an automobile. After that, a shopping trip to a mall outside Arlington, where he bought suitable clothing for Franc. This might not be the 1998 of his worldline, but he still knew how to get around.

"Maybe you will," Franc admitted. "You're a smart person." He fell quiet as a woman hastily strode past, then he walked a little closer. "But even if you do, where will that take you? You know how all this will eventually end."

"It doesn't have to be that way. A hundred . . . a thousand different things could happen that would prevent . . ."

"No." Franc shook his head. "I'm sorry, Zack, but you know better than that. You've seen the historical record. In a few years, David Murphy will publish a well-regarded science fiction novel which, in turn, will inspire his son to pursue time travel. Steven Murphy's theories will inevitably lead to the invention of timeships, which will result in Lea, Vasili, and me visiting 1937. The chain of paradoxes will begin there, and continue until . . ."

"Shut up!"

". . . And when it's all over, everything you've ever known, everyone you've ever loved, will be gone, and you'll be . . ."

Without really intending to do so, Murphy balled his right hand into a fist, swung it at Franc's face. He hadn't hit anyone since he was a teenager, though, and Franc saw it coming. He ducked the punch, but in doing so he lost his balance. His feet slipped on the icy sidewalk and he fell sideways, sprawling against the concrete basin surrounding the Reflecting Pool. He yelped in pain, then rolled away, wincing in pain as he clutched his left elbow

"Oh, Jesus!" His anger vanishing as suddenly as it had appeared, Murphy knelt down next to Franc. "I'm sorry, I didn't . . . I mean, I . . ."

"It's all right. I'm not hurt." Massaging his arm, Franc pushed himself up against the side of the basin. "I probably had that coming," he said, scowling as he gently flexed his bruised elbow. "If that's the best you can do, though, you've proven my point."

Murphy sat down on the wall. Like it or not, Franc was right. He was an old man . . . worse, an old man stuck out of time. For chrissakes, he couldn't even punch out someone anymore, not even in anger. If he was going to survive the winter streets of Washington in 1998, he was going to have to do better than that. A lot better.

"So . . . what's your idea?" he asked.

Franc didn't immediately answer. He gazed off into the distance, studying the thin spire of the Washington Monument at the far end of the mall. A few tentative flakes of snow were beginning to drift down from the slate sky. It was the beginning of a cold and sunless afternoon, with the threat of many more like it to come.

"There's nothing else I can do," he said at last. "At least, not now. I've got to return to the *Oberon*. You're going to have to take over from here."

"Okay." Murphy let out his breath. Like it or not, he was committed. "Now what?"

"Follow Murphy . . . David, I mean . . . after he leaves his office. He told me he rode the . . . the M, I think you call it? Is that a rapid-transit system?" Murphy nodded, and Franc went on. "He rode the M to work today, from where he parked his car in Virginia. Had something to do with local traffic conditions . . ."

"The Beltway." Murphy smiled. "Happens a lot around here."

"So I've been told." Franc reached to the front of his parka, unbuttoned its weather flap. "I want you to follow him from his office until you reach the place where he parked his car. Hopefully, the two of you will be alone by then."

"Then . . . ?"

"That's going to be the hard part." Franc unzipped the parka, thrust his hand inside. "But I'm going to give you something that will make the job a little easier . . ."

Consciousness returned as the gentle sensation of movement within darkness, interrupted now and then by an abrupt jar, a sporadic glimmer of light. From somewhere nearby he heard a wet flopping sound.

At first he thought he was at home and in bed—it was early morning, and Donna was nudging him awake; the alarm must not have gone off, and it was time to go to work—but then he opened his eyes and discovered the source of the sound: windshield wipers, brushing aside thick flakes of snow streaming past headlights like thousands of tiny stars.

Another pair of headlights appeared in the left lane, dazzling him for a few moments until they suddenly dimmed, then the other vehicle swept past. Through the windshield, he caught brief glimpses of lighted windows—farmhouses, a Mobil station, a Maryland Farms convenience store—which quickly passed by, disappearing like mirages into the cold winter night.

He was in the front passenger seat of his own car.

Murphy slowly turned his head, saw the old man from

the parking lot, his bearded face backlit by the dashboard. He drove with his left hand on the wheel, his right hand resting next to his thigh. Although Murphy wasn't aware of making any sound, the old man glanced his way, smiled slightly.

"You're awake," he quietly observed. "Feeling okay?"

He had a faint headache, but Murphy didn't answer at once. He looked to the right, peering through the side window. Wherever they were, it was out in the country—it looked like Virginia, but it could also be Maryland for all he knew. The headlights caught the reflective coating of a highway sign as it flashed by: *Route 234*. He knew the road; they were about twenty miles from Arlington.

"Don't worry," the old man said. "We're not far from home." He paused. "Bet your head hurts. Sorry about that. Don't you keep a bottle of Tylenol in the glove compartment?"

"Yeah," Murphy said, "I have some." His hands were folded together in his lap, but he was surprised to find that he could move them. His kidnapper hadn't bothered to tie him up. Which meant that, if he moved quickly enough . . .

"Don't even think about it," the old man said. "It's not a good idea."

"Think about what?"

The old man laughed: a dry, ironic chuckle, much the same as his own when he was amused by something which tickled him because it was so obvious. "Look at the speedometer," he said. "We're doing thirty-five right now. I'd drive a little faster, but the snow's coming down hard, and I don't think a plow's been this way in the last half hour or so. If you tried to grab the wheel, we'd probably skid out and go off the road. Or we might hit a car coming in the other lane. Either way, you'd kill both of us." He hesitated, then quietly added, "And jumping out is a bad idea, too. Remember what happened to Skip Baylor?"

Skip Baylor. Who the hell was . . . ?

A face flashed before his memory. Skip Baylor, one of his friends from junior high. A short, skinny kid with shag-cut blond hair. Used to love old Bruce Lee movies, especially when he was stoned. Skip was the class daredevil; he'd try anything once, so long as people were watching. One Saturday night, when Skip was out cruising with a bunch of guys, someone wondered aloud what it would be like to jump out of a moving car. Skip decided to give it a shot. He broke his neck and died instantly.

"How do you know about Skip?"

Long silence from the old man. "I know about a lot of things," he said at last, not unkindly, even a bit sadly. "Go on, get your Tylenol. It'll make you feel better."

Murphy reached for the glove box. His hand was on the knob when the old man spoke again. "It'll be stashed next to the New York and Virginia road maps. I think there's also an old Disney coloring book in there, along with some crayons. Steven liked to use them when you and Donna drove down to Florida to visit her mother, but even though he's grown out of them now, you haven't . . ."

"Who are you?" Murphy forgot about the glove box and the contents. "What are . . . who are you with? FBI? CIA? Army intelligence?"

Another dry chuckle, punctuated by a ragged cough. "None of the above. And, no, not the Russians or Mossad or . . . well, anyone you could think of."

"NASA," Murphy suggested.

"Gimme a break . . ." The old man gave him a skeptical look. "Unless, of course, you know something about NASA I don't." He waited a few moments for Murphy to answer, then he shook his head. "Okay, let's come clean here. I'm taking you someplace . . ."

"Where?"

"We're going to Manassas National Battlefield. It's closed this time of year, but someone's going to open the gate for us. My friends . . . our friends . . . are going to be waiting for us inside. They want to talk to you, David."

Despite the warmth of the car, Murphy felt a chill. "Who're your friends?"

"I could tell you, but you'd never believe me." The old man stared into the snow spiraling past the headlights. "I had trouble accepting it myself," he added. "It's that kind of thing. But you're going to have to trust me on this one . . . nothing bad is going to happen to you."

For reasons he couldn't explain, Murphy found himself beginning to trust the old man. By all logic, he knew that he shouldn't—after all, he had shadowed him on the train, trailed him into the parking lot, then somehow knocked him unconscious, after which he had abducted him and driven him clear out into the middle of nowhere (but not quite—hadn't he taken Steven out here a couple of times, using this route?). Yet his voice, his entire demeanor . . . it was much as if he was talking to a lifelong friend, someone he had known for many years. Every facial expression, every verbal tic, even the way he laughed, were strangely familiar.

And his face . . .

The Escort's high beams caught a large wooden sign on the right shoulder of the road: MANASSAS NATIONAL BATTLE-FIELD PARK. The old man began to slow down, easing his foot off the gas while not braking, just as Murphy himself would have done. "Here it is . . . Molasses Park." He glanced at Murphy. "Okay, for ten points, who used to call it that?"

"Stevie," Murphy whispered, feeling cold once more. "He still does."

The entrance came up, and the old man gently turned the wheel, steering the car into the snow-covered drive. He put his foot on the pedal again, and the car fishtailed a bit. "Damn," he mumbled. "Wished I'd . . . you'd bought snow tires for this thing."

"Sorry. Can't afford them."

The old man grunted as he turned into the skid. The car straightened out, then headed for the wooden gate which barred the park entrance. Yet now the gate was wide open; the Escort charged through, slewing snow as it passed the fieldstone fences on either side. "Not true," he said. "You have enough cash, but snow tires are one more expense you don't want to add if you didn't have to. I mean, this is Virginia, isn't it? Winter here isn't as bad as it was in Ithaca, when you had the old Volvo . . ."

Murphy looked at him sharply. "How did you . . . ?"

"Donna sometimes snores when she's asleep, and she doesn't like to make love while the lights are on, but she's got a thing for park benches. That's one of the reasons why you like coming out here." The old man flicked the wipers up higher. "On the way home, you always drop by a little roadside shack, where you can get fried clams and Stevie can use the pot. And sometimes you stop at the mall to rent a movie from Blockbuster. You always argue over what to get. She likes romantic comedies, but you prefer . . ."

"Who the hell *are* you?"

"You've got three guesses, and the first two don't count."

That had been one of Skip's favorite expressions.

The road was nearly invisible, but Murphy could make out the faint furrows of tire tracks; someone had come this way only a little while earlier. They followed the road into the park, passing trees whose branches sagged beneath thick blankets of snow, the headlights barely piercing the white squall. The road led them around a small hill toward a broad pasture; the headlights caught a metallic reflection: the rear bumper of another automobile, parked in the road just ahead.

The old man stopped behind the other car. "Okay, we're here," he said. He switched off the ignition, then opened his door. As the dome light came on, Murphy saw the odd gun with which he had been shot in the parking lot, nestled next to his thigh. The old man smiled as he picked it up. "Thanks for not making me use this on you again," he said, not pointing it at him. "I didn't like doing so the first time."

Murphy climbed out, shut the passenger door behind

him. Even in the darkness, he could make out the snow-covered hump of the other car. He expected someone to get out, yet no one did; so far as he could tell, they were all alone. "You said someone would be here," he said as the old man walked around to join him.

"You'll see." He pulled the bill of his Mets cap low over his eyes, then motioned for Murphy to follow him. "C'mon. This way."

Their boots crunched softly as they left the cars behind and trod into the pasture. Murphy's imagination briefly entertained a dark thought—his frozen corpse, found face-down in the snow in this very spot by a park ranger—yet he found himself more perplexed than afraid. Somehow, he intuitively knew that he wouldn't come to any harm.

About twenty feet from the road, the old man stopped. "Okay, we're here." He pointed into the darkness ahead. "Now watch . . . this is where it gets interesting."

Murphy stared at him, then turned to peer through the snow. At first he saw nothing.

And then a flying saucer materialized before him.

It appeared quietly, reverse-phasing out of the storm as if it had been there all the time. Indeed, it must have, for its upper fuselage was covered with snow and shallow drifts were piled around its wedge-shaped landing gear. Yet they were so close to it that, had he taken a few more steps, Murphy would have walked facefirst into one of the lowered flanges.

Murphy felt his heart skip a beat. Unable to breathe, let alone muster the startled scream that caught halfway up his throat, he staggered back, his legs obeying an instinctive urge to flee, until his numbed feet slipped out from beneath him and he toppled to the ground. He landed on his back, his arms sprawled out on either side; for an absurd moment he looked as if he were trying to make a snow angel.

"Oh, Jesus!" he croaked. "What? . . . What is that . . . ?"

"Exactly what it looks like." The old man chuckled. "It's a timeship, David."

"A . . . a timeship."

"That's right. A timeship. Just like you wrote about in your article." He bent down, offered his hand. "Nice guess. Couldn't have done better myself. Now, c'mon, get up. There's some people aboard who want to meet you."

Murphy didn't take his hand. Instead, he stared up the old man. His face lay in shadow, shrouded by snow and the darkness of night, yet suddenly it seemed as if he could see him as clearly as if it were high noon on a summer day.

"I know who you are," Murphy whispered.

"Yes," Murphy replied, "I expect you probably do."

"And that's why you're here," Franc finished. "Do you understand now?"

"Yeah, sure . . . sure." David Murphy slumped in one of the couches, gazing at nothing in particular. "It's perfectly clear."

"No. You're not getting it." Leaning against a bulkhead, Zack Murphy had remained quiet during the entire discussion. "You say you do, but you're still trying to find a way to fit this into your old worldview."

Franc glanced over his shoulder at him. "Dr. Murphy . . ."

"You think I don't know myself?" Zack crossed the crew compartment, sat down next to David. "Look here, son . . ."

"I'm not your son." David glared at the older version of himself. "Unless you've got another paradox you want to tell me about."

Zack grinned back at him. "Mom was pretty good-looking in her time," he said drily, "but I wouldn't go that far."

David surprised everyone by laughing out loud. Franc and Lea gave each other uncertain looks, and Metz stopped sniggering. Only Zack was amused. "Just a figure of speech," he added. "Sorry."

"Excuse me . . . sorry . . . didn't mean it." David shook his head. "But y'know, you're right. I didn't quite believe it . . . until just now, at least."

"So now we're straight, right?" Zack looked at him closely. "You know this isn't some CIA plot, anything like that? You know this is the real deal?"

"Uh-huh." David let out his breath, slowly nodded. "I knew it the moment I saw this thing. I just had trouble getting used to it." He hesitated. "The only thing I'm still unconvinced about is why I'm responsible."

"You're not," Franc said. "All of us share the burden. You're only the primary factor, and your role in this hasn't even begun yet. It's what you may do in the future that concerns us."

"That's the part I don't quite understand." David crossed his legs, bridged his hands together. "You say that, in a couple of years, I'm going to write a science fiction novel that will inspire Steven to become the scientist who figures out time travel. But I've already tried to write fiction, and everything I submitted to magazines was rejected. That's why I wrote articles instead."

"But you originally intended to write fiction, correct?" Lea asked, and he slowly nodded. "So it could be that, a few years from now, you try your hand at it again."

"And this time, you succeed." Clasping his hands together in a similar gesture, Zack pointed his forefingers at David. "Possibly because you used . . . could use . . . the article you published for *Analog* as the basis for your novel. At any rate, the solution is simple. Don't write a novel . . . or at least not *that* novel."

"So you're warning me not to do something I hadn't intended to do already." David slowly nodded, and Zack shrugged offhandedly. "Easy enough, but I'm not sure that's going to solve all your problems. Someone else may already be interested in time travel."

Franc raised an eyebrow. "How so?"

"Well, just this morning, I had a meeting with NASA's

associate administrator, Roger Ordmann. He's the chief of Space Science, my department, and . . ."

"Whoa! Wait a minute!" Zack Murphy raised a hand. "Did you say Roger Ordmann?" David frowned and nodded, and Zack gaped at him in surprise. "That's the Chief Administrator of OPS in my worldline."

"Another convergence," Lea murmured. They had already noted a certain reoccurence of names; Paolo Sanchez and Ray Sanchez, for example.

"One more indication that the worldlines aren't that far apart." Franc absently rubbed his chin with his forefinger. "In this frame of existence, he's a senior NASA administrator. In the other, he performs much the same function for the Office of . . ."

"Y'know, maybe you shouldn't be telling me this." David looked first at Franc, then at Zack. "I mean, you've already told me enough about the different worldlines. Maybe it's better if I don't know all the details."

"At this juncture, I'm not sure if it makes much difference," Franc said, "but if you'd rather not know . . ." David shook his head. "Very well, but what about this meeting you had with Ordmann?"

"He'd read my article . . . someone else at NASA had brought it to my attention . . . and he said he was concerned about it being published by someone who worked at the agency. Said it might cast NASA in a bad light and all that. But the thing that really struck me . . . especially later, after you and I had our little chat at the Air and Space . . ."

"I haven't apologized for that," Franc said. "Sorry. It had to be done."

"You scared the hell out of me, but . . . well, apology accepted." David grinned at him. "I'd love to know how you did it, but . . . I dunno, maybe that's one of those things I shouldn't know, right?" Franc smiled, and he went on. "What struck me later was that your questions were the same as his. Like, what led me to believe that UFO sightings were tied to time travel."

Lea groaned softly. "Oh, no," Metz said, closing his eyes and putting a hand over his face. "Here we go again . . ."

"No, no," Franc said quickly. "They're not necessarily linked. This could be exactly what it seemed to be . . . a senior government official concerned about public perception."

"But what if it isn't?" Zack asked. "Again, look at the convergences. In my worldline, in this very same year, the American government began a crash program to develop time travel. Does this mean that the same thing is going on here, in this worldline?"

Lea wrapped her arms around herself and turned away. "Nothing we do matters," she murmured. "No matter how this turns out, someone will eventually build a timeship."

"My point exactly," David said. "It may not matter whether I publish a novel or if my son becomes a physicist, because the idea's out there already. So what are you going to do? Go back to 1898 and kill H.G. Wells? You can, if you really want to, but what's to prevent another writer from coming up with the same concept? Or maybe you stop Einstein from developing the theory of relativity. You might, but does that necessarily prevent Stephen Hawking or Kip Thorne or someone else from investigating the same problems?"

"Free will," Zack said quietly.

"Pardon me?"

"It all comes back to the question of free will." Pushing himself out of his chair, the other Murphy clasped his hands behind his back. "We may be able to do certain things," he said, pensively staring at the floor. "In fact, it's almost a foregone conclusion that we will. The question is, *should* we?"

"Like . . . I dunno." David thought about it a moment. "Maybe like the decision to drop the bomb on Hiroshima and Nagasaki . . ."

"If you mean atomic bombs, that didn't happen in my worldline," Zack said. "About five thousand American

G.I.s were killed during the invasion of Japan, and nearly fifty thousand Japanese died defending their country, but no country has ever dropped a bomb in wartime . . . or at least not where I come from." He shook his head. "But you get the point. The technology may be inevitable, but the consequences aren't, and the consequences of time travel are far more hideous . . . at least in the long run . . . than nuclear war would ever be."

"So what do we do?"

"You already know what you have to do . . . or rather, don't do. It's up to you. These people have already made their decision." Zack took a deep breath, then turned to face the others. "Dr. Lu? You're still ready to go through with this?"

Franc hesitated, then glanced at Lea and Vasili. Both quietly nodded, Metz a little more reluctantly than the others. He smiled grimly, then turned back to the two Murphys.

"Yes, we are," he said. "We're staying here."

"What . . . ?" David Murphy rose from his chair. "Here? In this . . . I mean, in this year?"

"We don't have much choice," Lea said. "If we've succeeded, then the place we came from no longer exists. Or will never exist, technically speaking. The fact that we didn't board the *Hindenburg* is proof of that. If we attempt to go forward from this point in time, we may very well crash-land again in some place farther up this worldline, as we did the first time we attempted to leave 1937."

"Therefore potentially causing another paradox, with similar outcomes," Franc said. "The same thing would probably occur if we tried to go back in time. No matter where we go, regardless of the year or location, in all likelihood another paradox would result. We would survive, of course . . . but the consequences would be unimaginable."

"But . . ." David Murphy gaped at them in astonishment. "This is 1998. You're from 2314. You don't have a clue where you're going to go, what you're going to . . ."

"Sure they do." Zack Murphy turned toward him. "I'm staying with them."

"You're . . . what?"

Zack smiled. "What else am I supposed to do? Come home with you, claim I'm your long-lost uncle?" He shook his head. "No, I'm going where they're going, wherever that is. This may not be my 1998, but it's close enough. So far, we haven't done too badly. The currency's a little out of date, but we managed to buy some clothes, rent a car . . ." He frowned, then gave David a wry smile. "We're running a little low on cash, though. Think you could spare a few bucks?"

David hesitated, then reached into his back pocket, pulled out his wallet. A ten, three fives, and two ones. "That'll do for a start," Zack said as he took the money and folded it into his pocket. "Thanks. If Donna asks where you've been, tell her the car died and you had to call for a tow."

"And what about the ship? You're going to have trouble hiding something this big."

Vasili looked uncomfortable. He cleared his throat. "We're not going to hide it," he said. "We're going to destroy it."

Again, David's mouth fell open in surprise. "Do you know what you're saying? You're going to maroon yourselves here."

"I'm afraid so." Franc appeared no less discomfited by the notion. "But again, we've got no other choice. As you just pointed out, we'd have trouble concealing it. Its chameleon requires a constant energy input, and once the batteries drained below a certain level it would become visible once more. There's virtually no place on Earth where it could remain hidden without chance of discovery. Having someone stumble upon an operational timeship is far too great a risk for us to take. So destroying *Oberon* is the only option."

"I've already programmed the AI to fly it out of the atmosphere." Metz's eyes were sad, his voice bleak. "The chameleon will remain operational until it's achieved orbit. After *Oberon* reaches space, it'll open a wormhole that will take it straight into the Sun."

"Once it's destroyed," Franc continued, "for all intents and purposes, it will have never existed." He gazed at the pilot. "I'm sorry, Vasili," he added quietly, "but it has to be done."

Metz nodded, but said nothing. Franc turned back to David Murphy. "Which brings us to a final question. Besides us, you're the only person who knows anything about this . . ."

"Are you asking if I can keep a secret?" He shrugged. "Who would believe me?"

"Someone probably would," Zack said. "In fact, there's a lot of people out there who would be only too willing to suspend their disbelief, if they had any in the first place. You may be tempted to write a book about all this. Maybe you'd get lucky and it would become a best-seller. In any case, you could stand to make a few bucks."

Temptation stole across David Murphy's face. Zack noticed it; he frowned and shook his head. "Don't do it," he said quietly. "I beg of you, please don't. You don't know the things I've seen, but if you did, you'd never contemplate such a thing."

"All right, so I won't," David said, reluctantly. "I promise. Mum's the word. But you know, and I know, that the idea of time travel is already out there. Destroying this ship won't make any difference if someone is already trying to figure out how to build something like this."

"Which is another reason why we're staying here," Zack replied. "To make sure that no one does." He smiled grimly. "Remember, I've already been through all this. I know what to look for." Then he raised a finger and shook it at David. "And don't think for an instant we're going to forget about you. I know where you live."

David didn't reply. Franc studied him for a moment, then turned to the others. "I think that covers everything. Lea, is everything in the car?" She nodded, and he stood up. "Then it's time to go."

The storm had let up while they were in the timeship. Although the sky was still overcast, the only snow that fell was a few crystalline flakes the wind blew away from *Oberon*'s fuselage. Lea shuddered within her 1930s-style overcoat as she marched through the drifts away from the timeship. "I'm going to have to get used to this," she murmured to Franc through chattering teeth, then she looked at Zack. "Is it always this way, this time of year?"

"Usually. Sorry." He took off his baseball cap, gave it to her. "We can always head south. Florida's pretty nice in January."

David Murphy trailed behind them, reluctant to leave the timeship behind. As they approached the road, he stopped and turned around. Vasili Metz had just climbed down the ladder and was jogging away from the *Oberon*. He was the only one who didn't have a coat, and he wrapped his arms around himself in a futile effort to stay warm. On sudden impulse, Murphy pulled off his parka, offered it to him as he approached. Metz regarded it with surprise, then gratefully accepted it with mumbled thanks.

They trudged through the snow to the cars. "Mind if I

borrow your brush?" Zack asked David, then he opened the left rear door of the Escort and found the long-handled ice scraper. He had just finished clearing the front and rear windows of the rental Chevy when they heard a low hum from somewhere behind him.

Murphy turned just in time to see the *Oberon* lift off. The hemispheres beneath its hull gleamed against the white pasture as the timeship slowly rose, the negmass drive whisking away sheets of snow from the ground below. The flanges folded up against the bottom of the saucer, and for a few seconds it seemed to David as if he were watching a scene from one of the fifties science fiction movies he had relished as a kid.

Then the *Oberon* faded from sight. The last impression they had of its passage from Earth was a vague shadow slightly darker than the sky, quickly disappearing into the night.

"Well . . . okay. Let's go before we freeze to death." Zack opened the Chevy's rear passenger door, turned to help Lea inside. She stared at the place where the *Oberon* had once stood, then she allowed herself to be guided into the backseat.

Metz started to follow her, then he stopped. "I think this is yours," he said to David, and began to pull off the parka.

"Keep it," Murphy said. "You need it more than I do." The former timeship pilot nodded, then climbed in behind Lea.

Zack shut the door behind him. "That's awfully nice of you," he said, "but wasn't that a Christmas gift from Donna? Two years ago?"

"Umm . . . no, I bought it myself, at the outlet mall. Donna gave me a watch." He grinned at Zack. "Maybe the convergences aren't as close as we think."

"I hope not." He returned the smile, then handed the brush back to him, along with the keys to his own car. "Thanks, pal," he said, extending his hand. "We'll be in touch."

Murphy hesitated, then shook hands with himself. "Take it easy, friend. Give me a call sometime."

Neither of them seemed to know what to say next, so they left it at that. Zack turned and walked away.

Franc stood near the open front passenger door, still gazing into the sky. Murphy realized that he was looking upon a man lost in time, as homeless as any individual in history has ever been. When Franc lowered his face, Murphy noticed a faint wetness around his eyes. Franc saw him; he nodded once, distantly, then ducked his head and climbed into the car.

Murphy walked back to his own car, used the brush to clear the snow away from the windows. While his back was still turned, he heard Zack start the engine. The taillights flashed an amber glow across the windshield, then the tires crunched against the icepack as the car moved away, heading down the road out of the park.

Murphy resisted the impulse to watch them leave. Somehow, it seemed better that he not know which direction they were taking.

He was about to climb into his car when he detected a flash of light out of the corner of his eye. He turned around, saw an orb of light in the snow-covered pasture where the *Oberon* had rested. It remained for a moment, just long enough for him to realize what it was, then collapsed in upon itself like a mirage out of spacetime, finally disappearing with a faint thunderclap.

Murphy waited another moment, then he opened the car door and settled in behind the wheel. It had been a long Monday, and now it was time to go home.

AFTERWORD

For their assistance in the development of this novel, I'm grateful to the following individuals: Mark W. Tiedemann, Gregory Benford, Stanley Schmidt, Jim Young, Matt Visser, Scott Crawford, Ken Moore, Beth Gwinn, Judith Klein-Dial, my father-in-law Frank Jacobs, and my sister Rachel Steele.

As always, my wife Linda deserves special credit as my research assistant.

I also wish to thank my editor, Ginjer Buchanan, and my literary agent, Martha Millard.

—December, 1996–March, 1997;
St. Louis, Missouri; Sanibel, Florida
December, 1998–June, 1999;
Whately, Massachusetts; Frankfurt,
Germany

Sources

Allen, Hugh. *The Story of the Airship.* Goodyear Tire & Rubber Co., 1925.

Archbold, Rick. *Hindenburg: An Illustrated History.* New York: Warner/Madison Press, 1994.

Browne, Malcolm. "New Direction in Physics: Back in Time." *The New York Times,* August 21, 1990.

Campbell, Glenn. *Area 51 Viewer's Guide, edition 4.01,* self-published, 1995.

Cartmill, Cleve; "Deadline." *Astounding Science Fiction* (March 1944).

Comins, Neil F. *What If the Moon Didn't Exist?* New York: HarperCollins, 1993.

Cross; Colin. *Adolf Hitler.* London: Hodder and Stroughton, Ltd., 1973.

Darlington, David. *Area 51: The Dreamland Chronicles.* New York: Henry Holt & Co., 1997.

Deutsch, David, and Lockwood, Martin; "The Quantum Physics of Time Travel." *Scientific American,* (March 1994).

Forward, Robert L. *Indistinguishable from Magic.* New York: Baen, 1995.

Freedman, David H. "Cosmic Time Travel." *Discover* (June 1989).

Hawking, Stephen. *A Brief History of Time, second edition.* New York: Bantam, 1996.

Hoard, Dorothy. *A Guide to Bandelier National Monument, third edition.* Los Alamos Historical Society, 1989.

Hoehling, A. A. *Who Destroyed the Hindenburg?* Boston: Little, Brown and Co., 1962.

Ley, Willy. "Psuedoscience in Naziland." *Astounding Science Fiction* (May 1947).

Moody, Michael. *The Hindenburg.* New York: Dodd, Mead & Co., 1972.

Nahin, Paul J. *Time Machines, second edition.* New York: AIP Press, 1999.

Preston, Douglas. "Cannibals of the Canyon." *New Yorker* (November 30, 1998).

Shirer, William L. *The Rise and Fall of the Third Reich.* New York: Simon and Schuster, 1960.

————. *The Nightmare Years.* New York: Little, Brown & Co., 1984.

Sweetman, Bill. *Aurora: The Pentagon's Secret Hypersonic Spyplane.* Wisconsin: Motorbooks International, 1993.

Thorne, Kip S. *Black Holes & Time Warps.* New York: W.W. Norton & Co., 1994.

Whiting, Charles. *The Home Front: Germany.* Virgina: Time-Life Books, 1982.